# Ransom *my* Heart

**Mia Thermopolis**, also known as Her Royal Highness, Amelia Mignonette Grimaldi Thermopolis Renaldo, Crown Princess of Genovia, is the heroine of The Princess Diaries. Having cherished for many years a dream to be a published author, Mia has finally realized her ambition with the help of Meg Cabot. Mia lives with her family and her cat, Fat Louie, in New York City.

**Meg Cabot** is the author of the phenomenally successful The Princess Diaries series. With vast numbers of copies sold around the world, the books have topped the US and UK bestseller lists for weeks and won several awards. Two movies based on the series have been massively popular throughout the world.

Meg is also the author of the bestselling *Airhead*, *All American Girl*, *All American Girl: Ready or Not*, *How to Be Popular*, *Tommy Sullivan Is a Freak*, *Jinx*, *Teen Idol*, *Avalon High*, The Mediator series and the Allie Finkle series as well as many other books for teenagers and adults. She and her husband divide their time between Florida and New York.

Visit Meg Cabot's website at
www.megcabot.co.uk

# Ransom *my* Heart

by *Princess of Genovia*
MIA THERMOPOLIS
*with help from*

# MEG CABOT

author of *The Princess Diaries*

MACMILLAN

First published 2008 by Macmillan

This edition published 2009 by Macmillan
an imprint of Pan Macmillan Limited
20 New Wharf Road, London N1 9RR
Basingstoke and Oxford
Associated companies throughout the world
www.panmacmillan.com

ISBN 978-0-330-51100-1

A CIP catalogue record for this book is available from
the British Library.

Printed and bound in the UK by CPI Mackays, Chatham ME5 8TD
Printed on recycled paper

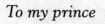

*To my prince*

# An Introduction to
# Ransom *my* Heart

As the person charged with the duty of chronicling the ups and downs of the life of Princess Mia Thermopolis, it is with great pleasure that I introduce *Ransom My Heart*. Those familiar with the journals of the Princess of Genovia (published in ten volumes as The Princess Diaries series) will be aware that it has long been the princess's secret dream to become a published author one day.

Well, that day has finally come. *Ransom My Heart*, the historical romance that Princess Mia spent twenty-one months (between *The Princess Diaries: To the Nines* and *The Princess Diaries: Ten Out of Ten*) researching and writing, has been published at last.

In this book, readers may find characters or incidents vaguely reminiscent of Mia's own life – the fact that the heroine's sister Mellana is an accomplished brew mistress, for instance (note Mia's unfortunate first experience with the single beer she consumes in *The Princess Diaries: Seventh Heaven*), or that the heroine's dog is named Gros Louis (French for Fat Louie, the name of Princess Mia's cat).

I'm certain the princess would not want readers to make the mistake of thinking that these things have any hidden meaning . . . that, for example, when creating the character of the hero, Hugo, Mia was thinking of any individual from her own life, particularly one who might have gone away for a long time and then come back (I'm certain the princess would point out that she and Michael Moscovitz weren't even going out during the time she wrote this book. Whether they are currently together is something readers can discover for themselves in *The Princess Diaries: Ten Out of Ten*).

It should be noted that all author proceeds from this book will go to Greenpeace, the princess's favourite charity. And though Mia will not, as she once dreamed, be spending her gap year working for Greenpeace, manning a rubber dinghy and keeping whales from getting harpooned, the income generated from this book will help someone else to do so.

So through this book the heartfelt dreams of a princess will be realized. And isn't that what books are for? So that readers can vicariously live their own dreams?

And for the millions of readers who have lived the dream of being a princess through Mia's diaries, with *Ransom My Heart* comes the chance to know what princesses dream of. I hope you will enjoy it!

*Meg Cabot*

# Ransom *my* Heart

# Chapter One

*England, 1291*

The hawk was back.

Finnula saw it the instant she pulled open the wooden shutters of her bedroom window and peered outside to see whether the sheriff and his men had yet ridden off. The evil-eyed, hulking brown bird was perched on top of the thatched roof of the henhouse, as cool as you please. It had killed two of Mellana's favorite hens the week before, and now was eyeing a third, the one Mel called Greta, as the speckled chicken scratched the muddy henhouse yard for leftover bits of feed. Though the hawk never stirred, even as the cold spring rain drizzled steadily down its back, Finnula knew it was poised to strike.

Quick as one of the earl's prize does, Finnula seized her bow and quiver from where they hung on the bedpost and centered the bird of prey in her sights, though her balance was a little off because the beams in the ceiling by the dormer window were so low. Drawing back the well-worn string of her bow, Finnula focused her entire mind on the target below her, the ruffled breast of the hen-murdering hawk. She didn't hear her sister climbing the stairs to the room they had once shared, or feel the scrape of the bedroom door being flung open.

"Finn!"

Christina's horrified voice so startled Finnula that she let go of the drawstring too soon. With a musical twang, the arrow sailed through the open window, arcing through the rain and planting itself harmlessly in the thatch at the hawk's feet, startling the indignantly squawking bird into flight.

"God's teeth, Christina!" Finnula cursed, jumping up from her archer's crouch and pointing an accusing finger in the direction of the shaft's flight path. "That was a perfectly good arrow, and now look at it! How am I going to get that one back? It's stuck in the henhouse roof!"

Christina was leaning back against the doorjamb, her plump face red-cheeked from the exertion of climbing the narrow staircase, one hand on her broad chest as she attempted to catch her breath.

"Fie on you, Finnula," she panted, when she was finally able to find her voice. "What were you thinkin'? The sheriff left not five minutes ago, and here you are, shootin' at poor innocent birds again!"

"Innocent!" Finnula slipped the battered leather strap to her quiver over one slim shoulder. "That was the hawk that's been killing Mellana's chickens, I'll have you know."

"Have you lost the brains the good Lord gave you, Finn? If the sheriff should have looked back and seen that arrow flyin' out of your bedroom window, he'd've turned round and arrested you on the spot."

Finnula snorted derisively. "La! He'd never. Imagine, arresting a sweet maid like myself. He'd fast become the most hated man in Shropshire."

"Not with the earl's cousin, he wouldn't." In her eighth month of pregnancy, Christina wasn't able to climb the stairs to her old bedroom with her usual swiftness, and now she sank down onto the bed her youngest sisters shared and sighed, the auburn curls that had slipped from her linen wimple swaying. "Can't you see reason, Finn? His Lordship knows it's you that's been poaching his woods—"

Again, Finnula snorted. "Hugo Fitzstephen doesn't know any such thing. How could he? He's been in the Holy Land these past ten years. No one's even heard from him since Michaelmas, when that filthy bailiff of his got word he'd been captured by Saracens."

"Really, Finn, you oughtn't to refer to your betters so coarsely. Reginald Laroche is Lord Hugo's *cousin*, and acting bailiff of the Fitzstephen estates in His Lordship's absence. How can you call him filthy? You know we are to accord him the same respect we would if he were our true lord. How can you—"

"Respect?" Finnula looked as if she might spit. "When he starts acting respectable, I'll respect him. In the meantime, do not ask me to call him my lord. For no lord worthy of the name would treat his vassals with such—"

Christina sighed again, this time in exasperation, and interrupted her outspoken sibling. "Very well, Finnula. I know there is no point in arguing with you over this issue. But think on this: Reginald Laroche told the sheriff he's got good reason to believe that it's you that's been picking off all of Lord Hugo's best game. All he needs is some little proof, and it's to the stockade you'll go."

Finnula kicked irritably at the wooden trunk that sat at the foot of the bed. Inside it were the kirtles and bliauts she eschewed for the more sensible garb she currently wore, tanned leather chausses and a well-worn woolen tunic.

"It isn't as if," she grumbled, "I was doing it for sport. If Hugo Fitzstephen were about, and he saw how poorly his serfs were being treated by that devil Laroche, he'd not begrudge the meat I provide them."

"That's neither here nor there, Finn." Christina spoke tiredly. It was an old argument. Essentially, it dated back to the day that the girls' oldest sibling and only brother, Robert, picked up a short bow and, mostly in jest, instructed then four-year-old Finnula in the art of targetry. Her first shot had been dead center in the rear end of her beloved wet nurse, Aggie, and ever since, no one had been able to pry a bow from the fair huntress's hands.

"Besides," Finnula went on, as if she hadn't heard her sister's interruption. "The sheriff's not going to find any proof. I never miss, so it isn't as if he'll ever get hold of one of my arrows and trace the markings on the feathers back to me. The only reason he even bothered calling today is that he's in love with Mellana."

"Finn, that simply isn't true. Monsieur Laroche told Sheriff de Brissac that another one of the earl's stags has gone missing."

"It hasn't gone missing at all," Finnula said, the corners of her sensually shaped mouth suddenly slanting upward in a smile. "That stag is right where it always was, on the properties of Stephensgate Manor. It just so happens that now it's resting in the bellies of some of Lord Hugo's serfs."

Christina blinked at her incorrigible sister. It occurred to her, not for the first time, that if Finnula would abandon her eccentric mode of dress and put on one of the silken gowns that had been purchased for her at the time of her ill-fated wedding, and brushed out her lovely auburn hair instead of keeping it tied away in that single braid, she'd be quite a beautiful woman. The girl probably wasn't even aware of it, and would most likely deny it if anyone broached the subject, but in Christina's opinion, it wasn't Mellana that was forever drawing the sheriff to the millhouse, but Finnula herself, and not just because of her poaching habit.

Christina sighed for a third and final time, and using the bedpost to swing herself awkwardly to her feet, she said, "Well, I've done what I could. Robert can't accuse me of not trying."

Finnula smiled again, and patted her sister fondly on her plump shoulder.

"Poor Christina," she said, sweetly. "I'm so sorry to cause trouble for you and your dear Bruce. I can't promise I'll stop, but I do promise you I'll never get caught, nor do anything to embarrass you in front of your new mother- and father-in-law."

Christina, forgetting her place as a married woman—and an important woman at that, being the wife of the village butcher—let out a snort not unlike one of Finnula's.

"That will be the day." She laughed, shaking her pretty head. "Well, I suppose you'd better get below stairs and make that same pledge in front of Robert."

"Robert?" Finnula pushed some loose tendrils of flame-red hair from her smooth white forehead. "What's Robert doing home at this time of day? Shouldn't he be at the mill?"

"Would have been, if it weren't for that visit from your greatest admirer, shire reeve John de Brissac." Christina's soft gray eyes took on a distinct sparkle. "But that hasn't been his only distraction today. Rosamund is here, and I believe she and Robert have something to tell you—"

Finnula gasped. Unlike her sisters, things like weddings and gowns had never held much appeal for her, but because she wor-shipped her brother, she was glad for him. "You don't mean . . . Rosamund's father agreed to it at last?"

Christina nodded, the mirth that she'd been trying to disguise as she chastised her little sister finally bubbling over. "Yes! Go now, go downstairs and welcome her to the family. She was quite confused by the presence of armed men in her future home. I had to assure her 'tis not a regular thing—"

Finnula, however, was no longer listening. Fairly flying down the steep stairs to the ground floor, where a tight knot of people were gathered at the fireside, she cried, "God's teeth, Robbie! Why didn't you tell me?"

The small crowd parted, and Robert, all six feet and then some of him, hurtled toward his much smaller, but quite a bit louder, youngest sister. Catching her up in arms rock-hewn from years of working His Lordship's mill, Robert swung Finnula high toward the rafters before setting her back on her feet and giving her pert backside a wallop that caused tears to sting her eyes.

"Damn you, Robert!" Finnula backed away from him, her hands slipping behind her to massage her throbbing skin. He'd hit her hard enough to wear a hole in her leather chausses. "What was *that* for?" she demanded hotly.

"For the stag," Robert replied, with a gravity that was quite at odds with his usual good humor. "If I have to lie for you one more time, Finn, you won't be able to sit for a week, mark my words."

This was hardly the sort of familial celebration Finnula had been hoping for. Blinking back tears that were more from anger than from pain, Finnula glared at her brother, trying to ignore the small, perplexed face of his bride-to-be, hovering near his elbow.

"Fie on you, Robert," Finnula snapped, furiously. "You can't prove it was me that shot that stag, any more than Sheriff de Brissac or that loathsome Reginald Laroche can prove it. I *was* going to wish you and Rosamund joy and felicitation, but now I think I'll just go after the sheriff and tell him to go right ahead and hang me, since it's clear I'm not wanted in my own home—"

And she turned toward the front door, knowing full well that Robert, though he'd tried to discipline her over the years since their parents' death, couldn't stand to see her unhappy. He was the only brother of six sisters, and each of them, in her own way, was capable of manipulating him. But the youngest one of all, Finnula, had it down to a science. Her older sisters watched with barely suppressed smiles as their brother's anger visibly melted beneath Finnula's fiery gaze. "We oughtn't," Robert ventured slowly, "to let anger mar this special day—"

"Nay," Rosamund chimed in, still looking a bit shocked at her betrothed's display of manly temper. "We oughtn't."

At the door, Finnula smiled to herself, but carefully schooled her features into an expression of contrition before turning around.

"You mean," she murmured, "that you'll forgive me?"

"Aye." Robert said, and nodded gravely, as if granting a reprieve to a convicted prisoner. "Just this once."

With a shout, Finnula threw herself once more into his arms. There she was joined by Rosamund, the angelic-looking daughter of the mayor of Stephensgate, the first girl Robert had ever wooed unsuccessfully, and therefore the love of his life. Perhaps understandably, Rosamund had been reluctant to attach herself to a family as odd as the miller's—Robert had six sisters, after all, *six*, something that would be considered a curse in many families, but something that his parents, before their deaths, had rejoiced over. But worst of all, there was the youngest sister, who gadded about in boyish garb and prided herself on the fact that she was the finest shot in Shropshire, despite the fact that at seventeen, she was far too old for such pursuits. And then of course there was the matter of Finnula's debacle of a marriage . . .

But the other five sisters all had reputations beyond reproach. There was the eldest, Brynn, at five and twenty a year younger than Robert, and happily wed to the village blacksmith. She had four boys already, each with his father's stocky build and mother's flame-red hair. Then came Patricia, wife to the local innkeeper and mother of three, and Camilla, who'd fought and wept and generally made herself unpleasant to live with until Robert had agreed to let her marry a winemaker two times her age. Then there was the newly wed Christina, who loved her butcher husband, Bruce, dearly, and the fifth daughter, Mellana, considered by many to be the family beauty, but, though approaching her twentieth birthday, who had yet to find a husband.

In all, the miller's family was not one against which Rosamund's father could have had many strong objections. Indeed, the mayor would have had no objections whatsoever, for a more promising young man than Robert Crais could scarce be found in Stephensgate. But there was the small matter of his youngest sister's oddly independent ways, her flagrant defiance of poaching laws, as well as that unfortunate incident between her and the late earl. How to overlook the fact that Finnula Crais, however wrongly, had been accused of murdering her own husband?

But Rosamund's affection for Robert was quite genuine, and, an only child, she eventually brought her doting father round to her way of thinking. If Finnula was his only objection, well, there was nothing to be done about Finnula. The girl was young, and it could be hoped that one day she'd grow out of her love for sport— and the leather chausses she insisted upon wearing. At least she had the sense to stay off the main thoroughfares while wearing them. And in the meantime, perhaps Rosamund's gentle influence could help her to see the error of her ways.

What with all the married Crais sisters and their spouses and progeny at the millhouse noisily celebrating Robert and Rosamund's impending marriage, it was perhaps understandable that no one missed one of the single sisters . . . at least, not right away. It was Finnula who eventually lowered her cup of ale and wondered aloud what had happened to Mellana.

No one, however, paid Finnula any mind, which wasn't unusual, since "Finn" was not only the family embarrassment but also the family storyteller, whose wild exaggerations were now believed only by her youngest nieces and nephews. Putting aside her cup, she went in search of her favorite sister, and found her by the kitchen fire, weeping into her apron.

"Mellana!" Finnula cried, genuinely shocked. "What ails you? Is it your stomach again? Do you want me to fetch you a tonic?"

From the looks of her pink and swollen eyes, Mellana had been crying for some time. Considered by many to be the loveliest of the miller's daughters, Mellana had had more admirers than anyone could count, but never an actual offer of marriage. Finnula had been unable to decipher why this was so, as she herself had been the recipient of one proposal, albeit ill-fated, and she in no way considered herself the beauty that Mellana obviously was.

Fair of face and trim of figure, Mellana was the only sister who had escaped the Crais family curse of bright red hair. Instead, she had lovely strawberry-blond curls that framed her heart-shaped face like a veil of reddish gold. Her eyes weren't the mist gray of her sisters and brother, either, but a deep, sapphire blue that looked almost black in certain lights. And somehow Mellana hadn't inherited the outspokenness of her sisters, being instead the mildest of creatures, an excellent cook and housekeeper who seemed to feel better suited to the company of the hens she loved than to actual human beings. At one time, there'd been some talk in the village of the next-to-youngest Crais girl being simple in the head. Robert and Finnula had soon put a stop to it, one with his fists and the other her bow, and now it was no longer mentioned by anyone—within hearing of the eldest and youngest Crais, that is.

"Mellana, sweetest, what is it?" Finnula bent over her most beloved sibling, trying to sweep some of the lovely girl's hair from her face, where strands of the blond curls stuck to her damp cheeks. "Why aren't you celebrating with the rest of us?"

Mellana hiccupped, barely able to speak through her sobs. "Oh, Finn, if only I could tell you!"

"What do you mean, if only you could tell me? Mel, you can tell me anything, you know that."

"Not this." Mellana shook her head with such force that her red-gold hair whipped her cheeks. "Oh, Finnula. I'm so ashamed!"

"You?" Finnula stroked her sister's shoulder through the soft material of her green bliaut. "And what have you, the gentlest creature in the world, to be ashamed of? Nothing to wear to the wedding? Is that it, eh, silly?"

Mellana tried to mop up her tears with the sleeve of her cream-colored kirtle. "I only wish it were that, Finn," she choked. "Oh, Finn, if only it were that! I'm afraid you'll despise me when I tell you—"

"I, despise you, Mel?" Finnula was genuinely shocked. "Never! Oh, Mellana, you know I never—"

"I'm late," Mellana gasped, and burst into a fresh shower of tears.

"You're late?" Finnula echoed, her slender eyebrows knit with confusion. "Why, you aren't late at all. The betrothal celebration has only just begun—"

Seeing Mellana's quick head shake, Finnula's voice trailed off. Late? She stared at the fractious girl, and understanding, when it dawned, was coupled with disbelief, disbelief that she couldn't keep from creeping into her husky voice.

"Late, Mel?" she asked, giving her older sister a shake. "You mean you're—*late?*"

Mellana nodded miserably. Still, Finnula needed clarification. She simply could not believe what she was hearing from her beautiful, sweet-tempered sister.

"Mellana, are you saying that you're . . . *with child?*"

"Y-yes," Mellana sobbed.

Finnula stared down at the bent golden head, and tried very hard to stifle a desire to shake Mellana silly. She loved her sister, and would thrash anyone outside the family who dared make light of her, but in truth, Mellana could be the most shallow of creatures, and Finnula was only too willing to believe that some rogue had taken advantage of that vapidity.

"What's his name?" Finnula demanded, her hand falling unconsciously upon the hilt of the six-inch blade at her hip.

Mellana only sobbed harder.

"His name, Mel," Finnula repeated, her voice hard. "The blackguard dies by nightfall."

"Oh, I knew I shouldn't have told you," Mellana groaned. "Finn, please, please don't kill him. You don't understand. I love him!"

Finnula released the dagger hilt. "You love him? Truly, Mel?" When the older girl nodded tearfully, Finnula frowned. "Well, that changes things, I suppose. I can't kill him if you love him. But why all the tears then? If you love him, marry him."

"You don't understand," Mellana wept. "Oh, Finn, I can't marry him!"

Back went the fingers to the dagger hilt. "Already married, is he? Right, then. Robert and I'll have him strung up before you can say Nottingham Town. Buck up, Mel. It'll be a lovely hanging."

"He's not married." Mellana sniffled.

Finnula sank down onto the hearth, exhaling heavily enough to blow a few stray tendrils of red hair from her forehead. Truly, she hadn't the patience today to deal with her scatterbrained sibling. Tracking a wild boar was ten times easier than trying to make sense of Mellana.

"Well, then what is the problem, Mel? If he's not married and you love him, why can't the two of you be wed?"

"It's—it's my dowry, Finn."

"Your dowry?" Finnula plopped both elbows down on her knees, and smacked her forehead into her palms. "Oh, Mel. Tell me you didn't."

"I had to, Finn! Five weddings, in as many years. And I hadn't a thing to wear. I wore the blue samite to Brynn's, the lavender silk to Patricia's, the burgundy velvet that I ordered from London to Camilla's, the rose-colored linen to Christina's, and the gold samite to yours—" Mellana looked up apologetically, remembering, even while consumed by her own grief, how intensely Finnula disliked mention of her own wedding. "I—I'm sorry, Finn. I'm certain it must seem petty to you. After all, you care only for bows and arrows, not ribbons and gewgaws. But I would have been the laughingstock of the village if I'd appeared at my sisters' weddings in gowns worn previously—"

Finnula thought it entirely unlikely that anyone in Stephensgate would remember what Mellana had worn to any of her sister's weddings, Stephensgate hardly being the fashion capital of the world. She refrained from saying so out loud, however.

"Are you telling me," Finnula said instead, her head still in her hands, "that you spent your entire dowry on bliauts, Mellana?"

"Not just bliauts," Mellana assured her. "Kirtles, too."

Had Mellana been speaking to any one of her other sisters, she might have received a remonstration for behaving in such a selfish and stupid manner. And though Finnula did indeed think that Mellana had behaved stupidly—no better, for instance, than her silly friend Isabella Laroche, that ridiculous creature whose father was so poorly managing Lord Hugo's manor house in his absence—she could not help feeling sorry for her. After all, it was rather a terrible thing to be pregnant and unwed.

When Finnula finally looked up, her face was expressionless. "Do you have any idea," she asked, "what Robert will do when he discovers what you've done?"

"I know, Finn! I know! Why do you think I'm crying? And Jack hasn't a gold piece of his own—"

"Jack?"

"Jack Mallory." Mellana blushed, lowering her eyes. "He's a troubadour. You remember, he played the lute so divinely at Christina's wedding—"

"God's teeth," Finnula murmured, closing her eyes in horror. "A *troubadour*? You've got yourself pregnant by a *troubadour*?"

"Yes, and you see, that's why we can't be married, not without my dowry, because all Jack owns is his rebec and some juggling balls. Oh, and his donkey, Kate. You know Robert will never allow me to marry a man who doesn't even own a change of clothing, let alone a home for us to live in—"

Finnula sighed, wishing heartily it had been one of her other sisters who'd found Mellana weeping by the hearth. Brynn would have sympathized, Patricia scolded, Camilla laughed, and Christina gasped, but any one of them would have been better able to handle the situation than Finnula. Finnula, never having experienced the emotion herself, hadn't the vaguest notion what it meant to love a man to distraction, the way Mellana apparently loved Jack Mallory. On the whole, Finnula felt she had the advantage. Being in love looked rather painful, from what she'd observed.

She said, "Well, instead of crying about something's that over and done with, why don't you scrape together what you've earned brewing ale—" She paused, noting that Mellana was energetically shaking her head. "What's the matter?"

Mellana's long eyelashes fluttered damply. "D-don't you see? I spent it."

"You spent it *all*?" Finnula's voice cracked. "But there were over fifty—"

"I needed new combs," Mellana whispered tearfully. "And ribbons for my hair. And that tinker came by the other day, and he was selling the loveliest girdles, of real gold they were—"

Finnula could hardly keep from cursing, and so she did so, roundly, despite the reproachful look it earned her from her sister. "You spent *all* of the money you earned brewing this winter on trinkets? Oh, Mellana, how *could* you? That money was to buy malt and hops for the summer's batch!"

"I know." Mellana sniffled. "I know! But a maid cannot always be thinking of beer."

Finnula's jaw dropped. Her sister was dim-witted, it was true, but surely this was the stupidest thing any woman in the history of Shropshire had ever done. For a while, the girl had had a very enterprising little business going out of her kitchen cellar. Mellana's ale was widely respected as the best in Shropshire. Innkeepers from neighboring villages thought it worth the trip to Stephensgate to purchase a barrel or two from the lovely brewmistress. But without any capital left to buy ingredients, Mellana's beer-brewing days were numbered.

"A maid," Finnula echoed, bitterly. "A maid! But you aren't a maid any longer, are you, Mellana? You're going to have a child. How do you intend to support it? You cannot expect to live always here at the millhouse with Robert. He'll be married himself soon, and while Rosamund's the sweetest of girls, she won't long tolerate a clinging sister-in-law who hasn't the sense God gave a chicken, let alone her fatherless child—"

Finnula instantly regretted her harsh words when Mellana burst into a fresh set of tears. Through her sobs, the girl gulped, "Oh! And you are one to talk, Finnula Crais! You, who were wed exactly a single night before returning to the mill—"

"A widow," Finnula pointed out, refusing to be manipulated by her sister's tears. "Remember, Mellana? I returned a widow. My husband died on my wedding night."

"Oh," choked Mellana. "Wasn't that convenient, considering how much you hated him?"

Finnula felt herself turning red with rage, but before she could march off in a huff, as she intended, Mellana grabbed hold of her wrist and beseeched her, her face earnest with contrition, "Oh, Finn, forgive me! I oughtn't to have said that. I regret it most sincerely. I know it wasn't your fault. Of course it wasn't. Please, please don't go. I need your help so much. You're so clever, and I'm so very stupid. Won't you please stay a moment and listen to me? Isabella told me of a way I might make some of my coin back, in a manner that I'm quite certain would work . . . only . . . only I'm much too timid to try it."

Finnula was only half listening to her sister. In the other room, Camilla's husband must have taken out his lute, for suddenly the strains of a merry tune reached the kitchen. Above the music, Finnula could plainly hear their brother calling their names. Curse it! He'd be in the kitchen in a moment, and Mellana was the worst liar in the world. The truth would be out, and there'd be no more celebrating. There would, like as not, be a murder. Finnula hoped Jack Mallory and his bloody donkey were nowhere near Stephensgate.

Mellana straightened suddenly, her blue eyes wide. "But *you* could do it, Finn! *You* aren't timid. *You* aren't afraid of anything. And it wouldn't be any different from trapping foxes or deer. I'm certain it wouldn't!"

"What wouldn't?" Finnula, sitting on the hearth with her elbows on her knees, looked up at her sister's suddenly transformed face. Gone were the tear tracks and puffy eyelids. Now Mellana's deep blue eyes were sparkling, and her red lips were parted in excitement.

"Oh, say you'll help me, Finn!" Mellana grasped one of her sister's hands, the one with the fingertips heavily callused from pulling back the drawstring of her bow. "Say you'll help!"

Finnula, quite distracted by her fear of her brother's wrath, said impatiently, "Of course I'll help you, if I can, Mellana. But I don't see how you're going to get out of this one, I really don't."

"Trust me. Promise?"

"I promise. Now let's join the others, Mel. They're calling for us. We don't want them to suspect anything—"

"Oh, thank you, Finn!"

Suddenly joyous, Mellana pulled her younger sister into an exuberant hug. "I *knew* you'd help me if I asked. You have always been good to me. I don't care what people say about you, I don't think you're a bit odd. And with your skills as a huntress, I'm sure you'll capture the richest man in Shropshire!"

Finnula looked up at her sister curiously. "Whatever are you talking about, Mel?"

Surprised that Finnula didn't understand, Mellana told her. And it took considerably more tears on Mellana's part before Finnula would even consider honoring the promise she'd made in a moment of distraction.

# Chapter *Two*

*H*ugo Fitzstephen might have spent the past decade in the Holy Land fighting for possession of Jerusalem, but that didn't mean that he himself was holy. Far from it. As ought to have been amply illustrated by the fact that he had bedded that innkeeper's wife, then refused to pay her husband recompense, as custom dictated, when the man "happened" to walk in upon the two of them.

Hugo had fled to the Crusades as the only recourse for the second son of an earl. His other option had been the monastery, which he steadfastly refused to enter, though it was his mother's fondest wish that he should seek oneness with the Lord. Hugo preferred seeking oneness with women, however, and he'd found plenty of them in the Kingdom of Jerusalem. The women of Acre, across the Jordan from Damascus, where Hugo had spent most of the decade he'd been away from England, had a curious habit of shaving their most private areas, and that alone had been incentive enough for Hugo to stay on.

Of course, being captured in Acre by the Muslim army hadn't been part of the plan, and by the time his ransom had been paid by the Crown, Hugo was particularly disgusted with the so-called Holy Land, and with crusading in general. By then, he'd learned of the death of his elder brother, followed by the extremely strange death of their father, making Hugo the seventh Earl of Stephensgate. He decided that he might as well go home to enjoy his new title.

But so far, he hadn't had much of a chance. He'd not yet so much as glimpsed the green pastures of Shropshire, and already he was in trouble again. This time it wasn't Saracens that were pursuing him, but the husband of that particularly well-endowed blonde with whom he'd dallied in London. "Dallied" wasn't the husband's word for it, however, and he was demanding a small fortune for his "humiliation." Hugo suspected this husband and wife worked as a team, she luring in wealthy knights, then her husband "discovering" them together and demanding recompense for his injured feelings. Well, Hugo was damned if he would give the man the satisfaction.

Now Hugo and his squire were being forced to take back roads and sheep trails to Stephensgate, avoiding the main roads for fear of being set upon by the innkeeper and his cronies. It wasn't that Hugo was afraid to fight; it was just that he'd had enough fighting in the past ten years to last him a lifetime, and wanted only to retire to his manor house and enjoy what he considered, in his twenty-fifth year, to be his old age.

Shunning inns and villages where the traitorous husband might happen upon them, Hugo and his squire slept out in the open air. Fortunately, except for the occasional thunderstorm, it was a mild spring, and sleeping outdoors was preferable to Hugo than what most country hostelries had to offer, anyway. The cramped, dark quarters that one shared with one's mount, the stale brown bread and dank ale served for breakfast, the lice-infested bedding—no, give him a bale of sweet-smelling hay and his cloak, and he was most comfortable.

Of course, Peter, his squire, used to the comforts of London, where Hugo had acquired him upon learning of the demise of the comrade-at-arms who'd sired him, complained bitterly about this ill treatment, feeling that each night spent beneath the open sky was a personal affront. Used to the crowded and foggy streets of London, the boy was frightened of the dark English countryside, terrified that they might be set upon by wolves—or worse, highwaymen—at any given moment. Recognizing his complaints for what they were, fear somewhat inadequately masked with insolence, Hugo put up with them, but felt the moment was soon coming when he'd give the boy the cuffing he so desperately needed.

They were, by his estimates, two days from Stephensgate when he felt they might risk stopping in the small village of Leesbury for supplies. He was not concerned for himself so much as for his mount, Skinner, a well-trained destrier who had been with him through thick and thin, and deserved better than grass day in and day out. Still, Hugo had to admit to a certain longing for good English bread and cheese, all washed down by that glorious beverage of which he'd had so little in Jerusalem: beer. And there was no other way to acquire oats and beer than to venture into a town.

Peter was beside himself with glee at the prospect of returning to "civilization," as he called it, though when he actually caught a glimpse of Leesbury, Hugo sincerely doubted he'd be impressed. After instructing his squire firmly that he was not to refer to Hugo as "my lord" in public, Hugo guided his exceptionally small entourage through the village gates and to the first establishment he saw that looked somewhat respectable.

Instructing the stable boy that his mounts were to get the finest oats available, and slipping a gold coin into the lad's hand to ensure it, Hugo nodded to Peter, and the two of them entered the Fox and Hare. At six and half feet tall, Hugo was an abnormally large man, and he not only had to duck his head upon passing the threshold, but turn his broad shoulders to one side in order to squeeze his bulk through the narrow doorway. His presence, however formidable, caused barely a stir with the besotted clientele inside, many of whom looked as if they, too, had spent a few nights out of doors.

With the owner of the establishment, however, it was quite a different story. Hugo's darkly tanned skin and heavily bearded face gave away the fact that he'd been in the Holy Land, and as the proprietor of the Fox and Hare knew well, no man returned from the Holy Land with empty pockets. Not relics of saints, or supposed shards of the Cross . . . no, religious icons held no interest for any sensible man whatsoever. It was the diamonds, the rubies, emeralds, sapphires, pearls, the gold and silver, the lapis and turquoise, the booty from Byzantium that one could almost smell on a man freshly returned from the Crusades that drew the owner of the establishment to Hugo's side immediately.

"Good afternoon, sir," the portly innkeeper cried. "Won't you sit yourself down at this table here and refresh yourself with a pot of me sister-in-law's best ale?"

"Gladly," Hugo replied, and indicated that Peter should sit at the table opposite him.

Peter sank gratefully into the wooden chair, feeling that finally he was being treated as the squire of a rich and powerful earl ought to be treated. The proprietor's fawning attention seemed to him only fitting, and he heartily dug into the fare that was placed before him, the thick loaf of freshly baked bread, the deliciously creamy, slightly biting cheeses, the crisp fruits, the steaming pots of stew. As he ate, he glanced around the crowded eatery, as his master had done when they first entered, but saw naught to cause undue alarm. In all, the clientele seemed rough, though not unmanageable. Sucking the foamy head from a tankard of ale placed before him, Peter leaned back in his chair and prepared to be pampered.

Hugo, however, did not relax. Well-used to battle, he knew that one trick of the enemy was to lull one's foes into a false sense of security, then attack. Sipping the brew the innkeeper had pressed upon him, he grudgingly admitted to himself that it was, truly, the best ale he'd had in ages, but his eyes never left the faces of the people seated around him, nor did they stray far from the door.

That was how he happened to see the creature who appeared on the threshold just moments after their arrival. At first he took the small figure for that of a young boy's. Surely no woman would be immodest enough to don a pair of form-fitting leather chausses. But that's precisely, he soon realized, what it was. A woman, and a young one at that, with a face like an angel and a mop of red hair that had been tied back in a messy braid that swung past an amazingly narrow waist, down to an equally amazing heart-shaped backside, readily visible thanks to the slim-fitting chausses. No wimple for this lass, or bliaut, either. She wore a white lawn shirt that was hardly opaque, and slung across her back was, of all things, a short bow and battered quiver.

If anyone else was surprised at this apparition, he gave no sign. In fact, the innkeeper greeted her as easily as one might a sister, casually offering her a stool and handing her a tankard of ale. And indeed, the sight of this comely—one could easily say beautiful— woman in boyish garb caused no more comment than a few laconic how-d'ye-dos. Glancing at Peter, Hugo realized that his squire, at least, was appropriately appreciative of this auburn-tressed vision.

"Slay me," the boy breathed, gazing over the rim of his tankard. "But that's a *maiden*."

"And an uncommon fair one, at that." Hugo shook his head, relieved that Peter was as shocked as he was. Ten years ago, when he'd left England, young women did not traipse about the countryside in men's clothing, and certainly did not frequent hostelries unaccompanied. So things hadn't changed around here as drastically as Hugo had at first thought.

The girl, then, must be a local eccentric, her odd ways accepted because they were familiar. Perhaps she was, in some way, related to the innkeeper. The two were engaged in easy conversation that seemed to be centered around the good fortune of someone named Robert. After a moment or two, the proprietor pointed to Hugo and said something in a hushed voce that caused the girl to turn her head in Hugo's direction.

He suddenly found himself raked by a gaze so piercing that, incredibly, he felt his cheeks warming. Women in Acre, though they might have shaved their privates, were too modest to look a strange man in the eye, and he was unused to such direct scrutiny. Lucky for him his thick blond beard hid his blushing cheeks.

As quickly as he was pointed out he was dismissed, the girl's restless gaze moving away from him and toward Peter, who choked on his mouthful of beer when he noticed the direction of the girl's look. Then the damned innkeeper was approaching, wanting to know if there was anything else he could get them.

"Nothing too good for our men fighting the good fight," was how he put it, making it perfectly clear that he knew Hugo was back from the Holy War. "If there's anything I can get you, anything at all, you just call out."

Catching the man's arm before he could move away, Hugo

pulled him down so that the innkeeper's ear was level with his lips. "Who," he demanded in his deepest voice, the one that brooked no disobedience, "is the maid in the lad's attire?"

The innkeeper looked surprised. "Finn?" He glanced over at the girl, who fortunately was looking the other way. "You mean Finnula? My brother, what owns an inn in Stephensgate down the road, is married to her sister. *Everyone* knows the Fair Finn."

As if to prove his point, an old crone who had been huddled by the hearth, in spite of the fine weather out of doors, got up and pulled on the sleeve of the girl's white lawn shirt. With practiced grace, the maid called Finnula flipped the crone a mark, and the hag cackled happily as she caught it, and went back to the fire.

"See that?" the innkeeper said happily. "Like I said, everyone knows Finnula Crais, the miller's daughter. Finest shot in Shropshire."

This was hardly a satisfactory answer, but Hugo handed the man a coin for it, just the same. Stumbling away, massaging his arm where Hugo had gripped it in his massive, ironlike fist, the innkeeper glanced down at the weight of the coin in his hand, and hesitated. It was a solid gold piece, the kind he hadn't seen in . . . well, *ever*. Like a man in a daze, he passed a couple of laggards at a nearby table, nearly tripping over their outstretched legs as he went by. When one of roughly garbed yeoman laughed a rebuke, the innkeeper righted himself and apologized, showing them the coin. The two drunkards whistled appreciatively, but it was the girl, noticing the exchange, who swung her intensely direct gaze upon Hugo once more.

Beneath the table, Peter kicked him.

"Look at that," the squire hissed. "That's twice she's looked this way. I think she likes me!"

"Get up," Hugo said woodenly. "We're leaving."

"What? But we only just got here!"

"We're leaving," Hugo said again. "We've attracted enough attention to ourselves."

Grumbling, Peter shoved bits of bread and cheese into his pockets, then tossed back the remainder of his ale. Hugo flung a few coins on the table, not even bothering to look at the denomination, then picked up his cloak and began to stride from the room, willing himself not to glance in the girl's direction again.

But he got no farther than the threshold before a raspy voice called out, "Oh, sir? I'm believin' ye've forgotten somethin'."

Hugo didn't have to turn around. He'd heard the brief scuffle, and, assuming it was only the innkeeper diving for the coins he'd tossed upon the table, had ignored it. Clearly, however, it hadn't been the Fox and Hare's proprietor who'd been responsible for all that scuffling.

Straightening, his eyes narrowing dangerously, Hugo laid a hand upon his sword hilt and said, still not turning around, "Let the lad go."

Behind him, the two drunken cutthroats chuckled. "Let 'im go, sir? Aye, we'll let 'im go. Fer a price."

Sighing, Hugo turned. He was so tired of violence, so very sick of death. He didn't want to kill the two village louts who had hold of his squire. Time past, he'd have slit their throats and laughed about it later. Not now. He had seen so much needless death during the Crusades that he could no longer kill so much as a moth without regret.

But that was not to say he wouldn't slit a throat if forced to.

The two men who'd been lounging at the table nearest Hugo's were on their feet, albeit unsteadily, and the bigger one had a heavy arm drape about young Peter's neck. Peter, for his part, was struggling against the viselike grip; his boyish face had turned a rather unnatural shade of crimson. He had been caught completely unawares, and for that would suffer both at the hands of these louts, and later, his master's.

"Don't mind me, sir," Peter choked, his thin hands wrapped around the burly arm that strangled him. "Go on, save yourself. I'm not worth it—"

"Bloody hell," muttered Hugo, rolling his eyes.

"Dick," cried the innkeeper, leaving his taps and glowering furiously. "Let the man alone. I won't have fightin' in me place—"

"If the bloke tosses us 'is purse," sneered the smaller man, who appeared to be known as Dick, "there won't be any fightin', Simon. We'll call it an even trade, won't we, Timmy?"

The giant grunted, giving Peter a shake. "Aye."

Three things occurred simultaneously just then. The first was that Peter, suddenly discovering that he had a backbone, or at least *teeth*, sank them into Timmy's arm. Timmy bellowed and released the boy, just as Dick, trying to illustrate to Hugo the seriousness of his intent, lunged at the squire with the business end of a very sharp stiletto. Hugo, witnessing the gleam of the knifepoint, unsheathed his sword and flung himself at the evil-minded Dick, only to find himself tripping over Simon, the innkeeper, who had decided to dive for the gold Hugo'd left on his table, in an effort to keep it from being lost in the fray.

The innkeeper ought to have stayed put. Hugo, in a desperate attempt not to kill some innocent soul with his blade, smashed a heavy shoulder into the table, shattering it and sending the coins flying across the room. Sprawled on his back upon the floor, Hugo found himself blinking at the crossbeams, the breath knocked out of him. The next thing he knew, the ferret-faced Dick had pounced, both of his scabby knees pressing down upon Hugo's sword arm before he could raise the weapon. Dick's small, rodentlike eyes sparkled with greed as his stiletto pressed against

Hugo's throat, recognizing the bigger man's unexpected disadvantage.

"Nice somersault, that," Dick complimented him with a smile that revealed a mouthful of rotting teeth. "Now cough up them coins—"

Out of the corner of his eye, Hugo saw that Timmy had caught Peter again, and was pulling out tufts of the lad's hair as recompense for biting him. Peter caterwauled while the rest of the inn's clientele scattered in four directions, with the exception of the innkeeper, who was still scrambling about the floor, looking for his money.

Hugo sighed. He still had his dagger in his left boot, tucked there for occasions exactly like this one. He'd draw the blade across Dick's throat before the footpad could whistle fare-thee-well, though Hugo didn't much like the idea of getting his cloak bloodied. Lord, he was sick of death.

"Very well." Hugo sighed again, feigning surrender. "Take it."

But the moment Dick's hand went for the purse at Hugo's belt, something whizzed past the cutthroat's cheek and buried itself through the thick sleeve of Dick's jerkin, pinning his arm to the floor just between Hugo's legs. Hugo had jerked his own hand back just in time to keep it from being impaled.

Staring down his long torso in disbelief, Hugo saw that a violet-tipped arrow had embedded itself deeply into the floorboards, missing not only his hand but his most prized treasure of all by a mere two inches. Dick's arm was trapped against Hugo's legs, and the shock of how close the projectile had come to splitting his hand in half caused the cutthroat to whimper.

Hugo looked up just in time to see the girl the innkeeper had called Finn turning to level an arrow at Timmy's broad back. This time, she calmly warned her intended victim.

"Let the boy go or I'll sever your spine."

The giant froze. Then, rotating slowly, Peter writhing in his arms, Timmy looked from Finn to his partner, trapped against Hugo and the floor.

"Gor," the simple man gulped. "Don't shoot, lass. Dick and I didn't mean nofink—"

He released Peter, who staggered away, clutching his head and moaning, Hugo thought, a bit louder than necessary.

The auburn-haired girl lowered her bow and approached Hugo, her lovely face as unconcerned as if she'd just brought in the washing. She studiously ignored Dick, despite his whimpered moans, and did not so much as glance at Hugo as she bent, wrapped slender fingers round the arrow's shaft, and gently worked the missile out of the wood in which it had been embedded.

While she was so close, Hugo could not help staring, and he did so unabashedly, taking in the smooth white skin, tinged pink at lip and cheek, the long, oddly dark eyelashes, the flowery fragrance of her. He was not generally dumbstruck in the presence of women—far from it, actually—but for the life of him, he could think of nothing to say to this maid, not even when her hand was but an inch from his—

"Ah," the girl said, finally drawing forth her arrow, intact, from the floor. She examined the tip critically, thumbing the point to check its sharpness. She was apparently pleased with the result, since her pretty face broke into a smile that revealed a set of even white teeth. "Well, look at that," she said to herself. "Thought for certain this one was lost for good."

The minute he was free, the hapless Dick scrambled to his feet, cursing fluently and flapping the arm that had been pinned to the floor.

"Damned bloody bitch," he howled. "What'd ye do that for? We was only havin' a bit o' fun. Weren't we, Timmy? Jus' a bit o' fun with the knight—"

Finnula Crais wasn't listening, however. She slid the undamaged arrow back into her quiver and calmly, with a last, appraising glance at Hugo, slipped out the door.

Hugo was on his feet in a split second, dodging the innkeeper, who was still on his hands and knees searching for coin, and the hopping-mad Dick, as well as the wreckage of the table he'd smashed. But though he reached the door perhaps a second or two after the girl, she had disappeared, as suddenly as she'd appeared in the first place. He looked up and down the cobblestoned street for some sign of the lass, but saw no trace of her.

He was swearing to himself when Peter approached, panting for breath.

"Did you see that, my lord?" the boy asked excitedly. "I never saw anyone in my life handle a bow like that. She lifted that thing like it was a part of her arm. Did you see it?"

Hugo, still scanning the crowded street for the girl, growled menacingly in response. The boy either did not hear him, or unwisely chose to pursue the topic in spite of his master's warning.

"Saved our lives, I think she did, my lord. Why do you think she bothered? Wee lass like that, you'd think it would be *us* that would be doing the rescuing, eh, my lord? But she fair took that Dick's hand off—" Then, in a different tone: "My lord, why do you look like that? Is aught the matter?"

Hugo shook himself. Was aught the matter? Who was this Finnula Crais, that she threw him into such a panic of emotion with a single look? Hundreds of women had looked at him in his lifetime, and he'd never reacted like this before. Nay, he'd quite naturally and happily lured them into his bed, and a pleasant time was had by all. What was it about that ridiculously dressed, cunning little redhead that had sent him chasing her, like a tom after a she-cat in heat?

"Come, my lord," Peter cried, excitedly. "She can't have got far. Let me run after her—"

Hugo caught the boy by the arm, nearly yanking him off his feet. "You'll do nothing of the kind. Go and fetch the horses. We're leaving this place posthaste."

Peter stamped his booted foot. He had gotten over the scare the giant had given him, and had looked forward to an exchange of pleasantries with the pert little maid in the leather chausses, the like of which even he, used to every type of woman London could afford, from nearly naked dancers to princesses of the blood, had never before encountered. But the girl had run away, and his master, in a fit of churlish pique, would not allow him to search for her.

"She wouldn't be hard to find," Peter grumbled. "A redheaded lass in braies is sure to be noticed wherever she goes. I wager we could find her in less than an hour. And we owe her our lives, my lord. Or at least a purse—"

Hugo's only response was to growl again.

"What ails you, my lord?" Peter demanded, unwisely. He could not, for the life of him, fathom why His Lordship wouldn't want to look for their rescuer. "Think you the maid a sorceress, that you run so feverishly from her?"

Hugo glowered down at the impertinent lad, his own gaze every bit as piercing as the maid's, though Hugo's eyes were a changeable hazel that even now glinted gold with anger.

"Nay," he snapped, taking long strides toward the public stables. "But she showed overmuch interest in us, a wandering knight, returning from the Crusades, and his raw squire."

"Aye," Peter readily agreed. "And I was enjoying her interest mightily."

"I could see that." Hugo's tone was sardonic, although the humor in his voice was not reflected on his stern features. "But of what interest could either of us be to so comely a maid, who is surely spoken for by some village smithy or local knight?"

Peter would have liked to reply that he himself would quite obviously be of romantic interest to any maid, however comely, but he didn't like to pass himself off as a braggart. He was quite certain that it was he, and not his master, that interested the auburn-tressed maid. Why would any girl be interested in a thickly bearded fellow likely twice her age, and dressed quite scruffily in spite of his fortune and title? Whereas Peter himself wore the shiniest gold necklace at his throat, and an expensive velvet tunic that, though not exactly suited to sleeping outdoors, clearly indicated his elevated rank of royal squire. What did it matter that both items had been purchased for him by his new lord? The girl didn't have to know that.

But now his master was speaking again, in that deep, rumbling voice that Peter alternately envied and feared.

"I do not wish us to attract undue attention," Hugo explained, in a tone he hoped did not sound condescending. Curse and rot his vassal for falling to that scimitar, and leaving him saddled with this pup! "Though any hope of that has been dashed by those men back there. Still, we'd best leave the girl be, since there is no attention worse than that of the father or brother of a virgin maid—"

"Ah," Peter said slyly. "Like that dancing girl what you had in London last fortnight, my lord? The one who called her procurer when you—"

Hugo glared down at the boy, his eyes tawny with impatience. "Nay, not like her, lad," he growled, but would not elaborate. Instead, he again bade Peter fetch the horses.

As he stood on the cobblestones, his hazel eyes alert for a

glimpse of auburn, all of Hugo's thoughts centered on the rounded derriere of the fetching Finnula. How had the girl learned to use a bow like that? And why had she taken it upon herself to save him? Women had certainly changed since Hugo had last been in England. Now they not only gadded about by themselves in boy's clothing, but slung quivers over their backs and arbitrarily shot at footpads. Although, Hugo thought, Lord knew that any woman who was going to dress like that needed to defend herself . . . most particularly from men like Hugo.

Trying hard to turn his mind to a higher plane, Hugo forced himself to think not of Finnula Crais's backside, but of Stephensgate Manor, and all the work that would be required of him to put right what his father had no doubt torn hopelessly asunder, as was his foolish wont. Still, those mist-gray eyes plagued him, even after he'd mounted his steed and urged the stallion forward. Had he looked back once more he'd have seen those very eyes boring a veritable hole into his back, as Finnula made some swift mental calculations of her own.

# Chapter Three

$\mathcal{F}$innula knew what it was she had to do. She had chosen her quarry, had protected it from being had by another, and now she would lay her trap. But she set about her task with a heavy heart—not out of pity for her prey, but out of anger at herself . . . and, though she'd be loath to admit it, at Mellana.

She knew she ought never to have agreed to this ridiculous undertaking. If Robert heard of it, and he was bound to, he really might wear a hole in the seat of her chausses, as he'd always threatened . . . or at least he'd attempt to catch her to try. Finnula was not some common-born milkmaid that she could act with such caprice and not expect the censure of her family. Though they were not titled or landed, the Crais family had operated the Earl of Stephensgate's mill for many a generation, and were one of the most respected families in the community. For a daughter of Phillip and Helene Crais to take part in something so . . . *common* . . . was unthinkable. Why, what would people think?

And Mellana's insistence that "all the maids in Stephensgate" were engaging in man-napping in order to buy ingredients for ale brewing was small comfort. Finnula hadn't the slightest regard for the maids of Stephensgate, who seemed to have little on their minds save collecting hair ribbons and husbands. And, of course, there was the small matter of the church, which expressly frowned upon the practice, a fact Finnula had pointed out to Mellana, that day in the kitchen.

"Mellana, you've taken leave of your senses," Finnula had declared tartly. "The fact that all of Stephensgate takes part in so pagan a practice means naught to me—"

"'Tis *not* a pagan practice." Mellana sniffed indignantly. "Isabella Laroche has done it dozens of times, and she—"

"Isabella Laroche is a trollop and a fool." Finnula's patience was wearing thin. "Don't you dare deny, Mellana, that she will lift her skirts for anything in chausses. God's teeth, she's mistaken *me* for a youth many a time and asked me into the manor house for a drop of ale. Of course a woman like that would think nothing of abducting a man and holding him for ransom. But you know as well as I that during his last sermon, Father Edward decried the practice most energetically—"

"And you know as well as I that Father Edward seeks his pleasure with Fat Maude in the village," hissed Mellana.

Finnula conceded the fact with an uncomfortable shrug of her shoulders. She had not known that Mellana was aware of such matters and wondered who'd told the girl. That damned Isabella, no doubt. That the priest was a hypocrite, Finnula would be the first to agree. But he was basically a good man, doing what he could with a poor parish and a manor that had been lordless for over a year. Seeing that none of her arguments bore any weight with her suddenly willful sister, Finnula accepted her fate with ill grace.

"All right," she grumbled. "I'll capture a man for you, and bring him here, and you can hold him for ransom and use the cursed gilt you get for him for hops or a dowry or whatever will you. Just don't, I beg you, Mellana, let Robert find out." Finnula shook her head. "He'll kill us both."

Mellana, her sapphire eyes sparkling with jubilation over her victory, chose to treat her younger sister magnanimously. "Oh, you exaggerate. Robert loves you best of all his sisters, sweet Finn. He lets you walk all over him."

"You didn't see him after the sheriff's visit." Sighing, Finnula looked down at her hands, which, despite the calluses on her fingertips, were quite slim and beautiful. "I'm well-used to trapping dumb animals, Mellana, but how am I ever to snare a man?"

Mellana, having gained her way, had lost interest in the details of the matter. "Lord, I don't know," she declared, fluffing out her hair so that she could join the rest of the family in their merrymaking in the room next door. "Just make sure he isn't from Stephensgate."

"*What?*" Finnula looked up, her large gray eyes filled with dismay. "Not from Stephensgate? You want me to abduct a *stranger?*"

"Well, of course. Isabella has already ransomed every man in the village at least once. And Shrewsbury and Dorchester, too. Their families won't pay a second time. The practice does lose its charm if overused—"

Finnula let loose some of her finest expletives, and Mellana, genuinely shocked, huffed away, leaving her younger sister glaring at the flagstones.

To abduct a stranger, Finnula fretted to herself, she'd have to travel the two days' distance to the nearest large village. She was a frequent visitor to Leesbury, of course, since her poaching forays sometimes took her in that direction, and Patricia's brother-in-law, Simon, ran the inn there and he wasn't stingy with the ale, but she didn't have much faith that the residents of the slightly more cosmopolitan village would find the practice of man-trapping amusing. *Their* parish priest wasn't nearly so liberal as her own, and might very well frown upon what in Stephensgate and Dorchester was considered a piquant custom.

But when Finnula saw the gold coin that the bearded traveler had thrown to Simon at the Fox and Hare, she knew that she'd found the ideal quarry. Obviously not from Leesbury, the tall man had both purse and a manservant, and, she soon saw, with just a little investigation, a fine destrier for a mount. Here was a man well-placed in life.

That she sparked an interest in the man equal to the one he sparked in her, she saw at once, though she knew it was for entirely different reasons. Finnula did not consider herself at all beautiful. No, Mellana, with her voluptuous figure and blond curls was the beauty in the family.

But Finnula couldn't help noticing that of late, she'd been attracting more and more masculine stares, and the fact was the cause of no little discomfort to her. Indeed, the change her passage from lanky girlhood into graceful womanhood had wrought on her looks was a primary source of irritation for her. It had, after all, caused the disaster that had been her short-lived marriage, and proven quite a hindrance during her pursuit of game: She was constantly being admonished by well-meaning husbandmen that she ought not to roam the countryside in chausses, and that it was a needle, not a bow, she ought to be wielding.

But conversely, her newfound attractiveness to the opposite sex had proven useful at times. She had all but charmed the shire reeve into overlooking her various violations of poaching laws.

And there wasn't a merchant in the village who wasn't paying more handsomely than ever for the legally obtained game she sold them, and boasting to his customers that the fowl had been shot by none other than the Fair Finn. Like Diana and Artemis, the pagan huntress goddesses of old, Finnula's reputation as a lovely archer did not harm as much as help in her endeavor to feed the hungry of Stephensgate.

And of course, now that she had gotten herself into the man-hunting business, she intended to use her own winsome beauty as bait.

That the tall, bearded stranger might not rise to the lure never crossed Finnula's mind. She had seen the way his eyes had raked her when she'd entered the inn. There was hunger in his glance, though she'd seen caution there, too. Not enough of the latter, since he'd managed to get himself into that scrape with that pair of footpads. Still, perhaps he'd learned from his mistake: When she'd followed him apace, she saw with approval that he steered clear of main thoroughfares.

His cautiousness, however, would be his undoing, because by sticking to sheep trails instead of the road, he'd be drawn directly into her most heavily hunted territory, the hills surrounding Stephensgate, and in particular, the earl's demesnes.

When the tall man and his boy set off in such haste from Leesbury, they unknowingly picked up a third member to their party. Finnula followed at a discreet distance, keeping to the shelter of the trees and allowing a slack rein to her mount, an unremarkable-looking mare she'd had since childhood that was nevertheless as highly trained as any knight's destrier. The horse, whom Finnula had named Violet in an unguarded moment of ten-year-old fancy, had learned to tread quietly over forest bracken and to stand as still as stone while her mistress was in pursuit of quarry, and also knew enough to amble back to the millhouse when Finnula set her in the right direction and whacked her on the rump. In all, the two made an awe-inspiring team, working together as well as any partners in crime.

Finnula watched the pair of travelers with keen interest, taking in as many details about them as she could. The man, the one she sought, was carefully dressed to reveal as little as possible about himself. Like the thick, tawny beard that hid his features, the untrimmed cloak, shapeless tunic, and plain chausses revealed nothing about the size of the purse carried upon his belt. There was no disguising his size, however, which was impressive. Why, he was probably taller than Robert, who stood over six feet tall.

The boy, however, hardly looked a challenge. Of medium height, he aped his better by overdressing in a velvet tunic and brightly colored hose. He, she thought, would definitely benefit from a treetop snare. The man, though. The man would require more finesse.

Unlike many hunters she knew, it was the pursuit, not the kill, that Finnula most enjoyed. The game she shot, she shot because she knew of families without meat on their tables. The good Lord had seen fit to give her unerring aim and a steady arm, so she felt it her duty to see those less fortunate well-fed.

But she didn't enjoy killing, and did so only when strictly necessary. Stalking prey was much more to her tastes, and trapping it in her own nonlethal traps even more satisfying. That she invariably released the animals she trapped few people knew, and even fewer were aware of the number of animals that, finding them in the traps of others, she also set free. She particularly disliked the cruel metal traps that the earl's woodsman set out to catch wolves, and whenever she encountered one, she quickly buried it where she knew old Tom would never find it again.

But there was something to be said for the chase, for the stalking, and though she never would have admitted it to Mellana,

Finnula thought there was a chance that she might just enjoy pursuing this particular quarry. How much more interesting to hunt an opponent of some intelligence, and not some dumb animal. Of course, he was a man, which automatically made him her intellectual inferior, since Finnula had never encountered a man whose wit rivaled her own—and that included her now-deceased husband. But still, it would be a challenge worthy of the Fair Finn, and it was with a happily thumping heart that she trailed him.

But when it became apparent to Finnula that the stranger seemed to know the countryside and was heading toward Stephensgate, she realized with a sinking feeling what she was going to have to do. She was loath to try it, since the last time it had produced such dreadful consequences. But if she didn't act soon, she'd lose her prey, and who knew when she'd find another so promising? She couldn't let Mellana down, not after she'd promised. Besides, she was a year older and wiser now. And this time, she would be in control. She'd be expecting him, and she'd be prepared.

Taking up Violet's reins, she urged the mare well ahead of the traveler and his servant, and hastily, but with practiced care, made the preparations.

# Chapter Four

*H*ugo wasn't certain how much longer he was going to be able to abide his squire's incessant whining. First about the girl in the inn, and now the fact that his horse didn't have the strength of Hugo's and needed a rest. Hugo himself had selected Peter's mount, and knew that the animal was as sturdy as his own, though not as highly trained. No, it was *Peter* who wanted to rest, though it was only just past midday and the weather fine, and they had been riding for only a few hours. What had Hugo done in this life to deserve the torment this sniveling youth was putting him through? Couldn't the lad keep his mouth shut and let them ride in peace?

"My lord," the boy called, from some distance behind. "My lord, hold up. We haven't had a bite to eat since Leesbury and I'm near faint with hunger—"

Hugo rolled his eyes. The boy's appetite, like his love of chatter, was insatiable.

"There's bread and bacon in your pack," Hugo growled, in his most menacing manner. "Gnaw on that awhile." Hopefully, the youth's mouth would be too full for conversation. Or, Hugo considered, brightening a bit, he might choke to death—

But they were entering familiar ground at last, and Hugo could not stay irritated long. Here was the grove where he had bagged his first stag some twenty years earlier, there the copse where he'd first laid Fat Maude, some ten years later. They were still a good two days' ride from the manor house, but it was two days of territory that was as familiar to Hugo as the back of his own hand. Ah! It felt strangely good to be home after a decade of fairly aimless wandering.

When they came to the turn in the sheep track that led to the rock formation that towered above the Spring of St. Elias, Hugo hesitated. The spring was a delightful place for a dip. Many a boyhood summer had been spent hunting in these hills, and the spring was where Hugo and his brother had bathed, learning to swim in the deep pool, and learning to dive from the towering rock outcroppings above the spring.

No longer tended by the church, St. Elias having fallen out of favor some fifty years back when water from his spring failed to cure a single leper, the pool was overgrown and desolately beautiful in its remoteness. Wildflowers flourished in the crevices of the gorge, and the branches of the trees that grew twistedly out of the rock skimmed the water's surface. It was a perfect place for a swim after a hot and dusty ride—and that's precisely what Hugo decided his charge needed.

Of course Peter had other ideas.

"Go for a swim?" he echoed, in disbelief, when Hugo imparted his plan. "What, *me*? Born and raised in London I was, don't forget, my lord. What do I know about swimming? Couldn't swim a stroke to save my life!"

"How fortuitous," Hugo rumbled, quite audibly.

"I mean it, my lord. I'm happy to water the horses while *you* swim, but you won't catch *me* jumping in for a dip. Besides, what would I want with a lot of icy cold spring water? It's just turned May, sir, not July. There's quite a distinct nip in the air—"

There wasn't, but Hugo wasn't in any mood to argue. Slipping from the saddle, Hugo grasped his mount's bridle and steered his horse first toward the rocky prominence that towered above the spring, so that he could gaze on it fully and see whether it had changed overmuch in the ten years since he'd last seen it. He left the boy grumbling behind him, and slipped through the fresh green grass alongside the sheep track and into the quiet solitude of the woods.

There, the bright afternoon sunlight slid in golden shafts through the ceiling of newly burst leaves overhead. The forest floor was sun-dappled and fresh with the scent of last year's mulch, and Hugo inhaled deeply. It had been too many years since he'd last smelled good English peat.

Heedless of the twigs and bracken crackling beneath his large boot soles, Hugo strode forward, hearing only birds calling to one another from the canopy of leaves above, the roar of water from the spring's cascade, and the sudden shouting of his squire behind. He stopped for a moment, wondering what ailed the boy, but decided it could only be more of the lad's foolish complaining. Rolling his eyes again, Hugo strolled toward the rock outcropping that overlooked the gorge in which the spring lay, and stood upon the gray stones, looking down.

With the exception of the trees, which seemed taller and more twisted than ever, the spring was much the same as when he'd last seen it. The water below was as clear as the air around him,

green in the golden light that streamed through the blanket of
leaves overhead, its glasslike surface disturbed only by the waterfall from the rocks upon which he stood. St. Elias's spring flowed
beneath the ground and bubbled up here through a crevice in the
rocky gorge, cascading in white froth a dozen feet down to the
pool below.

The sweetest, most refreshing water imaginable; one had to
catch it directly at the source, before it hit the pool below, to truly
divine its worth. Hugo and his brother had spent hours on their
stomachs on the very prominence on which he now stood, straining their arms down the cliff side to catch skinfuls of the cool
water.

Eyeing the nearly empty water flask on his saddle, Hugo decided to repeat the practice of his childhood, and fetched the skin,
emptying its stale contents on a bed of white violets. Striding back
to the outcropping, he lay full down on the sun-warmed stone,
stretching one long arm, flask in hand, to catch the burbling cascade at its mossy source.

It was as he was thus engaged that a flash of color, quite unlike
the cool greens and golds of the woods around him, caught his
eye, and he looked down into the gorge . . . and froze.

It was the girl from the inn.

He knew her instantly, though she wore neither chausses nor
white lawn shirt now. Indeed, her ivory flesh gleamed in the afternoon sunlight as she stretched languidly upon the stony banks
of the pool. Naked, all that glorious auburn hair unbound, she
looked as delicate as a water sprite: Her pert breasts were no larger
than would fit in a man's hand; her slim thighs, long and white,
met in a fluff of silky hair that echoed the shade of the curtain
of curls that fell around her slender shoulders; her waist was so
narrow his hands would fit around it, his fingers meeting in the

middle; her flanks were lean and white, and, as he'd noticed back at the inn, her backside distinctly heart-shaped.

All this he observed in the moment she hesitated upon the bank, first stretching and then coiling that long cape of hair into a knot on the top of her head. Then, with the grace of a porpoise, she slipped into the crystal waters.

It was then that Hugo realized he'd been holding his breath, so anxious was he not to break the spell of the moment. Lying flat as he had been, there was no possibility of the girl seeing him, but he had lain frozen just the same, afraid he might do something to alert the maid to his presence and cause her to flee.

That she would flee if he revealed himself he was quite certain. He readily equated her to the wild things that lived in the woods around them, most especially with the shy red foxes inhabiting burrows at the forest's edge. She had the look of a vixen about her, wild and sly and yet strangely diffident. Like any virtuous maid, she would not welcome intruders to her bath, and would surely run at the first sign of having been observed.

Hugo stared down at the lovely apparition swimming below him, his thoughts a-jumble in his head. Foremost among them was the question, *Who is she?*, though he knew the answer to that. Finnula Crais, the miller's daughter. There had been a family of that name in villenage to his father, Hugo remembered. This, then, must be one of their offspring. But what was this miller about, allowing a defenseless maid to roam the countryside unescorted and dressed in such provocative garb—or completely undressed, as the case now stood?

As soon as Hugo arrived at Stephensgate Manor, he would send for the miller, and see to it that the girl was better protected in the future. Did the man not ken the riffraff that traveled the roads these days, the footpads and cutthroats and despoilers of young women such as the one below him? Of course, the girl had more than proven her mettle back at the inn, but Hugo knew that most criminals were nowhere near as stupid as Dick and Timmy. The girl would not have lasted a second in London, and it was miraculous that she had not yet met with disaster here in Shropshire.

So fixed was Hugo upon his musings that for a moment, he did not realize that the maid had paddled out of view. Where the waterfall cascaded, the pool below was out of his line of vision, being blocked off by the rock outcropping on which he lay. He assumed that the girl had ducked beneath the waterfall, perhaps to rinse her hair, which he noticed she'd kept well above the water. Such a heavy mane would take hours to dry, and perhaps she preferred to cleanse it in the fresh water from the spring rather than in the slightly staler pool.

Hugo waited, pleasantly anticipating the girl's reappearance. He wondered to himself whether the chivalrous thing to do was to creep away now, without drawing attention to himself, then meet up with her again upon the road, as if by accident, and offer her escort home to the Stephensgate.

It was as he was deciding that he would do so, but not without a last glance at her slim beauty, that he heard a soft sound behind him, and then suddenly something very sharp was at his throat, and someone very light was astride his back.

It was with an effort that Hugo controlled his instinctive defensive reactions. Having been employed as a soldier for the past ten years, his senses were honed into pure fighting mechanisms, and whether he was partaking in a barroom brawl or rooting out Saracens, his instinct was to strike first, and question later.

But he had never before felt so slim an arm circle his neck, or such slight thighs straddle his back. Nor had his head ever been jerked back against such a temptingly soft cushion. When the curtain of auburn hair fell about him, caressing his face and filling his senses with the light fragrance of rose, he was glad he hadn't reached back and hurled his fair adversary over his head and down the gorge, where she would undoubtedly have split open her skull on the rocky banks below.

"Stay perfectly still," advised his captor, and Hugo, enjoying the warmth from her thighs and, more particularly, the softness of the hollow between her breasts, where she kept the back of his head firmly anchored, was happy to oblige her.

"I've a knife at your throat," the maid informed him in her boyish voice, "but I won't use it unless I have to. If you do as I say, you shan't be harmed. Do you understand?"

Hugo felt that a token of resistance must be made, though above all else, he did not want to injure the girl. So he attempted to lift his arms from where they hung, still holding the flask beneath the waterfall. But the diminutive fireball astride his back would have none of it, and stamped a pretty bare foot down upon his forearm, surprising him so that he dropped the flask into the pool below.

"Leave it!" she commanded, in an imperious voice. "I told you not to move!"

Hugo, admiring the slim arch of the foot, the only part of her that he could actually see, with the exception of the cloud of hair that enveloped them both, decided he ought to apologize now. Surely the girl had a right to be angry; in all innocence, she had come to the spring to bathe, not to be spied upon. And while he was greatly enjoying the feel of her nubile body against him, he was not enjoying her wrath. Better that he calm the spirited wench, and see her back on the road to Stephensgate, where he could make sure that she was kept from straddling other men's backs, and thereby getting herself into mischief.

"I earnestly beg your pardon, demoiselle," he began, in what he hoped was a contrite tone, though it was difficult for him to speak without laughing. "I stumbled upon you in your most private hour, and for that, I must ask your forgiveness—"

"I took you for simple, but not completely stupid," was the girl's surprising reply. Hugo was amazed to hear that her own voice was as rich with amusement as his own.

"I *meant* for you to stumble upon me, of course," she elaborated. Quick as lightning, the knife left his throat, and the maid seized both of his wrists and had them trussed behind him before he was even aware of what was happening.

"You're my prisoner now," Finnula Crais said, with evident satisfaction at a job well-done. "To gain your freedom, you'll have to pay for it. Handsomely."

# Chapter Five

*H*ugo could scarcely believe his ears. "What?" he demanded stupidly.

"You heard me. You're my prisoner."

So saying, she loosened her arm from around his neck, and he felt her draw away from him. A second later, his sword, still in its sheath, was detached from his belt, followed by the dagger he'd thought so well-hidden in his boot. Then the light weight of the girl returned, as once again she seated herself astride his wide back.

"So's your boy, for what that's worth," she informed him conversationally. "My prisoner, I mean. He stepped into one of my tree snares a quarter of an hour ago. I'm surprised you didn't hear him squalling. Quite a temper he has. You're much easier."

Hugo digested this small compliment, all the while conscious of the heat from the girl's thighs, the gentle weight of her on the small of his back, the soft scent of her, all clean and fresh womanhood. She had crept out of the pool and up a hidden trail in the rocks to where he lay. Somewhere along the way, she'd pulled on the chausses and whipped the white lawn shirt over her head—he'd felt the soft fabric against his cheek, where he'd thought to feel smooth skin. So she was not without modesty—but what manner of woman was this?

What sort of world had he stumbled into? When, in the name of God, had maids dressed in leather chausses started capturing grown men and holding them for ransom? He'd been gone from England a long time, he realized, but was it possible so much could have changed in that time? Why, ten years earlier, gentle maids blushed to *speak* to a stranger—they didn't strip before one, then leap upon his back and hold a knife to his throat.

Then a horrible thought occurred to him, and he blurted out, before he'd had time to think, "Those men at the inn. You are working with them?"

The girl snorted derisively. "Dick and Timmy? Certainly not. A stupider pair never existed. But I couldn't let them take what I meant to have myself."

"Do you mean to say," Hugo began, slowly, "that you—that all of this was apurpose?"

"Of course," the girl said, in some surprise. "I saw you at the inn, and decided you would make a good hostage. I'm not certain what to do with your boy. He's a bit of a nuisance, don't you think? Still, we'll think of something."

Hugo lay beneath her, hardly daring to believe his good fortune. He had been pursued by a great many women in his time, women more beautiful than Finnula Crais, women with more sophistication and worldly knowledge, but none of them had ever appealed to him as immediately as this girl. She boldly

announced that she wanted him for his money, and she wasn't
going to resort to seductions and stratagems to get it. Her game
was abduction, pure and simple, and Hugo was so amused, he
thought he might laugh out loud.

Every other woman he'd ever known, in both the literal and
biblical sense, had a single goal in mind—to become the chatelaine of Stephensgate Manor. Hugo had nothing against the institution of marriage, but he had never met a woman with whom
he felt he wanted to spend the rest of his life. And here was a girl
who stated, plain as day, that all she wanted from him was money.
It was as if a gust of fresh English air had blown through him,
renewing his faith in womankind.

"So it's your hostage I'm to be," Hugo said, to the stones beneath him. "And what makes you so certain I'll be able to pay
your ransom?"

"Do you think I'm daft? I saw the coin you tossed Simon back
at the Fox and Hare. You oughtn't be so showy with your spoils.
You're lucky 'tis me that's waylaid you, and not some of Dick's
and Timmy's friends. They have rather unsavory companions,
you know. You could have come to serious harm."

Hugo smiled to himself. Here he'd been worried about the girl
meeting up with trouble on her way back to Stephensgate, never
suspecting that she was sharing the same concern for him.

"Here, what are you smiling at?" the girl demanded, and to his
regret, she slid down from his back and prodded him, none too
gently, in the side with a sharp toe. "Sit up, now, and stop sneer-
ing. There isn't anything funny about me abducting you, you
know. I know I don't look like much, but I think I proved back at
the Fox and Hare that I truly am the finest shot with a short bow
in all the county, and I'll thank you to remember it."

Sitting up, Hugo found his hands well-tied behind his back.
There was certainly nothing lacking in the girl's knot-tying educa-

tion. His bonds were not tight enough to cut off the circulation, yet not loose enough to give way.

Lifting his gaze, he found his fair captor kneeling a few feet away from him, her elfin face pale in a halo of wildly curling red hair, hair so long that the ends of it twined among the violets below her knees. Her lawn shirt was untucked and sticking to her still-wet body in places, so that her pink nipples were plainly visible through the thin material.

Quirking up an eyebrow, Hugo realized that the girl was completely unaware of the devastating effect her looks had on him. Or at least aware only that naked, she made a fetching distraction.

"Well," she said, in that husky voice that hadn't a trace of flirtation in it, "I suppose that, seeing as how we'll be seeing a lot of each other over the next few days, I ought to introduce myself. I am Finnula Crais."

He couldn't help grinning, though he tried to hide his amusement by keeping one corner of his mouth down in a disapproving frown. "And does your father know that you roam the countryside, trussing up innocent men and demanding recompense for their freedom, Finnula Crais?"

"Certainly not," she snapped saltily. "My father is dead."

The corner of his mouth that had been grinning now fell to join the other in a frown. "Is he? Then who looks after you?"

"I look after myself," she said, with no little pride. Then, pulling a slightly comic face, she amended that statement. "Well, my older brother, Robert, tries to look after me, I suppose. But there are six of us—"

"Six of whom?"

"Six sisters. And it isn't easy for him—"

"Good God," Hugo cried. "You mean there are five more like you at home?"

"Of course not. I'm the youngest. Four of my sisters are already married, and the fifth, Mellana, would like to, only—" Here the chestnut-colored eyebrows, like winged birds in the smooth white sky of her forehead, gathered together in a scowl. "See here," Finnula said, in a voice that was heavy with disapproval. "You can't draw me out. I'm the interrogator here. Now tell me who you are."

Hugo had to think a moment. There was every chance that if he told her the truth, she'd release him at once, appalled. After all, her family owed their livelihood to the Earl of Stephensgate. She would have to be a very ungrateful—and stupid—chit indeed to hold her own lord for ransom. No, he wouldn't risk telling the truth to her just yet. He was greatly looking forward to being held captive by such a fair jailer.

"God's teeth," Finnula swore, with some impatience. "I only asked your name. If you're sitting there, thinking up some great lie to tell me, you'd better think again. Lies will only impede your return to freedom."

"Hugh Fitzwilliam," Hugo said, at once, and he told her he was the son of a knight situated in a manor near Caterbury, a village just beyond Stephensgate.

Finnula nodded knowingly, as if she'd guessed as much. "And you're returning from the Crusades," she said, touching her chin to indicate that only returning crusaders wore beards in this part of the country. Hugo had meant to shave, but the dispute over the innkeeper's wife had kept him too busy. "Were you imprisoned there?"

He nodded. "In Acre. For over a year."

If he'd hoped his woeful tone of voice would engender the girl's sympathy, he was disappointed. She didn't seem to possess any of the emotions he'd come to expect in women, pity among them.

"Well," she said cheerfully, "I'm certain that your wife will be happy to pay for your freedom, now that she has you so close to home. And you needn't fear, I won't charge her overmuch."

Hugo grinned. "But I have no wife."

The girl shrugged. "Your father, then."

"Dead."

Finnula looked so crestfallen that he wanted to laugh. Here she had gone to all the trouble of kidnapping him, and he had no relatives to pay ransom for him.

"Well, what am I to do with you, then?" she demanded, her asperity evident. "I can't go about with a giant clod of a man forever hanging on my shirttail. There must be *somebody* who would pay for your release. Think. Isn't there *anybody* who might want to see you again?"

Hugo glared at her. He didn't much appreciate being referred to as "a giant clod of a man." It didn't sound very complimentary, and he was used to receiving compliments from women—lots of them, as a matter of fact. And what did she mean, hanging on her shirttail? She made it sound as if she'd been saddled with some sort of invalid half-wit, and not the very good-looking, quite virile seventh Earl of Stephensgate.

"I'm sorry to disappoint you, madam," he said stiffly, and because he would not have her think he was a nobody, he added, carefully, "I do have a cousin who was instructed before I left for the Holy Land to pay any ransom demanded for me—"

"Oh, well, then," Finnula said, brightening. "That's all right!"

And she awarded him a smile so full of sunny warmth that he forgot all about being annoyed with her. He was so distracted that he didn't even hear the crunching of twigs nearby that warned of an interloper, not until it was too late.

Almost from out of nowhere hurtled the body of his squire. Peter collided against Finnula with stunning force, sending the girl sprawling beneath his vastly superior weight. Crushing the slender body down into the forest floor, Peter cried, "Run for it, my lord! Now's your chance!"

Hugo had never felt such all-consuming fury. Of all the times for his clodpated squire to try to prove himself—and against a helpless girl, no less! Hugo let out a roar that startled birds from the treetops, and sent his own mount's ears back flat against his noble head. Peter lifted his head from the girl stretched out prone beneath him, eyes closed, and had the grace to look sheepish.

"Get off her!" Hugo bellowed, struggling to his feet—no easy task, he found, with hands bound behind one's back. "You simpleminded fool, you've knocked her senseless!"

Peter looked down at the pale and limp form beneath him, and bit his lower lip. "I'm sorry, sir," he began, earnestly. "But I thought you were in real trouble. I stepped into a snare back there, that strung me up from a branch near five feet off the ground, and I only just cut myself free, and I thought—"

"And you thought I was in mortal danger from that girl beneath you? Get off her, I said!"

Peter clambered awkwardly from Finnula's body, and Hugo fell onto his knees at her side, peering down anxiously at her pale face. He could see no outward signs of injury, and no rocks nearby on which she might have hit her head, and decided that she must have only had the wind knocked from her, and would revive anon.

"Go and fill your flask from yon waterfall," Hugo instructed his squire curtly, "and dampen her face with it. At your peril she does not waken soon, or you will pay with your own worthless skull."

Shaken at the anger in his master's tone, Peter obeyed his instructions to the letter, filling his flask and lightly moistening the girl's lips and face with the cool, fresh water. St. Elias might well have fallen out of favor with the church for not having cured any lepers, but at the touch of his rejuvenating spring water to the fallen maid's skin, her eyelids fluttered, and color began to return to her high cheekbones.

"But I do not understand," Peter worried, kneeling at the girl's far side. "I saw that your hands were bound, and I stumbled upon your sword and knife, lain upon the ground, I thought those men from the inn had followed us, and that it happened she was one of their gang—"

"Nay," Hugo growled. "She captured me by herself and in all fairness. I will honor her demand for ransom—"

"Ransom!" Peter looked down at the fair form lying crumpled beneath him, and shook his head in wonder. "Don't tell me! I heard it, but I never believed it true . . ."

"Heard what?" demanded Hugo, his temper short. "Tell me now, you sniveling brat, or I'll—"

"I heard it said in London," Peter continued quickly, "that country maids were known to capture men and hold them ransom for monies they used to buy ingredients to brew ale—"

"Ale!" Hugo echoed, loudly enough to cause Finnula to groan at the word, as if it provoked an unpleasant memory.

"Aye, sir," Peter said more softly, nodding. "Ale they sell for profit, to pay for their weddings, as a sort of dowry—"

"I never heard of anything so ridiculous," Hugo declared. Truly, his country was well on the road to ruin if such practices were indeed taking place on a regular basis.

"Well," Peter said, "I can think of no other reason why this maid would risk her neck capturing strange men and demanding their ransom—"

"She wasn't risking her neck until *you* came along," Hugo declared, accusingly. "I wouldn't have laid a hand on her, and I'm sure she knew it."

"I still don't see—"

"No, you don't. Now listen to me, before she fully wakes, and listen well. You'll go on to Stephensgate alone, and wait for word of me there. Tell my bailiff I've been delayed, but that I'll arrive anon. And under no circumstance is the sheriff to be roused, or any such nonsense—" Hugo stopped speaking as Finnula became fully conscious. She blinked up at him dazedly, her large gray eyes filled with confusion.

Then of a sudden she was on her feet, bare as they were, leaping behind a startled Hugo's back and twining a slim arm around his neck, a small hunting dagger at his throat. Hugo was so tall that, kneeling, he was only a head shorter than she was fully standing, and so it was that he could feel the entire length of her warm body pressed close against his back, from the unsteady hammering of her heart beneath her rounded breasts, crushed up against his broad shoulders, to the trembling of her limbs as she regarded Peter from over the top of Hugo's head.

"I knew I ought to have checked your boots for knives," she said angrily to the squire, whose cheeks had been turning steadily a color not unlike umber. "But I thought you were too stupid to have a spare one. You did, though, and you cut yourself free, didn't you?"

Peter, for the first time since he'd been in Hugo's acquaintance, was actually tongue-tied. He nodded dumbly.

"I thought as much." Finnula's arm tightened around Hugo's throat, but he thought she did it unconsciously, as if by straining the master to her, she could keep the servant at bay. "Well, do not come any closer, or I'll have no choice but to cut him."

It was an obvious lie, which no one who looked into her angelic face would believe, but Peter remembered the men back at the inn, and stayed still. Besides, he'd been given his instructions by his master, and would not but obey them. Never again would he risk engendering His Lordship's wrath.

"I w-will do as . . . you say," Peter stammered, somewhat incoherently. "I am sorry for . . . for hurting you. You aren't— Is anything amiss?"

Finnula clung even closer to Hugo, who thought he might be strangled by the tight hold she kept on him. Truly, the girl did not know her own strength, which was considerably greater than one might guess, to look at her.

"You are Sir Hugh's squire?" she demanded, and Peter, though confused by the title and name change, nodded.

"Good. Then get gone with you to . . ." She paused, her lips not far from Hugo's ear, and turned her face toward her captive. "Where did you say you hailed from, sir?"

"You know where it is, boy," Hugo said, to hurry things along. "Go there, now—"

"And tell them," Finnula hurried to add, when it appeared that Peter was ready to fly from the clearing, "that they will be contacted in the matter of ransom for their master. And at Sir Hugh's peril do you contact Sheriff de Brissac," she took care to inform him, "because he won't brook any nonsense, and has more important things to do than trouble himself with so trivial a matter as this."

Hugo listened to this last with interest. It was spoken with a particular force that indicated that this maiden had tangled with Sheriff de Brissac in the past, and wished to avoid further confrontations. How many other men, Hugo wondered, had Finnula Crais abducted? Considering her tender years and obvious inexperience, not many, he thought. So what sort of troubles could she have gotten herself into that involved the reeve of the shire?

"Yes, madam," Peter was saying, backing away with no little haste. "I'll see to it that no one contacts the sheriff, never you fear."

"Get gone, then," Finnula said, with a wave of the dagger, and Peter nearly fell over himself in his haste to comply with her wishes.

Finnula never stirred from Hugo's back until the lad was well away, and the last sounds of his horse's hooves could no longer be heard above the roar of the waterfall. Then she withdrew her arm from Hugo's throat, but did not come around to face him.

He heard a sigh, and turning his head, saw that she had sunk down to rest upon the rocky shelf upon which he'd lain, observing her. Her elbows on her knees, her face resting in her hands, she huddled there, cloaked in her thick mane of auburn hair, no longer the spirited Diana who'd trussed him like a calf, but a small, defenseless maiden who had been taxed beyond her strength in the last few minutes.

Hugo, still kneeling with his hands bound behind his back, began to have misgivings about the entire situation. Damn that boy! He would never forgive him for scrambling the girl's brains so, and would see him duly punished when he finally reached Stephensgate Manor.

"Does aught ail you, Mistress Crais?" he asked gently. "Is there naught I can do for you?"

She looked up, her face pinched with pain. "'Tis nothing," she said stoutly, like a child too proud to share her hurts. "It will pass."

Hugo knew then that she was badly injured. So stubborn a girl would never admit to pain were it not of the worst kind. "Show me," he said.

"No." She shook her head firmly, the red hair bouncing wildly around her slim shoulders. "I told you, 'tis nothing. Come, we must move on in order to be at our destination by dark. 'Tis not safe to roam these hills after sunset—"

She started to get up, but pain creased her lovely visage, and Hugo lost all patience, and bellowed at her in the same manner he'd chastised his squire.

"Foolish girl, you're hurt. Unbind me and let me examine your wounds. I will not slip away from you, not when you have captured me in all fairness. I will play your game until the end, bound or unbound. Now, loose me!"

She snapped back at him, for all the world as if she were his wife of long standing. "Don't bellow at me! I am not your serf, that you can tell me what to do. 'Tis *I* that does the bellowing round here, not *you!*"

Taken aback by her considerable spirit, Hugo blinked. Never before had he encountered a woman so completely unmoved by his ire. He realized that she was immune to fear of him, and cast about helplessly, wondering how to proceed. Never had he dealt with so contrary a lass. There was no use trying to intimidate her, much less seduce her. Would she respond to logic?

None too patiently, Hugo snapped, "Around my neck you'll find a silken cord. Pull it out."

She stared at him round-eyed, as if he had taken leave of his senses. "I'll do nothing of the kind."

"Pull it out, I tell you. Upon it hangs an uncut gem of far more worth than any ransom, given to me by a daughter of the Sultan of Egypt."

"And tainted with some foul foreign poison, no doubt, with which you hope to kill me," she sniffed.

"Are you as stupid as that sniveling squire of mine? It will do nothing of the sort. Pull it out, I say!"

Seeing that she hesitated still, regarding him as suspiciously as

if he were the ferret-faced Dick, he roared, so thunderously that
his mount reared behind them, "Do it!"

"Don't tell me," she roared back, every bit as loudly, "what to
do! If you don't stop bellowing at me, I'll gag you!"

Hugo was so angry, he thought he might burst his bonds
through sheer frustration alone. Then, just when he thought he
might do himself—not to mention the intractable young miss
who'd captured him—a harm, she rose from her seat with a painful wince, stalked toward him, and did as he bid, plucking from
beneath his shirt the black cord about which he'd been speaking.
The large, uncut emerald fell heavily into her hands, and she
stared down at it in wonder, her lips parted moistly.

"'Tis yours," Hugo said, realizing he was breathing hard with
the effort of not knocking her about the head. "Until my ransom is
paid, in any case. Take it, Finnula. If I escape, then you may keep
it, to do with as you like. It will pay," he added, with ill grace, "for
a great deal of hops and malt."

Her eyebrows rose nearly to her hairline, so great was her surprise that he'd sussed out the true reason for her kidnapping of
him. "How did you know . . . ?"

"Untie me."

"But—"

"Untie me. Now."

Never taking her large gray eyes from his face, she carefully
dropped the silken cord from which the gemstone hung about
her own long, slender neck. Then she reached for the knife she'd
sheathed in the belt at her narrow waist, and, leaning so close
to him that he could once again smell the fresh scent of her, she
sliced cleanly through the rope that bound his wrists. Freed, Hugo
stood, pulling himself up to his full height, and looked down at
her. Finnula, who stood hardly past his elbow, regarded him with-

out trepidation, a rare occurrence for Hugo, who engendered as much fear as admiration in the hearts of the many women he had known. Perhaps that brother of hers had seen that she led a sheltered life, never knowing of the cruelty of which men were capable, he thought. Foolish boy! Better that the girl should know the truth, that most men would not have her best interests at heart.

"Show me where it hurts," he said, trying to keep his voice steady. There was something about her proximity, which was close indeed, that caused him no small degree of discomfort. He did not know whether he wanted to thrash her or kiss her.

Without a word, she sank back onto the rock outcropping, and lifting her white lawn shirt no higher than the beginning of the curve of her right breast, revealed a bruise already mottled. Hugo sank to one knee to examine it, then reached out a tentative hand to touch the sensitive skin. When Finnula drew away before he had even touched her, her expression clearly challenging, he looked into her wide eyes and asked politely, "May I?"

She looked scornful. "What do *you* know," she demanded, "of tending to wounds?"

"What choice do you have?" he snarled right back at her. "I don't see any of your many sisters about, do you?"

Capturing her lush lower lip between her white, even teeth, Finnula nodded, closing her eyes against the anticipated pain—or perhaps, Hugo considered, against the humiliation of his touch.

Carefully, he laid his hand upon the bruised flesh, feeling skin that was smoother than any he had ever encountered, as soft as silk, but as hot as a feverish brow. She had very little fat on her, her muscles well-honed from riding and hunting. Her ribs protruded slightly beneath her small breasts, and the one he felt was surely bruised from Peter's blow, though not likely broken. He had long experience with wounds, having spent so many years on battlefields, and he was well-versed in the arts of medicine.

But he had never, in all his healing experience, had so comely a patient.

Hoping that his voice carried no hint of the desire he felt at the touch of her bare, silken flesh, he asked, "Does it hurt when you breathe?"

She said, keeping her face turned well off to the side, so that all he saw was the curve of her high cheekbone, "A little. Is it my rib?"

"It is."

"Is it broken?"

"I think not," he said, straining to keep his voice light. "Bruised, surely, though. But such a slight wound is surely nothing to a woman of your stamina—"

The gray-eyed gaze swiveled toward him, the dark fringe of lashes narrowed suspiciously. "Do you mock me, sir?" she inquired.

"I, dare to mock a great huntress such as yourself? Forsooth!"

Her cheeks, which had been pale, flushed a hot pink. "You will regret making light of my hunting skills, sir, when I sup tonight on roast rabbit, and leave you to forage for yourself."

"Ah, but 'tis the responsibility of a captor to see that her prisoner is well-fed." Seeing her raised eyebrows, he added, to see how she'd react, "And even better bedded—"

She regarded him with just a trace of a smile on her lips. "Oh, you'll be well-bedded, sir," she assured him. "With the horses."

Hugo grinned back at her, liking her for her mettle. "If you will permit me, I will bind it."

She inclined her head regally in response, every bit as proud as the princess who'd given him the gem she now wore around her neck, and perhaps with more cause. After all, the sultan's daughter had possessed great beauty . . . but no skill with a short bow.

Tearing a wide strip of material from the lining of his cloak, which was satin, and ought not to irritate her delicate skin, he had her inhale, and wound the impromptu bandage round her narrow rib cage. It would suffice, he decided. Now he had only to convince her to take something for the pain—

"I have," he began, without preamble, "the essence of the poppy in one of my saddlebags. A few drops only will help lessen the pain. Will you take some?"

She eyed him narrowly, already clearly feeling better. "What kind of fool do you take me for? I know of a woman who took it, and remembered not what she did for twenty-four hours after, though all the village saw her skipping naked to the well—"

Tempting as that sounded, Hugo was already responsible for her bruised rib. He would not also be branded as her despoiler. There was that brother of hers to remember.

"Nay," he said lightly. "I would not let you take so much. Only a little, for the pain."

She was suspicious of him, surely, but what choice did the girl have, so far from home, and in such pain? Hugo felt a sudden and nearly overwhelming sense of anger toward this absent brother, who took such poor care of his womenfolk as to allow them to gad about the countryside, dressed in leather chausses and all but defenseless. He would do more than have words with Robert Crais when he returned to the manor house. Perhaps he might see that he spent a little time in the stockade, as well.

Of a sudden, Finnula capitulated, saying she would taste the medicine—if doing so would "shut him up about it." Swallowing a rebuke, Hugo hastened to his mount to fetch her the vial in which he kept the foul-tasting stuff. She balked at the smell, then finally allowed two drops to be placed on her pink and pointed tongue. She swallowed, looking unimpressed, and then, with no little urgency, insisted they be on their way.

"For," she said in her husky voice, "the sun is sinking fast in the west, and we've still a long way to go if we're to get to Stephensgate by nightfall next—"

"And what," Hugo wanted to know, regarding her seriously, "lies in Stephensgate?"

"Why," she cried, as if he were the simplest man to have ever walked the earth, "that's where I live. I must get you back to Mellana."

"Mellana? And who is this Mellana, who holds my fate so casually in her hands?"

"Mellana is one of my sisters. I promised her I would capture a man for her, so that she could ransom him—"

Hugo was not a little disturbed to hear this. "You mean you do not intend to ransom me yourself?"

She made a moue of distaste, wrinkling her small nose in a most illustrative manner. "Of course not!" She spoke as if he'd offended her by the very thought. "When I have need of coin, I have more sensible ways of earning it."

At Hugo's frankly questioning look, she shrugged, then winced when the gesture jarred her sore rib. "I merely bag a deer or two, to sell at the local inn. They always have a demand for venison, and the Earl of Stephensgate's woods are full of game—" She glanced up at him, her eyes wide at her indiscretion. "Not," she added, speaking like a child reciting its lessons, "that I kill the earl's game—that would be poaching. Poaching is very wrong."

Suddenly the reasons behind her reluctance to meet up with the local sheriff became all too clear to Hugo. But he did not want to raise her hackles, not yet, and so he pretended not to have heard the slip, and said only, "You must love your sister Mellana dearly to go to so much trouble for her."

"Oh," Finnula replied, a shadow darkening her light eyes. "Everyone loves her. Mellana is the beauty in the family—" This Hugo found exceedingly hard to believe, for though Finnula's

beauty might not be apparent to all, it would be hard to be outdone. "She isn't a bit like me. She wouldn't know how to draw a
bow to save her life—she is exceedingly maidenly. Or at least she
was, before she met that bloody minstrel."

"I beg your pardon?"

By way of reply, Finnula merely sighed. "But she does make
the nicest beer you ever tasted—"

Hugo laughed out loud at this assertion. Beside him, Finnula
shot him an aggrieved look, insisting, "You won't laugh once
you've tasted her ale. Mellana has a true gift for brewing—"

"And will I taste her ale?" Hugo wanted to know.

She looked arch. "Oh, I'll see that you get a tankard or two
before Mel turns you loose."

Hugo smiled down at the frank and open face beneath his, all
practicality and—albeit recently restored—good humor, quite
unlike any other female with whom he'd ever become acquainted.
"And it is for her that you are abducting me?"

"Oh, yes." Finnula waved a hand in irritation. "I promised
her, you see, in a moment of weakness. I was distracted by all the
stir over Robert's wedding—"

"Your brother is marrying?" Hugo wondered if this was excuse
enough for the lad's woeful neglect of his youngest sister's wel-
fare, and decided it was not.

"Most assuredly, and to the mayor's daughter. 'Twill be the
wedding of the year. Of course, 'tis likely to become a funeral, if
Robert finds out about that bloody minstrel—"

"That's the second time you've mentioned that unfortunate
person. Whatever did the fellow do to warrant such censure?"

She scowled. "Never mind. Suffice it to say, I made a promise to Mellana before I knew what it was she wanted me to do,
and now I am stuck with it, and so are you. I hope you do not
mind overmuch. I would not," she confessed, turning her great

gray eyes up at him seriously, "ever have *really* poked you with my knife. That was all for show. I think I did an admirable job of frightening your squire, don't you?"

Hugo smiled down at her, thinking her impossibly young, and very naive, that she spoke so confidently and so frankly with him, not knowing the least bit about him. But then it occurred to him that perhaps she did know a bit more than she let on. She had known that he would come to the spring, and she had known that he would look over the outcropping and see her bathing— but how?

When he asked, she shrugged and looked suddenly preoccupied, and busied herself with pulling on her boots, which she'd extracted from behind a clump of violets.

"I knew by the route you were taking that you were familiar with the land," she confessed reluctantly. "No one who has ever been in this area has not been to the spring, and no one who has been to the spring can resist going again. And besides . . . Well, you remind me a little of someone, and I met him much the same way as I met you—only not by knifepoint."

This oblique reference would not be elaborated upon, however, no matter how much he pressed. Eventually, in an obvious attempt to distract him from that line of questioning, she insisted that they be on their way; that if they were not on their way soon complications of grave magnitude would ensue; and would he please turn so that she could bind his hands again?

Hugo looked down at her in disbelief. "I thought we had settled that. I looked after your wound, and you untied me—"

"But I can't risk your riding away when my back is turned," she declared staunchly. "Surely, as a soldier of war, you can understand that."

Hugo stared down at her, unable to think up a reasonable argument in the face of such logic. Then suddenly it came upon him. She was a slight creature, and would do well situated in the saddle before him. He could not very well run away when she was seated right there with him.

He put the suggestion in just such a light, and though she balked at first, he knew it was just for show. Finnula Crais was a young lady who liked having things her own way, and she seemed quite keen on keeping his hands tied behind his back. Hugo wasn't certain if she considered having his hands tied a means of keeping him from escaping so much as a way of ensuring that those hands wouldn't wander where they weren't supposed to. Despite her earlier exhibitionism in the pool, Finnula was not without an inconvenient amount of modesty—quite a surprising trait, Hugo found, in a kidnapper.

Eventually Finnula capitulated, but only after some more grumbling about how she ought to have gagged him from the beginning, and how she'd never in her life met such a verbose knight.

"Aren't you," she demanded, every bit as peevishly as Peter might have, as she cautiously loaded his sword and dagger onto her mount's saddle pack, "supposed to be consumed with brawling and cursing and tossing bits of bone to your hounds?"

"Certainly not," Hugo declared. "A knight is a paragon of virtue, his sole pursuit that of justice for the good of the realm."

"Pshaw," Finnula snorted. "I never saw such a knight."

"That is your misfortune. I have met many such men," Hugo lied, "and enjoyed hours of enlightening conversation at their tables." Generally while dancing girls waved their bosoms in his face, if truth be told, but there was no reason she needed to know that.

Finnula snorted again. "I spent hours at the table of a lord once, and all I heard were belches. And he was an *earl*."

Hugo stared at her curiously. "What were you doing, dining with an earl?"

"Never mind," Finnula said, scowling. "You have an unnerving habit of drawing me out. I swear I never saw such a talkative soldier."

"And I," Hugo countered, watching disapprovingly as she tucked the trailing ends of her oversize shirt into her tight-fitting braies, "never saw such unmaidenly behavior in all my born days."

Finnula just laughed, and placing a dainty foot in the stirrup, swung herself expertly into his saddle, the bruised rib apparently not bothering her.

"Well," she said impatiently, looking down at him. "Are you coming, or not?"

Hugo glanced at the girl's mare. "And what of your mount? Should we not tie her bridle to Skinner's?"

"Certainly not," Finnula scoffed. "Violet will follow."

Hugo quirked up a single eyebrow. "Violet?" he repeated, with a mocking smile.

"Aye, Violet is her name, and I'd appreciate it if you'd wipe that smirk off your face. She's as well-trained as any destrier, and better tempered besides. I've had her since I was a child, and I wouldn't trade her for anything."

Hugo smiled at the loyal indignation in Finnula's voice. "Since you were a child, eh?" He laughed. "And what are you now, pray? You look hardly a week past your sixteenth birthday."

When Finnula pressed her lips into a thin line, obviously determined not to allow him to goad her into losing her temper, and haughtily tossed her long hair back behind her shoulders, he laughed again. She was a little fireball, this Finnula Crais, and he was going to be hard put to keep his hands off her. Perhaps he should have allowed her to truss him up again after all.

Grinning, Hugo swung himself into the saddle behind the indignant girl, and started to reach around her narrow waist for the reins, but received a sharp slap on the backs of his hands for his efforts.

"I will hold the reins," Finnula informed him tersely, and, indeed, she'd already gathered up the leather leads in her gloved hands. "There's no use you holding them. You don't even know the way."

Hugo shrugged and placed his hands on the girl's hips, liking the velvety feel of her leather braies beneath his fingers.

This time, he received an elbow in the midriff for his trouble.

"God's teeth, woman," he cursed, clutching his middle. "What was that for?"

"If you can't keep your hands to yourself, I'll tie them behind your back, I swear I will."

Finnula had turned in the saddle to glare at him, and in doing so, her pert backside pressed against the front of Hugo's braies, causing a reaction so immediate and unexpected that Hugo was momentarily nonplussed by it. Shifting so that she would not become aware of it, Hugo wondered at the instantaneousness of his body's response to her touch. What was wrong with him? The girl was attractive, yes, but it seemed as if every pore in his body was crying out for her touch. This was not how he usually responded to a beautiful woman. Usually he was master of himself, and his very self-restraint was what drove women into his arms. No beautiful woman could stand being ignored, and that was the trick in attracting them. Ignore her, and she will come.

But how could he ignore this girl when every fiber in him was twitching to strain her to him? How could he ignore her when the soft fragrance of her wildly curling hair was constantly in his nostrils, the memory of her slim thighs tightening around his waist constantly in his mind? And he didn't think it would matter if she were seated in a saddle before him or at a table in a tavern twenty leagues away; Finnula Crais, like a splinter, had worked her way beneath his skin with remarkable speed, and digging her out, he realized, was going to be no small task.

Shaking his head, aware that those gray eyes were fixed on him curiously, he clenched his teeth and tried to will himself to relax. He couldn't let her know the devastating effect she had on him.

But it was already too late. The sooty lashes lowered over those silver orbs, and Finnula demanded, staring below his belt suspiciously, "What is that?"

"What is what?" he inquired loftily.

"That," she said, and there was no mistaking what she was referring to when she wedged her hip up against it and lifted accusing eyes to meet his mortified gaze. "Is that a knife hilt? Do you have a weapon beneath your belt you didn't tell me about?"

Was the girl serious? He could tell by the angry set of her mouth that she was, that she honestly had no idea what lay beneath a man's chausses. Again, he felt a spurt of irritation against Robert Crais, for letting this child gad about the countryside in such ignorance. Surely one of those married sisters would have told her the facts of life—and yet she seemed truly annoyed that he had not surrendered to her his most prized weapon of all.

Hugo wasn't at all certain how to proceed. He had no experience whatsoever with virgins. And this one was armed. The very thought of what she might do when he unveiled the hard object about which she was making such a fuss made his blood run cold. She seemed to have no compunction about wielding that blade at her waist—

"It isn't a knife hilt," Hugo said finally, unable to keep wounded dignity from creeping into his voice. After all, it was considerably larger than a knife hilt.

"Well, what is it then?" Finnula demanded. "I can't ride comfortably with that thing poking at my back."

Hugo opened his mouth to reply, hesitating because he was uncertain exactly how to phrase what it was he wanted to say, and was relieved to find that no further explanation was required. Suddenly Finnula's cheeks flooded with color. Her eyes widened, and her jaw dropped. Yes, one of those five sisters *had* spoken to her about the facts of life. It seemed that this was the first time, however, she'd chanced upon an occasion that required her to put that information to practical use.

Turning quickly away, Finnula seized the reins, breathing a horrified "Oh!"

Hugo's discomfort was dissipating, but his amusement over the way it had unsettled Finnula mounted as the girl's cheeks turned an ever-deepening shade of red.

"I'm afraid that it's a natural reaction to your proximity, demoiselle," he said, delighting in her mortification. "Perhaps you haven't encountered such a strong response in any of your previous prisoners—"

Finnula's voice was so soft that he had to lean forward to hear her reply.

"I've never done this before," she whispered. "You're the first man I've ever—I've never—" She broke off, obviously frustrated. "Oh, bloody hell," she swore, and gave Hugo's horse a pretty vicious kick in the sides. "Just keep it to yourself, or I'll . . . I'll cut it off!"

Grinning, Hugo sat back in the saddle, well-contented with the way his day was proceeding. Who would have thought, when he'd wakened that morning in a hayrick with straw in his hair and dew in his clothes, that by evening he'd be the prisoner of so winsome a captor?

It amazed him to think that all those years ago, when he'd left

England, he'd ridden right by his father's mill, and given nary a thought to the possibility that years hence, the thatched roof might house so delectable a distraction as a Finnula Crais. He was going to enjoy his homecoming considerably more than he'd ever expected, thanks to this redheaded Valkyrie in the saddle before him, ignoring him so pointedly.

He chuckled delightedly to himself, not caring if the girl thought him mad.

# Chapter Six

The insufferable knight seemed actually to be *enjoying* himself, and that infuriated her.

It wasn't that she had hoped to terrify her captive, but, as a skillful—and fully armed—huntress, she did expect a little respect.

But this Sir Hugh's constant teasing showed that he did not consider her a serious threat at all.

She did not feel as if she were the party in control, even though *she* was the one with the dagger. Her authority had been usurped, first when that pea-headed squire had knocked her flat, and then when she'd had to undo Sir Hugh's hands so that he could tend to her wound.

That, she reckoned, had been her fatal mistake: not disarming the squire when she'd had a chance. But she'd felt sorry for him, squalling in midair, his arms flailing. She certainly never would have thought he'd have the gumption to hide a knife in his boot, let alone cut himself down. It was a drop of eight feet or more.

But he'd escaped, and she'd paid for her lack of farsightedness.

Surreptitiously pressing on her wounded side and finding it tolerably numb, Finnula supposed she ought to have thanked St. Elias for supplying her with a prisoner with so tender a touch. This Sir Hugh, despite his immense size—and alarming amount of facial hair—had surprised her with his gentleness, probing her sore rib with fingers that soothed. That brief glimpse into his true nature, the side of him that wasn't armored in cynicism, had been enlightening.

Still, she'd have traded all his sensitivity for a more civil—and less amorous—captive any day of the week.

It wasn't just his complete lack of fear of her that annoyed Finnula. There was something about the appraising way the knight's hazel eyes raked her at every glance, the slightly mocking curve of his lips, half hidden beneath that tangle of beard, that unnerved her, made her feel shy. Finnula was not, as a rule, a diffident girl, and she could not understand what Sir Hugh was doing to make her feel that way. She resented him for it. Deeply.

But despite the fact that her plan had not proceeded according to schedule, Finnula had to content herself with the fact that she did, indeed, have a prisoner to bring home to Mellana. True, he was entirely too sarcastic and far too forward for Finnula's taste.

But he would fetch a fair amount of ransom, enough to replenish her sister's dowry, anyway, and that was all that mattered. She didn't have to like him. She just had to deliver him. Intact.

Of course, the hardest part was going to be restraining herself from smacking him. He so roundly deserved to be put in his place, odious lecher. Imagine, pressing that . . . *thing* against her like that! The very memory caused Finnula's cheeks to burn. How was she going to put up with behavior like that for two days and nights? He might find himself trussed like a doe and slung over Violet's neck if he didn't watch it.

They had ridden for almost two hours, mostly in silence, except when Hugo asked her probing questions about her family and personal life that Finnula refused to answer, much to his amusement, when the slowly setting sun indicated that it was time to find shelter for the night. Finnula urged Hugo's mount, which she considered a truly fine beast, much more easily managed than his master, into a meadow that was already purpling in the twilight, and toward a hayrack.

"Our evening's accommodations?" Hugo inquired, an unmistakably hopeful note in his voice.

Finnula sighed tiredly. She was not looking forward to coping with the ham-handed knight come nightfall.

"It is," she said, trying to keep a threatening inflection in her voice. "I am acquainted with the farmer who tends this field, and he's given me permission to stay the night whenever I choose—"

"Generous of him," Hugo said, mildly. Finnula set her lips.

"In return, I keep his copses free of wolves," she said, disliking his insinuating tone. Behind her, she heard her prisoner chuckle.

"All I said," Hugo insisted, "was that it was generous of him—"

"I heard what you said," Finnula snapped. "Dismount."

Hugo looked about the meadow, already long-shadowed and growing cold now that the sun was sinking below the treetops along the horizon.

"What, here?" he questioned.

"Yes, here." Finnula waited until he was on the ground before swinging back a leg and slipping to the grass beside him. Once again, his towering height disconcerted her, and she went to Violet's side shaking her head, wondering at the fact that giants did indeed still roam the earth.

Reaching into her saddlebag, Finnula drew out a length of rope and turned toward the enormous knight.

"If you'll just sit there, please, at the base of the hayrack, I'll secure you."

Hugo stared down at her uncomprehendingly, his eyes glowing green in the failing light of dusk. "Whatever are you talking about?" he asked, a smile curving up the corners of his generous lips.

Finnula stamped an impatient foot. "I've got to build a fire and fetch us some dinner, and I can't do all of that *and* keep an eye on you—"

Understanding dawned. Hugo threw back his tawny head and laughed. "So you intend to tie me to a hayrack? Oh, that's rich."

Finnula glared at him. "It isn't amusing. What's to keep you from escaping while I'm hunting?"

"If you don't know, I'm certainly not going to tell you," Hugo declared, still laughing. When Finnula narrowed her eyes at him, he held up both hands, palms facing her. "Nay, don't give me that look, you hard-hearted wench. I swear to you I'll stay put. You have my emerald, remember?"

Finnula's fingers flew to the heavy stone she wore upon her neck. She had nearly forgotten about it, it nestled so comfortably between her breasts. Of course he wouldn't try to escape, not while something so valuable was still in her possession.

There was nothing, however, to keep him from sneaking up behind her and taking it away by force—but she supposed if he had been intent on doing such a thing, he'd have done it already. God knew he could easily have gotten away after his squire had knocked her senseless. No, as much as she didn't like to admit it, Sir Hugh Fitzwilliam apparently had *some* honor. He was the type to see a thing through to the end, if only for the pleasure of laughing at her some more.

"I'll make a fire," Hugo offered, reasonably, "while you fetch us something to eat. I'm looking forward to actually seeing these superlative hunting skills about which I've heard so much."

Finnula looked down at the length of rope in her hands. She *so* wanted to tie him up, and gag him, too, and spend a few hours in pleasant obliviousness to his presence. His aggressively male presence was grating. But there was no hope for it. She needed only to endure him for another forty-eight hours. Forty-eight hours was nothing. With any luck, she'd spend at least sixteen of them asleep.

If she could sleep in the presence of such a man.

Shrugging, Finnula went back to Violet's side and put away the rope, taking her bow and quiver from the saddle instead. She tried not to pay attention to the fact that she could feel her prisoner's eyes boring into her the entire time her back was to him. What was it, she wondered, that so constantly drew his eyes to her? It wasn't possible that he could still be attracted to her, not after she'd spent almost the entire afternoon being unpleasant to him.

But he didn't even have the grace to look away when she caught his stare on her hair, and, glaring at him challengingly, she quickly braided the mess of auburn locks, and tossed the plait over her shoulder and out of sight.

Hugo just smirked, as if her contrariness was charming. She glared at him some more.

"I hope you're partial to rabbit," she said irritably. "Because that's all you're getting for dinner."

Hugo bowed as if she'd said she'd be preparing boar in a delicate mushroom sauce. Fuming, Finnula whirled away, and began trudging toward a nearby thicket, muttering to herself. What was it about this infuriating man that kept provoking her? Normally she had the most steady of tempers. Normally it didn't bother her at all when people smirked at her: Isabella Laroche smirked at her regularly, and it had never irritated her a bit. But something about being the object of this man's amusement was very annoying indeed.

Stalking a particularly cunning hare in the half light calmed Finnula somewhat. She ignored several females for fear that she'd leave their little ones motherless, and went for a male instead. She dallied a bit, enjoying her time away from her lecherous prisoner, letting her prey escape several times before finally ending the chase by sending an arrow clean through the hare's brain. He never knew what hit him.

After skinning him expertly with her knife, Finnula washed her hands in a nearby brook, where she also paused to fill her water flask. By the time she returned to the hayrack, half hoping she'd find that Sir Hugh had cleared out, taking his smirks and insinuations with him, she found that he'd managed to start a fire and even had a pot of something bubbling merrily over it.

Hugo looked up from the small cauldron, from which the unmistakable odor of shallots was emanating. The sun had set, and except for the glow from the fire he'd started, the meadow was entirely in shadow. The firelight made his bone structure, which was difficult to see beneath the bristling beard, more pronounced, and Finnula realized, with a slight sinking feeling, that her prisoner was actually passably good-looking. Irrationally, this discovery annoyed her.

"I see you've been going through my belongings in my absence," she said coldly.

Hugo shrugged, salting his soup with a pinch from the bag of spices Finnula kept in her saddle pouch.

"Get to know one's enemy, I've always said." He smiled, supremely unconcerned by her irritation. "You've got quite an arsenal of cooking implements. I threw some of the turnips and shallots in here. You don't mind, do you? I figured that by adding the rabbit's carcass and letting the pot simmer overnight, we'd have a good, thick soup come morning."

Finnula tried to hide her surprise. Here was a man, a *man*, who knew how to cook? Why, Robert didn't know a turnip from a parsnip. Curiosity overcame her dislike of him, and Finnula asked bemusedly, "Where did you learn how to cook?"

"Ah," Hugo sighed, stirring his concoction with a stick he'd stripped of bark. "It wasn't always safe to eat the local food in Egypt. I saw many more men fall to illness brought on by consuming rancid meat than I saw fall by the scimitar. We learned to prepare our own dinners, cooking them in our helmets, most times." He chuckled at the memory. "Of course, that could prove dangerous as well, when one of us forgot last night's dinner was still in his headpiece, and went to put it on without first checking inside—"

Finnula couldn't help laughing at his wry expression. He grinned up at her, then lowered his gaze to the hare she'd skewered on a clean branch.

"Ah, the main course." Rising to his full height, the knight approached her, all of his attention focused on the rabbit she'd killed. He bent to take the skewer from her, closely examining it, then lifted his gaze to hers appraisingly.

"A clean shot," he said, the admiration in his voice evident. "You did this with that short bow?"

Finnula fingered her weathered bow, uncommonly pleased by the compliment, small though it was. Whatever ailed her?

"Aye," she said, unshouldering her quiver and showing it to

him. "'Tis all I need. A long bow is too much in the way. Besides, I've no need to pierce armor—"

Hugo flexed the bow experimentally. "Finely crafted. You made it?"

"Yes." Amazingly, Finnula felt her cheeks suffuse with color. His regard pleased her far more than it ought. What did she care what he thought of her? He was just a knight, and not a very chivalrous one, at that. He was nothing to her.

Of course, it was one thing to be admired for one's looks, which one couldn't help, and quite another to be complimented upon one's skills. Finnula took infinitely more pride in her hunting abilities than in her appearance.

Speaking quickly to hide her embarrassment, Finnula pointed out a notch she'd carved into each one of her arrows, a notch she claimed extended the curve of the arrow's flight.

"But," Hugo said, scrutinizing the violet-tipped projectile, "while it might lengthen your shot, it also makes your arrows highly distinctive."

Finnula shrugged, not understanding his meaning straight away. "Oh, aye, but it seems to work—"

"And Sheriff de Brissac hasn't yet learned how to identify your handiwork?"

Comprehension dawned. Suddenly uncomfortable with the shift the conversation had taken, Finnula took the quiver from him and turned her attention to dinner. "I'll rub this fine fellow with some herbs," she said, deliberately changing the subject. "With any luck, he should be done in half an hour—"

Hugo chuckled. "I see. Your troubles with the shire reeve aren't any of my business?"

Finnula sank to her knees by the fire and industrially began applying a layer of spice to her kill. She kept her eyes on her work, hoping that the red glow of the firelight hid her blush. "I have no troubles with the sheriff," she said nonchalantly. Then, flicking a quick glance in the knight's direction, muttered, "None that he can prove, anyway."

Hugo joined her on the hard ground, his joints popping in protest as he lowered his massive frame to the grass. He sat far enough away that their thighs were not exactly touching, but close enough that the chance of such contact occurring was a distinct possibility. Finnula regarded him nervously as she set the rabbit roasting over the flames, but all he did was lean forward, his broad shoulder suddenly blocking out all the firelight, and give his soup a stir.

"I see," her prisoner said, his deep voice inflectionless. "But all the man would need is a single shaft—"

"I don't leave my arrows lying about," Finnula said matter-of-factly.

"But surely you've missed from time to time—"

Finnula sniffed. "I don't miss."

"You can't *always* hit your mark, not every time—"

That stung. "I do," she snapped. "You think that because I'm a woman, there is something lacking in my skills as a hunter? I'll have you know that I'm the best shot in all of Shropshire. I have a golden arrowhead at home that I won at the Dorchester Fair to prove it—"

"I'm just saying that everyone misses now and again—"

"I never miss. I strike to kill, not maim." Finnula glared at him resentfully, forgetting to rotate the skewered meat. "There aren't any does roaming about the earl's lands with my arrows in their flanks. What I aim for, I kill."

It seemed to her that Sir Hugh took an intense interest in his soup all of a sudden. He dashed in a few pinches of the same herbs that Finnula had rubbed into her hare.

"And this earl, the one whose game you're poaching—"

Too late, Finnula realized her mistake, and she quickly bit down on her lower lip. *When* was she going to learn to keep her mouth shut? Verily, this knight was able to draw her out with the ease of the slyest village gossip.

"I didn't say I was poaching," Finnula grumbled.

"Didn't you?" Hugo's deep voice rumbled with amusement. "I believe you mentioned that that was the root of your troubles with Sheriff de Brissac."

Scowling, Finnula turned the skewer. She realized, as the aromas from the soup and the meat began to fill the air, that she was hungry. She hadn't had a bite to eat since the inn in Leesbury.

"It's not poaching, exactly," she explained reluctantly. "The game I kill never actually leaves the earl's demesnes—"

"What do you mean?" The look he shot her was uncomfortably sharp. In the firelight, his changeable eyes had gone yellow as amber. "What in God's name do you do with it?"

The intensity of his gaze was unnerving, and Finnula lowered her eyes, her throat suddenly dry. Using her free hand, she fumbled with the water flask that hung from her side, but Hugo passed her a flask of his own.

"Try this," he said shortly.

Finnula lifted the skin to her lips, only to pull it away a second later, feeling as if her lips were on fire. Gagging, she turned accusing eyes up at her prisoner.

"Are you trying to poison me?" she demanded, when she could find her voice.

Hugo had the grace to look sheepish. "I apologize. 'Tis only ale, though I admit it's a bit on the strong side. I would have thought that the sister of a beer maker would be accustomed to the vagaries of brewing—"

"Aye, but I thought 'twas water you were offering to me. Besides, this isn't ale. 'Tis dragon's milk. You bought it in London, I wager?"

Hugo inclined his head. "Guilty as charged."

"I thought as much. Whoever sold you this stuff let it sit too long, and now it's strong enough to turn the hair of the dog."

Annoyed that he had seen her sputtering reaction to the ale, Finnula took a long drink of the offensive stuff, just to prove that she was no lily-livered maid. Though her eyes watered, she managed to swallow several mouthfuls, then delivered a watery smile to her companion as she returned the flask.

"My thanks," she said hoarsely.

Hugo took the flask and said, "The earl's game. What do you do with it, if you don't remove it from his demesnes?"

Provoking man. Finnula winced to herself. He could not be swayed from this topic, no matter what she tried. There was no hope for it. She was going to have to tell him. She had only herself to blame for arousing his suspicions.

"You have to understand that the earl—the late earl, Lord Geoffrey—passed away over a year ago, leaving the estate in the hands of his bailiff—"

"This Lord Geoffrey didn't have an heir?" Hugo did not dare to look at her. He kept his gaze on the roasting meat on her skewer.

"Oh, aye, there's an heir." Finnula snorted disgustedly. "Only he's nowhere to be found. Got himself captured gallivanting about the Holy Land, not unlike yourself—"

"Gallivanting!" Hugo echoed beneath his breath, but Finnula heard him, just the same.

"Aye, well, you can't call it much more than that, can you? A sorrier display of masculine stupidity I never did see." She shot him a sly glance from beneath her eyelashes. "Did you know him, perhaps? Lord Geoffrey's son, I mean. Geoffrey, Earl of Stephensgate—"

Hugo pointed to the meat. "You'd better turn that. It's burning." After Finnula rotated the skewer, he said, "And so since Lord Geoffrey's son can't be located, the estate has lain lordless for a year?"

"And a little more. And the bailiff, one Reginald Laroche, Lord Geoffrey's cousin, he and his precious daughter live in the manor house—" Finnula was about to add, *And a finer pair of selfish pigs you never saw*, but restrained herself, remembering that her prisoner was not a stranger to Shropshire, and might very well know Reginald Laroche.

But apparently his acquaintance with the bailiff was either nonexistent or passing, because he asked, curiously, "This Laroche isn't performing his duties to your satisfaction, I take it?"

Finnula turned the meat, hunching her shoulders uncomfortably. She knew she should not complain about her betters, but somehow, though she herself was just a miller's daughter, she could not help thinking that she could do a better job of managing Lord Hugo's estate than that wet hen Reginald Laroche.

She felt her prisoner's elbow in her side. It nudged her tender rib, and Finnula let out an involuntary cry that caused the knight to look down at her, his shaggy blond eyebrows raised in surprise.

"I only meant to offer you another swallow," he said, holding up the flask of ale. "I'd forgotten about your rib. I'm very sorry. Is it still sore?"

Finnula eyed the leather flask. "Aye. But nothing that a drop or two more of that dragon's milk won't cure."

Chuckling, Hugo passed her the sack, and Finnula choked down a few more mouthfuls before handing it back to him and wiping her lips with the back of her hand. The ale was terrible, true, but it warmed her insides as much as the cheerful fire was warming her outsides.

In fact, despite her bruised side, Finnula was feeling quite nice, with the quiet night settling all around them like a blanket, and the stars twinkling coldly overhead, and their dinner cooking so aromatically before them. Her companion wasn't even annoying her that much anymore. He seemed to have adopted a less abrasive demeanor, and hadn't smirked at her in over half an hour. Perhaps she would actually begin to enjoy his company before the end of this trip . . .

"So this Laroche," Hugo prompted her, as if their previous conversation hadn't been interrupted.

"Oh." Finnula sighed. She supposed it didn't matter if she bad-mouthed the earl's relative to this man. Though there was a slight chance that Isabella, who had an uncanny ability to sniff out an eligible bachelor from leagues away, might find a way to wrangle herself an introduction to the knight, it was unlikely Sir Hugh would ever meet her father.

"Reginald Laroche seems to feel that the dues owed to Stephensgate Manor ought to be nearly twice what they were when Lord Geoffrey was alive," Finnula explained. "So instead of working three days in His Lordship's fields and four in their own, the peasants are forced to labor six days for Laroche, leaving only one for themselves. But that's nothing to compare with the tallages Laroche has instituted. I think it's done, don't you?"

Hugo had been staring at her intently, his hazel eyes yellow again in the firelight. She had to wave the skewered meat over the flames to get his attention.

"Does this look done to you?"

He tore his gaze from her face and glanced at the roasted rabbit. "Yes, it's done," he said, and, taking the stick from Finnula's hands, Hugo began to blow on the sizzling meat. "The tallages," he said, between breaths, his eyes, in his thickly bearded face, bright as the stars above. "He's raised the tallages, has he?"

Finnula wasn't certain she liked her meat blown on by anyone excepting herself, but she shrugged with good grace and contented herself with another swallow from her prisoner's flask. She really was feeling much better.

"Aye, raised the tallages by a third, and that, coupled with the extra three days' labor, well, it's caused a bit of bad feeling amongst the serfs." She accepted the hunk of rabbit Hugo passed to her, and, holding it in both hands, took a ravenous bite. "Hmmm," she said, though the meat was still too hot to eat comfortably. "That's good."

"Haven't the serfs complained to anyone?" Hugo demanded, his own mouth full of roast rabbit.

"Oh, aye, to Sheriff de Brissac. He's a good man," she admitted grudgingly, "for all he wants to imprison me, but there's naught he can do. Reginald Laroche had Lord Geoffrey in his pocket even before the old man died. He'll inherit, if Lord Hugo never returns from the Holy Land, and may God help us then."

Finnula wiped her mouth on the back of her hand and looked at her companion, then regretted it. The knight had bits of rabbit meat in his beard. She supposed he couldn't help it, his beard being so bushy, but it was really quite unattractive, and she couldn't understand why he hadn't shaved upon reaching England. Perhaps, she thought, her overactive imagination working furiously, he had a weak chin, and needed the beard to even things out.

Her prisoner seemed oblivious to the state of his facial hair, however. "So what you're telling me," he began, stabbing a finger at her for emphasis, "is that this Laroche is slowly starving the people of Stephensgate?"

"Well, the serfs, anyway," Finnula amended. "My brother,

and the other free folk in the village, aren't hurting too badly. It's the peasants who farm for His Lordship who are suffering the most—"

Hugo had quit chewing, and was staring at her so intently that Finnula began to feel uncomfortable again. There was something so familiar about his eyes, but for the life of her, Finnula could not say what it was. She rarely visited Caterbury, but she supposed it was possible she had met one of his kinsmen there. Or perhaps his uncles or cousins had stopped in Stephensgate to sample Mellana's brew. It really was quite famous, and on Tap-Up Sunday each October, the only day she could sell it legally without a license, the mill was crowded with men who'd traveled miles just for a taste of Mellana's beer.

"So you are killing the earl's game," Hugo said slowly, his deep voice a rumble, like distant thunder, "and giving it to his serfs, so that they don't starve."

Finnula's eyes widened, and she nearly choked on the piece of rabbit she'd just swallowed. "What?" she cried, giving herself a thump on the chest, then regretting it when she jolted her rib. "What did you say?"

"Don't act the innocent with me, little miss." The thunder in Hugo's voice was not so distant now. "That's how you can truthfully say the game isn't leaving the earl's demesnes. It's all lining the stomachs of the peasants who work the land—"

Finnula took another sip of ale, just to ease the digestion of the slightly stringy hare. She wasn't certain, but it appeared that Sir Hugh was upset about something. Since it did not seem wise to have such a very large man angry with her, she tried fluttering her eyelashes, which she'd seen Isabella Laroche do any number of times when caught in the glare of her father's disapproval.

"Had I not," Finnula said meekly, "they would have starved this winter. It was very cold—"

"Hell and damnation!"

Hugo's abrupt exclamation so startled Finnula that she nearly dropped her gnawed half of the rabbit carcass back into the fire. She watched in amazement as her prisoner did exactly that, flinging the meat to the ground and then climbing to his feet. He took several strides into the dark meadow, only to return a few seconds later, his large hands balled into fists at his sides.

She could not understand why a man who was a stranger to Stephensgate should be so disturbed by the mistreatment of its serfs, and so assumed that his anger was directed at her, for her flagrant disregard of poaching laws. The penalties for poaching were quite severe; those caught illegally hunting a lord's game could forfeit a hand or a foot for it, and it was not unusual for a poacher to pay for his crimes with his life.

Finnula instantly began to regret that she had ever opened her mouth about her hunting practices to this stranger. For all she knew, he could be some agent sent by the king to investigate the mysterious disappearance of game in Fitzstephen Forest. Why the king should take any interest whatsoever in Fitzstephen Forest, she could not imagine, but clearly, that was the only explanation for Sir Hugh's strange behavior. If Sir Hugh was even his name.

Finnula wasn't certain how to proceed. She supposed a girl like Isabella would have started to cry, using tears as a weapon against this large man's wrath, and had she been able to, Finnula would have feigned repentance. But she was *not* sorry for what she'd done, and she'd be damned before she acted as if she was.

So she merely slid what was left of her dinner into the pot hanging over the fire, since her appetite had abruptly left her, and waited quietly for the large man to vent his anger, bowing her head against the inevitable, but muttering rebelliously beneath her breath.

But when the barrage of accusations did not come, Finnula grew restless, and glanced up at Hugo just once before swiftly lowering her gaze. He was standing some feet away, his arms folded across his broad chest, his tawny gaze inscrutable, but most definitely fastened upon her. Finnula thought it might be wise to provide as small a target as possible for his rage, and so despite the discomfort it caused her side, she brought her legs up to her chest and circled them with her arms, resting her chin on her knees and gazing mutinously into the flames.

When Hugo finally spoke, the thunder was entirely gone from his voice. Instead, he sounded tired, and Finnula supposed that for a man his age, that wasn't so unusual. He had, after all, had quite a long day.

"Why did you do it?" he inquired.

Finnula was surprised by the question. As often as Robert had railed at her for poaching, he had never once bothered to ask her *why* she did it. That this stranger should put the question to her was really quite odd.

She looked at him, craning her neck to see his face, but his features were all in shadow, he stood so far from the fire.

"I told you already," she said. "If someone hadn't done something, they wouldn't have lasted the winter. There wasn't enough food in their stores, what with the high tallage set by Laroche—"

"But why *you*?"

Finnula frowned, looking away from him, back at the fire. She certainly couldn't tell him the truth. But she could tell him part of it, anyway.

"God gave me a gift." She shrugged. "It would be a sin not to use it. That's what my mother used to say, anyway." When he said nothing, she supposed he wasn't satisfied with that explanation, but it was all she was willing to give. She thrust out her chin obstinately, refusing to utter another word.

"You risk your life," Hugo said slowly, "for serfs."

Forgetting her resolve to be silent, Finnula corrected him tersely. "To you, perhaps, they are serfs. To me they are friends, people I've known my whole life, family almost. If their lord will not care for them, I will. 'Tis the right thing to do."

When he made no reply to that, Finnula pushed back a loose tendril of hair that had fallen over one of her eyes and glared at him, though he still stood in shadow and she wasn't at all certain he was even looking in her direction.

"You can't prove anything, you know," she said with reckless indignation. "Any more than Sheriff de Brissac can produce a shred of evidence against me. Ask any single one of Lord Geoffrey's serfs. They'll not say a word. So you can just go back to King Edward and tell him that if there is a poacher in Fitzstephen Forest, you couldn't prosecute for want of proof."

She was trembling by the time she got through with her speech, but not with fear. Good God, no wonder he'd been so amicable about being held hostage! He'd been hoping to goad her into a confession—and he'd succeeded, to a certain degree. But he still hadn't any evidence.

"What in the name of God are you talking about?" Hugo demanded, stomping back toward the fire in his enormous boots. He sank down beside her, took the flask from where she'd leaned it against a leg of the hayrack, and, unstopping it, took a few noisy gulps.

When he took the container away from his lips, the gesture made a smacking noise, which Hugo followed by wiping his mouth on his sleeve. His gaze was green-eyed now, Finnula noticed. It was disconcerting how his eyes were constantly turning different colors.

Finnula glowered at him, hoping to intimidate with her sadly unchangeable gray irises. "I know who you are."

Hugo looked taken aback. For several seconds he simply stared at her, his mouth moving strangely, before he finally echoed, in a voice that was too hearty by half, "Who *I* am? What are you talking about?"

"Don't play games with me," Finnula snarled. He seemed more amused than alarmed by her ire, but she wasn't going to let that stop her from delivering the lecture he so roundly deserved. "I think it's disgraceful, you taking advantage of me in such a manner. After all, I'm nothing but an innocent maid. You ought to be ashamed of yourself."

Hugo laughed outright. "Maid you might be, Finnula Crais, but I have serious reservations concerning your innocence. Point in fact, your method of distracting me at the Spring of St. Elias—"

Finnula flushed hotly at the memory, but refused to be distracted by embarrassment. "That is neither here nor there. When my brother finds out, you can count on him complaining to the king about your ill treatment of me—"

"*My* ill treatment of *you*?" Hugo's golden eyebrows slanted upward in disbelief. "Was it not *I* who was trussed, as you so delicately put it, like a pig? Was it not *my* life threatened at knife-point?"

"How you can be so indignant when 'tis you who are a sneak and a liar, I'll never know. I don't ken how you sleep at night." Leveling a narrow-eyed glare at him, she hissed, "Men like you are no better than the worms crawling below our feet this very instant—"

Hugo looked down, expecting to see the ground littered with night crawlers. "I apologize, demoiselle," he began carefully, "if I have done aught to offend you—"

"Offend me!" Finnula laughed humorlessly. "Oh, arresting me

will be an offense, all right. An offense against all that is sacred in this land—"

"*Arrest you?*" Sir Hugh's astonishment, which Finnula was certain was feigned, was nevertheless so convincing, she almost believed him. "Why would I *arrest you?*"

"Oh!" she cried, leaping to her feet at the cost of sending shooting pains through her side. "And still you play dumb!" She stabbed an impatient finger at him. "Are you not an agent of the king, sent here to root me out?"

To her surprise, her prisoner threw back his tawny head and laughed, long and loud. This reaction was so unexpected that for a moment, Finnula could naught but stare at him, openmouthed. He continued to laugh for some minutes, so uproariously that Finnula, who appreciated a good joke but disliked being the butt of one immensely, grew impatient.

"'Tis not amusing," she insisted.

But Hugo could not stop laughing. In a fit of pique, Finnula crossed the few feet of grass that separated them, until she stood over him, hands on her hips, her eyes snapping as hotly as the flames of the fire.

"Aye, that's right," she snarled. "Laugh all you want. We'll see how amusing you find it when my brother gets hold of you. He's got fists as big as flour sacks, you know, and he won't take it kindly if you bring me back to the millhouse in shackles."

This only succeeded in making the lion-maned knight laugh harder. Finnula stamped an impatient foot.

"I've got brothers-in-law, too, four of them, and Bruce is the village butcher. His arms are thicker than tree trunks—"

Before she realized what was happening, one of Sir Hugh's own arms, which, while not thicker than tree trunks, were among the longest and most muscular she'd ever seen, snaked around her legs. In the next second, he'd knocked her sharply in the backs of the knees, buckling them, while his other hand closed over her wrist, pulling her down into his lap. Finnula could not stifle a yelp of surprise.

But before she'd had time to recover herself from the igno-minious tumbling, before she'd had a chance to notice that his lap was not the most unpleasant place she'd ever been, being, among other things, rather warm, though uncomfortably hard in places, Finnula lifted her head to complain about this rude treatment . . .

. . . and found her protest silenced by a pair of very determined lips.

Finnula had been kissed before, it was true, but the few men who'd tried it had lived to regret it, since she was as swift with her fists as she was with a bow. Yet there was something about these particular lips, pressing so intently against hers, that caused nary a feeling of rancor within her. Indeed, what she felt instead could hardly be described, it was so foreign to her. But it was most definitely enjoyable, of that she was certain. She could not even bring herself to bite the audacious knight, she so enjoyed his caress.

He was an excellent kisser, her prisoner, his mouth moving over hers in a slightly inquisitive manner—not tentatively, by any means, but as if he was asking a question for which only she, Finnula, had the answer. Now there was nothing questioning at all in his manner; he'd launched the first volley and realized that Finnula's defenses were down. He attacked, showing no mercy.

It was then that it struck Finnula, as forcibly as a blow, that this kiss was something out of the ordinary, and that perhaps she was not in as much control of the situation as she would have liked. Though she struggled against the sudden, dizzying assault on her senses, she could no sooner free herself from the hypnotic spell of his lips than he'd been able to break the bonds with which she'd tied him. She went completely limp in his arms, as if she were melting against him, except for her hands, which, quite of their own volition, slipped around his brawny neck, tangling in the surprisingly soft hair half buried beneath the flung-back hood of his cloak. What was it, she wondered dimly, about the introduction of a man's mouth against one's own that seemed to have a direct correlation to a very sudden and very noticeable tightening sensation between her thighs?

Even in her heightened state of arousal, Finnula was not unaware of the fact that her prisoner seemed to be suffering a similar discomfort. She could feel that part of him which earlier she'd so foolishly mistaken for a knife hilt, pressing urgently against the softness of her hip. He had let out a low moan, smothered against her mouth, when she'd slid her hands around his neck, and now, as his need for her chafed against his braies, his strong arms tightened possessively around her. Callused fingers caressed her through the thin material of her shirt, and she realized they were moving inexorably close to her breasts. If she let him touch her *there*, what with the strange feeling she was experiencing between her legs, she'd be lost, she knew.

And she *had* to stop him, because she was no Isabella Laroche, who was loose enough to enjoy without compunction the lewd attentions of men she did not love or had any intention of marrying. She was Finnula Crais, who had a reputation to uphold. Granted, that reputation was not exactly a flawless one, but it *was* all she had. Besides, she would not end up in the same situation as Mellana, for whom she'd gone to all this trouble in the first place . . .

And then those strong, yet incredibly gentle fingers closed over one of her breasts, the nipple of which was already pebble-hard against the heat of his palm.

Tearing her mouth away from his and placing a restraining hand against his wide chest, Finnula brought accusing eyes up to his face, and was startled by what she saw there. Not the derisive smile or the mocking hazel eyes she'd become accustomed to, but a mouth slack with desire and green eyes filled with . . . with what? Finnula could not put a name to what she saw within those orbs, but it frightened as much as it thrilled her.

She had to put a stop to this madness, before things went too far. "Have you lost your reason?" she demanded, through lips that felt numb from the bruising pressure of his kiss. "Release me at once."

Hugo lifted his head, his expression as dazed as a man who'd just roused from sleep. Blinking down at the girl in his arms, he gave every indication of having heard her, and yet his hand, still anchored upon her breast, tightened, as if he had no intention of releasing her. When he spoke, it was with a hoarse voice, his intonations slurred.

"I rather think it isn't my reason I've lost, Maiden Crais, but my heart," he rasped.

Finnula snorted at this. He looked, to her, like a man who hadn't lost anything more serious than his judgment. "Do you think I'm a simpleton?" she demanded. "That I'll swoon at your pretty words and beg you to take me?" She laughed without humor. "Not bloody likely."

"'Tis going to be a long night." Hugo sighed. "Long and cold. Think of the comfort we could find in each other's arms—"

Finnula reached up and, with the heel of her hand, struck the knight soundly in the center of his forehead, sending his head cracking against the leg of the hayrack at his back. Hugo let go of her in his surprise, and Finnula scrambled to her feet, retreating a safe distance in the event that he chose to avenge his smarting skull.

"Don't make me have to hurt you," Finnula shouted, holding out a warning finger as Hugo staggered upright, using the hay-rack's wooden frame for support with one hand and clutching his head with the other. "I promised to return you to your squire un-injured if your ransom was paid in full, and it would be a burning shame if I had to deliver damaged goods—"

Hugo simply glared at her, all desire gone now from his face, his eyes a mocking amber once again.

"Remind me," he muttered, "never again to tangle with a virgin."

Finnula sniffed primly. "You have only yourself to blame. I never invited your advances."

"Like hell you didn't. What was that at the spring, then?"

"That was a trap."

"Yes, yes." He waved a hand at her dismissively. "A lure for the ignorant beast. Well, I certainly fell for it, didn't I? I have to admit that I'm a bit surprised that you, who seem to value hon-esty so highly, would stoop to such feminine trickery—"

Finnula stamped a foot in the soft grass. "I *told* you. My sister—"

"Yes, yes, yes." He rolled his eyes. "Your sister needs the money. What does she need it so badly for, anyway? Did she get herself in the family way?"

When Finnula, stunned speechless that he should have guessed so easily what she'd been trying to keep a secret from him, only stared at him, Hugo threw back his head and laughed mirthlessly.

"So that's it!" he crowed. "The beautiful Mellana has the face of an angel but the virtue of a trollop—"

Finnula took a half-dozen angry strides toward him. "You take that back!" she ordered him. "How dare you?"

"And this also explains your oblique references to that unfor-tunate minstrel. He would be the father, then? Well, no wonder the fair Mellana needs money so badly. Does Brother Robert know? I'd wager not—"

Finnula was so furious she could hardly refrain from launching herself at him and throttling his thick, stupid neck. Only the memory of how difficult it had been to extricate herself from his embrace the last time kept her from doing so.

"Mellana is no trollop," Finnula had to satisfy herself by hissing. "That damned troubadour tricked her!"

"Oh? Tricked her out of her maidenhead? I wish I was more intimately acquainted with a troubadour, that I might learn this trick that causes virtuous maids to so liberally bestow their favors. There's a certain maid I know who might benefit from such a trick—"

Finnula thought about hurling her knife in his chest, but that seemed a bit extreme. Murder, even of this cur, would only get her hanged.

But she could not possibly endure this man's company for another twenty-four hours. He was a vile, manipulative, rutting rake, and nothing would make her happier than never having to gaze upon his hairy face again . . .

"Here," she cried, reaching inside her shirt and drawing out the cord upon which dangled Hugo's emerald. She pulled the heavy stone from around her neck and hurled it, with unerring accuracy, into the grass at his feet. "Take the bloody thing back. I release you! You are no longer my prisoner. Take your horse and get gone with you. I never want to see you again!"

So angry that she was almost sobbing, Finnula whirled around, smugly satisfied by the dismay she'd seen on his face, and went to Violet's side, where she opened her saddlebags, looking for her cloak. While she was there, she noticed that his knife and sword were still tied to her saddle, and she set about undoing the knots that bound them, so that she could hurl them, too, at the churlish knight.

She heard him call her name, in a different voice than she'd ever heard him use before, but she wouldn't turn around. Instead she shouted, loudly enough to cause Violet to turn down her ears, "I told you, you're released! Get gone with you! The sight of you sickens me!"

A moment later, Hugo was speaking to her in a gentle voice that sounded only inches away. "Finnula. Turn around."

"I won't," Finnula declared hotly. She let first his sword, then his dagger fall to the earth, and enjoyed the cry of dismay he gave as each finely crafted blade clattered onto the grass.

Clutching her fur-lined cloak to her chest, as if the thick garment were protection against the wrath of a knight, she declared, to her saddle, "I want you to go away and leave me alone."

"I can't do that," Sir Hugh said.

There was no question that he was standing directly behind her now. She could feel his breath on the back of her neck, where her braid had fallen over one shoulder, and the heat emanating from his body warmed her back.

"What do you mean, you can't do that?" Taking a deep breath, Finnula turned around to face him, a little startled to find that he really was standing even closer than she'd suspected, literally just inches away. With his back to the firelight, his features were unreadable, and Finnula bit her lower lip. Oh, she'd been a fool, a blind, bloody fool, ever to have agreed to this undertaking. When she got home, she'd slap Mellana silly, pregnant or not.

"I can't leave you alone out here in the middle of nowhere," Hugo said, with quiet dignity. "Don't you know that there are cutthroats and footpads all over the countryside, looking for foolish maids like yourself to prey upon?"

Finnula snorted disdainfully. "Like Timmy and Dick? Let them try. I'd relish another chance to tangle with those two—"

"Worse than those two. Believe me, Finnula, you've been lucky up until now—"

"Lucky?" she sputtered, incredulously. "To have gotten myself saddled with the likes of *you*? Not likely!"

Hugo went on as if she hadn't interrupted. "I wouldn't be able to live with myself if I thought harm had come to you. After all, I *am* a knight." The wry grin, slightly lopsided, returned as he added, " 'Tis my duty to protect the innocent, and I suppose that means you, despite your excellent aim."

Finnula lowered her gaze, hoping that despite the fact that the firelight was full on her face, he could not see her blush. Why, oh why, did the slightest compliment from him cause her to redden like a milkmaid?

"I'm sorry I called your sister a trollop," Hugo went on seriously, in his deep voice. "Please forgive me. It was uncalled for. Now, as I am traveling in the same direction that you are, I do not see, prisoner or no, why we should not ride together. I promise to keep my hands to myself. You'll have to forgive my momentary lapse. You are, however, very distracting when you are indignant."

Without another word, he dropped the heavy emerald around her neck once more, letting the pendant fall with a thump between her breasts. Finnula looked down at the stone as it winked in the firelight.

What in heaven's name was she to do *now*? How was she to be rid of him? He was like a boy she'd known years and years before, who'd followed her for days until she'd finally had no choice but to jump on him and rub his face in the dirt until he promised to leave her alone.

But she'd *never* be able to get the best of Sir Hugh Fitzwilliam, not physically, anyway. She'd tried being unpleasant, she'd threatened violence, she'd even turned down an invitation to share his bed, albeit a straw one. But nothing had worked. What ailed the man?

"I'll see to tomorrow's breakfast," Hugo said, interrupting her mutinous thoughts. He left her to go and kneel beside the simmering pot hanging from the spit he had rigged. "You get ready for bed."

Finnula simply stared at him, astounded. She had released him, and yet he wouldn't go! What kind of man was he? A stubborn one, anyway. She was going to have to think long and hard of a way to be rid of him. Perhaps, if she rose early enough, she could simply slip away, and be gone before he woke. Yes, that was an excellent plan! She could be leagues away before he even stirred!

But then she'd have failed her mission for Mellana. That thought sobered her, even as she yawned from a tiredness she had not known she felt. If she did manage to shake off this clinging knight, who, in the name of St. Elias, was she going to hold hostage next? No, much as she didn't like to admit it, she needed this knight. She glared at him, as he, seemingly oblivious to her antipathy, salted his soup. Lord, how he irritated her! Stubborn, stubborn man!

It did not occur to Finnula that her prisoner wasn't any more stubborn than his captor. Instead of heeding his advice and preparing for sleep, she went silently round to the back of the hayrack and climbed inside it, sinking knee-deep into the soft hay. From that height, she could watch him, and she did that for a while, wondering what sort of knight he was, that he possessed what could, at times, be such a gentle manner, yet such grizzled looks. Surely he would not be half so bad looking if he shaved. Was he hiding from something—or someone—that he let his face get covered so with bristles?

After a few moments of such musings, Finnula thought she might be more comfortable lying down, and so she leaned upon her side, careful of her bruised rib, the hay beneath her pliant and sweet-smelling. Perhaps, she thought, watching Sir Hugh as he stirred his soup, he was escaping from an unhappy love affair of some sort. Perhaps the emerald really *had* been given to him by a sultan's daughter, as a love token. Most likely her father had not allowed the two of them to wed, being of separate faiths. She wondered if Sir Hugh had attempted to escape with the princess, and if the sultan had found the lovers out, and dragged them back to the palace for execution. Sir Hugh might have barely escaped with his life. No wonder he'd been so opposed to having his hands tied behind his back. Perhaps it brought back painful memories of the sultan's dungeon . . . .

Fingering the gem, Finnula rolled over onto her back to blink at the stars. They shined as brightly as the emerald, yet their light was cold, whereas when she looked down at the jewel around her neck, she saw a sort of fire in its center—not unlike the fire she had seen in her prisoner's eyes when she'd looked up at him, after they'd kissed. Did Sir Hugh's eyes burn that way after he kissed any woman, or was that fire for her, and her alone?

Turning her head, she stared at her prisoner through the slats of the hayrack. He was still puttering with his soup, pointedly not turning those green eyes in her direction. The fire bathed his face in a warm yellow light, bringing out, in sharp definition, the strength in his jawline, the lean spareness of his aquiline nose, the sensuous curves of his full lips. It was unnerving to recall the sensations those lips had aroused in her when they'd kissed. To look at him, one wouldn't suppose he'd be capable of rendering an otherwise sensible woman so giddy with desire. *She* would certainly never have thought it possible. Otherwise, she would have picked an entirely different quarry.

Finnula was not at all confident she would be able to turn down his advances a second time. No, she was going to have to make a break for it.

This was an encouraging thought, and she concentrated upon it happily until, despite all her intentions to the contrary, sleep overtook her.

Still, the last image that she saw before she drifted off was that of her prisoner, kneeling thoughtfully by the fire. She couldn't even rid herself of his memory, which seemed to be burned onto the backs of her eyelids. Fie!

# Chapter  Seven

ord Hugo Fitzstephen, seventh Earl of Stephensgate, looked down at the girl curled against his side and wondered how in the hell he had ever gotten himself involved in this ridiculous charade.

He had been in tangles aplenty in Jerusalem, many of them dangerous, more than a few of them purely lascivious.

But he could not remember ever having dealt with a virgin before, and the multifaceted problems this presented were threatening to overwhelm him, in more ways than one.

For one thing, when he'd wakened moments before in the hayrack into which he'd crawled late the evening before, careful not to jar the deeply sleeping Finnula, he'd found that the girl had rolled over in the night and snuggled up against him for warmth. Her curvaceous backside was pressed against the front of Hugo's braies, her back molded to his chest, her soft cheek resting upon his outflung arm. It seemed as if her small body had been created apurpose to fit against the curve of Hugo's. She slept beside him as comfortably—and as soundly—as a wife of long standing.

Hugo could not honestly say he was comfortable, however much he enjoyed the feel of her against him. The problem appeared to be that he was enjoying Finnula's close proximity a little *too* much. That part of him which most desired her touch was stiffer than on any morn of recent memory, and was anxious for relief.

But last night, Finnula Crais had made it perfectly clear that such relief was not to be found in her corner. It wasn't a question, Hugo knew, of her not desiring him. He was well-versed in the art of seduction, and he had tasted desire on her lips. Finnula was a woman with deep, as yet unplumbed, reservoirs of passion.

But—most likely because of what had happened to the conniving Mellana—exploring those depths was not an option.

And yet if she continued to curl against him like this, that option was going to *have* to be explored, because he wasn't at all certain how many mornings he could endure like this. He supposed when they reached Stephensgate tomorrow, he could seek out relief from the village whore—was Fat Maude still in business? he wondered. Surely by now she'd have retired, and someone younger would have set up shop.

But wait. No. He was lord of the manor now, and earls didn't seek their pleasure from village prostitutes. His father had certainly had consorts, but he hadn't shared them with the rest of the men in Stephensgate. No, that was it. Hugo was going to have to find a mistress, problematic as such an undertaking would surely prove. Mistresses required homes of their own, since they were generally demanding and therefore unpleasant to live with for long periods of time. And one was required to give them hand-some gifts of jewels and money. But this was no problem, since Hugo had plenty of both.

What he didn't have was the time. If what Finnula had been tell-ing him last night was the truth—and he couldn't imagine Finnula telling anything less than the strictest truth—Stephensgate Manor had been left by his father in sorry shape, made sorrier since the old man's death by his imprudent choice of a bailiff. Hugo knew his cousin Reginald Laroche well, and could easily imagine that the man was stealing from the estate funds. A little for himself, a little for the village mayor, in order to look the other way, understand, and soon Laroche had a healthy pot of gold to retire with upon the return of His Late Lordship's heir.

How the man could starve serfs, however, was beyond Hugo's comprehension. The families who had worked the fields of Ste-phensgate Manor for decades deserved better than Hugo's father had ever offered them, his tallages being among the highest in Shropshire. But to have that ridiculously high sum made even higher by a man who meant only to line his own pockets—well, Reginald Laroche was going to have some explaining to do when Hugo returned home, and much of it was going to be done from the stockade.

The last thing Hugo wanted to do was come home to place of dissension. But if that was how it was to be, he would cope.

Installing a mistress would necessarily have to wait until all these other matters had been attended to. How much simpler, Hugo sighed, looking down at his dozing companion, it would be if Finnula Crais were not quite so maidenly, and a little more will-ing to wriggle out of those temptingly tight leather braies . . .

A large drop of rain fell out of the leaden sky, which had long ago pearled with dawn and then clouded over, and landed smack against the side of Finnula's oddly patrician nose. She woke with a gasp, one hand flying to her face, the other curling around her knife hilt.

Hugo lay perfectly still, praying she wouldn't notice the swelling in his braies, and when those wide gray eyes turned upon him, filled with sleep and surprise, he wore his best mocking smile.

"Good morning," he purred, in his deepest voice. "I trust you slept well. Were you warm enough?"

Finnula's gaze flew from his face, down the length of his body, and then to her own. Startled, she raised accusing eyes, her fine eyebrows slanted downward, and her sensual lips curved into a frown.

"Don't look at me," Hugo said, quickly holding up both hands, one of which was hampered by the fact that her head was still resting against the curve of his biceps. "I had nothing to do with it."

With a smothered groan of fury, Finnula sat up, a host of unpleasantries poised upon her tongue, Hugo was certain.

But before she could get out the first ripe curse, her face paled, and she clutched her side.

Hugo was instantly contrite. He was well-aware that his squire had caused her an injury, and her tolerance for pain was remarkable. Amusing as she was to tease, Hugo preferred a sparring partner who was not doubled over in agony.

"Is it bad?" he asked gently, then chided himself for the question. Of course it was bad.

Finnula looked up at him, her eyes crackling with fury and almost the same color as the gray sky overhead. "Oh, no," she said, obviously lying. "'Tis fine."

"Let me see it," Hugo commanded.

She shook her head, straw falling from her long auburn hair, which overnight had come loose from the braid into which she'd twisted it. "Nay," she said. "I told you, 'tis fine—"

But Hugo was insistent. Too many times, he'd seen men ignore minor wounds, only to have them fester and eventually kill, when they should have healed harmlessly.

"I'll see it," Hugo said, gripping her soft upper arm in fingers of steel. Fortunately, in the cozy confines of the hayrack, there wasn't much chance of escape. And Hugo's massive frame took up most of the available space anyway, so she had no choice but to give in, though she did so with the ill grace that Hugo had come to expect from her.

"All right," she snapped, pulling the tails of her lawn shirt from her braies. "You can look, but don't touch."

"I haven't forgotten our agreement," Hugo said mildly, with a single raised eyebrow.

He kept his gaze carefully averted as she unwound the silk bandage from beneath her breasts. He'd been relieved to find that his discomfort was lessening, primarily due to the fact that she was no longer pressed up against him. He was still a long way from the relief he needed, but at least the necessity was not quite so crucial anymore. He did not want to run into similar temptations, however, and so stared hard at the darkening storm clouds over their heads until Finnula politely cleared her throat.

Finnula, her face turned primly away from him, lifted her shirt to reveal a mottled green and black bruise just under the curve of her small, round, breast. Hugo bent to examine the wound, and saw with satisfaction that the outer edges of the bruise had faded to a yellowish brown, which meant that it was healing. It might smart, but it wasn't fatal.

Leaning back, Hugo said complacently, "It's getting better. Let me bind it again, and I'll give you a few drops more of the poppy drink—"

"Getting better?" Finnula echoed, her throaty voice rich with disbelief. "But it feels even worse than yesterday!"

"Yes, but it *looks* much better." Hugo was slightly stunned at the fact that she'd finally admitted to some discomfort as he wound the strips of his cloak's lining back around her narrow rib cage. "Besides, you put yourself through quite a trial yesterday, with all that riding and hunting and despising me—"

Finnula turned her head toward him just enough to glare out of the corner of her expressive eyes. "I don't understand why you're still here."

Hugo didn't understand it himself, but he attempted a light-hearted quip to explain it. "I told you, I'm a knight. It's my duty to see that maidens are not taken advantage of—"

Finnula snorted, as he'd known she would. "Except by yourself, is that correct?"

Hugo ignored that, tying off the bandage and sitting back, admiring the way his handiwork thrust her tip-tilted breasts toward him.

"Now, breakfast," he said, feeling enormously self-satisfied, though not at all certain why. "Let's see how our soup fared overnight."

He climbed down from the hayrack, then turned to hold his arms out to her. As he might have predicted, she ignored him, climbing down without his aid. Then, as soon as her boots touched the hard ground, Finnula was off, stomping in the direction of a nearby copse. Hugo bent to test his soup. The fire had burned itself out during the night, but its embers still glowed warmly, and Hugo held out his hands, glad for a little relief from the morning gloom. It promised to be a gray day, and unless the light, drizzling rain let up, they'd be soaked through come nightfall.

The soup turned out better than Hugo would have expected. The addition of Finnula's rabbit carcass thickened it, and lent it a hearty flavor it might have lacked with just vegetables. The herbs from her saddlebags, however, were what made the difference. However frustratingly virtuous she was, Finnula appeared to be as seasoned a traveler as he himself was, packing such necessities that, though small, could make the difference in a meal cooked on the road.

He'd been surprised at the number—and diversity—of provisions he'd found in Finnula's saddlebags the day before, everything from dried herbs to a hairbrush and comb, and from spare arrowheads to a wrinkled kirtle of the softest linen. Everything in her possession smelled of roses, and he found a number of dried buds in the bottom of her leather saddlebags, which explained why. The contrast between a girl who could hit a hare in the eye with an arrow at fifty paces, and a maid who kept dried rose blossoms in her saddlebags to keep her kirtles smelling sweet, caused Hugo to shake his head in wonderment.

When Finnula returned, Hugo saw that she'd washed in the stream, combing the straw from her hair and scrubbing the sleep from her eyes. The long red mane swayed loose upon her narrow shoulders, and already the light drizzle had collected within the thick curls, each drop sparkling like a diamond. Her cheeks were flushed from the morning chill, and she'd draped her cloak about her shoulders to ward off the cold.

Her freshness made Hugo wonder what kind of sight he looked, with his unkempt hair and beard. He was going to have to do something about his appearance at some point, since occasionally he caught Finnula staring at him in dismay, a reaction he was not at all used to. Normally his looks engendered glances of admiration from comely women, not curled lips.

"Here," Hugo said shortly, when Finnula approached. He thrust the warm pot of soup in her hands, along with a wooden spoon he'd dug out of his own saddlebags, and the vial of the poppy syrup. She struggled to keep from dropping everything, looking up at him as if he'd lost his mind. "Two drops," he advised, as he stalked toward the stream. "No more."

A glance at his own reflection in the stream revealed what he suspected. He looked like a crazed old hermit. Despite the fact that there wasn't hint of white in his fine gold hair, he looked a decade older than his actual age. There was nothing he could do about it now, however. He couldn't very well shave in the rain, though he did his best to brush out his beard and shoulder-length hair. He didn't know why it mattered to him, what this eccentric miller's daughter thought of him, except that she attracted him like no other woman he'd ever met. He supposed that was just because he knew he couldn't have her. Forbidden fruits were always the best, or so he'd been told.

When he returned to the hayrack, Finnula glanced up at him, the spoon poised at her lips, and if she noticed his attempt at grooming, her face didn't register it. Instead, she said, indicating the pot, "This is good. Do you want some?"

Hugo did, and he took the pot and spoon from her, hunkering down in what little shelter the hayrack provided from the drizzle. "'Tis a miserable day," he announced, between bites of the stew. "What say you we find an inn and spend it before a nice, roaring fire?"

Finnula had been administering her drops of painkiller, her tongue extended to catch the ruby liquid. After she'd swallowed, making several dramatic faces to indicate to him her dislike of the stuff, she said, with a wrinkled nose, "I would say nay."

"Just like that? No consideration?"

"I considered it." Finnula shrugged. "And dismissed the idea. I have to get to Dorchester by nightfall—"

"Why?" Hugo demanded. "What's the hurry? Is Mellana starting to show?"

She gave him a sour look, and passed the vial back to him.

"Nay, nothing like that. Only if I'm gone too long, Robert gets suspicious—"

"Suspicious of what?" Hugo lifted an eyebrow. "Seems to me the sister he ought to be worried about is the one waiting back home at the hearth—"

"Aye," Finnula conceded, with surprising bitterness. "Robert never has paid Mellana much mind. *I'm* the one he always frets over. Mellana never gives anyone any trouble. I'm the one the sheriff is constantly threatening to imprison."

"Perhaps if Brother Robert had minded Sister Mellana a little more, she wouldn't be in the position she's in now."

Finnula looked up at him appraisingly, as if he were a deaf-mute who had suddenly begun to speak. "Aye," she said. "That might well be true." Then she sighed, lifting a wave of rain-heavy hair from her eyes. "But be that as it may, I've still got to get at least as far as Dorchester today, so I can make it to Stephensgate by tomorrow. I'd best be off."

"*I?*" he echoed. "*I'd* best be off? Aren't you forgetting someone?"

She cocked her head to one side as she regarded him sarcastically. "No, I'm not. You're not coming with me."

"What do you mean?" Hugo felt cut to the quick. "I'm still your prisoner, am I not?"

"You're not. I released you last night, remember?"

He felt absurdly disappointed. He'd hoped she'd forgotten about last night. "But what of Mellana?" he asked quickly. "How will she scrape together enough money for hops and malt without my ransom?"

Finnula glared at him, then bent and, to Hugo's surprise, took the empty pot from his hands. The argument appeared to be over, but he wasn't certain who had won. Without another word, she turned and traipsed down to the stream. He supposed she considered it an even labor exchange—he made the stew, and she washed the pot. The domesticity of the gesture moved him, however, because Finnula was not someone he could picture performing household chores like a goodwife. What was going to happen to her? he wondered. She was of marriageable age, after all. She could not possibly hope to find a husband who would approve of her hunting and her leather braies and her extended trips across the countryside. Not unless, he supposed, she married someone who was wealthy enough not to require his wife to perform housekeeping.

Someone like himself, for instance.

Shaking his head, sending a fine spray of rainwater droplets flying, Hugo berated himself. What was he thinking? He could not, *would* not marry Finnula Crais. Marry the miller's daughter? His father would turn over in his grave. No, Hugo was going to marry a wealthy widow and add to the Fitzstephen fortune and estate. The only thing Finnula Crais could provide him was children—who'd inevitably be carrot-topped—and game for dinner every night.

Upon her return from the stream, however, Hugo couldn't help offering to allow her to tie his hands again, in the hope that she'd take him prisoner once more, an offer at which Finnula turned up her nose. She further dismissed his suggestion that they both ride on his steed, as they'd done the day before, to better ward off the cold and rain from each other. She pointed out, with no little sarcasm, that he was no longer her prisoner, and therefore she didn't need to keep him from escaping. In fact, he was free to ride away whenever he chose, and she'd wish him well.

Hugo knew it was absurd, but he was chagrined. He'd looked forward to once again sharing a saddle with her. She was a pleasant companion, when she wasn't whacking him in the head with the heel of her hand. She never bored him. Her contrariness was a relief from the fawning attentions he normally received from women of his acquaintance.

"What I don't understand," Hugo said, when they'd finished cleaning up their campsite and were mounted and moving away from the hayrack, "is how you're going to provide your sister with the financial assistance she requires now that you've released me."

Finnula was hunched beneath the fur trim of her cloak, blinking against the drizzle. She seemed to be pointedly ignoring him, except when he thrust himself directly into her line of vision. "God's teeth," she swore, though whether at him, the rain, or his reminder, he wasn't certain. "I don't know. I suppose I'll have to find someone else."

"Someone else?" Hugo guided Skinner closer to her mare's flank, not certain he'd heard her correctly. "Did you say you're going to have to find someone else?"

"Aye." Her profile, what he could see of it above the cloak's fur collar, was grim. "Though I don't know where I'll find another as promising as you. Isabella Laroche has apparently already held every man in the vicinity hostage at least once. I'm afraid their families won't pay a second time. Not handsomely, anyway."

Hugo nosed his destrier closer to Violet's head. "Who are you considering? Because I'd like to make a suggestion."

"Oh?" She looked at him, her slender eyebrows raised questioningly. "This ought to be interesting. And what might your suggestion be?"

"Don't use the same lure you used with me. You have a reputation to think of, you know. You can't go around allowing the entire male population of Shropshire see you in your altogether. It will make it difficult to find a husband, when the time comes for you to marry."

The smile she quickly suppressed was not lost on him. "Oh? That's your advice, is it?"

"It is. And I suggest a younger man than myself."

"Ah," she said knowingly. "You found the role of hostage too rigorous for a man of your advanced years, did you?"

"I most certainly did not," Hugo snapped, stung. "I meant only that a younger man might be more manageable, and less apt to make trouble for you."

"Less apt to make advances, you mean."

"I didn't say that—"

"You didn't have to. Your concern for me is touching, Sir Hugh, it truly is, but I believe I am capable of making my own selection as far as future hostages go—"

"If I might be of assistance, you needn't hesitate to ask."

"Thank you, but I believe that this undertaking is traditionally a purely female concern. Your assistance will not be required."

Hugo was not put off by her dismissive tone. "If you would allow it, I'd gladly offer my squire, Peter, for your next hostage."

She looked at him, wide-eyed, before she burst out laughing. Hugo glared at her, failing to see anything humorous in the offer.

"What's wrong with Peter?" he demanded. "He's my charge. I'll gladly pay whatever ransom you ask for him—"

"I can hardly be assured of that," snickered Finnula. "Why, your squire is even more tiresome than you are! I'd have to keep him bound and gagged, just to keep from killing him myself, and I sincerely doubt that anyone, including you, sir, would ever pay money to get him back—"

Hugo didn't much appreciate being called tiresome.

"Besides," Finnula went on, oblivious to his ire. "Your Peter's the one who wounded me. I'd hardly be likely to take him hostage.

He might murder me next time. Chivalry is one thing you've yet to teach your squire, sir."

"Who will you kidnap next, then?" Hugo demanded hotly. "Some brawny-armed smithy, who'll be so smitten with you that he'll probably follow you about like a puppy even after he's ransomed?"

Hugo was relieved when she didn't point out that that, in fact, was what he himself was doing. "And what would be so wrong with that?" Finnula inquired.

"If that's how you see yourself, nothing's wrong with it, I suppose. I can't picture you as the wife of some thick-chested blacksmith, but if that's the future you've chosen for yourself, I shan't try to stop you."

Finnula laughed, the bell-like sound sending ripples up and down Hugo's spine.

"I'm looking for a hostage, not a husband," she reminded him with an infuriatingly condescending smile. Giving Violet a gentle kick in the sides with her heels, she trotted a few yards ahead of Hugo and his mount, her horse's footing amazingly steady on the mud-slicked track. "Besides," she called gaily over her shoulder, "you oughtn't speak so contemptuously of blacksmiths. They perform many vital functions in the community. I'd be honored to be married to a smithy."

Hugo rolled his eyes derisively, mimicking her. "'I'd be honored to be married to a smithy,'" he murmured, loud enough for her to hear. "We'll see how honored you feel when you're fat with your thirteenth brat and your husband the smithy is just rolling in from the local tavern, stinking of beer and ordering you to make him supper. Oh, yes, we'll just see how honored the Fair Finn feels then."

When she didn't turn her head, he could not help adding, "But then, the stink of beer oughtn't offend your sensitive nostrils, since it's probably a smell you're uncommonly accustomed to, what with your sister the brewmistress—or should I say, brewmatron?"

Finnula gave Violet another kick, and suddenly, she was cantering away at a pace that, in the mud and rain, probably wasn't wise. Hugo urged his destrier to follow, the bigger horse less sure of his footing in the foul weather. It was some minutes later that Finnula, glancing over her shoulder and seeing that he still followed, allowed her mount to slow. When Hugo caught up, he was winded and resentful.

"That was a damned fool thing to do," he accused her, between breaths. "What were you thinking, putting your horse in jeopardy like that? She could have slipped and broken a leg."

Finnula didn't say anything. She had pulled her hood up over her head to shield her hair from the rain, and he could see only the tip of her pointed nose.

"Not speaking to me, eh?" Hugo observed, wiping rainwater from his forehead. "Hit a bit close to the mark, did I, calling your sister a brewmatron?"

Finnula turned her furious gray eyes toward him.

"Why won't you leave me alone?" she demanded. "Why do you hang about, insulting and mocking me? I gave you your freedom, I told you to go. Why do you persist in tormenting me?"

"For one thing, you still have my emerald. For another, I wonder why you persist in believing a lie?" he countered.

She turned her attention back to the muddy road before them. "I don't know what you're talking about," she said.

"This sister of yours, this Mellana. She's using you."

Finnula flicked a rain-soaked tendril of hair from her eyes. "She is not," she said loftily. "I can't imagine what you mean."

"You know exactly what I mean. You're too intelligent, Finnula, not to know. She tricked you into embarking on this ridiculous mission. *She's* the one who got herself pregnant, and yet *you're* the one who's riding around in the cold and rain with a strange man while she's safe and snug at home. And you say she isn't using you?" He laughed shortly.

Finnula glared at him. "She's my sister," she said, through teeth that almost, but not quite, were beginning to chatter from the spring cold. "Sisters do things for one another. You wouldn't understand."

"I think I understand all too well. I had a brother, you know."

That got her attention. She blinked at him. "Did you?"

"I did. An elder brother. He was my father's heir. Anything he wanted, he got. Me, I was the younger son. I was expected to enter the church—"

Finnula's bark of laughter was so explosive that Hugo's mount laid back his ears and whickered questioningly. When the girl had calmed down sufficiently, Hugo continued. "Yes, amazing as that may sound to you, Finnula, my mother's fondest wish was to see me a monk."

Finnula, he realized, had been laughing so hard that she was now dashing tears from her eyes. "You!" she giggled. "A monk! Oh, God have mercy!"

"Amusing, isn't it?" His mouth twisted sardonically, Hugo gripped Skinner's reins in one white-knuckled hand. "Nevertheless, that was her intention. I begged her to reconsider, and my father, too, but they wouldn't listen. A monk I was to be, and they wouldn't fund any other endeavor, least of all my ambition to become a soldier."

Finnula said, a little more warmly than she'd ever spoken to him before, Hugo thought, "Well, that's wrong. If you wanted to be a soldier, they ought to have let you. After all, it was your life."

"My sentiments exactly. So I appealed to my brother, who by that time had come of age, and asked him to take my part, and explain to our parents that I could not possibly take the vow. And do you know what he did?"

Finnula shook her head, a droplet of rain flying off the end of her nose.

"He hired a couple of footpads to sneak into my chamber late one night and spirit me away to a local monastery."

Finnula gasped. "Nay, but that isn't so!"

"'Twas so. When I overpowered the cads, they told me. I packed my few belongings and left for London that very night. And I haven't returned home since."

Finnula's face was grave. "Your brother did you a grievous wrong, but it's well that you leave the past behind and make peace with him now."

"I'm not making peace with him," Hugo said. "He's dead."

"Oh."

"They're all dead. My mother and brother fell to a fever years ago, and my father died just last year."

Finnula said quietly, "So now you are alone."

"Yes. And heir, despite my brother's best efforts. So do not tell me that siblings are incapable of doing one another harm. Your sister is using you, and you are allowing her to do so."

Finnula was staring down at her hands, upon which she'd pulled a pair of close-fitting leather gloves. She looked so miserable, so unhappy and cold, that Hugo felt sorry for having spoken to her so harshly.

"What happened to your sister's dowry?" he asked, in what he hoped was a kindlier voice.

"She spent it," Finnula said sorrowfully. "On gowns and trinkets. I suppose 'tis true that Robert does not watch her as closely as he ought."

*Brother Robert,* Hugo thought, *is a fool who might just join Reginald Laroche in the stockade when I return to the manor house.*

"But," Finnula said, looking up at him with eyes that were as large as the emerald she still wore between her breasts. "But whether or not she is using me, Mellana is my sister, and I've got to help her, if I can." A simple shrug. "And I can. So I will."

Hugo stared at her. She looked so small perched atop her spotted mare, engulfed in a cloak that was too large for her, her red hair plastered to the sides of her skull. It amazed him to think that such a tiny vessel was capable of containing the passion he'd sensed kissing her the night before, but it was there, all right, and suddenly he knew he'd be damned before he'd let some other man tap it.

"I don't see why you can't continue holding me hostage," he said, his voice carefully toneless. "I think I made a very fine prisoner."

She glanced over at him, and the smile she flashed was so sunny, yet so brief, that it dazzled him.

"Aye," she said, turning her eyes back to the road with a studied frown. "You had your moments."

"I never tried to escape, did I? I could easily have overpowered you, and yet I restrained myself—"

"*Most* of the time," she corrected him.

"And I don't remember that you particularly *minded* the one time I did overpower you—"

Again the smile, not directed at him this time and accompanied by a blush. She said, with obvious reluctance, to her hands, "I suppose, since you won't leave me be . . ."

"My sense of chivalry won't allow it," he said quickly. "I will see you to your very door."

She winced as though that was something she'd been afraid of. "Well." She sighed. "I suppose that since we are traveling in the same direction—"

"Caterbury is but a half day's ride beyond Stephensgate," he pointed out.

"I suppose it only makes sense—"

"And 'twill save you a good deal of time. Not to mention that fact that if you were to disrobe in this weather, in order to catch yourself another hostage, you might very well catch a cold—"

"All right." She laughed. "I'll keep you as my prisoner, then. But you must promise not to be so . . . *irritating* . . . this time."

"I never meant to be *irritating* at all," he said, with a sly grin. He knew what she meant by irritating. "I was only being myself."

She sighed heartily. "That's what I was afraid of."

"If it makes you feel better, you can bind my wrists," Hugo offered, holding up both his hands. "Only then I won't be able to guide Skinner, so you'll have to ride with me . . ."

"No." Finnula laughed. "That won't be necessary, I'm sure."

Hugo shrugged as if it didn't matter to him one way or another, but he could not help feeling self-satisfied with the turn of events. It had taken him nearly two hours, but he'd finally goaded her out of her anger with him. A woman who could stay angry at a man for no longer than two hours was a rare find indeed. He deliberated over the meaning of this discovery.

Something was very wrong. Normally, if a woman expressed no interest in him—and that, though rare, had occurred once or twice in Hugo's past—he promptly lost all interest in her as well. But this girl, with the big gray eyes and the very sharp knife, intrigued him as much as she frustrated him. He'd had a perfect opportunity to leave her, and yet he'd stayed. Why had the thought of her taking some other man prisoner angered him so irrationally? He wasn't normally a jealous man—he'd shared women in the past, happily. Why did the thought of sharing this one annoy him so much, when she wasn't even his to begin with?

He had a lot of time to mull over these topics, since the mud on the road was deep, and the rain in their faces pelting at times. The way was slow, and even Finnula, determined as she was to be at Dorchester by sundown, began to look longingly at the smoke curling from the chimneys of the small farms they passed.

It wasn't until they were riding past a field that was undergoing tilling by an ox-pulled plow that a voice broke through the steady hissing of the rain, and Finnula jerked on her mount's reins and looked about, startled.

"Your Ladyship!"

Finnula, Hugo saw, sat so stiffly in the saddle, her eyes so wide, that she looked a statue. He turned his head and saw that the man operating the plow and his ox-crier were hurrying toward them through the thick mud, the man waving his hat.

"Your Ladyship!"

The rough-shod farmer stumbled upon the road before them, and, clutching the rim of his hat to his chest, peered up at Finnula. He was a young man, Hugo saw, no more than twenty, and though his garments were soiled—no small miracle for farming in this weather—they were of good quality, neither threadbare nor much patched.

"I thought 'twas you, m'lady," the farmer cried, giving a stunned-looking Finnula a toothy grin. "I said to Evan 'ere, Evan, I says, Like as not that's t' Lady Finnula, the Fair Finn, passin' by—"

Finnula's astonishment had ebbed enough for her to smile graciously at the farmer and his assistant, who could not seem to lift his head, he was so cowed with embarrassment.

"Good day to you, Matthew Fairchild," Finnula said, with a graciousness she'd never exhibited toward Hugo. "And to you, too, Evan. 'Tis a sorry day for plowing."

"And for ridin'," Farmer Fairchild pointed out, laying hold of Violet's bridle like a man who knew he might. Hugo glared. "I says to Evan, I says, If'n that's t' Lady Finnula passin' by, my Mavis'd 'ave me 'ead if'n I don't invite 'er inside for a bite—"

Though the man's rough dialect had Hugo's head spinning, Finnula seemed to understand it perfectly. She had already begun shaking her head before the invitation—for that's what it seemed to be—was fully out of the peasant's mouth. "Oh, Matthew, 'tis kind indeed for you to ask, but I must be in Dorchester by sunset—"

"What sun?" chuckled Matthew. "You'll make it in plenty o' time. Come inside, warm yourselves, 'ave a cuppa—"

"A cuppa?" Hugo inquired, since this sounded promising.

"Aye, a cuppa my Mavis's cider. My Mavis brews t' best. An' like I said, she won't take kindly to knowin' you passed an' didna stop to see the wee one—"

Finnula, drenched to the skin, looked sadly at the road before them, and Hugo could almost see her making the swift mental calculations necessary to determine how long they could stay and how soon they'd have to take their leave. Then she sighed, though her smile was bright.

"Thank you, Matthew," she said. "Sir Hugh and I would be honored to join you and Mavis."

Matthew chuckled happily and, hitting Evan lightly in the head with his cap, cried, "Run an' tell your mistress to expect company, an' be sure an' tell 'er it's Lady Finnula. I'll just bring in Goliath. You know the way, surely, m'lady?"

"I know the way," Finnula said, with a smile, and she turned Violet around with a gentle tug on the reins, and headed toward a dirt track leading off the main road that seemed to be made up of nothing but mud.

Hugo followed on Skinner, a crooked grin twisting his mouth. "Your Ladyship?" he couldn't help calling. "Oh, Your Ladyship, I'm sorry to trouble you, but is there something you haven't been telling me?"

Finnula's lips, he saw, when Skinner caught up with the girl's mare, were set grimly. "Mind your own business, *sir*," she suggested, with a sneer.

Hugo was unruffled by her disdain. "Had I known I was traveling with a noble personage, I'd have insisted upon your putting me up in an inn, instead of that hayrack—"

"They use the title as a courtesy," she said, with a sigh, keeping her eyes on the mud, through which Violet picked her way daintily. "I've asked them not to, but they persist. 'Tis really quite silly. Matthew is very sweet, though—"

"This Matthew seems to know you quite well," Hugo said, and he was amazed at the testiness in his voice. "Was *he* ever one of your prisoners?"

Finnula glared at him, the anger in her gaze hot enough to warm his hands by. "I told you, you're the only man I ever—"

"And so what's this Matthew to you? An ardent suitor, from the looks of it." His tone was sharp, and Finnula raised her eyebrows at him. Cursing to himself—*why* could he not act disinterested where it concerned this girl?—he tempered the accusation by adding, ungraciously, "If you don't mind my asking, that is."

Finnula shook her head. "For a knight, you have a rather active imagination. Matthew is a freeman, a farmer who works that plot of land you saw by the road. Last year, he fell in love with the daughter of one the Earl of Stephensgate's serfs, Mavis Poole. When he asked for her hand, Laroche demanded that a ridiculously high tallage be paid before he would release her from the earl's service—"

"Let me guess the rest," Hugo said, holding up a hand. "You scraped the necessary amount together by selling off meat poached from the earl's demesnes."

Finnula looked haughtily away. "I don't know what you mean," she sniffed.

"Ha!" Hugo snorted, in disgust. "No wonder they m'lady you.

You've done more for them than any chatelaine Stephensgate Manor's ever seen . . ."

Finnula ignored him. "Mavis gave birth to her first child not too long ago. 'Twould have been rude to have passed by without pausing to look at it."

Hugo shook his head. Was there no end to this girl's talents? She reminded Hugo of the stories his childhood nurse had told him of the legendary outlaw Robin of Loxley. Only this particular criminal was not only a perfect shot, a provider to the poor, but also apparently a matchmaker. And all encased in that delectably slender frame and topped by that amazing mass of auburn hair.

Hugo was surprised when the Fairchild home appeared before them. Instead of the rough hovel he'd expected, he saw a cheerful cottage with a thatched roof and swept yard, circled on three sides by tall pine trees. Smoke curled promisingly from the chimney, and the strong odor of baking bread sent Hugo's stomach churning in anticipation. It had been a long time since the rabbit soup, and he was ravenous.

Matthew Fairchild, freeman, appeared to be doing quite well for himself. He even had a structure other than his own home in which to keep his livestock, a rarity in farming communities. Usually a farmer and his family shared the same floor as their pigs and sheep.

Finnula dismounted, and led Hugo toward the small barn, through the muck into which the yard had turned. Once in the meager shelter provided by the enclosure, they rubbed down their mounts in companionable silence, filling the feed trough and making sure the horses had fresh water to drink. It wasn't until their mounts were comfortable that Finnula took her dripping cloak from her shoulders and shook it, sending a cascade of rainwater in Hugo's direction.

Throwing up an arm to ward off the unexpected shower, Hugo

barked, "See here!" When Finnula smirked at him, he lowered his arm and glared at her. "You did that apurpose."

"I?" Finnula's gray eyes widened in feigned innocence. "You are my prisoner, remember? I can treat you however I see fit. And you looked to me like a man in need of a dunking—"

"I'll show you a dunking," Hugo declared, and he lunged for her—only she was too quick for him. Ducking, Finnula ran laughing through the rain to the cottage's front door, where she stood hugging her arms to her chest and grinning at his lumbering attempt to follow her, his large feet at odds with the sucking mud of the yard.

Perhaps hearing all the ruckus outside her door, the matron of the house flung open the portal and let out a glad cry. "Lady Finnula!"

Mavis Fairchild was an apple-cheeked woman no older than Finnula herself, with dark hair and eyes and a blissful expression. She flung her plump arms around a startled-looking Finnula and hugged her soundly.

"Oh, 'tis a delight to see you, m'lady, and on such a gray an' barren day. Oh, but you're wet through, m'lady. Come in, you must come in, and get yourself dry—"

Spotting Hugo loping toward her doorway, Mistress Fairchild paused, her expression revealing all too clearly how unrespectable Hugo looked, with his wild hair and beard and mud-spattered cloak and boots.

"Mistress Fairchild," Finnula said, with a smirk Hugo did not miss. "This is Sir Hugh Fitzwilliam, of Caterbury. He is lately returned from being imprisoned in Acre."

Mavis Fairchild's face brightened. "Ah! A knight returned from the 'Oly Land! Well, that explains it."

Hugo stood in the rain, glaring at the two women who gazed pityingly at him from the dry doorstep. Mavis Fairchild bit her lower lip and said, "Well, if you cleaned 'im up a bit, 'e might not be so bad, m'lady."

Finnula looked dubious. "I suppose so."

"I mean, 'e's terrible large, but wi' a 'aircut, an' rid o' those awful clothes an' that beard, 'e might look presentable, anyway."

Finnula wrinkled her nose. "You are a generous woman, Mavis."

Mistress Fairchild whispered, loud enough for her words to be perfectly audible to Hugo, "Is 'e simple, that 'e just stands there in t' pourin' rain like that?"

Finnula sighed. "I'm afraid so."

Hugo took umbrage at that. Throwing back his broad shoulders, he cleared his throat. "Mistress Fairchild," he said, in his most impressive voice, "I am neither simple nor uncouth. Might I enter your abode and warm myself by your fire, as your husband suggested I may?"

Mavis Fairchild's eyes went round as eggs. "Of course, sir." She stood aside, and a giggling Finnula slipped past her into the cottage.

Hugo followed, nodding politely to his hostess as he passed her. He had to duck his head to enter the cottage, but when he straightened, he saw that the home was neat and more prosperous than he'd expected. The Fairchilds had a wooden floor, a rarity in Shropshire, and their cottage was divided into two small rooms, the common living space in which Hugo stood, and what was probably a bedroom beyond it. They even possessed a few sticks of furniture, including a solid table, upon which cooled several loaves of bread.

The fire on the hearth was a large and cheerful one, and Finnula had gone to it at once, spreading her wet cloak before it and, removing her damp gloves, warming her hands before the leaping flames. There didn't appear to be much hope for the rest of her; her leather braies were damp, and gave off the smell only wet leather created, and her white lawn shirt clung moistly to her skin.

The sight was quite appetizing, actually, and as Hugo joined her at the fire, warming his own hands, he couldn't help stealing glances at her. Traveling with a female companion was proving to be far more interesting than Hugo would have ever thought.

"Here, you must be chilled to t' bone." Mavis Fairchild pressed steaming tankards into their hands, and when Hugo brought his to his lips, he found the promised hard cider, hot and spiced with cloves. He sucked at the liquid greedily, and felt it warming his insides at once.

Finnula was a little better mannered. She thanked the housewife before tasting the mulled drink, and inquired after the health of the baby. This brought a stream of excited jabber from the plump Mistress Fairchild that Hugo could hardly follow, though when she bent over a rough wooden cradle he hadn't previously noticed off to one side of the hearth, he assumed she was waxing poetic about her progeny. A glance told him that the child in question was large and healthy, all anyone could ask for of an heir, and he lost interest immediately and stared instead at his fair captor.

In the orange glow of the fire, Finnula's hair gleamed lustrously, and as she bent to examine the baby, Hugo was awarded with an excellent view of her heart-shaped backside. The leather braies might have proven to be inappropriate rainwear, but they were very fetching indeed on a woman of Finnula's proportions, which were exactly, in Hugo's opinion, what a woman's proportions ought to be: slender in the waist, full in the hips, and if her top half wasn't quite as full as the bottom, it didn't much matter, seeing as how what she had up top was so perfectly suited to Hugo's tastes.

The abrupt entrance of the farmer and the abashed Evan interrupted Hugo's reverential leering, but it hastened the introduction of a meal. From out of nowhere, pots of creamy cheese appeared, along with a barrel of pickles, and that, accompanied with the crusty loaves of still-warm bread, proved a better luncheon than Hugo expected to receive.

Sitting upon the hearth with the ever-silent Evan and his master, young Matthew, who prattled away about crop conditions and his hopes for a fruitful summer, Hugo hardly heard a word the farmer said, because all his attention was focused upon a single object. That object was at the other end of the hearth, cooing over a fat baby and listening to the gentle gossip of the farmer's wife.

Finnula seemed to feel at home with these people, and there was no change in her easy manner to mark the fact that she was conversing with people who were quite a few rungs below her own social standing. From what Hugo could remember, the Crais family were freemen of long standing, having been released from servitude to the earls of Stephensgate by one of Hugo's forefathers, grateful, apparently, for some act of bravery Finnula's great-great-grandfather had performed.

What struck Hugo as odd was the deference Matthew and his wife paid this young girl. But he supposed the couple owed her their current undeniable happiness. As much as it discomforted her, it amused him when they m'lady'd her, and several times he caught her eye and winked. Finnula only suppressed a smile and looked away.

When Mistress Fairchild began pressing a third "cuppa" upon them, and Hugo was already beginning to feel pleasantly sleepy from the first two, Finnula stood and, politely declining the offer, insisted that they had to go. Her hair had dried to form a thickly curling aurora around her head and shoulders, undoubtedly due to the dampness in the air, and Hugo could not help admiring the slender curve of her throat where her shirt collar opened. Occasionally, the shirt parted enough to reveal a tantalizing glimpse of a breast. Hasty glances at Matthew and his apprentice assured Hugo that he was the only male present who noticed the delightful phenomenon.

Though both Matthew and his wife urged them to stay the night, insisting that the day was too rainy for travel and that Dorchester was too far for them to get to before nightfall, Finnula would not be swayed from her original plan. Even Hugo's longing looks at the hearth wouldn't change her mind, and they left amid cries that they visit again soon.

"And next time bring some of your sister Mellana's ale," teased Matthew, and Finnula cheerfully assured him that she would.

Hugo was uncommonly pleased by the fact that he was able to make it all the way across the muddy yard and into the barn, out of sight of his host and hostess, before taking hold of Finnula's arm and spinning her toward him.

"What—?" she demanded, raising her thick eyelashes and looking up at him in astonishment. But before she could utter another sound, Hugo brought his lips down over hers.

He felt her body tense, but when she tried to back away from him, two things happened simultaneously to thwart her escape. The first was that she came up against Violet's solid flank. The mare only looked back at them, placidly chewing on some loose straw, and would not move. The second was that Hugo's arms went around her, half lifting Finnula off the ground even as his tongue slid into her mouth.

Finnula let out a mew of protest that was quickly stifled by his mouth . . . but her protest seemed short-lived. Either Finnula was a woman who appreciated a good kiss, or she liked him, at least a bit. Because a second after his mouth met hers, her head fell back against his arm, and her lips opened like a blossom. He felt her relax against him, her hands, which previously had been trying to push him away, suddenly going around his neck to press him closer.

It wasn't until he felt her tongue flick tentatively against his that he lost his careful control. Suddenly, he was kissing her even more urgently, his hands traveling down her sides, past her hips, until they cupped those leather-clad buttocks and lifted her full up against him.

Her firm breasts crushed against his chest, her thighs clenched tightly around his hips, Hugo molded Finnula against him, kissing her cheeks, her eyelids, her throat. The sensuous reaction he'd evoked from her amazed and excited him, and when she held his face between both her hands and rained kisses upon him, he groaned, both from the sweetness of the gesture and the fact that he could feel the heat from between her legs burning against his own urgent need.

Holding her to him with one arm, he swept open the collar of her shirt and placed a hand over her heart, feeling the hard bud of a nipple against his palm, surrounded by the silken heaviness of her breast. Finnula let out another sound, this one a sigh of such longing that Hugo could not stifle a wordless cry of eagerness, and he looked about for a pile of hay thick enough for them to lie in . . .

. . . and turned to see the witless Evan standing in the open barn doorway, his jaw slack, his ears as red as fire as he stared at them.

Finnula let out a strangled cry and elbowed Hugo, hard, in the midriff. Grunting, he dropped her to seize his middle, and Finnula hastened to close her shirt.

"Y-ye fergot yer gl-gloves," Evan stammered, holding up Finnula's riding gloves. "M-mistress sent me to br-bring 'em to ye—"

Finnula darted forward and snatched the gloves from Evan's hands.

"Thank your mistress for me, will you, Evan?" she said, in a breathless voice. "'Twas very nice to see you again."

"Aye," Evan said, and he gave Hugo one last, curious glance before turning and walking back out into the rain.

"God's teeth," Finnula groaned as soon as he was out of sight. She buried her burning cheeks in Violet's mane. "What have you done?"

Hugo pressed tenderly on his stomach. "I believe you've caused me an internal injury," he said.

Finnula lifted her head from the horse's neck, her expression one of consternation. "He's bound to say something! Evan will tell Matthew and then Matthew will say something to one of my brothers-in-law, and they're bound to tell Robert, and then I'll never hear the end of it!"

Hugo eyed her hungrily. Her hair was in total disarray, her shirt tucked half in, half out of her braies. There were spots of bright color in her high cheekbones.

She looked, in other words, like a woman who needed to be tossed down in the hay and thoroughly loved.

And that's exactly what Hugo desperately wanted to do. Only the miracle that had occurred, making her pliant in his arms, had passed, and now she looked as if she'd sooner ram a fist in his gullet than kiss him again. Fussing with Violet's saddle, she radiated hostility, as if Evan had caught them doing something considerably more serious than simply kissing.

Hugo sighed. It was probably just as well that the boy had interrupted them. A horse stall was no proper place to perform a seduction. No, a woman as fine as Finnula Crais deserved better than a bed of hay upon which to lose her maidenhead. If Hugo had his way, he'd take her in his own bed back at Stephensgate Manor. It was a wide, canopied structure with a springy mattress of goose down spread over an intricate webbing of rope.

How he wished they were in Stephensgate already! More than anything in the world he wanted to spend this cold, wet day in bed with this woman, tasting every inch of her, exploring her, inhaling her . . .

But she'd turned virtuous on him again, and was now busy fastening her cloak and tugging on her gloves.

In a sudden fit of furious temper, Hugo lifted a booted foot and slammed it against the barn door.

Finnula looked up with a startled exclamation. Her eyes widened when she saw the loosened board Hugo had made. He was a bit surprised by it as well, and stood back, wondering what had possessed him.

"Why in the bloody hell did you do that?" she demanded, her mouth set angrily. "It isn't Farmer Fairchild's fault—"

Hugo reached into his cloak pocket and pulled out a coin.

"There," he said churlishly, hurling the gold piece into the drinking trough. "That will pay for a whole new barn. Are you satisfied?"

Glaring at him, Finnula swung herself up into her saddle. "You, sir," she said, haughtily, "grow too big for your braies."

Hugo glowered at her as she rode past him.

"That," he hissed, giving his braies a frustrated tug, "is entirely the problem."

# Chapter Eight

$\mathcal{F}$or the rest of the day, Finnula tried as best she could to ignore her traveling companion. It wasn't a simple undertaking.

It seemed as if Sir Hugh was determined to make as much of a nuisance out of himself as possible. He was forever letting his mount drift over into Violet's path, causing the horse to start and whinny. Or he'd brush his knee against Finnula's and then mouth apologies that were insincere or, worse, teasing.

She didn't know what she'd done to warrant the furious glowers she caught him giving her from beneath his hood. Was he angry that she'd elbowed him? That had been a purely instinctual reaction. Much like kissing him. In all her life, Finnula had never met a man who was able to provoke such physical reactions from her. It seemed that her desire to hit him was equal to her desire to kiss him, though kissing, she'd discovered, was infinitely more satisfying . . .

And yet, strangely not so.

Her cheeks burned at the memory of their embrace in Matthew Fairchild's barn. What would Mavis think, when Evan told her of it? For Finnula was certain that he would. Mavis was a sweet woman, but surely she'd be shocked, almost as shocked by it as Finnula herself was. Why, she'd put her tongue in a man's mouth! The fact that Sir Hugh seemed to quite like it being there hardly mattered. Sir Hugh seemed to like all sorts of things that weren't in the least proper. His hand had been on her breast, and Finnula had *wanted* it there! Surely Mavis Fairchild would never understand that. Well, Mavis might.

But Robert never, ever would.

And knowing Mavis, she'd probably assume Finnula was in love with this scruffy-looking knight, an assumption that couldn't be more wrong. How could Finnula be in love with such a foul-tempered, ill-mannered person? He was old enough to be her father, surely, and rude enough to be her brother. The man she fell in love with certainly wouldn't dream of fondling her in a stable. The man she fell in love with would court her properly, with poetry and flowers and small gifts, such as hair ribbons. Not that Finnula ever wore hair ribbons.

But that was beside the point.

No, she was not in love with Sir Hugh Fitzwilliam—though she did have to admit that she admired him physically. Not his face—Lord, no. She couldn't make out one feature from another, he was covered with so much hair.

But he had rather nice eyes, she'd decided, even though they were forever changing colors. When he'd winked at her in the Fairchilds' cottage, his eyes had been a gentle green, full of mirth and friendliness. She had liked him then, for listening to Matthew's boring farming stories with such patience, and for admiring Geoffrey Fairchild so gamely, and for generally being pleasant to everyone, including herself, for a change.

And if Finnula was being strictly honest with herself, she had to admit to a certain liking for his arms. He wore a close-fitting woolen shirt beneath his tunic, and the muscles of his arms were plainly visible beneath the sleeves. His biceps, she'd noticed that morning, when she'd woken with her face resting against one, were the size of Mellana's favorite gray-speckled hen. For a man of such advanced years to have such well-developed muscles— well, Finnula had to admire him for that.

His legs weren't spindly, either, something she'd noticed about some men. She couldn't stand a man who looked spindly or bandy-legged in a pair of braies. Sir Hugh's were solid as tree trunks, well-formed and, for being so long, surprisingly graceful. Even when he'd been battling the muck in the Fairchilds' yard, she'd noticed that he wasn't at all awkward in his own skin. She supposed that was what came from being a soldier. He couldn't afford to be clumsy, because clumsiness might have gotten him killed.

No, Sir Hugh Fitzwilliam was a fine figure of a man, one that any woman would be proud to call her husband—any woman except Finnula, that is.

Why she'd reacted the way she had to his kiss, she'd never know. It had seemed right, somehow, to kiss him back, and then, when he'd lifted her against him, well, that had seemed right, too. Lord only knew what would have happened if Evan hadn't interrupted them. Was that how Mellana had gotten pregnant? Finnula wondered. Jack Mallory had started kissing her, and no Evan had interrupted them? Finnula couldn't condemn her sister

for her foolishness anymore, since she was beginning to understand only too well how difficult it was to resist temptation.

Sliding a glance at her huffy prisoner, Finnula saw that he was
glowering at her again. He looked utterly miserable, wet to the
bone. She was certain she looked a sight, as well. Any warmth
that had returned before the Fairchilds' fire was gone again, and
she could hardly stand the damp smell of her own clothing.

It had rained nonstop all day, the sun never once showing its
face from behind the clouds. While May was supposed to be a
month of sunshine and flowers, Finnula supposed the flowers
wouldn't grow without a good drenching. Now that darkness was
falling, it had grown even colder, and it seemed hard to believe
that winter was behind them.

Summoning up a cheerful smile that her eyes did not echo,
Finnula called, through the steadily hissing rain, "Should we
stop, Sir Hugh, and look for shelter for the night? I know a shepherd's lean-to not far from here."

Hugo let out an ill-tempered guffaw. "Shepherd's lean-to," he
sputtered. "What do you take me for, a duck? I'm not stopping until
we've reached Dorchester, and there I'm taking a room at an inn."

Finnula felt herself growing irritable, but tried to calm her
temper. *He's just a man, after all*, she said to herself. *He can't
help being so contrary*.

"We can't stay at an inn," Finnula reasoned, gently. "I haven't
any coin for a room."

"I'll pay for a bloody room," Hugo declared.

Finnula glanced at him, then shrugged. "I'll stay with the
horses."

"Like hell you'll stay with the horses," Hugo exploded. "You'll
stay in the inn with me like a decent, God-fearing woman, and
not some sort of demented Diana—"

Finnula felt her cheeks growing hot, but whether it was from indignation or embarrassment, she wasn't sure. She chose to think of it as icy rage, and spoke accordingly.

"I am not sharing a room with you, Sir Hugh," she declared. "I'd sooner sleep with the horses."

Hugo shot her a surprisingly humorous look for one who'd so recently been glaring balefully in her direction. "Separate rooms, then. Be sure to bolt your door. With the sort of riffraff that lurk about inns these days, I hardly think you'll be safer by yourself than with me. And I fail to see why you'd be content to share a shepherd's lean-to with me, but not a comfortable room—"

"Not in Dorchester, where everybody knows me!" Was the man dense? "You may not think much of my reputation, but I assure you, I do have one, and 'twould be sullied beyond repair were I to share a room in an inn with a wandering knight."

Her traveling companion chuckled to himself, his good humor mysteriously restored. "Separate rooms, then, like I said. Christ's toes, but virgins can be tiresome."

Finnula kicked Violet into a trot, but the odious knight followed, not getting the message at all.

"I don't care where we stay," Hugo informed her. "So long as I can get out of these wet clothes and into a hot bath."

Finnula stared back at him through the darkening gloom. "Baths cost extra," she couldn't help reminding him.

"I think I can afford it." Sir Hugh, though a seasoned campaigner, seemed to have grown soft in his old age. "I'm sick of rain and I'm damned sick of mud. I'd forgotten how bloody muddy England can be in the spring—"

Finnula thought it best to keep quiet after that, lest she should find herself targeted to receive a stream of the expletives the tawny-headed knight was muttering beneath his breath.

Fortunately, they were only a league or two from Dorchester. Before long, the desolate road along which they traveled grew more populous, as despite the rain, villagers rushed about with their errands. There was Vespers to attend, supper to prepare, friends to gossip with. The rain didn't slacken as they passed through the gates to the prosperous village, but Finnula's heart lifted anyway. The prospect of a hot meal and a soft bed was a welcome one, and she didn't even mind the fact that a strange man would be paying for it all. She figured that after the mortification he'd put her through back at the Fairchilds', Sir Hugh owed her a good supper, at the very least.

Her hopes, however, were soon dashed. No sooner had Hugo entered the Hearth and Hare, leaving Finnula to hold the horses, than he emerged again, his expression grim.

"They haven't got two rooms left," he told her, without preamble. "Just one."

Finnula, still holding the horses' reins, began leading them back to the stables, the rain pelting her shoulders.

"Have a pleasant night's rest," she called back to him, over her shoulder. "I'll give your regards to the fleas—"

"Finnula!"

Hugo splashed across the cobblestones to reach her, laying a heavy hand upon her arm and spinning her around to face him in a manner reminiscent of earlier that day, in the Fairchilds' barn. Only this time, Finnula didn't think he was going to kiss her.

"Finnula, listen to me." His eyes, she saw, in the dim light cast by the torch over the stable door, were green again. "There's no reason why we can't share the room. I won't lay a hand upon you. You have my word."

"Ha!" Finnula, still holding on to the horses' reins, jerked her arm from his grasp. "You gave me your word once before, remember? No, I'm far safer sleeping with Violet. She may not smell very nice, but at least she's not preoccupied with what I've got on beneath my braies."

Stomping across the courtyard, Finnula flung open the stable doors, hauling the horses into adjoining stalls. She was beginning to unsaddle them when she saw that Sir Hugh had followed her into the dimly lit barn. Fearing a scene like the one that had occurred the last time they'd been in a barn together, Finnula seized a cloth and began to furiously dry Violet's back, keeping the horse as a barrier between herself and the man.

"Finnula," the knight said, leaning against the stall door. "You're being ridiculous."

"I'm not," she snapped.

"You are. Listen to you, your teeth are chattering."

"They aren't."

"They are. And was that a sniffle I just heard?"

Rebelliously, Finnula wiped her nose with her sleeve, before bending to rub her mare's forelegs. "It wasn't."

"And your rib is hurting you. I can tell by the way you bend."

"It isn't," Finnula lied, through teeth gritted against the pain of her bruised side.

"You can have the bed. I'll sleep on the floor."

Finnula snorted.

"All right, on the hearth, then. Finnula, I won't have you sleep in the stables. My sense of chivalry won't allow it."

"Then let me have the room to myself." Finnula looked up to see how he bore that suggestion, and saw the amusement that flashed across his face.

"What?" He chuckled. "I pay for a room for you, whilst I spend the night in the company of nags? No, thank you. My sense of chivalry is not *that* deep."

"Then the answer is still no." Finnula set about filling the feed trough with oats from a bucket hanging on a peg.

"What are you afraid of?" he asked, in a deep voice that actually sent a ripple down Finnula's spine. Then again, she was freezing, and her hair was dripping frigid rainwater down the back of her cloak, so that could easily explain the chill she'd felt.

"What am I afraid of? My brother, Robert, for one thing."

He didn't look as if that was the answer he'd been expecting. "What has Brother Robert to do with it?" he demanded.

"Everything." Finnula had moved to unsaddle his destrier, but with an impatient gesture, Hugo himself saw to his mount's needs. Finnula, whose teeth, despite her denial, really were chattering, retired to the stall door against which he had been leaning. "If Robert were to hear I'd spent the night with a man, he'd see to it I never left the house again. Or *try* to see to it, anyway."

Hugo used the same cloth she'd employed to rub down his own mount. "But you spent last night with a man," he reminded her, with a furrowed brow.

"Aye, but who's to tell of it? Here, in Dorchester, I'm well-known. I've sold game to this very inn—"

Hugo gave her a stern look over his destrier's flank. "The earl's game?"

Finnula could not help blushing. "Aye, from time to time. The point is, someone'll tell Robert, and he'll make my life a misery. He's marrying soon, and . . . well, it took him a bit to get the girl to come around, and if I did something *more* to upset her, or her parents . . . well, I'd just as soon not get him in a lather."

Hugo muttered something. Finnula didn't catch what it was, but when she asked him what he'd said, he leveled an enigmatic stare at her and demanded, his voice without inflection, "Is that all that frightens you? Brother Robert finding out?"

Finnula stuck out her chin bravely. "Aye," she lied. "What else would I be afraid of?"

"Me, for instance."

He said it tonelessly, but Finnula saw his glance flick up from his horse's feed, the green eyes arresting her with the intensity of their glow, and she knew that her answer mattered, perhaps more than anything else she'd said that evening. She could not meet his gaze.

Was she afraid of him? Yes, certainly, but not in the way he meant. She wasn't afraid that he would hurt her, or even frightened that he might try to seduce her. She was fairly certain that he would attempt the latter, and equally certain that, if she wanted to, she could stop him. And that was the problem:

She wasn't at all certain she'd want to stop him. And then where would she be? In the same spot of trouble as Mellana.

Looking down at her gloved fingertips, Finnula shrugged, and lied with as much bravado as she could muster, "You? You don't frighten me a bit."

Hugo said, "Good," and suddenly, he'd left his horse's stall and come round to where she leaned. Placing a hand on either side of her waist, he gripped the frame of the stall door against which she leaned, entrapping her within the confines of his arms but not touching her. Not at all.

"Because I think I know of a way we can both sleep in relative warmth and comfort tonight, without ruining your reputation, or Brother Robert finding out," he went on, his breath warm.

Finnula tried to act nonchalant, as if his close proximity did not affect her in the least, though she did have to tilt her chin at a considerable angle to look up at him.

"Oh?" Fortunately, her voice did not tremble. It was better, she decided, to curtail her syllables while he was standing so near.

"Yes. It's fairly simple, really." He smiled at her, and she noticed that his teeth were fairly even and quite white. Nice teeth, really, to be hidden beneath that tangle of a beard.

"Everyone at the Hearth and Hare knows Finnula Crais," he

said. "But no one here knows me. And no one here knows my wife."

Finnula stared up at him, her mouth suddenly dry. "*Wife?*" she echoed.

"Aye, my wife."

Not understanding the grin he was giving her, Finnula continued to stare, feeling suddenly—and ridiculously—like crying.

"B-but . . ." she stammered. "But when I asked you yesterday, at the spring, you said you hadn't any wife—"

"And I haven't," Hugo said, his grin turning into a delighted smile. "But the proprietors and patrons of the Hearth and Hare don't know that, do they?"

Finnula couldn't stop staring at him. She found herself unable to decide whether he'd finally slipped over the edge into insanity, or if she was the one the being incredibly dense. He must have seen her incomprehension, because he let go of the stall door and put his hands on her shoulders.

"Don't you see, Finnula?" he asked, still wearing that crooked grin. When she mutely shook her head, not trusting herself to speak, he let go of her and went to the low wall where she'd thrown her saddle. "Here," he said, "let me show you."

And without another word, he opened her saddlebags, withdrawing first her hair comb and pins, and then the spare kirtle she always carried with her. "The folk at the Hearth and Hare know the Fair Finn, in her leather braies and braid," Hugo said, giving the kirtle a hearty shaking, so that the worst of the creases in it snapped. "But if I'm not mistaken, they've never met my wife, the Lady . . ." He paused. "Lady what?"

Comprehension dawned, and Finnula was quick to put out both her hands. "No," was all she said.

"Why not?" Hugo looked down at the gown in his hands. "If they're used to seeing you in braies, they'll never recognize you in this. With your hair up, and a hood over your head, they'll just think you're Sir Hugh Fitzwilliam's modest lady bride—"

"I said no," Finnula reminded him. "How many times do I have to repeat it before you listen? No, no, no—"

Hugo shook a finger at her. "I thought you said you weren't afraid of me."

Finnula stuck her chin out again. "And I'm not. But—"

"I thought you said the only thing you were afraid of was Brother Robert finding out."

"I did, but—"

"Perhaps," Hugo said, looking mournfully at the cream-colored gown, "the Fair Finn is not as courageous as I've been led to believe."

"I am," Finnula insisted. "It's just that—"

"Just that what?" Those bright green eyes were upon her, mocking her. One of his tawny eyebrows had lifted skeptically, and Finnula knew, with a sinking feeling, that she'd lost.

"Oh, *all right*," she snapped peevishly, stalking forward and ripping the kirtle from his hands. "But wait outside while I change."

"I shall do better than that," Hugo declared, awarding her a gracious smile that she didn't feel she deserved. "I shall go and secure the room, and baths for the both of us. I will be back momentarily to escort you, Lady . . .er . . ." He looked at her, his eyebrow raised quizzically now, rather than dubiously, and said, "Well, I'll think of it upon my return."

"Just get out," Finnula ordered, and he complied with a laugh.

Alone in the stable with only horses and a lone cow to watch her disrobe, Finnula sighed to herself. How she got herself into these situations, she couldn't fathom. Here she was, the Fair Finn, stripping off her soaked shirt and braies so that she could slip into a kirtle she hadn't worn since—well, she didn't like to think of the last time she'd donned it—and pose as a strange man's wife, all so that she could spend the night in an inn with that same strange man . . .

It was too much. This adventure was by far the most complicated she'd ever encountered. She blamed Mellana for it, then amended that decision, and blamed Jack Mallory instead. If Jack Mallory hadn't seduced her innocent sister, getting her with child, then Finnula would not be disrobing in a stable, preparing to spend the night with a man she hardly knew.

Not that she'd really be spending the night with him. She would be spending the night in the same room with him, but certainly she wouldn't be sharing his bed. If it came to that, she'd sleep in a chair. Or on the hearth, as he'd suggested. Oh, no, if she'd learned anything in the past few days, it was that the worst possible thing in the world was to be in Mellana's position, unwed and pregnant. Almost, she thought, as she peeled off her braies, as bad as being *wed* and pregnant.

Not that Finnula had anything against the institution of marriage. But when Hugo had teased her about her husband the blacksmith, he hadn't been far wrong in his picture of domestic felicity: the wife fat with another pregnancy, the husband drunk and demanding his supper. Most marriages, Finnula thought, turned out not unlike that picture, her own sisters' perhaps notwithstanding. But her sisters were all clever, and had chosen husbands whom they could bully. Finnula did not think she could respect a man whom she could bully.

But the alternative, to marry a man who bullied *her*, was equally as unappealing.

And how could she ride and hunt with a child forever in her belly? It wouldn't be seemly. So what would she do for nine months? She couldn't sew, and despised housework. She could cook a little, but infinitely preferred catching the game to preparing it.

No, better to avoid the entire situation, she decided.

Standing in the chilly stable in only her boots and bandage, for she wore no underthings beneath her shirt and braies, she flung the soft kirtle over her head and squirmed into the close-fitting garment. The sleeves were tight and descended halfway down her palm, the waist nipped in closely to follow her womanly curves. The skirt was so long that she had to lift it to keep the hem from dragging in the stable muck, but when she had to use both hands to tackle her hair, she resorted to tying the ends of the skirt into a loose knot at her knees.

Her hair was a disaster, wet and full of tangles, and in the end, Finnula gave up, wringing it out and then piling the sodden curls on top of her head and jamming wooden pins in it, willy-nilly. She had no mirror, so she couldn't judge the effects of her new coiffure, but when Hugo returned to the stable a few moments later, the cheerful tune he'd been whistling quickly died on his lips when he saw her, so she knew she must look very bad indeed.

As she turned quickly at his entrance, her hands flew instinctually to the place where, had she owned one, a girdle of braided leather or chained metal would have sat. But since her gown was a simple one, of ivory linen without ornamentation of any kind, save his emerald, which she still wore upon its black cord, she had to satisfy herself with smoothing the wrinkled fabric over her flat belly.

It was cold in the stable, though warmer than outside, and without her cloak, Finnula felt the chill, especially on the back of her long neck, bared now to the elements. She was distinctly aware, even before Hugo's gaze dropped there, of her rebellious nipples, which had sprung fully erect from her nervousness and the damp cold. The thin linen did nothing to hide them, the bodice being tight-fitting and meant to mold itself over all her attributes, bringing them fully to the attention of any who watched her.

Only Finnula would have given a lot if her attributes had been just a little better covered, for Hugo's gaze was bold, and a hot blush sprang to her cheeks before she could dive for her cloak, seeking what meager protection the damp wool could afford her from that searching gaze.

But Hugo, recovering himself from whatever had afflicted him a moment before, was faster, whipping off his own cloak and laying it gently over her shoulders.

"Mine's a bit dryer," he said, by way of explanation of the chivalrous gesture. He had to clear his throat, as something appeared to have become momentarily lodged in it.

Finnula clutched the heavy garment gratefully with one hand, holding up the train of her gown with the other. Sir Hugh's cloak was indeed dryer than her own, and richer, as well, the fur lining thicker and more plentiful than on her own well-used cape. Hugo folded that garment across his arm, and held out his arm the way Finnula had seen courtiers at the Dorchester Fair hold out their arms to ladies.

"If you'll allow me," he said, and though Finnula looked for it, she could find no trace of mockery in his features.

Uncomfortable with this change in Sir Hugh's attitude toward her, Finnula laid her hand upon his arm, but gave him a wary look as she did so. He didn't appear to notice it. Instead, he hefted the shoulder bags, and, guiding her around the many piles of manure that lined the stable floor, he led her back out into the rain and across the courtyard to the inn.

Finnula had been in the main room at the Hearth and Hare so many times that she could hardly count them, but it wasn't until she walked into it on the arm of a knight that she'd ever seen a hush fall over the crowded dining room. All her old friends were there, including the innkeeper, Mr. Pitt, operating the taps on the kegs, as were most of the men whom she'd once drunk under the table one Saturday, on a dare. Even the village prostitutes, Mary Alice and Kate, were leaning against the bar, eyeing her with open hostility. Normally, they treated Finnula with friendly ease. What had happened to turn that companionship to animosity?

What had happened was that no one recognized her. None of them had ever seen Finnula in a gown before, and with her face hooded, she looked, as Sir Hugh had assured her she would, like the modest young bride of a wealthy knight. She had doubted him, thinking that her friends would recognize her under any circumstances, but now she saw that he'd been correct. There wasn't a reason in the world that any of them should have suspected that it was the Fair Finn beneath that cloak, and, accordingly, none of them did.

Mistress Pitt, the proprietor's wife, was the first to break the spell Finnula's presence seemed to have cast over everyone. The portly woman rushed from the back of the inn, where, from the floury appearance of her apron and hands, she'd apparently been rolling dough. Brushing loose tendrils of dark hair from her plump face, she bobbed a curtsy at Finnula.

"Oh, m'lady, come in, won't you, out of that nasty rain—" Mistress Pitt, who had always heartily disapproved of Finnula's leather chausses and who'd once threatened to burn them if she ever happened to come across an opportunity to do so, was all solicitous concern for the well-being of the wealthy knight's young wife.

"I've got a nice 'ot bath for you steamin' in me own chamber— your 'usband says as 'ow you'd be wantin' a nice soak after the dunkin' you received on the road, and I can't says as I blames you. What you need is a nice 'ot bath and a good warm supper, and then to bed. I've got the supper on the stove, and I'll be bringin' it up to your room so's you can enjoy it in front of your very own fire, after your bath——"

Finnula, the hood of Sir Hugh's cloak drawn so far over her face that she could hardly see where she was going, tilted her head so that she could deliver a baleful glare in his direction, but he only grinned and said, "Lady Fitzwilliam is most grateful for your kind attentions, Mistress Pitt. You'll have to excuse her if she seems a bit on the quiet side, but we're newlyweds, you see, and she's quite shy——"

"Poor lamb," Mistress Pitt cooed, patting Finnula's shoulder. She had once called Finnula a spawn of Satan for tracking deer blood over her newly scrubbed kitchen floor. It was interesting that now she was a poor lamb, where previously she'd been a child of the devil.

"You come with me— No, never fear, Sir Hugh, she's in good 'ands. There's 'ot water waitin' for you, too, sir, upstairs." Taking hold of Finnula's cold, slim hand, Mistress Pitt began steering her down a short corridor, back to the private section of her inn. "I'll return 'er to you presently, sir, warm and scrubbed——"

In the entire history of the Hearth and Hare, Finnula could not imagine that there'd ever been an occasion for the Pitts to prepare two separate baths on the same night, and she wondered exactly how much Sir Hugh had been forced to pay them to receive this kind of servile attention.

She was conducted by the still prattling innkeeper's wife to a pleasant bedchamber with a well-lived-in look, in the center of which a crude wooden tub had been placed. That then, Finnula realized, was her luxurious bath. But upon closer examination, she saw that the water was clean and steaming hot, and that the bath would be deep enough for her to sink into up to her neck. Perhaps it would be luxurious after all. She assumed that it was

Mistress Pitt's own bath, since there was no way such a large amount of water could have been boiled so quickly.

"There's scented oil for you, m'lady, and some soap, and clean cloths to dry yerself with, and plenty o' water—don't you worry about rinsin' your hair, Peggy's on 'er way with two more buckets. You'll be wantin' my 'elp out of your wet things, won't you?"

But when Mistress Pitt began tugging on Sir Hugh's cloak, Finnula shook her head and backed away, her heart hammering hard within her chest. Just imagine what the old woman would say when she discovered it was Finnula Crais for whom she'd sacrificed her own bath!

"Ah," Mistress Pitt said, with a twinkle in her eye. "You *are* a shy one. Your 'usband wasn't exaggeratin', then, was 'e, lamb? Well, never you mind. I was shy meself, me first few months of marriage. Didn't let me 'usband see me naked for over a fortnight. But that's just plain foolishness in your case, m'lady, since any soul can see you're pretty as the flame on a candle. Ah, 'ere's Peggy with the rest o' your water—"

A young girl Finnula didn't recognize hurried into the room, her plain face very serious as she hauled in two more steaming buckets of water. These she left by the side of the tub, and, bobbing a clumsy curtsy at Finnula, the serving wench fled, to Mistress Pitt's apparent approval.

"Well, that's all then, if you can manage yerself." Mistress Pitt indicated a bolt on the back of the bedchamber door. "No one ever slips this far back into the 'ouse, but just to be safe, slide this bolt into place after I've gone. No one'll disturb you. They're a rough lot, but good-'earted. Mostly."

Finnula uttered a few quiet words of thanks, which seemed to please Mistress Pitt very much, since the woman beamed as she left. Mistress Pitt did not beam very often, and Finnula supposed she was happy that the clientele of the Hearth and Hare was moving up a notch. At this rate, the Pitts would be entertaining royalty soon!

As soon as the proprietress had left, Finnula slid the bolt on the door into place and threw back her hood with a sigh of relief. So much fuss for a bath and a bed! If Finnula'd had her way, they'd be sleeping under a lean-to, using their saddles as pillows and the rainwater to wash in.

Still, she thought, when she slipped into the hot water of her bath, she had to admit Sir Hugh had been right. This was entirely more civilized. And if one had the money, why not? Finnula wondered precisely how much money Sir Hugh had in his possession. It seemed to be an awful lot, for a simple knight. Then again, he was heir to some kind of estate, or so his story of his brother had led her to believe. And he'd been in the Holy Land for quite a long time. Finnula's parish priest had told his congregation stories of the treasures that were to be found in Egypt and the lands surrounding it, tales of tombs filled with gold and jewels. Finnula wondered if Sir Hugh had ever stumbled across one of those tombs. She wasn't at all certain she now believed his tale about the emerald he'd given her being a gift from a sultan's daughter. She was quite sure that if she were a sultan's daughter, she could easily find someone more attractive than Sir Hugh Fitzwilliam upon whom to bestow her most treasured jewel. Although if he'd ever kissed her, Finnula could see how the princess might be swayed in his favor . . .

Though it was lovely to simply soak in the wooden tub, the water quickly cooled, despite the bright fire on the hearth a few feet away. Besides, Finnula was hungry, and looking forward to some of Mellana's ale, which she knew the Hearth and Hare stocked. Quickly employing soap and sponge, she washed, even giving her hair a thorough scrubbing, then rinsed with the water from the buckets Peggy had provided.

Toweling herself off with the linen cloths Mistress Pitt had left for her, Finnula began to feel like a human being again. She couldn't bandage herself, but she found that upon examination, her wound was healing, the bruise not so florid, the skin no longer so tender to the touch. She pulled the kirtle back on, and was wrapping one of the linen cloths around her wet head in a sort of turban when there was a timid knock at the door.

Instead of asking who it was, since Finnula was afraid the person might recognize her voice, she slid back the bolt and opened the door a fraction of an inch—keeping her hunting knife, which she clutched in her right hand, out of sight.

But it was only Peggy, who curtsied nervously and said, "Me mistress says to see if you be needin' anythin'."

Finnula shook her head, feeling the turban slip. Peggy saw it, too, and said, brightening a little, "I could comb out yer 'air, if ye be needin' it. Mistress says I'm right talented wi' a comb."

This seemed like a harmless enough concession, since Peggy didn't know her, and Finnula waved the girl into the room, then bolted the door behind her.

Peggy was as good as her word. She set to work on Finnula's hair with the focused concentration of a metalsmith, and though she wasn't gentle, she managed to tame the wet curls, smoothing all the tangles and finally patting the thick mass into a long, single braid down Finnula's back.

"There," Peggy said, her satisfaction at a job well-done evident.

And she got up from the bed upon which they'd been sitting and went to Mistress Pitt's trunk, from which she removed a small, jagged piece of glass that she presented matter-of-factly to Finnula.

"It's a looking glass," Peggy explained reverently, in the event that Finnula did not know what to do with it. "It cost a *fortune*. 'Tis the only one in the whole of the village."

Finnula had only rarely caught a glimpse of her own reflection. With her wet hair dragged back so severely from her face, she expected to look a fright, but she saw in the dark glass that a few curls had already dried and were frizzing around her forehead and ears in snaky tendrils, framing her heart-shaped face and lending it a softer look than she was accustomed to. Finnula nodded and handed the mirror back to the girl, who restored it to its place of honor in Mistress Pitt's trunk, then turned and said, "Mistress says I'm to take ye to yer room, now."

Finnula almost laughed at the girl's serious expression, but instead she thanked her, recognizing that the child was desperately hoping to please her. Gathering up Sir Hugh's cloak, Finnula pulled the hood over her head and followed the child up a back stairway, the sounds of laughter and masculine conversation drifting up from the taproom.

Peggy paused at a door at the end of a corridor and tapped shyly. A gruff voice barked at her to wait a moment, and Finnula was amused to think that they'd interrupted Sir Hugh in a moment of privacy at the chamber pot.

But when the door was flung open a second or two later, she realized it wasn't Sir Hugh they'd interrupted at all, but a much younger, much handsomer man.

Only half dressed, the clean-shaven stranger stared at her with Sir Hugh's unmistakable greenish-amber eyes, but the face of someone else entirely. His strong, squared jaw was all that a knight's should be, his chin clefted and broad. The mouth was familiar, but far too attractive to be Sir Hugh's, the lips full and sensual. They were lips that promised things, things Finnula had only just recently begun to understand. Were those the same lips, she wondered, that only a few hours ago had clung to hers so tenaciously? No, it wasn't possible—

He had a neck thickly corded with tendons, and a broad, muscular chest crisply matted with tawny hair that tapered down to a point above his flat stomach before widening again as it approached the loosely tied laces of his braies. But it was his arms Finnula's gaze kept returning to. Bared, they were golden in color, like his eyes, like his long, loose hair, but so sinewed and muscular that he looked capable of lifting the heaviest of bows, and shooting with it, too.

But this was the face and body of a man years younger than Sir Hugh! Why, this man was no older, surely, than Finnula's brother, Robert, who at barely six and twenty, was considered a prime candidate for marriage. And this man was handsome— breathtakingly handsome, a magnificent male specimen, one that would have made Isabella Laroche weak at even the thought of spending the night with him. Indeed, the sight of him sent Finnula staggering back until she hit the wall, which she gripped tightly with moistened fingers, her breath suddenly shallow.

"I'm sorry," she murmured faintly, unable to tear her gaze from the stranger's arms, which she couldn't help picturing wrapped around her own body. "We must have the wrong room."

"Nay," Peggy insisted truculently. " 'Tis the right room. Mistress told me—"

"No," Finnula said, feeling color rush into her cheeks. "No, there must be some mistake—"

The handsome young stranger looked down at the serving girl and grinned, but there was no amusement in the gesture. "See what happens?" It was Sir Hugh's voice, but coming out of a man who was no more Sir Hugh than Finnula herself was. "A fellow shaves, and his own wife doesn't recognize him. Come along, sweetheart—"

Snaking out one of those long, well-formed arms, the stranger took hold of Finnula's wrist and yanked her from the wall, propelling her across the hallway and into his embrace. Confused, Finnula flung up both her hands, and found them pressing down upon thick chest hair and warm muscle. Craning her neck, she looked up into what were unmistakably Sir Hugh's eyes.

"Hullo, love," he said, those golden eyes twinkling wickedly. "All cleaned up now, eh?"

Finnula's bemusement was quickly turning into another emotion altogether. Fear. She had been worried before that she might be unable to resist Sir Hugh if he attempted to seduce her. Now that worry turned to full-blown alarm as she inhaled the unfamiliar fragrance of clean man, felt the brand-new sensation of bare flesh beneath her fingertips, heard his quick intake of breath when the tips of her breasts accidentally skimmed his furred chest.

That was it. She was getting out, while she still could.

Panicking, Finnula tensed, preparing to back away and follow Peggy downstairs with a lame excuse about having forgotten something. Then, once in the stables, she was going to saddle Violet and head for home, rain or no rain.

But some of her panic must have radiated to Sir Hugh, because he tightened his grip on her arms and pulled her even closer to him, so that her cheek was crushed to his bare chest, her eyes just inches away from one flat, brown nipple, half hidden in all his chest hair. The sight of it caused her even more alarm, but though she struggled to be free from him, he hung on, speaking calmly to Peggy, as if there wasn't a half-wild woman in his arms.

"Thank you very much for your trouble, my dear," he said, placing a coin in the child's cupped palms. "My wife needs a good deal of looking after."

Peggy agreed, gazing piteously at the struggling bride. "Mistress says she'll get over it," Peggy assured him, and the knight thanked her again, as politely as if he'd been addressing a queen.

As soon as the girl was out of earshot, Hugo leaned down and hissed in Finnula's ear, "What the devil is the matter with you? You nearly ruined everything—"

Finnula could think of nothing but escaping the touch of his bare chest, and with another frantic motion, she was free, leaving him holding nothing but his own cloak.

But somehow, she'd ended up on the wrong side of the door! Instead of being out in the corridor, where she could have made her escape, she was inside the bedchamber! And there, she could see all too clearly, the trappings of her seduction had already been laid.

A roaring fire snapped upon the hearth, while a small table, set for two, basked in its glow. A thick bearskin covered the floor, and the bed, wide enough for three, was piled high with down-filled pillows and comforters. Expensive wax candles lent a romantic air, since they weren't needed in the strong glow from the fire, and the room was rich with the odor of roasted meat, which sizzled in a covered pot upon the table. Turning, she saw her braies and blouse hanging on a peg near the hearth, lending a coziness to the room that belied what she knew was inevitably going to occur within it.

"What's gotten into you?" Hugo demanded, closing the door and sliding the bolt home. The sound of the metal lock clanking was the one, Finnula knew, that sealed her doom.

"You looked scared as a cat out there," he grumbled, going to the bed and seizing a white lawn shirt that had been lying atop it. "What's the matter? Did Mistress Pitt recognize you?"

He pulled the garment over his head, and Finnula was given a tantalizing glimpse of the thick, golden patches of hair beneath his arms. The skin there was not so tanned as the rest of him, and looked silken, like the lining of his cloak.

Abruptly, Finnula's knees buckled, and she sat down hard upon the hearth.

His head appearing through the shirt's opening, Hugo eyed her, his long, blond hair a damp tangle about his handsome head. "Are you all right, Finnula? Your side bothering you again? I've never seen you so quiet," he commented, scrutinizing her amusedly. Walking toward the low table, he hefted a tankard and passed it to her. She took it without thought, hoping he wouldn't notice her trembling fingers.

"This should loosen that tongue of yours a little," he said, with jovial ease. "It isn't dragon's milk this time, but something they call Mel's Brew. Your sister Mellana, I take it?"

Finnula put the wooden tankard to her lips and tasted the ale. It was Mellana's, all right. Just the feel of it in her mouth set her a little more at ease. At least *something* in this room was familiar.

"I thought that came off rather well, didn't you?" Hugo smirked, seating himself upon one of the low stools that Mistress Pitt had set up around the table and helping himself to a crusty roll. "They didn't suspect a thing. I told you they wouldn't. You don't look anything like the Fair Finn. In fact, you clean up rather nicely, considering."

She stared at him owlishly. "Considering what?" She was surprised to find that her voice was quite steady.

"Well," Hugo said, clearing his throat. "Considering what we had to work with, I mean. A wrinkled kirtle, a brush and comb, and look at you. A knight's lady. You could easily pass for the wife of an earl, for all that——"

Finnula nearly dropped the tankard. Did he *know*? How *could* he know?

But no, he wasn't paying the least bit of attention to her, just picking at the pot of cheese in the center of the table, oblivious to her nervousness.

"Are you hungry?" he asked, lifting lids and peering into pots. "Because there's a lot of food here. That looks like stewed venison. One of yours, I presume. And there's glazed carrots, and roasted turnips, and plenty of bread, and that looks like parsnips, and—"

Finnula asked, keeping her voice low to hide her fear, "Why did you shave?"

He looked up at that, and Finnula wished she'd kept her mouth shut. She wasn't at all comfortable with his bright gaze upon her, and the comic twist to those sensuous lips didn't soothe her much, either.

"Why did I shave? Because I was tired of looking like a demented hermit. Why? Don't you like me like this?"

Finnula took a long gulp of ale. "You're assuming," she said, with some of her old asperity, after she'd swallowed, "that I liked you before."

"True," Hugo agreed, with a chuckle. He speared a turnip with his knife and bit into it. "But I did rather get the feeling that you liked me, back there, at Farmer Fairchild's barn."

Finnula blushed hotly, and was glad that the heat from the fire disguised her high color. "I thought you were much older," was all she said in reply.

"Did you? I suppose I looked it. But you sound disappointed."

She shrugged, and reached over to pick at the glazed carrots.

"You *are* disappointed." Hugo set down his tankard with a thump and stared incredulously across the table at her. "God help me, you liked me better before, beard and all!"

Finnula, careful not to look at him, shook her head. "No, you look quite nice without a beard," she said politely.

What she did not add was that without the beard, he looked like someone whom she'd have given a wide berth, back when she'd been hunting for a hostage. One did not want to hold for ransom someone who looked as dangerously handsome as he did. No, such a kidnapping might lead to all sorts of complications. In fact, it already had. Look at the situation she was in now! She was having dinner with—sharing a room in an inn with!—a man who was so good-looking that she wanted to leap across the table and devour him. This had been a slight concern before, but now . . . *now* she had to hang on tight to her beer tankard to keep herself from doing so.

"I'll be damned," Hugo said, and she did not think she was mistaking the mournful expression on his face. "You liked me better with a beard." Then, brightening, he shrugged. "I'll grow it back."

Finnula raised her eyebrows. "I hardly think we'll be seeing that much of one another," she said mildly, "once you're ransomed."

He stared at her. "I see," he said, in an offended way.

"I mean, I hardly ever travel as far north as Caterbury," she hastened to explain, pausing as she ladled herself a serving of Mistress Pitt's stew that she knew she'd never finish. "And I don't expect you'll have a lot of time for traveling to Stephensgate, what with managing your father's estate."

"No," Hugo said, his gaze downcast. "I suppose you're right."

Finnula could not understand what ailed the man. Did he really think they could be *friends* after this? Why, she had a good many male friends, but none of them looked like *him*. She couldn't possibly be friends with a man that good-looking. She wouldn't be able to concentrate on anything except how very much she wanted to kiss him. He was either completely oblivious to the effect his looks were having on her, or dense as a board.

"I suppose," Hugo said, taking quite a large gulp of ale, "that you'll be marrying your smithy, then."

It was Finnula's turn to stare. "What smithy?"

"The village blacksmith. The one you're going to have the thirteen children with—"

"Oh," Finnula said. "The drunk one, who'll demand his supper and beat me if I fail to produce it promptly? No, I don't think I'll be marrying a smithy. I tried it once already, you know."

She had the satisfaction of seeing him drop his knife. At least she'd managed to shock him as much as he'd shocked her.

"You tried what?" he demanded, bending to retrieve his knife.

"Marriage." Finnula sipped a little more ale. She'd never much liked discussing it in the past, but then she'd never before had such a handsome conversation partner to keep at bay.

Hugo stared at her, his amber eyes turning, for the first time that she could remember, a dark brown. "You were married before?" he asked slowly.

She nodded, her heart in her throat. Lord, she hated this subject. But she supposed she owed him the truth. "Briefly."

"I don't believe it," he scoffed dismissively. "This is a fabrication, an invention on your part purely to annoy me."

"I wish it had been a fabrication," Finnula said. She leaned one elbow on the tabletop and rested her chin in her hand. "Unfortunately, it was very real."

"I don't understand this," Hugo declared irritably, leaning forward until his face was just inches from hers. "How old are you?"

She lifted her eyebrows. "Nearly eighteen. What has that to do with anything?"

He looked worried. "How long were you married?"

"A day."

He let out a bark of laughter and leaned back, strangely relieved. "I thought as much. What happened? Brother Robert forced an annulment when he heard of it?"

She scowled. "No, nothing like that."

"Then where's your husband? Surely no man, once he had managed to win the Fair Finn, would willingly let her go."

Finnula frowned. "Well, this one did. He died."

"Died?" Hugo sat up straighter, his eyes amber again, and fastened upon her as inexorably as brambles. "What do you mean, he died?"

"He just died, that's all. As you can guess, it was hardly an enjoyable experience for me. So I won't be trying it again."

"Try what again? Marriage?" Hugo's voice, as well as his expression, was incredulous. "Not ever?"

"No, never." That said, she took a big bite of her stew, found it delicious, and washed it down with another swallow of Mel's Brew. Suddenly, she seemed to have recovered her appetite, and she ate hungrily, aware that the knight was eyeing her, but trying to ignore him. It wasn't easy.

"Strange," Hugo mused, after a considerable silence. "I never would have taken those leather braies for widow's weeds."

"Why should I mourn him?" she questioned indignantly, sampling a bit of cheese. "I didn't love him."

Hugo let out something that sounded like a hoot. "Apparently not! Who was this unfortunate fellow, who died on his wedding day to a woman who didn't love him?"

"He wasn't a blacksmith," she admitted.

"I assumed that. Was it an arranged marriage, then?"

"If you mean did I have any say in the matter, no, I hadn't, obviously. Why would I marry someone I didn't love?"

He looked up at the ceiling. "People marry for reasons other than love, Finnula."

"Oh, of course. People like you." When she noticed his wounded expression, she hastened to explain herself. "I mean landowners. You marry for wealth or property. But people like me and my sisters and brother, we marry for love."

"And you don't think you'll ever fall in love, Finnula?" The soft question was accompanied by a smile of such gentle compassion that for a moment, Finnula was rendered breathless. How could this man, who had irritated and plagued her for two days straight, suddenly make her sigh with a glance, make her blush with a single word? Her gaze flickered to his hands, wrapped around his beer tankard, and she remembered the way those strong, callused fingers had felt on her skin.

Was it possible that she was in love with *him*? When he wasn't maddening her with desire, he was infuriating her with his words. She feared his touch because she longed for it, and she knew that she wouldn't be able to resist him again if he kissed her. He was the most exasperating man she'd ever met, an incurable tease, but he made her laugh, just the same. Was that love?

She turned the question upon the one who'd asked it.

"What about you?" she inquired. "Will you ever marry?"

"Most assuredly," he said. "It's my duty to continue the Fitz, er, william line."

"And will you marry for love?" Finnula teased. "Or money?"

"That remains to be seen." His glance was bright. "I rather think that I have enough money, don't you?"

"You do seem to throw it about quite a bit," Finnula agreed.

"Yes, it's a bad habit I have. When I see something that I want, I'm afraid I'll spend any amount I have to in order to get it." He held up the pitcher containing the beer. "More of Mel's Brew?"

Finnula nodded, holding out her tankard. Now that she had eaten something, she felt a little more relaxed. She was slowly becoming accustomed to Sir Hugh's new appearance, and it did not seem nearly so threatening anymore. Talking to him had helped. He was still the same irritating man he'd always been, just with a better-looking face.

Hugo poured her the last of the ale, and she blew on the foamy head as she watched him pick at the remnants of the food on his plate. He'd eaten even less than she had, and he was twice her size. She wondered what ailed him.

"What did you think of it?" she asked, indicating the beer.

Hugo smiled, though the smile didn't reach his eyes. "A fine brew, overall. Not too rich. I'm honored to be kidnapped in an effort to make more of it."

Finnula giggled. She stopped herself, realizing she shouldn't have had so much to drink on an empty stomach.

"How is your side?" Hugo inquired.

Finnula smiled at him sleepily. "Fine," she said.

"Do you want me to bandage it again before we go to bed?"

*Before we go to bed.* How domestic that sounded! As if they were an old married couple who climbed into bed together every night. "No, thank you," Finnula said, and she could not think of the intimate way his fingers had probed her flesh without blushing. She had blushed so many times this evening, he must think her face was always ruddy in hue.

"Finnula," he said, but when she glanced up at his face, it was unreadable. He looked quickly away. "Never mind."

He stood up, the legs of the stool scraping against the floor. "Mistress Pitt said to leave the dishes in the corridor."

"Oh," Finnula said, setting down her tankard. "Let me."

"No, I'll do it," Sir Hugh said, a little snappishly, she thought.

The blond knight collected the dishes and then carried them, rattling, to the door, where he bent to stack them in the corridor. He made several trips, but never said another word to her. Finnula wondered what she'd done to offend him. Perhaps she oughtn't have told him of her ill-fated marriage. It was a topic she was generally loath to discuss. The fact that she'd brought it up with him surprised her. He seemed to have a talent for drawing her out on subjects she generally preferred to let alone. Perhaps that was one of the reasons that she liked him: She had the feeling she could say anything to him, however shocking, and he would not think ill of her.

But obviously, she'd done something to annoy him, because he was studiously avoiding her gaze. Well, if he wanted to sulk, she wasn't going to stop him. Shrugging, Finnula left the hearth and went to the bed, pushing experimentally on the feather tick. She could not sleep on too soft a bed. This one seemed firm, but not uncomfortably so. Finnula felt they'd been lucky that on so horrid a night, there'd been such a nice room left, even if they did have to share it.

There was a single window in the room, much like her dormer window back at the millhouse, only smaller. This one was paned in wavy, expensive glass, against which the rain and wind outside beat. In the only pane that was not cracked, Finnula could see her reflection, a slim girl in a white dress with a large green stone hanging from her neck. Her red hair hung in a single braid across her left shoulder. She looked, even to her own eye, small and woefully defenseless. This, though, was only a distortion of the glass, because Finnula knew herself to be far from defenseless.

When the door closed and the bolt slid back into place, Finnula didn't move, watching Sir Hugh's reflection. She wasn't entirely surprised when she saw him come up behind her. Her heart thumping, she spun around to face him. She knew what was about to happen.

She also knew she had no intention of stopping it. God help her—she now understood exactly why Mellana had acted such a fool with that idiot troubadour.

And yet there didn't seem to be a bloody thing she could do to stop herself from doing the exact same thing over this exasperating, heart-stoppingly handsome . . . and yet frustratingly kind knight, who *would* see that he did the right thing by her, even if it meant driving her to distraction.

"Finnula," he said again, and this time she recognized the need in his voice. It matched the need she felt in her own heart, in the thrum of her own pulsing veins. "I know I gave you my word I wouldn't touch you, but—"

Finnula wasn't at all certain how what happened next transpired. It seemed as if one minute she was standing looking up at him, wondering if he'd ever stop talking and just *do it*, for heaven's sake . . .

. . . and the next, she was in his arms. She didn't know if he'd moved or she had.

But suddenly, her arms were around his neck, drawing his head down toward hers, her fingers tangled in his soft hair, her lips already parted to receive his.

Those strong golden arms, the ones she'd longed to have round her, imprisoned her, clasping her so close to his broad chest that she could hardly breathe. Not that she could catch her breath anyway, since he was kissing her so deeply, so urgently, as if she might at any moment be torn away from him. He seemed to fear that they'd be interrupted again. Only Finnula realized, with a satisfaction that surely would have shocked her brother, had he known of it, that they had all night long. Accordingly, she lengthened the kiss, conducting a leisurely exploration of those arms she'd so admired. Why, they really were every bit as perfect as she'd imagined.

Abruptly, Hugo lifted his head, and looked down at her with eyes that had gone an even deeper green than the emerald around Finnula's neck. She was panting from lack of breath, her chest rising and falling quickly, color bright over her high cheekbones. She saw the question in his glance, and understood it all too well. He didn't know that she had already made her decision, that it had been irrevocably made for her the second she'd seen him without that beard, and her heart—or something very like her heart, anyway—had been lost for good.

Well, maybe her decision had been made the second that bolt had slid into place. What did it matter? They were strangers in a strange—well, strange enough—place. No one would ever know of it. This was no time for his oddly misplaced sense of chivalry.

"Not *now*," she growled, knowing full well why he'd stopped kissing her, and what his questioning look implied. "God's teeth, man, it's too late—"

Whatever Hugo had been planning to say, her impatient cry silenced him upon the subject forever. Tilting her body back in his arms, Hugo rained kisses upon her cheeks and the soft skin beneath her ears, his mouth tracing a fiery path down the column of her throat to the neckline of her gown. Finnula, still anxious for the taste of his lips on hers, drew his head toward hers again, then gasped as his fingers closed over one of her firm breasts.

The sensation of his mouth devouring hers, his hands on her straining breasts, was threatening to overwhelm Finnula. It was everything she'd suspected it would be . . . only so much more. The room seemed to sway around her, as if she'd drunk too much of Mellana's ale, and Hugo remained the only stationary, solid mass within her line of vision. She clung to him, wanting something . . . and she was only just beginning to understand what that something was.

Then, when his knee slipped between her weakening legs, and she felt his hard thigh against the place where her legs joined together, the resulting shock that shot through her was like nothing she'd ever experienced before.

Suddenly, she understood. *Everything.*

And the next thing she knew, both his hands had slipped beneath her, and he was lifting her in the air. Finnula squealed instinctively as her head neared the timber beams overhead, then gasped as Hugo's mouth pressed hotly over one of her nipples, caressing it through the linen of her kirtle with his tongue. Laughing, she looked down at him, admiring his clean-shaven face from this new angle, then felt guilty for giggling. Surely, what they were about to do was no laughing matter . . .

And then, suddenly, he tossed her onto the bed, where she bounced for a few seconds, before he joined her there, bereft of his shirt and braies.

Finnula stopped giggling at once. She'd seen naked men before—she and her sisters had done their fair share of spying at the village pond—but never one as incredibly well-made as Hugh Fitzwilliam of Caterbury. Bronzed all over from the Egyptian sun, his skin was stretched taut over rippling muscles, marred only by a few long-healed, but vicious-looking scars. The golden hair that furred his chest and arms was echoed on his legs, and a thick patch of it nested between his legs, where—

Finnula quickly lifted her gaze, her lips parting. But Hugo wasn't about to give her a chance to reconsider. Lifting her skirt up to her knees, he pulled off her boots with quick, precise tugs. Finnula wouldn't be distracted, however. Rising up on her elbows, she said, "Perhaps—"

But Hugo had already taken up one of her bare feet in his hands, and began kissing its delicate arch. Finnula gasped and tried to pull her foot away, shocked by the intensity of the sensation—and her body's instant reaction to it.

But Hugo stopped kissing the sole of her foot only to burn a trail of kisses up her legs, his tongue branding her calves, the backs of her knees, the insides of her thighs—

That was when Finnula fell back against the pillows, certain he would stop. Surely this had gone far enough. But instead of stopping, Hugo took hold of one of her wrists, pulling her into a sitting position, and in a single, practiced motion, whipped her kirtle over her head, leaving her naked to his glance—all but the emerald pendant—as well as to his touch.

Finnula instantly tried to cover herself with her hands for modesty's sake, forgetting that he had already seen her undressed, back at the spring, and that all this had been her idea in the first place. But Hugo kept hold of her wrist, and a second later, his heavy, masculine weight was pressing her down against the bed, making escape impossible. Again, his hard leg pressed against the slick crevice between her thighs, and again, she felt a jolt of desire throughout her entire body. She arched instinctively against him in response, and it seemed as if just seconds later, instead of his thigh, it was the velvet head of his penis that pressed against her.

Finnula had thought initially, based upon her first view of it, that incorporating Hugo's length was going to be a daunting prospect. But now she found that she didn't care . . . her desire outweighed all anxiety and inhibitions.

As for Hugo, he seemed unaware of her initial hesitation. His mouth hot on hers, he slid smoothly inside her. Finnula gasped, recognizing that perhaps this wasn't going to be quite as easy as she thought . . . until, hearing her quick inhalation of breath, he withdrew a little, and looked down at her uncertainly, and she realized that she had, in fact, been wrong. She *could* contain all of him without being broken in half . . . and also that the pain of losing one's maidenhead—which, apparently, had been lost long ago, no doubt on the back of Violet—had been grossly exaggerated by her sisters. Now she felt only completely filled by him, and her need for release was of primary concern.

But Hugo had no way of knowing that. "Finnula?" he asked uncertainly, aching to continue, but not at all certain what her feelings on the matter were—though he rather hoped she was game. "Are you—"

Rather than reply verbally, she arched against him, silencing him with her lips and signaling her need. And Hugo, with a cry that might have been one of exultation (though it was difficult to tell, since it was muffled against her mouth), plunged deep within her.

She climaxed almost at once, crying out against his mouth as wave after wave of release crashed over her. His own release came just seconds after hers. His heart pounding, his breathing hard, his first words were of concern for her, as he asked raggedly, "Did I hurt you, Finnula?"

"Hurt me?" she echoed dazedly. "I should say not."

His head sagged in relief, until it lay upon her slender shoulder. Finnula didn't know how long they lay like that, but the fire had died to a ruddy glow and all the candles had burned themselves out before Hugo finally lifted his head and kissed her again, this time gently.

"You changed your mind at the last minute, didn't you?" was his unexpected observation.

Finnula reached up to stroke some of his overlong blond hair from his eyes. "Only for a second." She paused, embarrassed. "'Twas a fairly daunting prospect," she went on vaguely. "I didn't believe it could be done, or that if it could, I'd survive the accomplishing of it. But I did"—she shrugged—"and I enjoyed it."

"You are a strange woman, Finnula Crais," Hugo said, one finger lazily tracing circles around her shoulder, sending shivers up and down her arms. "So stubborn in so many ways, with your leather braies and your poaching and your temper. Yet beneath it, so kind and giving—"

Finnula sighed. He was very heavy, and now that their desire had been sated, and she was no longer buoyed by passion, her weight could no longer support his. She pressed a thumb to his bare hip.

"Move," she said, and he obligingly rolled from her, but, wrapping a brawny arm around her waist, brought her with him, until her body lay in the curve of his, her back to his chest, his arm beneath her cheek. He let out a satisfied grunt that she didn't understand until she saw the faintest of pink stains upon the mattress.

"Oh, no!" she cried with dismay, rising up one elbow. "Mistress Pitt won't like that at all."

Hugo pulled her down again, and studied the stain over her shoulder with some surprise. That had not, apparently, been the source of his good humor.

"Explain to me again," he queried, one tawny eyebrow lifted, "how it is that a widow should be a virgin?"

"I told you," she said sleepily. "I was only married for one day. My husband died before—well, before."

"Unfortunate man," Hugo murmured, pressing his lips to the spot beneath her ear that made her toes curl pleasantly. "Fear not for Mistress Pitt and her bedclothes. I will leave her coin as recompense."

Finnula smiled again, her eyes drifting closed. Her last conscious thought, before sleep overcame her, was that it was strange how well their bodies fit together, her and Sir Hugh's. It was almost as if they'd been made for each other.

# Chapter Nine

$\mathcal{H}$ugo was amused the next morning when Finnula, waking slowly next to him, stiffened and tried to roll away from him, as if nothing had changed between them. Catching hold of her arm, he pulled her back into bed, and found her giggling and compliant once he'd reminded her of the pleasure his body was capable of giving hers.

Never, Hugo knew, had he met a woman more passionate in bed, both giving and demanding in equal portions, than Finnula Crais. She was as bold as the bawdiest prostitute, yet gentle as the untried virgin she'd been before Hugo had robbed her of her innocence. She did not seem to regret the hours they'd passed together, however. Indeed, when she looked up at him now with those mist-gray eyes, they seemed filled with self-satisfaction, as if she'd learned the joke of a lifetime.

Seeing her translucently pale skin in the bright morning sunshine that slanted through their room's single window, Hugo could think of nothing but making love to her again. It was exactly the way he'd felt upon waking yesterday morn, the only difference being that today, he could act upon his desire. He did so, promptly, vowing to himself that it was a pleasure he was going to experience every morning, for as long as possible.

Sliding a hand between her slim thighs, Hugo lowered his head to capture Finnula's lips with his. She stiffened against the pressure of his fingers, as he'd known she would, then melted against them a minute later, when his other hand moved to caress her small breasts. Guiding her with his hands, Hugo urged her to straddle him, and when her slick tightness encompassed him, sheathing him in her warmth, it was his turn to writhe.

The braid in which Peggy had tied her hair the night before had come undone during their loving, and now all those glorious auburn curls cascaded around her face and shoulders, forming a sweet-smelling curtain around them as they moved together. Hugo watched Finnula's beautiful face as she experienced yet another climax, holding on to her slim hips and plunging himself deeper and deeper into her, until at last he followed her into mindless pleasure.

This time it was she who collapsed against him, and he wrapped his arms around her, marveling at her fine-boned beauty and wondering at how such a petite maid was capable of arousing this raging lust within him. He felt that he would never be sated of his need for her, and this thought was a sobering one.

After all, he was not Hugh Fitzwilliam, simple knight of Caterbury. He was Hugo, Earl of Stephensgate, and this girl was the daughter of his miller. Finnula Crais, though she wasn't aware of it, was his vassal, and he had a feudal duty to protect and nurture his vassals. Granted, his father had abused those very people he'd been sworn to protect, but Hugo was not his father, and would right all of Lord Geoffrey's wrongs as soon as he reached Stephensgate.

That didn't change the fact, however, that he had deflowered this girl, an act which rendered her unmarriageable to any other man.

Not that Hugo would ever now allow such a marriage to occur.

No, Finnula Crais and her fate was his responsibility, and his only concern was how he was going to get her to give up the leather braies. They looked very charming on her, but he certainly wasn't going to allow his wife to traipse about, dressed like a boy, for any man to leer at. No, she was going to have to start wearing gowns, like the one she'd worn the night before, the one that had clung to her curves so tantalizingly.

On top of him, Finnula stretched, catlike, and said, "If we're going to get to Stephensgate by nightfall, we should leave here soon."

Hugo grinned at her, and gave her bare bottom a smack. "Still your prisoner, am I?"

"Don't get the idea that anything's changed." She slid down from him, resting her head upon his bare chest, and stared down at the source of their pleasure, now lying limp against Hugo's thigh.

"I think I understand Mellana a little better now," Finnula said, thoughtfully.

Hugo looked down at her long eyelashes and small, expressive mouth. "You mean how she came to be pregnant?"

"Aye. I couldn't understand how she could do such a thing before, but now I see how it might happen. If Jack Mallory pleasured her half as much as you pleasure me, that is."

For a moment, Hugo was tempted to tell her the truth about his identity. After all, Finnula could be as pregnant as her sister now, and Hugo wanted to assure her that if that was the case, she needn't concern herself over the fate of the child. But somehow, he thought the revelation that he was the Earl of Stephensgate might spoil what would otherwise be one of the finest mornings in his memory.

And so he remained silent, watching with pleasure as Finnula rose and began to pad about the room, as unconcerned by her nakedness as she'd been at the spring.

They washed and dressed, Finnula donning her wifely disguise once more, hampered this time by Hugo's frequent caresses. The sight of her in a gown rendered him positively mad again with lust, and what should have taken them a few minutes took them more than an hour. By the time they left Dorchester, Finnula riding sidesaddle out of deference to her kirtle, the sun was high in the southeast, all of the previous day's clouds blown away, the sky a vast canopy of blue overhead.

Finnula chattered amiably about their luck that no one had recognized her or her mount, since apparently Violet was as well-known in the community as she herself was, and Hugo only half listened, admiring instead the way the sunlight brought out the gold highlights in her curls. Hugo found himself envying the emerald between her breasts, winking in the sunbeams, nestled so comfortably where he only an hour before had lain his head.

Such thoughts, he told himself, were maudlin and nauseating, and he couldn't understand why he was mooning over this girl, when he'd already bedded her. He was usually cured of any admiration for a woman the minute he was through making love to her, but his regard for this girl seemed to increase with every passing hour. Making love to her had only added fuel to his feelings for her. He was in a sorry state indeed, and he knew, with a sinking heart, that there was only one cure for it.

They had ridden for some time before Finnula complained of a cramp in her leg, and insisted upon stopping so that she could change back into her braies. Hugo rolled his eyes, wishing he'd burned the leather garment back at the inn while she'd slept, but the sight of Finnula's bare bottom in the sunlight caused him to forget his disapproval of her, and he dismounted and joined her in the little copse in which she'd hidden to change clothes.

Making love out of doors had never been very satisfying for Hugo, since in the past his partners had invariably complained of dirty hems and the hardness of the ground, but Finnula didn't seem concerned about either, once he'd managed to arouse her to a point where it didn't matter what lay beneath them. She was reluctant at first—until he touched her between the thighs, and then she seemed to melt against him, becoming as pliant as a kitten. It was an interesting trait, and one that Hugo intended to remember for future occasions. It would be a handy tool to use, he thought, to cool her ire when he revealed his true identity.

After that brief bout of lovemaking in the woods, Finnula, suddenly affectionate, agreed to his suggestion that she ride in the saddle before him, and they were seated thus together upon entering Stephensgate at last, a few hours later.

Finnula had taken to pointing out landmarks to him, proudly showing off her village and the demesnes surrounding it, and Hugo, who hadn't seen his home in over ten years, enjoyed the tour. The village seemed smaller than when he'd left it, instead of bigger, which he knew to be the case. As at the spring, the trees seemed larger, but the cottages smaller and the people older— much older. He'd been shocked to learn from Finnula's not-very-respectful description of the parish priest the fact that Fat Maude, from whom Hugo had learned all that he knew of the art of plea-suring a woman, was still conducting business from her cottage on the far side of the village.

But he was in for an even bigger shock when they rounded a bend and approached the millhouse, situated on the gently flowing river and looking very much as it had ten years previously, when Hugo had passed it without a thought to its inhabitants, one of whom he now had perched rather intimately in the saddle before him. Gathered in the yard before the neat, two-story house was a multitude of men and their mounts, including, he learned when Finnula stiffened before him and whispered it, the shire reeve.

"Oh, no," Finnula groaned, burying her face in her hands. "And all my brothers-in-law. What can they think I've done *now?*"

Hugo kept a firm grip on her narrow waist, guiding Skinner steadily toward the house and the group of men clustered outside it. A rowdy band they looked, too, each one larger than the next, and all of them pointing and glowering at them.

"Whatever it is, I know you're innocent," he said, trying to keep his voice from revealing the amusement he really felt. "You've been with me the past three days. Unless it's something you did before you left—"

But Hugo's assurance was broken off by a thunderous shout. One man tore free from the group and came hurrying toward them. Hugo recognized him by his bright red hair and furious expression. Brother Robert. There was no doubt about it.

"Finnula!"

The man was surprisingly tall, nearly as tall, Hugo judged calmly, as himself. He was strong, too, his shoulders thick from years of hauling wheat and flour sacks. As Hugo pulled Skinner to a halt in front of the millhouse's watering trough, Brother Robert and about a half-dozen other men approached at no mean pace, their faces masks of anger.

Hugo felt Finnula panicking against him, and as if she were a nervous pony, he shushed her.

"You don't understand," she fretted. "He's like to kill me!"

"He won't lay a hand on you," Hugo assured her.

Brother Robert halted about a foot from the trough, and, glaring up at Hugo with narrowed gray eyes that were an echo of his sister's, he growled, "Is this the bastard, Fairchild?"

From out of the crowd of brothers-in-law stepped Matthew Fairchild, nervously holding a weather-beaten hat in his hands.

"Aye, Robert," he stammered. " 'Tis the one I told you of."

"Unhand my sister, sirrah," Robert snarled, "and dismount. I've a score to settle with you—"

"Robert!" Finnula cried, all her fear forgotten as she rushed to Hugo's defense. "How dare you speak that way to Sir Hugh! Apologize at once!"

"I'll apologize and be damned," Robert declared, his massive hands curled into fists at his sides. "His name isn't Hugh, and there's no sir about it. Will you unhand my sister, man, or must I drag her down myself?"

Hugo wasn't amused anymore. The presence of Matthew Fairchild could mean only one thing: that the serf Evan had told what he'd seen in the Fairchilds' barn . . . only Hugo's stolen kiss had been interpreted by Finnula's protectors as something considerably more serious. He realized that Robert had every right to be furious with him, however misconstrued the provocation.

"What do you mean, his name isn't Hugh?" Finnula's voice was rich with scorn. "You don't know what you're talking about. His name is Hugh Fitzwilliam, and he's a knight just back from the Crusades. He lives in Caterbury—"

"He isn't, Finnula," rumbled a man almost as large as Brother Robert, only portly, besides. From the richness of his garments, this man Hugo judged to be Sheriff de Brissac, the one Finnula feared. He seemed to have a certain regard for the girl, however, as he looked up at her, his mouth set grimly within a thick—though neatly trimmed—black beard. "Why don't you come down from there, Finn, and let your sisters take you inside?"

Hugo saw Finnula lift her head. Crowded in the doorway to the millhouse were five women, each crowned with a head of flame-red hair, except for one, who wore braids of pale gold. This one he judged to be Mellana, for she was weeping energetically and crying, " 'Tis all my fault! Oh, Finn, will you ever forgive me?"

"No one's taking me anywhere," Finnula announced stubbornly, digging her hands into Skinner's mane, "until someone tells me what this is all about."

Hugo bent to speak into her ear. "Finnula, you'd best do as the sheriff says. This is a matter for men to settle. Go inside with your sisters."

"There is no matter to settle," Finnula declared hotly. Her gray gaze swept the group of men until it landed upon the one she sought. "Matthew Fairchild, what tales have you been spreading about me?"

"None but the truth, m'lady," the nervous farmer insisted. "My boy Evan saw it all—"

"Your boy Evan saw nothing," she said scornfully—and rather boldly, considering she was telling an outright lie.

"Nothing! He said he saw that man kissing you," Robert declared, jabbing a furious finger at Hugo, "and that afterward you hit him, trying to escape his embrace. But when Evan brought Matthew out a few seconds later, you had gone already, taken against your will by that bastard—"

"That is the most ridiculous pack of lies I ever heard," Finnula scoffed. " 'Tis true we kissed, but 'twasn't against my will, and as for being taken—"

"Finnula," the sheriff said calmly. "I've been to Caterbury this morning. There never was any Sir Hugh Fitzwilliam hailing from there. There isn't any Fitzwilliam family for miles around."

Hugo felt, rather than heard, Finnula's gasp. She'd gone still as a statue in the saddle before him. This, he knew, was bad. Very, very bad.

For him.

"Now be a good girl," the sheriff went on, "and get down from there, so I can speak to this man in private."

Hugo prodded Finnula gently. "Do as he says, love. I'll explain it all to you later, but for now, go to your sisters."

Finnula's face was a mask of such misery that Hugo longed to snatch her to his chest and comfort her.

But he wasn't at all certain that at that particular moment, such a gesture would be welcome. Finnula's hand had drifted to her knife hilt at her hip. Torn between loyalties, she hesitated, glancing first at her brother, then at Hugo.

"Go on," he urged. "All will be set right, I promise you."

With a roll of her eyes, Finnula swung her leg around Skinner's neck and jumped lightly to the ground. She hadn't even straightened before Robert Crais was upon her, his fury driving him to seize her roughly by the shoulders.

"What madness is this?" he demanded, shaking the slight girl in his hold. "What could you have been thinking, you stupid, stupid maid?"

They were very nearly the last words Robert Crais ever uttered. The next thing the miller knew, Finnula had been pulled from his grasp, and there was a two-foot blade pressed to his throat. Hugo had drawn his sword and dismounted before anyone else could move, his reactions second nature, honed from a decade of warfare. Thrusting Finnula behind him, he stood between brother and sister, the sword loose in his grasp, but the grin upon his face dangerous.

"You may heap all the blame you like upon me, Brother Robert," Hugo said, his voice chilling in its deadly calm. "But touch not the girl. She's innocent of any wrongdoing, and the only man who lays a hand upon her is me."

"The hell you say," exploded Robert, with admirable spirit for a man at whom a blade was pointing. "She's *my* sister!"

"She's going to be *my* wife," Hugo informed him.

Behind him, he heard Finnula inhale a sharp protest at this, but the only person he had eyes for at that moment was the miller. He saw the younger man's gray eyes go flat with rage, and almost felt sorry for him. It was a terrible thing, he supposed, to lose a sister to a complete stranger. But Hugo could not see that the man had done much to deserve better treatment. After all, he'd been the one who'd allowed Finnula to wear those blasted braies, courting all sorts of disaster. It was lucky for Brother Robert that more serious danger had never befallen her.

"Well, well, well," chuckled Sheriff de Brissac, bringing his large hands together in resounding smacks. "That is quite a different matter altogether. Rape, after all, is a crime. But marriage is cause for celebration. Put away your sword, young man. Robert won't lay a finger on the girl . . . Will you, Robert?"

Robert looked as if the only person he wanted to lay a hand upon was Hugo. "I won't touch her," he said. "But he'll marry her over my dead body."

"That can be arranged, you know, Crais." Hugo said, sheathing his sword.

"I—" began Finnula, but Sheriff de Brissac intervened, coming between the two men and laying a hand upon each of their shoulders. "Harsh words, harsh words indeed between two men who might one day be brothers. There is a simple enough way to handle this situation, I believe."

Looking down at Finnula, the sheriff smiled. "Now, Finnula, why don't you tell us what happened. Did this man rape you, dear?"

Finnula shook her head. "No, but—"

"Did he harm you in any way?"

"No, but I—"

"Well, then." Sheriff de Brissac released the miller's shoulder, but retained his grip on Hugo's. Hugo didn't mind, because he was beginning to like the corpulent lawman, who wouldn't allow Finnula to let loose the outburst that Hugo could readily see was brewing. He thought he could see why it was that, though the sheriff seemed perfectly aware who was doing all the poaching in His Lordship's wood, he had never arrested the offender. "I believe that the only question remaining is who, sir, are you?"

Hugo stared steadily at Finnula as he said, with quiet dignity, "I am Hugo Geoffrey Fitzstephen, seventh Earl of Stephensgate, recently returned from imprisonment in Acre to lord over my late father's demesnes."

The silence that this announcement engendered was broken only by a cry of outrage, which, Hugo realized with a start, came from Finnula.

When he turned to look over at her, the last thing he expected to see was that she'd burst into angry tears. But that's precisely what had happened. The Fair Finn, frightened of no man or beast, was sobbing furiously, and when Hugo said her name and started toward her, she turned and ran, fleetly as a doe, toward her sisters.

Those auburn-haired matrons enveloped her in their arms and, giving him a communal look of pure, unadulterated hatred, slammed the millhouse door in his face.

Sheriff de Brissac was the first to throw back his head and laugh. He was joined a moment later by Finnula's brothers-in-law, then by Matthew Fairchild, and finally, most heartily of all, by Robert Crais. Hugo stood in the center of the yard, staring at the firmly closed door, and wondered how in the hell he'd ended up the lord of a village of lunatics.

"Ah," Sheriff de Brissac cried, the first to recover from being doubled over with derisive laughter. "Ah, but that felt good."

Hugo glared at the older man. "Doesn't anyone believe me?"

"Oh, aye, m'lord, aye. We all believe you. Who else could you be? That's not what we all find so amusing."

Hugo had placed his fists on his hips and regarded the guffawing men impassively. "Well, perhaps you'd care to enlighten me, then, as to what, precisely, does so amuse you."

"Well, 'tis the fact that you think you're marryin' Finnula, if you must know." The very idea seemed nearly to send Sheriff de Brissac over the edge again, but he must have noticed Hugo's frown, since he controlled himself. "Beggin' your pardon, m'lord. Can you honestly not know?"

Hugo could never remember feeling such rage in his life. It took an almost superhuman effort to control his desire to tear across that yard, kick down a door, and drag out his weeping bride-to-be.

"I honestly don't know," he said through gritted teeth.

"Well, perhaps you ken that Finnula was married before?"

"Yes," Hugo said, shrugging. "What of it?"

"And she didn't tell you to whom it was she was wed?"

"She didn't say."

"She wouldn't. Worst day of her life, I believe." By now, all the men had ceased laughing, and were staring at Hugo with a wide variety of expressions, from Robert Crais's self-satisfied smirk to Farmer Fairchild's anxious pity. Pity? Hugo wanted to put his fist through something.

"Well?" Hugo demanded. "Aren't you going to tell me who the bloody hell it was she was married to?"

Sheriff de Brissac looked almost sorry he had to be the one to break the news.

"Your father, my lord."

# Chapter Ten

$\mathscr{F}$innula lay on the bed she and Mellana had shared for nearly all their lives and scowled. She had cried for nearly a quarter of an hour, her sisters clucking around her like hens, but Finnula had never been a weeper, and couldn't keep up a steady stream of tears for long.

So after having endured Brynn's coddling and fended off Patricia's scolding, having allowed herself to be disrobed by Camilla—"These leather braies are a disgrace!"—and dressed again by Christina—"You have such lovely bliauts, why do you not wear them?"—she lifted her head from a damp pillow and abruptly stopped weeping. Rolling onto her stomach, oblivious to the wrinkles she was making in her dark green bliaut, Finnula scowled at the headboard while her sisters chattered around her.

"'Twas a nasty trick he played on you, Finn," Christina was

saying, running a brush through her little sister's thick hair as she sat beside her on the wooden-framed bed. "But you can't blame him—"

"Aye, how was he to know about you and Lord Geoffrey?" Brynn sighed. "The poor man—"

"Poor nothing." Patricia, who was the family scold, was happy with neither Finnula nor the earl. "He *would* have told her, if he hadn't been so enchanted with the idea of being held for ransom by a winsome redhead—"

"Patricia!" The ever-gentle Brynn was shocked. "How can you say such a thing?"

"How can I? Because it's the truth, you goose."

"But he's an earl!"

"Oh, and earls aren't men? I believe we know only too well, from Finnula's experience with the late Lord Geoffrey, that earls are men first, lords second—"

"'Tis ridiculous to suggest he didn't tell her because he liked being held hostage by her," Christina said, giving a tangle in Finnula's hair a playful tug. "Perfectly ridiculous."

Patricia had folded her arms across her chest. "Obviously he liked it, or he would have escaped."

"He couldn't escape," Brynn said. "It was Finn who had him, remember. Finn would never allow a hostage to escape. That's why Mellana asked her in the first place—"

"Oh," wailed Mellana, from the far corner of the room to which she'd been banished by her older sisters. "'Tis all my fault!"

"'Tis true," Patricia snapped, completely without compassion for her second youngest sibling. "'Tis your fault entirely, Mel. No one's denying that. Imagine, spending your entire dowry on trinkets. Whoever heard of such a thing? I'm ashamed to admit I'm related to you. You just sit in that corner until we've figured out what we're to do with you."

Mellana wailed some more, and Finnula glared at her. She hadn't yet let slip the reason behind the urgent need to replenish Mellana's dowry, but she had already resolved that if worse came to worst, she would.

"Oh, Finnula." Brynn was biting her lower lip worriedly. "I don't know how to put this, but, Finnula, you and the earl didn't . . . I mean, nothing . . . *improper* . . . occurred whilst you were traveling with him, did it?"

Finnula only scowled more deeply.

"Don't be a goose, Brynn," Christina advised. "The earl would never have made improper advances toward one of his own vassals."

"He would if he intended to marry her, as he announced below," Patricia said dryly.

"Did he, Finn?"

"Yes, Finn. Did he?"

"You can tell us, Finn. We won't tell Robert. Did he, dear?"

Fortunately, Finnula was spared from having to make a reply by footsteps on the stairs just outside their door. Camilla burst into the room, her pretty eyes glowing. The gossip of the group, Camilla had been sent downstairs to spy upon the men, and from the look on her face, she'd heard plenty.

"Oh, Finn," she cried, running to the bed and leaping upon it like an exuberant child, oblivious to Finnula's prone body and her own fine silk bliaut and carefully coifed hair. "You'll not believe what a ruckus your Lord Hugo's making! He's demanding that you be brought below immediately, and threatening Robert with the stockade! It's simply too delicious!"

Finnula's other sisters crowded round the bed.

"What did he say?"

"Does he still want to wed her?"

"Robert can't deny him—"

"How could he wed his own father's widow?"

"Tell us what you heard, Camilla!"

"Yes, tell us!"

Camilla held up two hands, commanding silence. A born thespian, she lowered her voice dramatically and whispered, "Well, when I got to the doorway of the gathering room, Bruce was standing there, guarding it, and he had the nerve to say, 'Get upstairs with your sisters, woman. Your prating prate isn't needed here,' to which I replied—"

"No one cares what Bruce has to say," Patricia scoffed, and then added, with a slightly apologetic smile, "Begging your pardon, Christina—"

Christina waved a dismissive hand, and Camilla continued.

"Well, Sheriff de Brissac was telling Lord Hugo about how Finnula and his father met—"

Finnula groaned and, lifting the pillow, crammed it over her head.

"Sheriff de Brissac was telling him?" Brynn was confused. "Why wasn't Robert telling him?"

"Robert won't speak to him. Just glowers at him over his tankard—"

"Tankard?" Brynn was shocked. "They're *drinking*, at a time like this?"

"Lord Hugo himself demanded a barrel of Mel's Brew be opened. Will you please let me finish?" Camilla was impatient to get on with her performance. "So as Sheriff de Brissac described how Lord Geoffrey came upon Finn swimming that day at the Spring of St. Elias, and how he spied upon her and became besotted with her and followed her all the way back to Stephensgate"— Finnula groaned again from beneath the pillow—"Lord Hugo grew quite red in the face, and then he said, 'That old devil,' about his own father, mind. Then Sheriff de Brissac told him how Robert did everything he could think of to keep Finnula from having to marry the old goat—his words, not mine—because she did nothing but weep at the prospect of such a marriage, but how nothing would dissuade the old man and how finally, Lord Geoffrey issued a feudal command, on sheepskin, no less, informing Robert that if he didn't deliver up Finn the mill would be taken away—"

Beneath the pillow, Finnula let out a muffled groan, then kicked her bare feet against the bed until Patricia reached down impatiently and seized both her ankles.

"Keep still, you impertinent cuss. We're listening."

Finnula said, her words barely intelligible, since she was speaking into the feather tick, "Can't you all go away and leave me alone?"

"No," Patricia snapped. "Go on, Camilla."

"Well, you could tell Lord Hugo was right shocked to hear that his father had intended to exercise his feudal rights in that respect, since he spat out all his ale, nearly hitting Matthew Fairchild in the face—"

"He didn't!" Patricia was shocked by this unlordly behavior.

"He did. But when he recovered himself, Sheriff de Brissac assured him it was true, and that Finnula prepared for her wedding day as if it was her funeral—"

Finnula kicked her feet some more, and Camilla said, "Oh, I am sorry, Finn, I'd forgotten how much you hate to hear about that day. But the telling's necessary this time, don't you know. In any case, Sheriff de Brissac told how Finn and Lord Geoffrey were wed, with the whole village in attendance, and how afterward there was that feast in the manor's great hall, and then Finnula and Lord Geoffrey went up to bed, and then—"

Finnula whipped the pillow off her head and sat up, her bliaut twisted so that much more of her chest was exposed by the low neckline of her tight bodice than was proper.

"What did Lord Hugo say then, Camilla?" Finnula demanded, seizing her sister's slim wrist. "When the sheriff told him?"

Camilla, pleased her narration was being appreciated by at least one enraptured audience member, preened a little, smoothing her auburn curls and examining a fat diamond ring with which her winemaker husband had gifted her last week. Then, seeing that all four of her other sisters were also watching with bated breath, she clapped her hands together.

"Well! Sheriff de Brissac told how Finnula came screaming from the bedchamber, all her hair streaming down her back and looking like it was on fire—I liked that bit, about how her hair looked like fire—crying that Lord Geoffrey was dead. You should have seen Lord Hugo's face then. White as snow, it was, and his mouth hanging open. 'Dead?' he repeated, and Sheriff de Brissac nodded. 'Aye. Dead.' And then the sheriff went on to describe how everyone ran upstairs and there was the earl stretched out on the floor, dead as a donkey, and Finnula in hysterics swearing she hadn't laid a hand on him, and how Reginald Laroche straight off accused her of poisoning the old man, and—"

"*But what did he say?*" Finnula took hold of Camilla's wrist again. "*What did Lord Hugo say to that?*"

"He looked the sheriff in the eye and said, in that deep voice of his— Oh, Finnula, he really is quite handsome, your Lord Hugo. And his voice is so rich and low, like thunder it sounds. It sends chills up the back of my neck—"

"*Never mind that now. What did Lord Hugo say?*"

"He said, 'No one could honestly believe Finnula Crais capable of poisoning anyone, even someone as odious as my father,' and Sheriff de Brissac said that he had always believed in your innocence, and that it was a bad thing, a very bad thing that had happened—"

"What did he mean by that?" Finnula wondered.

"La, I don't know. But the sheriff told him that no poison was ever found and that no one else died that night, and we'd all eaten the same food, so he ruled Lord Geoffrey's death a natural one—after all, the man was nearly sixty—"

"And your husband's how old, Camilla?" inquired Patricia, wickedly.

Camilla glared at her. "Fie on you, Trish. Gregory's only two score and ten—"

"*What did Lord Hugo say?*" Finnula hissed, through gritted teeth.

"Oh, well, he said, 'Of course no one honestly believed Finnula would have done something like that,' and the sheriff said that only the Laroches believed it . . . You remember how that bitch Isabella was going about, calling us sisters of a murdering whore and all of that?"

In the corner, Mellana made a sound, and Camilla threw her a disparaging glance.

"Oh, Mel, I don't care if Isabella is your friend. A crueler slut never walked the earth. Remember how her father went into that rage when the sheriff wouldn't arrest Finnula for murder? But then when Father Edward ruled that the marriage was void, on account of it never having been consummated, Laroche quit complaining, and that was the end of it. That was when Lord Hugo said a curious thing."

"What?" Finnula's face had gone white as the sheets beneath her. "What did he say?"

"He said, 'You mean Finnula didn't get her third?' and the sheriff said, 'The marriage was never legal,' and Lord Hugo said, 'Meaning that the entire estate fell to Laroche,' and the sheriff agreed, saying, 'You were being held in Acre, my lord, and the common belief at the time was that you were going to die there.'"

Patricia elbowed Finnula, hard. "Your Lord Hugo thinks Reginald Laroche murdered his father and tried to make it look as if you did it, so you'd go to the gibbet and he'd get the estate. Mark my words, there'll be blood spent over this."

Finnula glared up at her sister, rubbing the tender spot on her rib where she'd prodded her. "Ow."

"Did you hear me?"

"I heard you. Don't poke me there, I've got a bruise."

"Lord Hugo won't be able to prove Reginald Laroche had anything to do with Lord Geoffrey's death, Patricia, any more than Sheriff de Brissac was ever able to," Christina said, shaking her head. "Oh, Finn, this is nasty business—"

"What happened then?" Finnula asked Camilla, trying to keep her eagerness from showing.

"Well, then Lord Hugo said something else I didn't understand. 'So that's why they m'lady her,' and the sheriff laughed and said how Finnula took her oath to protect Lord Geoffrey's vassals very seriously, and Lord Hugo said that it looked as if Finnula'd never stopped carrying out her duties as chatelaine to Stephensgate Manor and that it was a good thing, too, because when he married her it wouldn't be such a dreadful change for her—"

"*What?*" cried Finnula.

"Which is exactly what Robert said. 'What?' And he came rising up out of his chair, screaming, 'You can't still mean to marry her!' to which Lord Hugo replied, 'If she'll have me,' and then the sheriff started to laugh again and Robert lunged across the table, like to kill His Lordship, only Bruce stopped him, and reminded him it was the earl he was speaking to, not some wandering minstrel who'd asked for his sister's hand—"

In the corner, Mellana let out a whimper.

"And Robert said that he didn't care, he'd see Finnula dead before he'd let her wed another Fitzstephen, since she did naught but weep for days at the prospect of marrying the first one, and that she was already upstairs weeping at the idea of marrying his son. And then, you wouldn't have believed it, Lord Hugo threatened to have Robert thrown in the stockade for his impudence! He even called our brother an interfering pup, and then started chastising him for letting Finnula wander the countryside in braies, to which Robert replied, 'If you think you can manage her better, my lord, you're welcome to her!' And Lord Hugo said, 'Thank you very much,' and Sheriff de Brissac straight off proposed a toast to the happy couple!"

Christina shook Finnula excitedly. "Did you hear that, Finn? Did you hear?"

Finnula nodded dazedly, then sat back, feeling limp. Well, of course he had to say he wanted to marry her, after all that! But he couldn't possibly mean it. He was only doing it out of honor. And Finnula wouldn't marry a man simply to assuage his sense of honor. She was going to do the right thing, and tell him it wasn't necessary. If she was with child, she'd simply go somewhere—to a convent, she supposed. She could tell everyone she'd gone on a pilgrimage to purify her soul. Though she rather doubted anyone would believe it. And she'd have the baby, and see that it was given to some childless couple, then come straight back home.

Oh, yes, better that than a loveless marriage—

"Finnula, what is the matter with you?" Brynn shook her gently from her reverie. "Aren't you happy, sweet? Don't you like him?"

Finnula looked at her eldest sister grimly. "Brynn," she said. "I thought him a stranger . . . a hapless knight from Caterbury, and now I learn he's Lord Geoffrey's son? How am I supposed to feel?" Honestly, she'd never have bedded him if she'd known! Look at the mess she was in now!

"What difference does that make?" Camilla demanded. "He's still the loveliest man I've ever seen . . . ."

"Men aren't lovely," scoffed Patricia.

"Well, handsome, then. Oh, Finnula, think how different it will be to be lady of Stephensgate Manor with Lord Hugo, rather than his father, at your side. Why, he's not someone I'd begrudge a place in my bed—"

"Camilla, you are a bigger slut than Isabella Laroche," Patricia declared.

"Finnula," Brynn said, chewing worriedly on her lower lip. "Think on this. Was his masquerade such a heinous one? Who did it harm? No one. He seems to love you—" Finnula let out a snort. "Well, to care for you, anyway. Why else would he fight so for your hand?"

Finnula said nothing, just glared at the window, which showed that twilight had fallen outdoors. He'd fought so hard for her hand because he'd dishonored her, and he was only doing what, as her lord, he owed her. It was no less than she'd do for any serf of hers.

"'Tis true that if you wed him, there'll be sacrifices," Brynn began, slowly.

"Aye," Patricia agreed. "No more leather braies."

"No more hunting," Camilla said.

"No more disappearing for days on end on the back of Violet," Christina said.

Finnula was certain she died a little, just listening to them.

"But think what you'll be getting in return," Camilla cried, her gray eyes glittering. "Think what jewels and bliauts! Think of how lovely it will be to have servants to comb your hair and pour your bath and prepare your food! Why, you'll be the richest woman in Stephensgate—"

"Isabella Laroche will die of envy," Patricia said, with relish.

"Oh, you've *got* to marry him, Finn," Camilla said. "You'll learn to love him, honestly you will. Look at me and Gregory."

Patricia snorted. "I'd hardly hold *that* up as an ideal marriage."

"But it is. It began as a business arrangement. Gregory fell madly in love with me, and I agreed to marry him if he met certain stipulations—"

"Like that necklace?" Patricia asked, acidly.

"Why, yes," Camilla replied, laying a hand on the ruby and pearl choker at her throat. "That was one of them. And little by little, Finnula, I've come to appreciate Gregory for his other qualities—"

"Like what?" Patricia laughed. "The man's old enough to be your—"

A thunderous shout broke through their bickering. It was Robert's voice, and he was calling, "Finnula! Finnula Crais, get down here at once!"

Finnula gazed up at her sisters with widened eyes. "Oh, no," she cried. "Lord Hugo must have left. And now Robert's going to wring my neck! Quick—I must slip out the window—"

Christina hurried to the small window and bent to look out into the yard. "Nay, His Lordship's horse is still here."

"He must want your answer to Lord Hugo's proposal," Brynn said. "Oh, Finnula, you must go to him."

But Finnula only sat back against the pillows, her face a mask of rebellious obstinacy. "I shan't," she sniffed.

"Oh, Finn!"

But Finnula was adamant. "I'm not setting foot outside this room until that man is gone. And I mean it."

Brynn and Camilla exchanged glances. "Finnula." The eldest sister hesitated. "Are you quite certain nothing, er, *untoward* occurred whilst you were traveling with Lord Hugo?"

Finnula stared. "Why do you ask?" Did losing one's virginity show? Finnula had detected no change in Mellana's appearance, and she was pregnant!

"Well, it seems to me that you are unreasonably angry at him for lying to you. After all, 'twas not so strange a thing he did. Perhaps he never tells women that he is an earl, for fear 'twill make them, er, like him for his purse, and not himself—"

This sounded very like the conceited Sir Hugh—or Lord Hugo, as she now had to refer to him. How stupid, how blindly stupid she'd been! A man and his squire, returning from the Crusades, and headed for Stephensgate—*of course* she ought to have known it to be none other than the long-absent Lord Hugo. And then he'd changed his name just the tiniest bit—Hugo Fitzstephen to Hugh Fitzwilliam—and she still hadn't caught on!

And the story of his brother, none other than Henry, Lord Geoffrey's eldest and most beloved son. That was a well-known story in her village, and still she hadn't made the connection! Oh, he must think her the dimmest wench in the shire. She had even noticed something familiar about him at the spring, but never realized that the familiarity was due to Lord Hugo's slight resemblance to his father.

Well, he'd shown her what a silly, ignorant maid she was, and she thanked him for it. The next time she met a man, she'd be far less trusting.

"Finnula!" roared Robert, the timbre of his voice almost shaking the rafters.

"You had best go to him," Finnula advised Brynn, "and tell him that although I am conscious of the great honor the earl has bestowed upon me, I have no intention of marrying him, and that Lord Hugo can just go home now."

Brynn rose reluctantly. "Finnula, I think you're making a mistake. Do not allow pride to stand in the way of your happiness—"

"Thank you for the advice," Finnula said stiffly. "But my happiness is right here, at the millhouse."

Sighing, Brynn left the room to deliver Finnula's message. Patricia, who'd been pacing the small chamber, stopped in front of Mellana and said coldly, "Well, I hope you're happy. What could you have been thinking, sending Finnula out on such a ridiculous errand? Fetch you a man to ransom. Ha! I think you've spent entirely too much time in the company of that slut Isabella. I intend to tell Robert not to allow you to see her anymore. What do you have to say to that?"

"I do not care." Mellana wept into her skirt. "I never want to see her again anyway."

"Oh, *now* you come to your senses. You know, it's just fortunate for you, Mellana, that Finnula happened to kidnap a man with a sense of chivalry. Suppose she'd kidnapped someone like Reginald Laroche? Do you think she'd be entertaining marriage proposals from an earl? No, she'd have lost her maidenhead, and be with child now, probably—"

"Patricia!" Finnula cried. "Let Mel alone."

"Well, you know 'tis true."

Another shout rattled the house, and this time, it was accompanied by heavy footsteps on the stairs. Since the second floor of the millhouse was primarily the domain of the female Craises, they were unaccustomed to hearing masculine footsteps on the stairs, and all five of them froze, their eyes on the door.

"Finnula!"

This time, the thunderous bellowing of Finnula's name didn't come from their brother, Robert, but from Lord Hugo . . . and he appeared to be standing directly behind her bedroom door. Finnula exchanged astonished glances with her sisters, but didn't move.

"Finnula," Lord Hugo growled menacingly. "Will you open this door, or do I have to knock it down?"

It was Mellana who hopped up from her chair in the corner and hurried to the door, one hand over her mouth, her eyes wide with alarm. When she swung open the heavy portal to reveal a very irritated-looking Lord Hugo, she bobbed a graceful curtsy and babbled incoherently, "Oh, my lord, please don't be angry with Finnula. 'Tis all my fault. You see, I made her do it. She didn't want to, but I cried, and she—"

"Yes, you cry very prettily," Lord Hugo observed dryly. "And you're quite right, it *is* all your fault, you and your Jack Mallory."

Mellana gasped, her bright blue eyes flying accusingly to Finnula, who sat still as a statue on the bed.

"You told!" Mellana cried. "Oh, Finn, how could you?"

"Aye, she did tell," Hugo said, and Finnula did not miss the smugness in his tone. "And lucky for you she did, or you wouldn't be receiving *this* right now, along with my blessings—" Lord Hugo dropped a fat purse of coins into the hands an astonished Mellana hastily extended.

"This should pay for your dowry and for a few other sundries. I suggested to Brother Robert that he find a place for your husband at the mill, since troubadouring is hardly steady work, and your Jack will need something a bit more regular, with the babe on the way—"

Mellana gasped again, and Patricia's nostrils flared.

"Mel!" she cried, outraged. "*You*—"

But Lord Hugo interrupted her. "Your brother, Robert, is waiting below, Mellana—I may call you that, may I not, as we are shortly to be related? Brother Robert would like a few words with you."

Mellana was too frightened to start weeping again. Instead, clutching the bag of coins he'd given her to her chest, she crept from the room with her head ducked. When Hugo glanced at Finnula and saw her expression, he said lightly, "Never fear.

Brother Robert assured me he would never strike a pregnant woman."

Finnula thought she'd had about as much as she could take. Scrambling from the bed, oblivious to the twisted bodice of her gown, she cried, "You blithering idiot! What did you tell Robert for? Now he'll make her life hell!"

"Better hers than yours, Finn." Hugo glanced at Camilla and Patricia, who, with Christina, were staring at him as if he was something that had just crawled up from the depths of the watering trough—or tumbled down from the heavens. Finnula couldn't entirely read their expressions. But Hugo could, apparently.

"If you ladies will excuse us," he said, bowing, "Finnula and I have some things that need discussing in private."

"Oh, of course," Camilla said, dipping a quick curtsy and darting toward the door. "Of course, my lord!"

"Please excuse us, my lord," Christina breathed, moving less gracefully because of her pregnancy, but no less quickly.

Patricia was the last sister to leave, and she paused with her hand on the leather strap that served as a doorknob and looked slyly at Lord Hugo.

"Kiss her," was Patricia's cryptic advice. "She'll come around."

And then she shut the door firmly behind her.

Alone in her bedchamber with Lord Hugo, Finnula could not help feeling at a distinct disadvantage. She'd forgotten how physically intimidating the man was. Why, he had to stoop to avoid striking his head on the wooden ceiling beams, he was so tall. His massive frame seemed to take up far more room than all five of her sisters put together.

Hugo himself seemed aware of how awkward he looked in this vibrantly feminine room, and he glanced from the dried bouquets of roses hanging from the rafters to the curtains with raised eyebrows, though he said nothing. His amber gaze roved from her loosened hair to her bare feet, hesitating only at the low neckline of her dress, which, Finnula realized, only then had slipped to reveal more than was proper.

Reaching up quickly to adjust the bliaut's bodice, her cheeks flushing hotly, Finnula snapped, "I'd have thought you'd seen enough of me to satisfy you for one day."

Hugo's grin was slow and suggestive. "But therein lies the rub, Finnula. I don't think I'll ever get enough of you. That's why I think marriage the wisest answer—"

"Marriage?" Finnula turned away quickly, unwilling to let him see what effect his words had on her face. "I told you before I never wanted to be married again. Or weren't you listening?"

"And I would ask why a maid so intent on avoiding marriage would behave as you have in the past day or so."

Finnula felt the warmth in her cheeks, which only seemed to grow, rather than ebbing, and avoided his eye with even more determination. "I couldn't help that," she said.

"Couldn't help what? Making love with me?"

"Aye," she admitted shamefacedly.

"Look at me, Finnula."

She shook her head, keeping her face averted, her gaze on the yard outside, in which Sheriff de Brissac was laughing and clapping her brothers-in-law on the shoulders.

"Would you have married Hugh Fitzwilliam?" he asked.

Would she have married that irritating knight? The surprising answer was that she might have, if he'd asked. She shrugged.

"That's no answer."

"'Tis all the answer I have," Finnula snapped, turning angry eyes upon him. "I do not know. I cannot predict what might have been, any more than I can tell you what will be. But I will tell you that I will never set foot in that house again, and so a marriage between us is impossible."

"What house? You mean Stephensgate Manor?"

"Aye," Finnula said, and couldn't help shuddering at the name. "The hours I spent there were the worst of my life. I swore when I was released I would never again cross that accursed threshold—"

"Finnula, I know what passed between you and my father—"

"No," she cut him off, vehemently. "You do *not* know, *no one* knows. Your father was mad, completely mad, and thought I was your mother. Did Sheriff de Brissac not tell you that? Lord Geoffrey never called me by my name, he called me Marie. Wasn't that your mother's name?"

When Hugo nodded, dumbly, Finnula said, "It wasn't *me* he loved at all, he didn't even know *me*. But in his demented mind, I was the Lady Marie, and so he would have me, and nothing I could do or say would dissuade him—"

"Finnula," he said, taking a step toward her, but she held up a hand, palm out, to stop him.

"I'm sorry to tell you this, but I felt it then, and I *still* feel that a miracle occurred to save me that night. No sooner had we stepped into His Lordship's bedchamber than he collapsed upon the floor. I was so frightened, I did not know what to do—"

"Finnula, listen to me. We'll lock up that room. You need never enter it again—"

But Finnula spoke like one in a daze, as if she hadn't heard him. "I stood over him as he clutched his chest, trying to breathe. I ran for Sheriff de Brissac, praying he had not yet left the hall—but by the time I'd fetched the sheriff, Lord Geoffrey was dead." Finnula realized that she'd begun weeping as she spoke, and stared in bemusement at a single tear that splashed upon her sleeve. "And then I was accused of—of *murdering* him, and Reginald Laroche wanted me hanged on the spot! Only Sheriff de Brissac wouldn't allow it—"

This time Hugo wouldn't let her stop him. He was across the room and at her side in one long stride. He snatched her up into his arms, crushing her to his chest and murmuring into her hair, "I know, I know. John told me all about it. But we can put that behind us, can't we? We can forget all that and start anew. The first thing I'm going to do when I get to the manor house is dismiss Laroche, and then I'll board up my father's bedchamber. No one will ever enter it again, least of all you. Oh, Finnula, do not weep—"

But she couldn't help it. She clung to him, sobbing, and despising herself for it. How could she show such weakness before him? Hadn't her pride been wounded enough? Did she have to disgrace herself in front of the man? Wiping her eyes on her sleeve, she tried to get hold of herself, and pushed ineffectually at his chest to get him to release her.

Only Hugo wouldn't let go. If anything, he only held on to her more tightly, saying, "Listen, Finnula. It isn't as if anything will change. Oh, you'll no longer live at the millhouse, but Stephensgate Manor will be yours, to do with whatever you like. And you'll still be responsible for all my vassals. They already think of you as their lady. Wouldn't it be better for you to be Lady Finnula in truth? You can help me return what was so wrongfully stolen from them. I need your help, you know. I've been away ten years. I can't trust Laroche. I need someone to tell me how things ought to be done . . ."

Finnula twisted to be released from his grasp. "Ask Robert. Robert can tell you. And John de Brissac. You don't need me—"

"But I do." He kept his hands tight around her waist. "Forsooth, Finnula, I may not be Sir Hugh in name, but I am the same man beneath the new title. Why do you suddenly hate me so?"

"Because," she grunted, writhing against him. "You lied to me!"

"That was before I knew who you were," he explained. "Besides, you had a knife to my throat, remember? You couldn't honestly expect me to tell you I was an earl when you were holding me hostage as a knight. Act your age, Finnula."

"*And* you only agreed to marry me because my brother threatened to kill you—"

"I beg your pardon, Finnula, but I believe *I* was the one holding your brother at sword point, not the other way around. And God's truth, I meant to have you any way I could the moment you straddled me at the spring and announced that I was your prisoner. And since marriage is the only way I can have you and still be respected by my vassals, then marriage it has to be—"

"Ha!" Finnula tried to find a way to lever an elbow into his stomach. "See, I told you so. You don't want to marry me—"

"No man wants to marry, Finnula. There are just some women they can't have any other way, and so it is a sacrifice willingly made in order to attain a particularly choice—"

"Ooh!" Finnula was so angry, she'd have bitten him, if she could have found a portion of him that wasn't so hardened and muscular that she feared to break her teeth upon it. "I knew it!" she cried. "Well, I'll have you know, there are some women who don't care for marriage, either! And I'm one of them! I'm telling you right now that I shall make you a miserable wife. I can't sew and I don't know how to clean and I'm disaster in the kitchen. I shall leave the house every morning at dawn and hunt all day and return home at night muddy and tired, and I'll look such a sight, you won't want to come near me—"

"If that's what you think, you are far more innocent than you led me to believe last night." Hugo said, and grinned, and before she could draw breath for another barrage of threats, he kissed her, as her sister had advised.

Finnula squirmed in his embrace, intent upon making it clear to him that by marrying, they'd be making a horrible mistake.

But it was so difficult to remember how angry she was when his lips were on hers . . . especially when first one of his callused, knowing hands dipped beneath the wide neck of her gown, and then another cupped her backside, drawing her even close to him until, really, she had no choice but to wrap her arms around his neck, merely for fear of losing her balance.

Things got even worse when, with a knee, he parted her legs, thrusting an iron-hewn thigh against the crevice where her legs met. And Finnula, though she tried to resist it, could not help sighing and relaxing against him, feeling the pleasant wave of desire that passed over her as it always did when he touched her there. Fie! Had the sultan's daughter taught him that devil's trick?

She gave up after that, all the fight gone from her trembling limbs. She didn't care if they married or not, so long as he kept touching her there, sending such delicious sensations through her body.

Hugo felt her surrender, and took full advantage of it. He hadn't fought as a soldier these past ten years not to know enough to seize whatever victories came his way. Perhaps it wasn't fair, this power he had over her, but he wasn't about to feel any guilt over it, not while he had her exactly where he wanted her. Laying her pliant body back against the bed and lifting her skirt, he caressed with his hand now what he'd previously stroked with his thigh, eliciting soft murmurs of pleasure from Finnula, who, in some distant part of her mind, thought it a little wicked of them to be making love in her childhood bedroom.

But it didn't seem to matter where they were when Hugo wanted her and made her want him, too.

Before she was fully aware of what Hugo was about, he'd dipped his head between her thighs, and was caressing with his mouth what he'd previously caressed with his fingers. The feel of his tongue on her most sensitive area had a poleaxing effect on Finnula. She had to grasp the quilt beneath her fingers merely to have something to hang on to as his tongue sent her into ever widening spirals of orgasmic pleasure. She was doing her best not to cry out—and alert her entire family as to what the two of them were up to—when suddenly Hugo was unlacing his braies, and that part of him which she had grown to appreciate most fondly of late sprang free from the confines of his chausses.

She gasped as he filled her. His repeated thrusts soon sent her over the edge once more, into that place she'd been only with him. Though this time she tried to be quiet about it.

When Hugo, too, found release, he collapsed atop her, and they lay in a damp pile, breathing hard and barely able to see each other in the darkening room.

Still, Hugo's green-eyed gaze sought out hers, and he asked, panting, "*Now* will you marry me?"

She could barely speak, her throat was so dry from their passionate exercise. "I don't suppose I have much of a choice," she said.

"No. I'll force you, if I have to. On sheepskin."

Finnula thought about this. "I won't give up my braies," she said.

"Yes," he panted. "You will, if I have to burn them."

"You wouldn't dare!"

"I would. And I want my emerald back."

Finnula looked at the ceiling. "I don't know where it is."

"'Tis round your neck. You think I can't feel that thing pressing into my gut?"

Finnula frowned, noting that the house seemed oddly silent. "You don't think they heard us, do you?" she wondered anxiously.

"With you gasping like that? They probably think I was up here killing you."

"Or that *I* was killing *you*—"

"You were the one crying, 'Oh, yes, please—'"

Finnula gasped. "Oh, no! I wasn't. I tried to be so still . . ."

"You failed. The whole village probably heard you—"

Finnula looked at him in the twilight. "You did that apurpose, didn't you?"

"Did what?" he inquired innocently, rising and straightening his braies.

"You know."

"No, Finnula, I don't know. And now I suggest you start packing, because I'll only give you this one night of reprieve. Tomorrow we wed."

"Tomorrow!" she cried indignantly, rising to her elbows.

"Aye, tomorrow. And don't try to run off, because I'm of a mind to flay you if you disobey me."

"I thought you told Robert—"

"I told Robert the only man who'll lay a hand on you from now on is me." He leaned down and kissed her hard on the lips. "I didn't say I'd never take you over my own knee if you were ever so unwise as to disobey me."

Finnula considered this and decided that, overall, being taken over Hugo's knee would not be the worst thing that had ever happened to her. Still, she thought it better not to tempt him.

# Chapter Eleven

*I*t had been ten years since Hugo had last seen his home, if one could call Stephensgate Manor a home. Hugo himself could not. The memory of his brother's betrayal was still as fresh in his memory as if it had occurred yesterday. And though his brother was long gone, and his parents as well, Hugo could not help giving a shudder as he approached the manor house's gates.

Though the village church bell had struck eight, there was still plenty of light in the sky. It was only the second week of May, but the sun stayed above the western horizon well past Vespers, and in that purple light, Hugo could make out only too well the twin towers that flanked the stone walls surrounding the structure that had come to be known as Stephensgate Manor. Not quite a castle, lacking moat and drawbridge and the normal accoutrements one came to expect from a well-fortified structure, it nevertheless was an imposing building, looming over the village of Stephensgate like a bird of prey.

Constructed entirely of stone, including the roof, which consisted of piled slate, and the six-foot-tall wall surrounding the house and its adjoining stables, bakehouse, and storehouses, Stephensgate Manor been built as a shelter for Stephensgate's lord and his minions during a time of warfare, but the only concession to that purpose were the towers that flanked the two-story structure. Topped by battlements jutted with merlons, behind which archers might crouch, the towers served no purpose other than a military one, as the only thing existing within them were curling staircases to the platform roof.

Since Stephensgate hadn't known feudal warfare in over a century, the towers had fallen into disuse before Hugo's father's lifetime, and except when Hugo or his brother, Henry, had climbed those stone-carved stairs to enact some boyhood prank, Hugo could not remember anyone ever having entered the towers for any reason whatsoever.

Which was why, when he and John de Brissac passed through the manor house's gates and dismounted, Hugo was surprised to hear a voice call down to him from the battlements.

"Hullo, there."

Looking up, Hugo squinted in the half light, and saw the face of a towheaded boy staring down at him from between two merlons.

"Hullo," Hugo said. It was a quiet evening, the stillness broken only by the occasional cooing of doves that nested, as they'd done when Hugo'd been a boy, between the slates on the manor house's roof. His voice sounded unnaturally loud in the silent yard.

"Hullo, there, Jamie," Sheriff de Brissac called jovially. He had dismounted, and his mare, relieved from the burden of her master's immense girth, danced a little on the cobblestones. "Fetch old Webster down here, would you? We need someone to put away the horses."

Jamie's head didn't budge. "Who's that with you, Sheriff?" he demanded. The boy couldn't, Hugo judged, have been more than nine or ten years old, but he had a commanding presence, even from twenty feet overhead.

"That?" Sheriff de Brissac chuckled. "That's His Lordship."

The boy's tawny eyebrows rose with interest. "Give over. Lord Hugo?"

"That's him."

The boy stared down at Hugo a second or two more, and then the golden head disappeared. Hugo flashed the sheriff a look of mild amusement.

"Who was that?" he asked, removing his riding gloves and slapping them loosely against his thigh.

"That? That's Jamie."

"How many hangers-on is Laroche allowing to hole up here, anyway?" Hugo looked about the yard, amazed at how little anything had changed in ten years. The stables, the bakehouse— everything looked the same. A little shabbier, perhaps. Certainly not more prosperous. But oddly, strangely, homelike.

"Ah," the sheriff sighed. "All sorts, all sorts. Including that squire of yours you sent ahead—"

"Oh? Peter made it here all right, did he?" Hugo was surprised. He wouldn't have counted on the boy to find London Bridge without getting into some scrape or another.

"Arrived yesterday, with quite a tale to tell. Said you'd been waylaid by highway robbers who'd be sending notice of your ransom sometime in the near future. Laroche didn't know what to make of 'im, and sent for me. Of course, when the boy clapped eyes on me, he shut up like a clam."

Hugo chuckled to himself. "Finnula told him at peril of my life was he to say anything to the shire reeve concerning my, er, disappearance."

"That would explain it, then. Ah, here's Webster."

The old servant, who'd managed the Fitzstephens' stables since Lord Geoffrey's father's lifetime, shuffled toward them, his milky gaze on Hugo.

"That you, my lord?"

"Aye, Webster." Hugo's heart swelled with unexpected emotion at seeing the old man, still up and around and performing his duties at the manor house, in spite of the fact that it had lain lordless for a year. One year or twenty, Hugo doubted Webster would have left until he was certain all his beauties, as he referred to just about any horse that wasn't swaybacked, were taken care of.

"Well met, old man," Hugo said, striding forward and taking hold of Webster's spindly arm. "Well met!"

"'Tis you, all right," Webster said, apparently unmoved. "I'd recognize that grip anywhere. Never did know your own strength. Well, you're back, then."

"I'm back," Hugo assured him, dropping the arm. "To stay."

"'Tis about time, I'd say." Narrowing a disapproving look at Hugo, he nodded. "Me beauties were beginning to suffer. But now 'at you're t' home, they'll be right enough."

Without elaborating further, the old man turned and collected the reins to both horses, shuffling toward the stable door and muttering to Skinner beneath his breath. Hugo stared after the old servant, his lips pressed into a frown of disapproval.

"I suppose," he said to the sheriff, "I should be happy they kept him on. God knows they could have turned him out, blind as he is. But why they haven't taken on a boy to help him—"

"Another mouth to feed?" John de Brissac grinned beneath his dark beard. "Not your cousin Laroche. No, he kept him on, since he couldn't find another to work so well so cheaply. Devoted to those horses, the old man is. And doesn't cost your bailiff more'n a milkmaid's salary—"

"So that's how it is, is it? I should have guessed. What about that boy Jamie?" Hugo looked about the yard for the inquisitive mite. "He's not a stable boy?"

"Jamie? Nay."

"Not one of Mistress Laver's, surely? Mistress Laver's still in the kitchen, is she?"

"Aye, workin' for her keep and a pittance besides. Nay, Jamie ain't hers, but he lends a hand where he may, though without doubt he causes more harm than help." Sheriff de Brissac clapped his palms together, a favorite gesture of his, Hugo had learned, and rubbed his hands together. "Well, now, my lord, shall we knock, or merely enter?"

Hugo could tell that the sheriff was anxious to get to the business at hand, not out of any impatience to be home—nay, John had told him, quite without self-pity, that he had no wife to come home to, only an aged mother who was known as a scold—but for the action to be under way.

Unlike the sheriff, Hugo was not looking forward to the scene awaiting him. He'd witnessed more than his fair share of death and violence abroad, and longed for nothing more than a life of quiet domesticity, which certainly would not be guaranteed by his choice of a wife, but he supposed he might hope to attain it by the time he and Finnula were grandparents. Watching over his vassals, engaging in a tournament or two, and rearing children would be all the excitement he needed for the remainder of his life.

But the ousting of Laroche from his home was necessary to achieve that peace, and so Hugo squared his shoulders and said, "Fie on you, John. Why should I knock upon my own door?"

So saying, he bent to throw open the heavy portals, but found the iron latch moving before he ever even touched it. Creaking, the oak doors parted, and a familiar blond head peeped out between them. Hugo saw now that the face the towhead tipped up at him was as filthy as any he'd seen.

Standing no higher than Hugo's hip, Jamie said, in his high-pitched voice, "Well, come in, then. Don't just stand there."

Hugo frowned down at the boy. "Quite at home here at Stephensgate Manor, aren't you, lad?"

"I should hope so," Jamie said. "I was born here."

"Were you now?" Hugo stepped past the boy and entered the manor house's Great Hall, nothing more than a vast dining area, surrounded on all four sides by a gallery that skirted the second floor and allowed those gathered there to look down upon the heads of those dining below. The Great Hall took up nearly all of the manor house's main floor, but only the very center of it featured the vaulted ceiling of a cathedral, from which hung two or three tattered banners, left over from some battle long since forgotten.

At the far end of the hall, opposite the doors, stood a wide fireplace, high enough to warm the entire room, or most of it, anyway. It was in front of this fireplace, in which roared a fire too hot for so fair an evening, that two high-backed chairs had been placed. In one, Hugo saw at once, though the boy's back was to him, lounged his squire, Peter. In the other was hunched a man Hugo thought he recognized as his father's cousin, Reginald Laroche.

At the sound of their entrance, Peter turned his head, and let out a glad cry.

"Why, look here!" the squire called out, his voice echoing in the vast chamber. " 'Tis my master!"

Coming unsteadily to his feet, Peter crossed the flagstones to greet Hugo and the sheriff, the former of whom realized immediately that the boy was drunk. What fool had opened the wine cellar to this cocksure lad, Hugo could only guess, but the boy could barely stand, he was so intoxicated. Still garbed in his velvet tunic, the boy had at least removed his chain mail, though he'd replaced the ermine-lined cloak with a new gold necklace Hugo had never seen before. He hoped Laroche hadn't given it to the boy in an attempt to win his loyalties. Hugo was only too certain such a ruse would succeed, knowing Peter's vanity. Showering the lad with gifts and keeping him drunk as a pig in mud would win him over very nicely.

"Look, here he is, monsieur," Peter said, pointing at Hugo, a ridiculous, toothy smile on his youthful face. "No ransom n-necessary, I s-see. D'ja give 'er a tumble, my lord? Lord, I wish I'd been in your boots! I tol' you she was a choice piece—"

Hugo ignored the boy, his gaze going past him to the man who had stood up as well, and was coming toward them more slowly, but with his arms spread wide in the age-old gesture of welcome.

"But this can't be Hugo Fitzstephen," Reginald Laroche cried. "Not the raw youth who left here ten years ago, in such a fury. Laid a curse upon every head within this hall, you did that morning, did you not, my lord? And now look at you. Twice as broad as your father ever was, and taller than our towers, I swear. What a joyful homecoming this is, is it not, John? I see you rescued our lord from those vile highwaymen Peter told us of—"

"No highwaymen about it, Reginald," John said, and grinned, purposefully using the English pronunciation of the bailiff's name, to irritate him, Hugo had no doubt. "Just the work of our favorite little huntress."

The bailiff's face clouded over a bit at the mention of Finnula.

He was a tall man, though not as large as Hugo, mustachioed and lean, with a dark head of hair just going gray in front. Hugo remembered him as ever-present back in his father's day, more than a family member, an adviser, overseer of the estate, but Geoffrey Fitzstephen's best friend. A friend who, if what Hugo suspected was true, just might have murdered the old man to gain control of the manor, and then blamed the crime on the dead earl's innocent bride.

"Ah," Reginald cried, the dismay in his voice only half feigned. "And your squire told us it was cutthroats!"

"She said she'd kill him if I told," Peter slurred happily. "Only, what a way to go! I'd've gladly died a thousand deaths for just one kiss from 'er—"

Reginald's grin seemed frozen on his narrow face. "Ah. Well, we were expecting a missive demanding your ransom, my lord, but happily, here you are instead. Fortunately, my daughter— you remember Isabella, I'm sure? She's grown into quite a young lady since you last saw her—had your father's old bedchamber made up for you—"

Hugo quirked up an eyebrow. "Weren't you using it, Reginald?" he asked, following the sheriff's cue.

"What, me? Well, yes, but now that we have you back, my lord, 'tis only fitting—"

"Quite."

Hugo saw how Laroche intended to play it. The loyal cousin, who had struggled to keep the manor running smoothly after His Lordship's untimely death, now delighted to be of service to the late lord's heir. Laroche could have no idea that Hugo had been briefed already concerning the state of his demesnes and vassals. John de Brissac would have no reason to say anything, and no one else would have dared. Except, of course, for the Fair Finn. But she was suspected of murdering Lord Geoffrey. Who would be foolish enough to believe *her*?

Hugo said, slapping his riding gloves loosely against his thigh and glancing about with seeming indifference, "The place looks fine, just fine, Reginald. I was happy to see old Webster outside. But you must find he's a bit slow these days. You never thought to get him a hand?"

"Well, things aren't quite the same as they were when you left, my lord. No, not at all, not at all." The bailiff shook his head mournfully. "Your father sold off most of the horses shortly before he died. Didn't see the use in keeping such a large stable when it was just him, you know—"

"Strange he'd have done so, don't you think?" Hugo flicked his gloves at a shield mounted against the wall, bearing the Fitzstephen crest of two falcons and a lamb, and frowned at the dust the gesture produced. "Considering he was marrying. He must have expected his bride to have use of a mare, at least. And there'd have been children—"

Reginald hesitated, but only for a second. "Ah, the sheriff told you about that debacle, did he? Yes, a dark day in your family's history, my lord. A sort of madness seized your father in those unhappy weeks leading up to his ill-fated wedding to that little chit—" The bailiff's face darkened at the memory, then, with a sigh, he brightened, like a man who wished to put an unpleasant thought behind him.

"But it won't do to dwell on those sad days, not when you've so many happy ones before you, my lord. Now, we must celebrate your homecoming. Jamie—" This, sharply, to the towheaded boy. "Run and tell Mistress Laver that His Lordship has returned, and see to it she prepares a meal fit for an earl. Tell her she has my permission to slaughter one of the suckling pigs—"

Jamie, who'd been watching the proceedings with hazel eyes wide as crabapples, looked startled. "One of the pigs, sir? Mam'selle Isabella won't like that—"

"Tell Mademoiselle Isabella that His Lordship has arrived. She'll understand." Reginald spoke slowly, hissing the words between his teeth in the manner of someone used to having his orders carried out without question. The boy darted away, and the bailiff turned with a sigh.

"'Tis so difficult to find reliable help these days," Reginald said, shaking his head.

"I can imagine it must be quite difficult." Hugo folded his arms across his chest. "Particularly when you are only willing to pay them a third what they're worth."

"My lord?" Reginald looked perplexed.

"You heard me." Hugo jerked his head at his squire. "Peter, go out to the stables and give Webster a hand with our mounts."

Peter was so drunk he could hardly stand, but he was still as intractable as ever. "Give Webster a hand?" the boy whined. "Why? The old man can care for two horses. There's only three others in the stable besides—"

"Do as I say!" roared Hugo, his voice thundering through the hall.

Peter jumped, ducked, and ran. Hugo had never seen the lad move with such speed, and was pleased that, even drunk, the boy was quick on his feet.

"My lord," Reginald said, when the vast oak panels had clanged shut behind the hurrying squire. "Is aught the matter? Excuse my forwardness, but you seem . . . displeased."

Sheriff de Brissac, always ready to appreciate a good joke, chuckled at that, and Hugo unfolded his arms and began slapping his gloves into his right palm, slowly, methodically, but with increasing force as he stared at the bailiff.

"Honestly, my lord," Reginald stammered with an unctuous smile, "if it's the sale of Lord Geoffrey's horses that worries you, I can say only that His Lordship's last weeks of life were not his best. He seemed like a man possessed—"

"Or a man whose brain was slowly being destroyed by poison," Hugo said, mildly.

"Poison, my lord?" The bailiff raised his black eyebrows in surprise. "Poison, did you say? Aye, there was talk of poison at the time of his death. It was my opinion that the little chit he wed slipped something into his chalice—"

"Oh, no," Hugo said confidently. "The poisoning began long before his marriage. 'Twas the poison that made him mad enough to desire the wedding in the first place."

"But, my lord," Reginald said, licking his thin lips with the pink tip of his tongue. "Know you what you say?"

"Indeed I do." Hugo began to pace a wide circle round the bailiff, still slapping his glove rhythmically into his palm. "In the history of my family, Monsieur Laroche, there is no record of madness. Not my grandfather, not his father, nor his father's father ever took leave of his senses—"

"Well, there are many things that can drive a man to madness," Reginald Laroche insisted, turning to watch Hugo pace. "In your father's case, it was the trickery of a young girl. A witch, some might have accused her of being, in a less enlightened age—"

"Nay," Hugo said, never taking his gaze off the bailiff. "Finnula Crais wasn't the cause of my father's madness, but a symptom. The cause was poison, pure and simple."

Reginald inhaled sharply, his gaze flying to the sheriff. "You told him, then, of what I said after the old ma— I mean, Lord Geoffrey died? That I thought 'twas the girl who slipped him something. Oh, Lord Hugo, you should have seen how she despised him. Wouldn't stand to let him touch so much as her hand.

A strange girl, most unwomanly. Have you told him, Sheriff, how we suspect her of poaching my—His Lordship's game, as well? A murderess, a poacher, perhaps even an enchantress—"

"You lay many accusations at the feet of a simple maid," Hugo observed, pacing more quickly now.

"Simple maid, my lord? Oh, no, Finnula Crais is no simple maid. Flaunts her womanhood for all to see in a pair of braies, rather than donning a gown like a God-fearing Christian—"

"That is quite enough," Hugo barked, coming to a standstill directly in front of the bailiff. "You'll not utter another word against that young woman. What you *will* do is produce the bills of sale for my father's horses. You will bring me the account books, and explain to me just why it is that tallage of my father's serfs has increased by a third. You will also inform me why it is that this winter, so many of them would have starved were it not for the kindness of the very person whom you so foully maligned a moment ago."

Reginald Laroche must have been expecting a scene of this kind. He must have thought, did Hugo survive the Crusades, that he would be made to account for his actions following the death of Lord Geoffrey. Hugo could not prove that the bailiff had poisoned his father, though he strongly suspected that was, indeed, the case.

But he could easily make a case proving Reginald Laroche guilty of extortion and embezzlement, and it was for that reason he'd wanted John de Brissac at his side while making the accusation.

"My lord," the bailiff cried, surprising Hugo with a smile, however wan. "My lord, what is this? You've been listening to village gossip. I'm surprised. You were never one to judge a man before giving him a fair hearing—"

"Ah!" Sheriff de Brissac turned one of the chairs away from the fire and positioned it so that he could watch Hugo and his cousin. Lowering his bulk into the chair, he chuckled, reaching for Peter's abandoned wine chalice. "So let us hear your version of things, Monsieur Laroche. This should make an amusing tale, indeed. Lord Hugo, won't you sit with me and enjoy the performance?"

"I'll stand, thank you, John," Hugo said, unable to restrain a grin at the sheriff's obvious relish of the situation. "Well, let's hear it, Reginald," he said, folding his arms again. "Start with the horses."

"Well, 'twas so long ago, I can hardly remember, but I seem to recall one of them sickened, and then the others, until finally, near all had to be destroyed—"

"And so my father didn't sell them?"

"'Twould seem I was mistaken in my initial statement, my lord—"

"And the increased tallages?" What would be his excuse for that? Hugo wondered, and couldn't help being impressed when the man came up with, readily enough, flooding.

"Aye, my lord, flooding. The river overflowed last June, flooding near all of your property, destroying more than half the crops. I had to increase tallage, my lord, if only to replace the ruined crops and keep the manor house stocked through the winter months—"

Hugo glanced at Sheriff de Brissac, who looked thoughtful. "Aye, the river overflowed last June," he agreed. "And it did flood a field or two. But I don't recall anything other than a wheat field being destroyed—"

"Oh, sir, the damage was much more severe than that. Whole areas of land were under water for days—"

"And it was for this reason you demanded so much money from Matthew Fairchild for permission to marry Mavis Poole that he had to accept charity in order to pay it?" Hugo's eyes were hard.

"Matthew Fairchild?" Reginald Laroche's black eyes looked beady as a bird's, and panicked as a crow's in a snare. "Mavis Poole? My lord, there must be some mistake. These names aren't familiar to me—"

"Mavis Poole's family has been tilling the same piece of land for the Fitzstephens for over fifty years," Hugo informed him disparagingly. "And yet you say her name is not familiar to you? You were my father's bailiff for years before his death. What did you do, if it was not to familiarize yourself with the names of those employed to serve you?"

Reginald stammered some reply, but Hugo cut him off, furiously. He had had more than enough. This man, if he hadn't murdered Lord Geoffrey, had murdered his memory, by allowing his people to starve. Hugo's anger reached boiling point, and he had to succumb to it for the moment, come what may.

With a growl of pent-up rage, Hugo fell upon the bailiff, clutching his velvet tunic in fists of steel. Lifting the terrified man from the flagstones, the earl held Reginald Laroche above him, glaring, with eyes that had turned a murderous yellow, at the whimpering man.

"I could crush you," Hugo snarled, "like a twig. I could toss you against that wall and break your neck—"

"My lord—" Sheriff de Brissac half rose from his comfortable chair, his expression alarmed.

"I could justly accuse you of crimes easily proven," Hugo went on, in the toneless inflection of one who has been angered beyond expression. "And happily watch you rot in prison for the rest of your days. But I'd much prefer to run you through with my sword, and then wipe your blood from the blade upon your sorry carcass—"

"My lord!" the sheriff cried, genuinely wary now, his chalice of wine forgotten. "No!"

"But instead," Hugo rasped, still keeping the smaller man lifted from the floor with the force of his grip, "I'll tell you what is it that you did, since you play the innocent so convincingly—"

Placing his cousin upon his feet, Hugo wrenched the older man to him, still gripping him by the tunic. "*Nothing*," he hissed, so softly that Sheriff de Brissac had to lean forward to catch his words. "You did *nothing* for this estate and nothing for my father. You did not concern yourself with the lives of those my father was sworn to protect and which, in turn, he willed you to serve. Your only concern was lining your own filthy pockets with Fitzstephen gold. Well, it ends tonight."

Tossing the smaller man away from him, Hugo watched the bailiff as he hit the far wall, then went sliding down it, whimpering, his body curling into the position of an infant. Completely without compassion for the man who'd harmed so many, Hugo intoned, passionlessly, "I want every coin you extorted from my people returned to me by the end of the year. I want every scrap of paper recording every transaction you made in Sheriff de Brissac's possession by dawn. And I want you out of my house no later than noon tomorrow. Am I understood?"

For a moment, Reginald Laroche looked up from his hands, and it was then that Hugo saw something pass across his cousin's face that was not fear, or even agitation, but hatred, pure and cold as the killing hatred Hugo had seen in the eyes of the Saracens against which he'd fought. Only this hatred was somehow more terrible, since it was natural to be despised by one's enemies.

But to be hated so by someone in one's own home—that was different. Reginald Laroche despised Hugo, and had probably despised his father before him. How Lord Geoffrey hadn't seen that naked contempt in his cousin's flat black eyes, Hugo couldn't imagine.

But no sooner had he himself spotted it than it disappeared,

Reginald's features schooled into an expression of anxious offi-ciousness, as he scrambled to his feet.

"My lord, my lord," the bailiff murmured, brushing himself off as if he'd merely tripped accidentally, and not been thrown bodily across the room. "All that I've done in your absence has been for the good of the manor. Indeed, many of your serfs com-plained, but you must know that your father coddled them. Why, they are the best kept vassals in the shire, even the sheriff will grant me that—"

"Were," John corrected him. "*Were* the best kept."

"There, you see? Your father, God rest his soul, was a kind man, but he had no business sense. I'll gladly show you whatever papers you wish to see, my lord, but I cannot help feeling myself sorely used. Think you upon it overnight, my lord. You are tired from your journey, and perhaps your ear has been turned by some lips that are against me—"

"There's no need to think upon it," Hugo said, shaking his head in wonder. Verily, this man had a death wish, if he thought he could talk Hugo out of the killing rage he was in. "Tomorrow you'll be gone, or by God, Laroche, you'll feel the point of my blade at your back, forcing you out—"

"Father?"

A musical voice lilted toward them, and Hugo lifted his gaze toward the staircase on the right-hand side of the hall. There, with one slim hand resting on the polished wooden banister as she de-scended the stairs, floated a vision in purple. Skin pale as cream complemented by hair black as ebony created the appearance of delicate femininity that few women could rival. Isabella Laroche, whom Hugo remembered only as an obnoxious ten-year-old in braids, had grown up into a lovely woman indeed.

"Father?" she questioned again in her soft voice. "Is aught the matter?" Then, noticing Hugo, the girl placed a hand upon her well-developed bosom and let out a startled gasp.

"Why, Lord Hugo!" she cried, and in a few swift, graceful steps she was before him, sunk onto the flagstones into a curtsy that sent her wide purple skirts puddling around Hugo's feet.

"Oh, 'tis like a dream! I heard that rascal Jamie say that you were here at last, and yet I could not believe it, lest I saw it with mine own eyes!"

Rising from her curtsy, her black eyes shining like onyx, Isabella smiled beatifically up at him. Hugo was amused to see that her perfectly shaped lips were rouged, since they appeared unnaturally red, the color of the pomegranate seeds Hugo had sometimes eaten in Egypt.

"Oh, cousin, how very tall you are now! I thought 'twas just a trick of my girlish fancy, remembering you as tall as that, but after all this time, to find that— Well, like a tree, you seem, just as when I was small. How well he looks, doesn't he, Father?"

Reginald Laroche growled, no more officious groveling in his voice, "Go to the kitchen, Isabella, and see how Mistress Laver gets on with the preparation of supper."

"Oh, Father, you can't be serious! It's been ages since Cousin Hugo and I have seen each other. We have so much to talk about." Isabella made a fetching moue of disappointment at her father. "After all, Cousin Hugo's been halfway around the world. I want to hear all about it, and about the Saracens he killed, and the sights he saw. Did you see the pyramids, Lord Hugo? I've so longed to see them myself. Are they truly all that people say?"

Hugo looked down at the bewitching creature his father's cousin had sired and understood well the dislike Finnula and her sisters felt for the girl. Beautiful and sly, Isabella Laroche was, in her own way, even more dangerous than her father, and any maid who didn't know better would be jealous of both her looks and her station in life. Isabella appeared to have made quite an effort this evening, donning a silken kirtle and a bliaut with a neckline to rival Mellana's in indecency, along with enough gold jewelry to weigh down her wrists and fingers.

"But I see my forgetful father hasn't even offered you a sip to drink," Isabella cooed, taking hold of Hugo's arm and pressing a heavy breast against it. "Let me fill a chalice for you, my lord—"

Sheriff de Brissac laughed outright at the suggestive tone the girl had employed, and she shot him an aggravated glance, her slender eyebrows descending over her fine-boned nose in a frown. "Oh," she said flatly. "'Tis you. I hadn't seen you there. Well, what are you laughing at, pray?"

"Ah, demoiselle," sighed the sheriff. "If you don't know, I shan't be the one to tell you."

"Isabella," Reginald snapped. "Get gone with you."

"Father!" The black-haired temptress stamped a small, velvet-shod foot. "You are being rude to our host!"

"Lord Hugo and I are discussing a matter of importance that does not concern you! Go to the kitchens and see how Mistress Laver fares with his supper—"

"Actually, monsieur," Hugo interrupted, "I will dine at the *millhouse* this evening. So you needn't concern yourselves—or Mistress Laver—with my supper, though I'm certain Sheriff de Brissac, who'll be staying here to help you, monsieur, with your packing, would appreciate a bite to eat."

"Dine at the *millhouse?*" cried Isabella, her tone horrified. She'd heard nothing beyond that. "Whatever will you be dining *there* for? We can prepare a better supper for you than can be had at the *millhouse*—"

"Possibly." Sheriff de Brissac laughed. "Possibly, demoiselle.

But you cannot provide the kind of company His Lordship's been keeping these past few days."

"Whatever does he mean?" Isabella turned accusing eyes up at Hugo. "What is he talking about, Your Lordship?"

Hugo, reluctant to bring up Finnula's name, which had been bandied about much too liberally for his liking in recent conversation, only shrugged dismissively. "You'll remember what I said, monsieur," he said, leveling a deadly glare at the bailiff. "No later than noon tomorrow."

Hugo did not need to add, *Or you'll live to regret it*. The threat was there, in his voice, without the need to speak the words.

"But, my lord, I beg you—"

A heavy hand fell upon Reginald Laroche's shoulder, and the bailiff turned angrily, only to find himself staring up into the shire reeve's wide, bearded face.

"Conduct me to your account books, my dear fellow," John ordered him, pleasantly enough. "And if you can find a skin or two of wine along the way, all the better."

"But—" Reginald called after Hugo, who'd already turned and was heading for the doors. "My lord, wait—"

But Hugo was outside, in the cool evening air, before the bailiff got out another word. Inhaling deeply, Hugo filled his lungs with the scent of pine and wood smoke, the English night sounds as familiar to him as his own voice. Somewhere, a nightingale trilled a thrilling song, and nearby, another answered. This, then, was what he had missed those cold nights in the desert. Not his family, not his home, but good English countryside, the warning hoot of a wood owl, the soft lowing of the milk cow in the stable. This, then, was what he'd come home to. And this was what he would share with Finnula, and their children, God willing.

Hugo looked in the direction of the stables, and was about to

go and kick his squire awake, assuming that the young jackanapes had passed out from his excesses, when a small voice
stopped him.

"You're leavin', then?"

The towheaded boy appeared as if from nowhere, and Hugo
squinted down at the lad's shabby tunic and threadbare chausses,
his dirty cheeks and wide, hazel eyes.

"Just for a little while," Hugo said calmly. "I'll be back after
your bedtime."

"I can go to bed whenever I want," Jamie assured him. "I'll
wait for you."

Hugo lifted an eyebrow. "As you wish then."

Strolling toward the stables, Hugo had the distinct impression
the boy was following him, and when he turned and caught the
child stooping, pretending to be interested in a mouser that had
been strolling nearby, he asked curiously, "Who do you belong
to, young man?"

"What, sir?" The boy gulped, looking up from the cat's tabby
back. "Me?"

"Yes, you. Whose are you? Mistress Laver's? Laroche's?"

"Oh, no, sir," the boy cried, straightening to his full height.
"I'm yours."

Hugo nodded, unimpressed. Some scullery maid had got herself with child and dropped this pup among them. Hugo would
pay for the lad's upkeep until the day he died. Unless, of course,
he could apprentice him out. The lad looked sturdy enough,
though undeniably dirty.

"Right, then," Hugo said, rubbing his chin. It had been so long
since he'd gone smooth-shaven that he still wasn't quite used to
it. "There's something you can do for me while I'm gone."

The boy nodded eagerly. "What, sir?"

"You can keep an eye on Sheriff de Brissac. See that he doesn't doze off or anything, before I return. You see, lad, I'm making Monsieur Laroche and his daughter clear out, and I don't want them playing any nasty tricks on me—"

"I understand, sir," the boy said. "I won't let anything happen to the sheriff. He's nice to me, Sheriff de Brissac. Takes me fishing."

Hugo raised his eyebrows at that, but refrained from comment. Instead, he tossed the lad a coin, which the boy caught expertly.

"Good lad," was all Hugo said, and then he went in search of his squire.

# Chapter Twelve

$\mathcal{D}$inner at the millhouse that night was a draining affair. Shire tradition dictated that Hugo wasn't to sit near or speak to the bride-to-be until the wedding, and since it was Finnula alone that drew him from his own hearth, this was disappointing, to say the least.

Shire tradition further dictated that Hugo, as the bridegroom, be subjected to numerous humiliations enacted by Finnula's family. While her brothers-in-law held Hugo in too much awe to play pranks upon him, their wives did not hesitate to tease him, at every opportunity, about Finnula's capture of him, both literally and figuratively. That, coupled with his unease over what had occurred with Laroche—he had come so close to killing the man, after swearing off violence forever, that he could still feel the longing quake in his limbs—made Hugo a surly dinner guest, and he did not smile once during the whole of the dinner, a fact the impertinent Patricia pointed out to him.

"Verily, for a bridegroom, you look glum, my lord," she teased.

Hugo looked the sharp-tongued woman straight in the eye— eyes the same color as Finnula's, actually, but lacking the warmth and humor he'd become accustomed to seeing in gray irises— and said, simply, "When she is mine I will rejoice. Until then, I dare not."

Patricia had only looked sly. "It seems to me," she'd said archly, "'tis Finnula you ought to be tellin' that to, my lord, not me."

Hugo looked across the wide wooden table, its surface whitened from so many vigorous scrubbings, at Finnula, who was protesting quite strenuously something her brother had said. Her color high, she pounded the tabletop, insisting that the papal ban on crossbows had been misinterpreted from the start. What sort of woman was this that he was marrying, whose conversation consisted of hunting techniques and weaponry rather than babies and pie recipes?

Hugo grinned for the first time all evening, suddenly inordinately pleased with himself. Exactly the sort of woman with whom he wanted to spend the rest of his life, that's what sort she was. What interest had he in babies and pie? None at all.

He watched Finnula's easy banter with her brothers-in-law and envied her her family. Even though there was the irritable Robert and the vapid Mellana to consider, overall, the Crais brood was a happy one, the sort of family Hugo had always longed for. If he and Finnula could produce a family as large and as boisterous, he'd die a happy man indeed.

It was close to midnight when the very loud and drunken party broke up, and Hugo, after an attempt to kiss Finnula good night that was thwarted by her giggling sisters, found his way to his horse. He mounted and pointed Skinner in the direction of the manor house, reflecting that, considering what awaited him there, he ought not to have had quite so much to drink. Ah, well, tomorrow he would be well-rid of the Laroches, replacing them with a winsome wench who had already proven herself a worthy wife.

It wasn't a trick of the moonlight or of the vast amount of ale he'd consumed that evoked an image of that very person before him, however. Somehow, Finnula had managed to evade her sisters, and was gesturing to him from the shadow of a large oak tree behind which she'd hidden herself.

Hugo urged Skinner to her side, and leaned down to grasp the hands she stretched toward him.

"Step on my boot toe," he whispered, and Finnula did as he bade her, swinging easily into the saddle before him, with the athletic grace of a cat.

"Good evening," Hugo said, and smiled, wrapping strong arms about her waist and nuzzling her neck beneath the vast amounts of flowing red hair.

"Good morning, you mean," said his bride-to-be.

"Aren't you risking rather a lot, sneaking out to meet me like this?" Hugo wanted to know, noticing that she still wore the green bliaut, though, unfortunately, its neckline was no longer twisted so interestingly. "Won't the wrath of your sisters rain down upon us if we're caught?"

"Don't be stupid," Finnula said. In the moonlight, which was very strong, Hugo saw that her pretty face had grown troubled.

"What is it?" he demanded, groaning inwardly. He had already bedded her multiple times that day, and he didn't think he had the stamina to go again. Bedding her seemed to be the only way, however, he could keep her in line.

"I just—" Finnula craned her neck to look up at him, her gray eyes wide and shining in the moonlight. "I just wanted—"

Hugo smiled and stroked her hair. "You wanted what? To tell me again how very much you don't want to be my bride?"

Finnula frowned. "I thought perhaps you might have reconsidered."

"Will being wedded to me be such a hardship?" Hugo could not help swearing beneath his breath. "Faith, I never met a maid so loath to wed. Generally, 'tis the only thought in a wench's head!"

"I have many thoughts in my head," Finnula said, indignantly. "And none of them concerns weddings."

"No, but I'll wager a good many of them concern things only a married woman ought know." He frowned down at her. "You need a husband more than any lass I ever saw. 'Tis a wonder to me you remained a virgin as long as you did—"

Finnula gasped and struggled against him. "Forsooth! What are you saying? That I'm wanton?"

"You most certainly are." Hugo chuckled, keeping a firm grip on her. "But fortunately, thus far I've been the only man to catch on to it. And, being of a chivalrous bent, I intend to make an honest woman of you. So count your blessings—" He gave her a hearty kiss, then slapped her backside as she scrambled angrily down from his saddle. "And don't get up to mischief between now and the wedding."

Huffing indignantly, Finnula whirled around to leave him, but Hugo leaned down and caught a handful of her gown, stopping her short. She looked back at him, her cheeks, even in the silver moonlight, aflame.

"What?" she demanded.

"Remember, Finn. You gave your word."

She grimaced. "I know it," she snarled, and snatched her train from him. "I'll be there."

Hugo laughed and let her go, watching amusedly as she stalked across the yard and into the millhouse, where she gave the door a healthy slam. Little witch! Lord, how she made him laugh. No other woman of his acquaintance had ever delighted him as much.

Hugo was able to hold on to his good spirits all the way back to the manor house, where he found, to his astonishment, that the stables were filled with horses. Further inspection revealed that the Great Hall was crowded with men Hugo didn't recognize, all of whom had gathered round the long dining table, at the head of which sat John de Brissac, roaringly drunk and keeping one heavy hand on the shoulder of a very dour-looking Reginald Laroche.

"Ah, His Lordship, at long last!" Sheriff de Brissac staggered to his feet, the chair in which he'd sat falling over backward. His deep voice boomed through the vast hall. "Gentlemen, raise your cup. Here comes Lord Hugo Geoffrey Fitzstephen, seventh Earl of Stephensgate."

Chair legs scraped against flagstone as each man stood, holding a flagon aloft and looking pointedly in Hugo's direction. Hugo was just drunk enough to burst into guffaws.

"De Brissac," he managed to snort, between brays. "What welcome is this? Who are these men?"

Grinning a bit self-consciously, the sheriff shrugged. "My men, of course. It's been a long while since the wine cellars of Stephensgate Manor were opened—"

Hugo was still laughing when a chalice was thrust into his hand. Each of John de Brissac's deputies—and there appeared to be over twenty of them—tipped his flagon in Hugo's direction.

"Long life to you, Hugo Fitzstephen," the sheriff declared. "And much happiness with your little bride, the Fair Finn—"

"To the Fair Finn!"

The lusty cry echoed throughout the hall, and then the men drank, all except Reginald Laroche, who had not risen with the

others, and looked, in fact, as if he was not feeling well. When
Hugo had drained his own cup, he approached John de Brissac
and asked after the bailiff's health.

"What, him?" The sheriff looked down at Monsieur Laroche
with distaste. "Ah, he's feeling no pain, believe you me. Showed
me his books, he did, and what receipts he didn't burn in the
great bonfire you might have noticed when we walked in earlier
today."

Reginald Laroche looked up at Hugo, and the hatred burning
in his eyes was palpable.

"Welcome back, my liege," he sneered, clearly the only sober
person in the room. "Might I have your leave to retire? There is
much still needs doing if my daughter and I are to be away from
here before noon tomorrow—"

Hugo was feeling the effects of the wine on top of all the ale
he'd consumed, and he waved dismissively at his father's former
bailiff.

"Get thee gone," he said. When Laroche scurried to obey him,
Hugo leaned over and requested that a few of the sheriff's men
be assigned to watch the man, a request that de Brissac instantly
honored, sending three men, armed with a skin of wine, to keep
an eye upon the former bailiff.

It was after two in the morning when Hugo finally mounted
the stairs to the second floor, where the bedchambers lay. He
wasn't precisely staggering, but did have to lean rather heavily on
the banister. Below him, John de Brissac snored before the fire,
as did a number of his men. Hugo had found young Jamie curled
on a pile of dusty pelts in a far corner, and laid his cloak over the
boy, to protect him from the spring chill. The manor house was
quiet, and Hugo, guided by the light of a torch he'd lifted from a
sconce upon the wall, searched for a bed upon which he could lay
his spinning head.

His father's former solar was out of the question. Hugo would not spend the night in the bed where Lord Geoffrey had died. His brother's solar held bitter memories as well, for it was there that he'd been urged—nay, nagged—to join a monastery time and time again. Hugo finally decided that his old room, a drafty corner space that was lovely in summer but in winter was impossible to warm, would suit until he could have an addition applied to the house.

He found the room not unlike he'd left it ten years earlier, down to the threadbare blue velvet bed curtains and battered wolf-pelt spread. The space needed airing, and so Hugo opened the wooden shutters over both windows, neither of which had ever been glassed in, and inhaled the fresh English night air for a few moments before stripping naked and pulling back the musty pelts that covered the wide bed.

He had just extinguished the torch and slid between the cool sheets when a soft tap sounded upon his door. Hugo, annoyed, barked, "What is it?"

The portal eased open, and a circle of light that could only have been thrown from a wax candle spilled across a far wall, revealing a tapestry Hugo hadn't noticed before but recognized as his mother's stitching.

"Who's there?" Hugo demanded, sitting up in bed and narrowing his eyes against the candle's bright glow.

A slim hand, clutching the candle, appeared from behind the heavy door, attached to a slender arm clothed in a sleeve of some diaphanous material. At first, a fuzzy-headed Hugo thought he was being visited by the fair ghost of a long-dead ancestor, but then he remembered that ghosts had no need of candles. And when his early morning visitor stepped fully into the room, he recognized her, despite the fact that the long black hair was loose about her shoulders and the rouge had been toned down somewhat.

"Lord Hugo," Isabella Laroche whispered, her dark eyelashes

fluttering. "Oh, Lord Hugo, I thought you were never coming to bed. I must speak with you, my lord!"

Hugo couldn't help grinning. "Speak with me?" He chuckled, taking in the girl's attire, which consisted of a slim sheath of a gown of the thinnest possible silk, covered by a robe that might have been made of gossamer, for all it hid from the eye. Isabella was not dressed for conversation, but for something quite a bit more intimate.

"Oh, Cousin Hugo," Isabella breathed, coming toward his bed, the candle held high. "I am so afraid there has been some misunderstanding—"

"There most certainly has been," he said, lifting an eyebrow at the way the girl's bosom was rising and falling dramatically beneath her nightdress. "Apparently, you've lost your way, and wandered into my solar by mistake. You had best hurry on back to your own bed, cousin, before a chill takes you. You are hardly dressed for visiting."

Isabella ignored his warning and rested one bold knee against his mattress, a hand flattened to her bosom provocatively.

"Oh, Lord Hugo," she cried softly. "My father tells me that you have commanded him to leave this house by noon tomorrow—"

"Today, actually," Hugo corrected her dryly.

"But I cannot believe this to be truth! My lord, this has been my home for half my life. Surely there must be something I can do to change your mind?"

As she said the word "something," Isabella lowered her back-side onto the bed, and, leaning upon one hand, fluttered her eyelashes at Hugo again. Hugo, who had never seen such an inept attempt at seduction, hid a smile.

"Nay, demoiselle, there is naught you can do. Return to your chamber now, as I have need of a good night's rest—"

"If I may be so bold to suggest it," Isabella whispered, reaching out and running a finger down one of Hugo's darkly tanned arms, "I might be able to help make your night's rest very good indeed—"

Again, Hugo could not stifle a grin. "Oh? And how might you do that?"

The finger tangled in the coarse mat of hair upon his bare chest. "I think we both know that, Cousin Hugo." Isabella smiled suggestively, her rouged lips parting to reveal a pink and darting tongue. "I have been chatelaine of this manor for some time now. I would be invaluable to you in that respect, as well as . . . others . . ."

Hugo did not need to venture as to what others she meant, for her dark-eyed gaze dipped boldly to where the sheet covered his lap. All at once, Hugo was no longer amused. He wondered if the girl's father had put her up to this, and despised the man even more for using his daughter in such a manner. Then Hugo remembered the contempt in which Isabella Laroche was held by Finnula and her sisters, and he wondered if her father had, in actuality, had anything to do with this early morning visitation.

"Mademoiselle Laroche," he said carefully. "Have you any idea why I am so badly in need of a good night's rest?"

She shook her head, dark hair falling about her face in an ebony wave.

"Tomorrow I am to be wed."

That stopped her finger from drawing little circles upon his chest. "Wed?" she echoed, in quite a different tone than she'd employed before. "But you are only just returned to—"

"Aye. But the fact remains. Tomorrow I wed."

"I don't believe you." Isabella snatched her hand away. "That is a deliberate lie. Who do you wed?"

Hugo smiled. "Finnula Crais."

"Finnula—" Isabella leaped from the bed, her beautiful face

contorted as if she were choking. "Finnula Crais?" she screeched. "Are you mad? Have you taken leave of your senses? Finnula Crais was married to—"

"My father, I know." A wave of tiredness overcame Hugo, and he heartily wished the girl would continue her histrionics elsewhere. "Good night, demoiselle."

"That witch!" Isabella spat. "That little witch! First Lord Geoffrey, now you. I don't understand it. It's got to be witchcraft!"

"Far from it," Hugo said coldly. "Now, if you'd be so kind as to—"

*Close the door on your way out* was what Hugo was going to say, but he found the words unnecessary as the enraged woman stalked from his chamber, giving his door a very hard slam behind her. Darkness once again fell over Hugo's bedroom, and he sighed, and lay back down upon the pillows. He sincerely hoped that Finnula had no compunction about using her bow upon feminine adversaries, because, judging from the look on Isabella Laroche's face, such action might very well prove necessary.

*D*awn had just turned the eastern sky rosy and sent the birds in the treetops into their shrill morning cacophony when Finnula crept down the stairs from her bedroom. Avoiding the bottom step, the one that creaked so, even though she knew perfectly well that the entire household was still abed, she stole into the kitchen, where she skewered a hunk of black bread with her knife and gnawed on one end of it while tugging on her boots. She had just downed a cup of leftover ale and was wiping her lips on her sleeve when the back door swung open and, to her dismay, Robert came in.

"What ho," he said cheerfully, seeing that his little sister wore both braies and quiver. "Going a-hunting on your wedding day? Forsooth, Finn."

She glared at him. What was he doing up so early? Last night's feast ought to have rendered him semiconscious. He'd drunk over two pitchers of ale on his own. Why wasn't he prostrate in bed, moaning?

Lowering a heavy bag of flour he'd had slung over his back, Robert straightened and eyed the small bundle that rested on the bench by Finnula's hip.

"Not running away, are we, Finn?" Loping toward her, Robert reached for the bundle, but Finnula snatched it from his reach, holding the cloth bag to her chest.

"What if I am?" she demanded hotly. "Are you going to stop me?"

"I'll most certainly try." Robert sat down where the bundle had rested, too close for Finnula's comfort. She scooted farther on down the bench. "What can you be thinkin', love? Runnin' away from Lord Hugo? I thought you liked the fellow."

Finnula scowled at the stone floor. "I do," she admitted.

"Then what do you want to run away for? Has the man hurt you in some way?"

Finnula shook her head.

"Cheated you somehow?"

Again, a negative shake of her head.

"Robbed you?"

Finnula considered confessing that Hugo had indeed robbed her of her maidenhead, but remembering that it was Robert she was speaking to, she thought it wiser to remain silent. Besides, she hadn't exactly been robbed of her virginity. She had, more accurately, thrust it at Hugo, in a manner that still caused her to blush when she recalled it.

"Then what is the matter?" Robert wanted to know. "He seems a fine man to me. I know you don't want to be married to another Fitzstephen, but the son's a spot better than the father, don't you think?"

Sullenly, Finnula shrugged.

"So what are you running away for? You should be the happiest girl in the shire. You've snagged yourself a rich and handsome husband. Mellana is beside herself with jealousy."

Finnula lifted her head and said, "But that's just it, Robert. He *is* rich and handsome. He could have any woman he wanted. So why *me*?"

"Why you?" Robert looked down at his little sister with a constricted brow. "What do you mean, why you?"

"What I said. Why me? I'm not rich. I'm not beautiful. I've got nothing that would tempt a man like Lord Hugo—"

"Obviously you've got something," Robert interrupted. "Or the man wouldn't be marrying you."

"I don't know why he's marrying me," Finnula insisted. "Except that he said he couldn't get me any other way."

Robert's eyebrows lifted at that. "Ah," he said. "He loves you, then."

"Loves me? Bah!" Finnula sprang up from the bench, violently pitching her bundle into a far corner of the kitchen. "I have yet to hear any such sentiment from his lips. Love! He knows not the meaning of the word."

She saw her brother smile. "Ah," Robert said again, passing a hand over his mouth to hide a smirk. "So that's the way of it, then?"

"What do you mean?" Finnula stamped a booted foot. "What do you mean, that's the way of it?"

"Only that you're quibbling over trifles," Robert said. He leaned back, so that his spine rested against the tabletop. "You want him to declare his undying devotion to you, to go about crying how much he needs you, as if he were Mellana's bloody troubadour. You want him to write verse praising your beauty and sing songs of unrequited—"

"God's teeth, Robert," Finnula said scornfully. "That isn't what I want, and you know it. A simple 'I love you, Finnula' would suffice."

"That's what all you women want," Robert disagreed, in disgust. "You want romance. You want flattery. Well, the only way you're going to get those things out of Lord Hugo is if you play the part."

Finnula, who'd been pacing the kitchen with a scowl upon her face, halted and stared at her older brother. "Play the part? What part?"

"The part of the fair damsel," Robert said, waving a dismissive hand. "The highborn lady, with the creamy white skin and helplessly fluttering eyelids."

"What?" Finnula looked at him as if he were demented. "What are you talking about? What about my eyelids?"

"Finnula, if you want him to sing the praises of your beauty, you've got to look beautiful . . . or at least look like a *woman*, for God's sake. Bashing about in those leather braies isn't going to inspire words of worship from him." Robert stared at her critically. "And why don't you do something with your hair, instead of tying it up in that donkey's tail?" Finnula's hands flew defensively to her braid. "Can't you wear it down, with some gewgaws in it? Mellana knows how to do it—"

"And look where it's gotten her," Finnula observed, dryly.

"Precisely. Finnula, I don't know why you're feeling so sorry for yourself. You've got your man. If he isn't everything you'd like him to be, 'tis up to you to change him. That's what you women seem most keen on, anyway."

Fingering her braid, Finnula stared at him. Surprisingly, her brother's words made a certain amount of sense. She certainly hadn't acted much like a maiden worth worshipping; more like a maiden in need of a horsewhipping.

"Rather than running away," Robert said, with a glance at her bag, crumpled in the corner by the woodpile, "why don't you stay and fight for what you want?"

Finnula had no reply for that. Instead, she crossed her arms over her chest and, leaning on one hip, regarded her brother with narrowed eyes. "You knew I'd try to run away this morning, didn't you?" she demanded. "That's why you got up so early. You didn't really have work to do at the mill, did you?"

"Lord Hugo warned me you'd try to make a run for it," he admitted, with a grin.

Finnula inhaled sharply. "What? He *told* you—"

"He mentioned something last night." Robert stretched out his long legs, crossing them at the ankles and looking, for the first time, like a man with a headache.

Finnula snorted disgustedly. "Well, I like that! After I gave him my word!"

"A lot of good your word is," Robert sneered. "You tried to make a break for it in spite of your promise not to."

Her shoulders slumped dejectedly, Finnula sank down onto the bench beside him. After a short silence, during which both brother and sister studied their boots, she asked, shyly, "Robert?"

"Aye, Finn."

"Will you help me?"

"Help you what, Finn?"

"To act more . . . maidenly."

Robert made a face. "Can't you ask one of the girls? You've got five sisters to choose from. Four of 'em've already won husbands, so they obviously know what they're doing. Why ask me?"

"Because." Finnula swung her legs back and forth, in the same manner as when she'd been small. "I trust you most. Please?"

Robert sighed. "Finnula, my head's about to split in two—" Seeing his little sister's crestfallen expression, he sighed. "Oh, very well. Though what you think I know about these kinds of things, I can't imagine . . ."

As it happened, Robert Crais knew a great deal about those kinds of things. After granting him a reprieve of a few more hours of sleep, Finnula consulted him regarding her toilette—hair straight or curled? up or down? were her fingernails clean enough?—and her wardrobe—was her kirtle too tight? her bliaut too loose? flowers or jeweled combs in her hair?—and found that after twenty-five years in a household full of women, her brother had garnered a vast wealth of opinions on such matters. When his sisters were through scrubbing, anointing, perfuming, grooming and dressing their youngest sibling, Robert inspected the results and found, with a minor adjustment here and there, that Finnula passed muster.

"I don't know why you think you aren't beautiful," was his comment, when Finnula, resplendent in her wedding clothes, made her final trip down the stairs from her bedroom.

Looking down at herself with skeptically raised eyebrows, Finnula said, "What, me? Mel's the beauty in the family, Robert."

Robert snorted. His headache had not gone away, and he'd been forced to imbibe in some hair of the dog in order to temper it. Tankard in hand, he circled Finnula, critically examining every aspect of her habiliment.

Her wedding clothes were not new, though they'd been worn only once before, nearly a year ago to the day. A simple white kirtle of the finest linen fit her with glovelike closeness. Over that she wore a bliaut of white samite, with sleeves so wide and full that they fell almost to the floor. Around her waist was anchored a girdle of silver-link, her only ornament, save a coronet of fresh wildflowers that had been twined through her loosely flowing auburn curls.

Finnula looked, to Robert, like every man's dream of a blushing bride. Satisfying himself on a single point, he demanded that she lift her skirts to her knees, and when he saw only bare leg and no braies, he relaxed.

"Well, Finn." He hiccupped. "You've outdone yourself. A more beautiful bride I've never seen."

This assertion caused indignation among the other Crais sisters, who'd gathered in the kitchen to view the results of their morning's labor, but Robert waved their protests away.

"She's got the richest groom," he insisted. "That makes her the prettiest. And now, if mine ears don't deceive me, that's the church bell, tollin' the hour. Methinks Her Ladyship's carriage awaits."

Finnula's sisters ushered her into the yard, where their husbands waited with a dogcart festooned with ribbon and flowers. Following village tradition, the dogcart was hitched to a small white donkey, and though Finnula balked at actually seating herself in such an undignified conveyance, she gave in with ill grace eventually, and the merry party—many of whom were holding pitchers of Mel's Brew even as they approached the church—made their way to the pulpit.

# Chapter Fourteen

The banging sound that woke Hugo shortly before noon was not, he soon discovered, a result of the pounding within his own skull. No, someone was knocking on the door to his solar, and the throbbing in his head was the result of either too much wine or too much ale—or rather, too much of both.

Lying perfectly still, Hugo stared up at the cobwebs in the canopy over his bed and bellowed, "Enter!" He instantly regretted bellowing, even before he saw that his visitor was neither comely nor carrying anything edible.

The boy Jamie peered at his new lord with very wide eyes as he approached the great bed. "Hello," he said warily. "Sheriff de Brissac sent me to wake you. Said as you wouldn't be likely to throw anything at a wee lad like myself."

Hugo, glowering at the boy with bloodshot eyes, said, "John's right. Now what'd he send you to wake me for?"

"Monsieur Laroche and his daughter're leavin'," the boy said amiably. "The sheriff thought you might want to bid 'em farewell."

Hugo groaned. The last thing he needed was another scene like the one last night involving the Laroche wench. But he had a duty as lord of the manor, and so, head pounding, his joints creaking in protest, he rose from the bed, and even managed to find a clean pair of braies and a tunic to cover his nakedness.

All this was observed by the boy Jamie, whom, Hugo noted, wore exactly what he'd had on the day before and didn't look as if he'd seen a bit of soap in his lifetime. He also didn't appear to have anything in particular to do except stare at Hugo as *he* washed, and this was somewhat annoying.

"Who do you belong to, little man?" Hugo asked, eyeing the scamp as he shaved.

"Why, I already told you. To you, my lord," the boy answered promptly.

Hugo rolled his eyes. "But what function do you perform here at the manor house?" Hugo asked. "Do you help Mistress Laver in the kitchens? Give old Webster a hand with the horses? What?"

"All those things." The boy shrugged. "There's naught I ain't been asked to do except help Mam'selle Isabella with her toilette—"

"Ah." Hugo grimaced. "I would guess not."

His own toilette complete, the earl fastened on his belt, making sure his sword was attached to it, in case he was called upon to look intimidating. Then he headed down the stairs, to see his cousin off.

In the stable yard he found Reginald Laroche and his daughter slumped upon the seat of a rude wagon, surrounded by Sheriff de Brissac's men, none of whom looked as if their heads hurt any less than Hugo's. The back of the wagon was filled with bric-a-brac that might or might not have originally belonged to the Laroches—indeed, Hugo saw a tapestry he thought quite probably had belonged to his mother. But he was too hungover for much arguing, and after checking to make sure that at least the horses pulling the vehicle weren't his own, he slapped one on the rump and couldn't stifle a grin.

"So," he said to the Laroches. "Know you yet where you go? For I'll be expecting full recompense in the coming year—"

"I know it," snarled the former bailiff. The man looked almost as bad as Hugo felt. Dark circles rimmed his eyes, and his hair appeared not to have seen a comb in some time. "I told Sheriff de Brissac."

The sheriff, standing with his thumbs hooked into his belt, opened an eye swollen from lack of sleep and too much ale and said, "Aye. He's got a sister in Leesbury. Says she's married to a cousin of—What was it now, Laroche?"

Reginald Laroche eyed Hugo bitterly. "Cousin of the queen's favorite lady-in-waiting. The King will hear of this outrage, Cousin Hugo. Rest assured."

"Ah." Hugo smiled. "And no doubt, when he does hear of it, the King will take your side? I think not, monsieur."

The sheriff chuckled. "In any case, we'll be able to find 'im, if we need to. But we won't need to, am I right, Laroche? Because you're going to be makin' those payments to 'Is Lordship in a timely manner, or into the jailhouse you'll go . . ."

"You'll be hearing from me," Laroche snarled. "I guarantee it."

Beside him, Isabella lifted a wimpled head, and Hugo saw that her face was splotchy with tears, her fine black eyes red from crying. She was dressed in what undoubtedly were her oldest clothes, and looked no more like the vibrant beauty of yester eve than Fat Maude.

"You'll hear from us," she shouted, quite vehemently, at Hugo. "You vile, horrible man!"

Hugo quirked up an eyebrow. He hadn't been called a vile, horrible man since . . . Well, probably since the last time he'd seen Finnula. Quite used by now to being reviled by young women, he only snapped his heels together and gave the girl a mocking bow.

"Mademoiselle," he said. "I wish you the best. If I may offer this piece of advice—"

"You may not," snapped Isabella.

"—abandon your father at the earliest opportunity. Marry an honest man, if one can be found who'll have you, and use your talents and beauty for good, not mischief."

Isabella pursed her lips as if she were about to spit, and Hugo stepped fleetly out of the projectile's path.

"Ah," Sheriff de Brissac cried, coming out of his stupor with a laugh. "She's got spirit, that one!"

"Verily," Hugo agreed, looking down at the glistening globule that had landed just inches from his feet.

Reginald Laroche whipped his horses, and the wagon lurched forward, causing some items in the back of the cart to tinkle ominously. Isabella cried out for her father to stop so that she could better pack whatever was threatening to break, but Laroche ignored her. The undignified processional disappeared through the manor house gates, and the moment it did so, a cheer erupted from the general area of the kitchens.

Hugo glanced around and saw Mistress Laver and the aged groom, Webster, standing side by side, looking after the departing Laroches with delighted grins across their faces.

"Good riddance to ye," Mistress Laver called.

"Don't come back soon!" Webster rasped.

Hugo, his eyebrows lifted to their limits, glanced at the sheriff. "I see there's no love lost between the servants and my father's cousin," he observed.

"Cheated them out of their wages every chance he got," de Brissac said mildly. "'Tis a wonder they stayed as long as they did. Waited for you, I think, my lord."

"And they shall be rewarded," Hugo declared, and, making good on his promise, he called to the ancient groom and the somewhat less aged cook and, thanking them for their faithful service, poured a small fortune from a pouch at his hip into the palms he had them cup.

Mistress Laver was beside herself with gratitude, but Webster managed a toothy grin, and a pull on his forelock. "I seen as 'ow it would be, m'lord, the minute I seed you in the yard last night," he said, through toothless gums. "I tol' that squire o' yours, 'im won't be lettin' that Frenchman walk all over 'im like 'is father did, mark me words, nor did ye. Bless ye, m'lord!"

"I shall be asking for your blessings again later this afternoon," Hugo said. "I intend to bring my bride here anon, and will need your help in making her feel at home."

"Your bride!" cried Mistress Laver, clapping her hands. She'd shoved the gold he'd given her deep into her apron pockets. "What a 'appy day indeed! I'll need to get straight to work, then, if it's a wedding feast that's called for. Might I have your leave, m'lord, to ask in my nieces to 'elp?"

"Ask as many of your relatives as you feel necessary, Mistress Laver," Hugo said, with a wave of his hand. "'Tis not just a wedding feast we'll be needing, but this entire house aired out, if we're to live here comfortably. See that something gets done about the dust in there, if you would. And the cobwebs. And the mice—"

"And the empty wineskins," the sheriff added, thoughtfully.

Mistress Laver clapped her hands again, she was in such high spirits, and set off with a great many mutterings about carpets and seedcakes and bed linens. Old Webster shuffled away, and it occurred to Hugo that a member of his household was missing. He had only, it seemed, to glance right or left and there stood Jamie, his dirty face blinking up at him.

"And where is my trusty squire this fine morning?" Hugo inquired.

"He's asleep in the washtub," was Jamie's chirpy reply. "He had a whole barrelful of wine to drink last night, and snored enough to wake the hounds—"

Grimacing, Hugo ran a hand through his long hair, and noticed that Sheriff de Brissac was signaling for his men to mount up.

"With your leave, my lord, we'll escort you to the church and then some of us'll be off," John de Brissac said, with a mighty yawn he didn't even bother to stifle. "Only got an hour or so of sleep last night, what with keepin' an eye on your man, and whatnot—"

"But you'll all return tonight for more whatnot," Hugo urged. "If there's any wine left in my cellars, I hope to drink to the health of the new Lady Stephensgate."

"You couldn't keep me away, my lord." The sheriff grinned.

And so it was that Hugo arrived at his wedding under armed escort, a hungover squire at his side and a painful throbbing behind his own right eye. The headache let up a little, however, when he glimpsed his bride waiting for him quietly in the nave, looking even more angelic than she had that stormy night in the hostelry, when he'd sworn to himself to make her his own.

Indeed, if it hadn't been for a familiar glint of rebelliousness in those gray eyes, Hugo would have thought some sort of devilry afoot, for the girl who met him at the altar was even more beautiful

than he remembered Finnula Crais to be. She looked so feminine
and even ladylike in her spotless white gown, it was hard to imagine that this winsome wench had ever held him at knifepoint. She
repeated her vows in a soft voice, hardly ever glancing in Hugo's
direction, and he was left to suppose that one of her nosy sisters
had got hold of her, and filled her full of lies about how a proper
wife ought to behave. He had every confidence that by evening,
she'd be his own Finnula again. He wondered if she was wearing
the leather braies beneath her bridal gown, and looked forward
to the moment when they were alone, and he'd be able to find out
for himself.

By the time they were pronounced man and wife, the little
church of Stephensgate was as packed as ever Hugo'd seen it,
jammed not only with Finnula's innumerable relatives, but by
his own vassals, who'd somehow heard of the impending nuptials
and had shown up in droves to wish the couple well. There were
so many people present that they couldn't all fit in the pews, and
spilled out into the aisles and even into the churchyard. When
Hugo, as directed by Father Edward, bent to kiss the bride, a
cheer erupted that fairly shook the rafters.

And then the earl and his bride were caught up in a surge of
well-wishers, who pressed forward with earnest congratulations,
and at length, Hugo was forced to bellow an invitation to one and
all to sup at the manor house, simply in order to clear a path out
of the church.

Outside in the fine spring air Finnula looked, if such a thing
were possible, even more lovely. But as Hugo had expected,
her usual asperity was not hidden deep beneath that virtuous
exterior.

"What can you be thinking, inviting all these people to dine?"
she demanded, as he placed her on the saddle before him. "Mistress Laver can't be expecting them—"

"As it happens, my love, she is," Hugo said, slipping an arm around his wife's narrow waist. She blushed delightfully at the contact, as if the two of them had never so much as kissed before. Hugo couldn't help grinning, anticipating an interesting wedding night. "And if you can convince Mellana to provide us with a barrel or two of ale, we ought to get by admirably—"

Finnula scowled darkly at the mention of her sister's name. Hugo's invitation had served to empty the church, but one late arrival had captured the attention of Robert Crais and his brothers-in-law. Word of the wedding had not only reached the ears of Hugo's vassals, but had stretched to outlying villages, bringing such unlikely hangers-on as a traveling tinker, hoping to make a few sales, and several wandering minstrels, one of whom turned out to be none other than Jack Mallory.

It was as they were thanking Father Edward for agreeing to conduct the ceremony on such short notice—an act for which Hugo had seen the church was amply compensated—that a whisper in the crowd first alerted Robert to the presence of Mellana's lover. Though he might have thought differently, fortune was smiling upon Jack Mallory that day, in that the shire reeve was present. John de Brissac alone kept the minstrel from being killed outright by his lover's enraged brother, for the troubadour was greeted not with applause and tossed coins, as custom dictated, but with fists and boot toes.

Sheriff de Brissac broke up the fight before Mallory suffered too many contusions, but there was no calming down the shrieking Mellana.

"Murderer!" she cried at her brother, throwing her arms around the semiconscious minstrel. "Look what you've done! His beautiful face! Oh, Jack, your face!"

Robert, brushing off his hands, regarded his handiwork with satisfaction. "He's not dead," he said, and there was no denying the regret in his voice. "Not yet, anyway. But when I get him to work for me at the mill, he'll be wishin' he were."

"Oh, you brute, you brute," Mellana moaned. She buried her golden head in Jack Mallory's neck, and made a very pretty picture there in the churchyard, with her bright skirts spread upon the ground, and her lover's body in her arms.

"Am I to take it that there's soon to be another wedding in the Crais family?" Father Edward stepped forward to inquire, eagerly anticipating a full collection box.

"You can stake your surplice on it, Father," was Robert's acerbic reply. "Soon as the groom comes to, we'll be needin' your prayer book opened again."

"Ah," said the priest, and he made the sign of the cross over the troubadour's supine body, hoping to speed along the fellow's recovery, as Father Edward was anxious not to miss any of the revelry up at the manor house.

Finnula, who'd bucked against Hugo in her eagerness to join her brother in the minstrel's beating, complained bitterly all the way back to the manor house, insisting that she hadn't wanted to hurt Mallory much—just a few kicks. Hugo, however, would have no part in the squabble, having sworn off violence. Besides, he secretly harbored a feeling of gratitude toward the troubadour, who, in impregnating Mellana, had been the reason behind Finnula's abduction of himself. Hugo could not but be thankful to a man who had brought him such unexpected bounty, and he had already resolved to reward the minstrel somehow, as soon as he regained consciousness.

By the time they reached the manor house, however, Finnula had nearly forgotten her pique. It was difficult to pout when one was jouncing along the road in the arms of one's new husband, especially when the legs of Hugo's mount were surrounded by village children and Finnula's own nieces and nephews, bearing garlands and singing songs. It wasn't until Hugo turned in the saddle to shoo some of them away—they were intent upon humiliating his noble mount by entwining wildflowers in his mane and tail—that he noticed they were also followed by the largest, ugliest dog Hugo had ever seen.

"What," Hugo cried, noticing that none of the children seemed particularly frightened of the beast, "is *that*?"

Finnula glanced casually over one shoulder. "That? That's a dog."

"I can see that it's a dog. Why is it following you?"

"He's my hunting dog, Gros Louis," Finnula said stiffly, "and of course he's going with me to the manor house. My sisters didn't much care for him, and made him sleep in the barn, but I was hoping, being a man of the world, you'd have a more open view. He does so enjoy sleeping with me."

"The hell he does. I'm not sharing my bed with that beast." Hugo eyed the panting animal uneasily. "Where was he when you set off on your quest to kidnap me?"

"I couldn't bring him," Finnula said, in horrified accents. "He'd have only got in the way. He's a tracking dog. He picks up scents and follows them. I could hardly have used him, when I didn't know who I was tracking."

"Does he have to come with us now?" Hugo complained. "Couldn't he follow you upon the morrow, with the rest of your things?"

"He won't be in the way," Finnula said airily. "You'll hardly know he's about."

Rolling his eyes, Hugo relented, thinking that he'd have his revenge later in the evening—if Mistress Laver managed to get his solar aired out, anyway.

He needn't have concerned himself over Mistress Laver's ability to accomplish all she'd set out to do, however. By the time the

wedding party arrived at Stephensgate Manor, the succulent odor
of roasting pig was in the air, all the shutters in the stone structure
had been thrown back, and garlands of flowers were strewn across
every arch and doorway. Even Finnula, who'd been so loath to
return to the accursed place, smiled when she saw the happy faces
of the vassals she'd helped through the cold winter, gathered at
long, laden tables in the Great Hall. Cries of "Lady Finnula!" and
"Fair Finn!" filled the air, as cups were raised to toast the wife of
the new Earl of Stephensgate.

It was Matthew Fairchild and his wife who thrust chalices into
the hands of the bride and groom, and Hugo thankfully drained
his, feeling the tension from his altercation with the Laroches
slipping away. Seated in flower-festooned chairs at the head of
one of the tables, he and Finnula were subjected to all the humiliations traditionally wrought upon the newly wed. Broad jokes at
the expense of the supposedly virginal bride, and even lewder
ones concerning Hugo's anticipated performance that evening
ran rampant.

Finnula, to Hugo's surprise, took the ribbing with good grace,
and did not so much as raise her dinner knife in a threatening
manner when a few braver souls made light of the fact that a year
before, she'd been seated upon the same dais with Hugo's father.
When her family arrived, carting a confusedly blinking Jack
Mallory along with them, she smiled quite sweetly at her newest
brother-in-law and said nary a word concerning his treatment of
Mellana.

The dancing started at nightfall, by which point, Hugo later
learned, a dozen pigs had been roasted, thirty wineskins opened,
and ten barrels of ale tapped. Hugo, having been out of the country for the past ten years, hadn't the slightest clue as to how to
perform the complicated reels, and Finnula at first disparaged the
activity, since it was Jack Mallory's rebec to which the couples

danced. But after some considerable amount of pressure was exerted by his subjects, Hugo was forced to join the revelers, and Finnula proved a patient dance instructor, who did not seem to mind having her toes trodden now and again.

It was nigh on midnight when Finnula's sisters came to her and gigglingly led her off to Hugo's solar, explaining that they had to "ready" her for the wedding night. Hugo, despite his enormous size—and respected title—was raised upon the shoulders of a half dozen men and carried off in the opposite direction, and it wasn't until he offered to pay the men a goodly reward that they changed their minds, and instead of depositing him in the middle of the woods, as custom dictated, detoured back to the lord's own chamber.

There he found Finnula dressed in nothing but a nightdress that was every bit as diaphanous and revealing as the one Isabella Laroche had worn the night before. Her sisters were plucking limp flower petals from her hair, and their astonishment at seeing Hugo back from the forest so soon was great, but they hastily left the couple alone, and only stood for a little while outside the solar door, banging on pots and shrieking. At that point, Sheriff de Brissac, doing as Hugo had instructed earlier in the evening, called out that there was a wineskin for every man who let His Lordship and lady be. The retreating footsteps of the revelers, in their haste to secure a wineskin, sounded like thunder.

Alone with his wife at last, Hugo glanced about his bedchamber, and saw that Mistress Laver had outdone herself. The drafty chamber had been transformed into a bridal bower, with newly washed bed curtains and linens, the cobwebs swept away, and flowers strewn everywhere. A cheerful fire crackled on the hearth, though the night was fair, and wall sconces burned brightly. The only item out of place was Finnula's mastiff, stretched out upon the hearth like a great hairy carpet, looking distinctly at home.

Hugo chose to overlook this, seeing as how the canine's teeth were as big as Skinner's, and he didn't much fancy having them fastened to his backside.

"Well," Hugo said, sinking down upon the bed, his gaze on Finnula. "That wasn't so bad, was it?"

Finnula looked at him as if he'd lost his mind and said nothing.

"In any case"—Hugo shrugged, defensively—"you're not dead, are you?" Never had he met a more contrary woman. He had married her, and all he received for his trouble was a shrug.

Finnula added to her repertoire by rolling her eyes. Then, glancing about the room, she asked, in a curiously diffident tone, for a woman so handy with a knife, "Was this where you slept as a boy?"

Hugo grunted, and bent to pull off his boots. "Aye. It's damnably cold in winter. Mayhap my brother's solar would be more comfortable. I haven't had a chance to look at it yet."

"One of them should rightly go to Jamie," Finnula said, as she ran a brush through her long hair.

"Jamie?" Hugo, barefoot, reached to remove his tunic. "That scamp? Whatever has he done to merit a bed in a Fitzstephen solar?"

Pausing with the brush in mid-stroke, Finnula eyed him. "Well!" she declared. "I like that! And I suppose our children— if we have any, which I sincerely doubt—won't merit solars, either?"

"What are you talking about?" Hugo asked, slipping out of his braies. Her doubt at his capability to sire offspring ought, he thought pridefully, to be banished with one glance at the large package between his legs.

Finnula laid the brush aside, staring at him. Hugo did not think her steady gaze was the result of lust after his fine masculine form, but rather of dread, though why she should dread going to bed with him, when she'd done so happily so many times over the past two days, he couldn't ken.

"Hugo," Finnula said slowly, and he realized, with a rush of pleasure, that it was the first time she had ever called him by his given name. She said it, however, as if the word felt odd on her lips. "Don't you know who Jamie is?"

"No." Hugo gave the sheets an irritated flick, then slid between them, thinking that it was a fine thing when a man was treated like a veritable stranger by his own wife.

"Hugo," Finnula said, biting her lower lip. "Jamie is your son."

# Chapter Fifteen

"My what?"

Finnula jumped as Hugo's voice thundered through the solar. Never in her life had she heard such a bellow.

"My *what*?" Hugo roared again.

He threw back the sheets, revealing his large, tawny body in all its naked glory. But he seemed unconscious of his nudity as he stalked toward her, where she leaned against the windowsill. Before Hugo could lay a hand on her, however—if, indeed, that had been his intention—Gros Louis was up and growling before his mistress, the hackles on his back rising like a hedgehog's quills.

"Christ's toes, Finnula," Hugo shouted, backing up hastily. "Call him off!"

"Down, Gros Louis," Finnula said, and the dog sat back on

his haunches, but did not take his eyes off Hugo. Nor did he stop growling.

"I think I understand a little better how you managed to remain a virgin so long, my love," Hugo remarked dryly, "despite gadding about in those braies."

"He thought you were going to hit me," Finnula said, giving the dog a fond scratch behind the ears.

Hugo grimaced expressively. "Hit you? Someone ought to be hit, for keeping this from me. Why did no one think to mention to me the small detail that I have a son? Like you, for instance? Or were you saving it up for our wedding night all along?"

"I find it hard to believe you didn't realize it for yourself right away. He looks exactly like you."

"'Tis rather hard to tell, beneath all that dirt." Hugo strode from one side of the solar to the other, as rapidly as a caged wolf Finnula had once seen in Leesbury. "The boy would be what, ten years old, then?"

"Just."

Hugo stopped pacing of a sudden, and focused his inscrutable amber-eyed gaze upon her with a directness that was disconcerting. "And his mother would be?"

Finnula rose from the windowsill and moved to the bed. Her brow was knit with annoyance, and she forgot all about Robert's advice that she act more womanly before her husband. "You forget your lovers so soon?" she sniffed. "I wonder how long 'twill be before I'm forgotten!" She knew she sounded a petulant wife, but she could not still her tongue. How was it that a man could bed a woman, and ten years later not remember her name? Finnula would never, did she live to be one hundred, forget Hugo.

"My lover?" Hugo echoed. "I was fifteen! I had no lover then." Then he grinned rakishly at her. "But *you* I wouldn't dare forget. You're too well-armed."

Finnula, turning down the sheets on the opposite side of the bed, glared at him. He appeared to be joking, but she could never really tell. He was very strange, this man she had married. For the life of her, she could not decide why he had agreed to wed her. Except, she supposed, to prevent scandal.

"Well, tell me," Hugo said. "Who is this woman I supposedly got with child?"

"There is no supposedly about it," was Finnula's tart reply. She slid beneath the sheets and looked at him, unabashedly staring at his nude body, and wondering what it would be like to have that great thing hanging between her own legs. Mayhap, had she one, she, too, would be unable to recall the names of the women into whom she'd inserted it.

"Your father himself recognized Jamie as his grandchild," Finnula went on, circling her knees with her arms and sitting up in the great bed. "'Tis only because Maggie died giving birth to him that the boy was left to run wild—"

"Maggie," Hugo said, his brows constricting. "Her name was Maggie?"

Irritated because he still looked blank, Finnula said, "Yes. *Maggie*. I don't know the whole of the story, being myself but seven years old at the time, but you supposedly dallied with her in the milking barn—"

"The milking barn," Hugo repeated. And then, loudly, he cried, "Not *Maggie*! Not the *milkmaid*!"

Finnula regarded him calmly. "Aye, Maggie the milkmaid. Does it begin to come back to you now?"

This news seemed to stagger Hugo, and he sank onto the end of the bed, oblivious of the fact that he'd nearly trodden upon Gros Louis's front right paw.

"Maggie," Hugo echoed, like one from whom a fog has lifted. "Maggie the milkmaid. Ah, sweet Maggie . . ."

Finnula hadn't thought she'd spend her wedding night discussing her husband's past loves, but as her only other wedding night had been even more unpleasant, she imagined she should be grateful things weren't worse. Plucking up the wolf pelt, since a breeze had been rattling the shutters and the chamber had grown a bit chilled, she huddled down beneath it, blinking sleepily against the light from the wall sconce.

"Maggie," her husband murmured again, and had Maggie still been living, Finnula would have gladly run her through with a shaft from her quiver.

"Aye," she said irritably. "Now put out the sconces, will you? I'm tired and want to go to bed."

Hugo turned as if startled, and looked at her over his naked shoulder. She tried to keep her face impassive, but something Hugo saw in it caused him to grin in a completely infuriating manner. "Jealous, are you, love?" he asked, reaching out to give one of her feet a poke through the bedclothes.

"Certainly not," Finnula sniffed, and she kicked at the hand that teased her. "You think a mite too much of yourself, my lord."

"Oh, do I?"

There was something distinctly lascivious in his grin, which Finnula chose to ignore, turning to beat her pillow into a plumper shape. "There's no use your looking at me like that," she informed him sharply. "And since I'm not going to swoon at the sight of your naked body, you might as well put on a bed robe—"

"You're very proper now, aren't you?" Hugo stretched his long frame onto the bed beside her, his eyes glowing unnervingly gold in the light from the hearth. "Quite the prim lady, now that you're married."

Finnula shrugged. "I told you that you'd regret marrying me."

"Oh, yes, I'm already beginning to." Hugo lifted the wolf pelt and looked beneath it. "And wearing clothes to bed, too! How novel! I must say I preferred what you wore to bed that night at the inn—"

"That night," Finnula snapped, sitting up, "was a mistake—"

"Oh, most certainly. A very grave one."

"—and 'tis not too late to rectify it," Finnula went on, as if he hadn't spoken.

"Not too late?" Hugo grinned quizzically. "And how might that be? If I recall rightly, Father Edward pronounced us man and wife—"

"But the marriage has yet to be consummated," Finnula hastened to explain, "and can still be annulled . . ."

A single raised eyebrow joined its twin in a downward rush as Hugo glowered at her. "I see," he said, and his deep voice no longer held any amusement.

Finnula eyed him uncertainly, hoping that she hadn't angered him overmuch. He ought, if he was any sort of man at all, to be overjoyed that she was again offering him a way out of this ridiculous marriage. He had already told her that no man wished to be saddled with a wife. Here she was, generously agreeing to release him from the unwanted shackles of wedlock. But, alas, no! Judging from his expression, he wasn't pleased at all.

And yet, as if she hadn't said a word, he reached forward, seemingly unconsciously, and found a limp flower petal that lay tangled in a curl of her long hair. Finnula watched as his large, callused fingers gently drew the white petal down the length of the curl, his knuckles brushing one of her breasts as he did so. Her rebellious nipple sprang erect at the contact, pressing insistently against the thin material of her nightdress. Finnula looked down at it, nibbling on her lower lip. Fie! Was she so wanton that his barest touch set her aflame?

She was only too aware of the answer to that question.

If Hugo noticed her body's reaction to his touch, he didn't say anything. Instead, successfully removing the petal from the loosened auburn curl, he held up the fragile leaf, and examined it in the firelight.

"And you would be released from this marriage," he said, looking at the flower and not at her, "because you despise and revile me?"

God's teeth! The man was impossible.

"Nay, not that," Finnula said, making an effort to keep her voice steady and low. "I am . . . fond enough of you."

"Fond of me?" The golden gaze swiveled toward her, and Finnula was uncomfortably aware that, with his back now to the fire, she could not quite make out his expression. "Are you? Then why this urgency to annul what I have spent so much time—and coin—to arrange?" When Finnula, frustrated, did not formulate a reply with enough alacrity to suit him, Hugo went on, "Is it because of the boy?"

Finnula hesitated. "Nay . . ."

"Is it because of his mother?" Hugo leaned forward and captured yet another flower petal between his thumb and forefinger. Extricating it from a silken tress, the back of his hand brushed her other breast, and the nipple reacted as sensitively as its twin. "Do you not ken how much I regret what happened to her? Maggie was sweet . . . but she was older than me by a good five years, and I won't say she didn't know what she was doing. Far more than I did . . . But I regret I was not here to see that she was better taken care of . . . she and the boy . . . but you'll recall my family did try to send me off to a monastery."

He was having a bit more trouble removing this flower petal than he'd had with the last. His thick fingers worked with surprising dexterity, but occasionally, Finnula felt the gentle warmth of his hand against her throat, or excruciatingly close to her earlobe. She swallowed, her mouth gone suddenly dry.

"Aye," she said, and her voice was oddly hoarse. "But you have amply proven that you care not how many women you bed—"

"That was once so," Hugo said, gathering her lock of hair toward him, ostensibly to better examine the tangled leaf. "And I am fortunate that, with the exception of poor Maggie, no one was harmed by my amorous adventures. But now that I have a wife, I shall cleave only unto her, as the priest so instructed me, not twelve hours ago."

Finnula snorted, though it was difficult to keep her head about her while he lay so close, playing with her curls, the firelight casting his naked flesh in bronze. The mat of golden hair that carpeted his chest, then tapered down toward his flat belly, was particularly distracting. "A wife who brings you no fortune, no property?" Finnula shook her head. "A wife who can neither cook nor sew? Verily, my lord, you have been too long away from England, and have lost all sense of practicality. Such a wife is nigh useless—"

"Useless?" The fingers Hugo had been running through her hair dipped suddenly to close over one of her small breasts. Gasping at the sudden contact, Finnula raised startled eyes to meet her husband's.

"I believe the outpouring of folk who came to our wedding today proved how useful you have been to many in the past, Finnula," Hugo said, his fingers kneading the soft flesh. "Not least with a bow. Nay, I can think of many things at which you are quite useful—"

So saying, he lowered his head and, through the thin batiste of her gown, delicately tasted her taut nipple with his tongue. Finnula, suddenly feeling quite warm, pushed back the wolf pelt, revealing long legs bared from the thighs down, since the hem of her nightdress had become twisted round her hips.

Noticing this, Hugo lost no time in sliding his free hand between those slim white thighs, before Finnula, her cheeks blazing, could adjust the gown. Then, when she made a movement as if to snatch away from him, Hugo rose up suddenly, and lowered his heavy body over hers, effectively cutting off all escape routes.

"Nay, madam," he said, his laughing amber eyes gleaming down at her. "I'd say you are quite useful at other things not requiring a bow, as well . . ."

Finnula struggled to keep her wits about her, but the introduction of a hardened thigh between her legs once again made rational thinking impossible. Hugo's body was weighing down upon hers, and it was a weight she welcomed, for her body was instantly reminded by it of pleasure received in the recent past. Before she could stop herself, her arms were curling around his neck, her legs spreading to better accommodate him between them. God's teeth, but she wanted him. Perhaps it was just as well that they stay wed after all . . .

And then Hugo's lips came down over hers, and all ability to think left her. She closed her eyes, feeling a familiar rush of warmth between her thighs as Hugo insinuated first one, then another finger within her. Instinctively, she arched her pelvis against him, and had the satisfaction of hearing him moan.

"Not yet, my love," he whispered raggedly against her mouth. "Not yet."

His hands moved to the neckline of her gown. Finnula's eyes flew open as she heard the fabric rend. Gasping as he tore her nightdress down the middle as effortlessly as if it were made of parchment, Finnula cried, "Hugo! Are you mad?"

Now that her creamy skin, tip-tilted breasts, and the silken patch of red hair between her thighs were revealed to him, Hugo grinned, eminently satisfied. "Nay. Let that be a lesson to you, love." He chuckled. "Wear naught when you come to bed with me, or all your gowns, however pretty, will meet a similar fate."

Finnula eyed him, thinking that she'd married a barbarian, and was about to make her feelings on the matter known when, of a sudden, the lips that moments before had ravaged her mouth suddenly settled over a pink nipple. The sharp words that had been on Finnula's lips turned to a moan of pleasure as Hugo's mouth, hot on her tender skin, burned a trail of kisses down her flat white belly, and then even farther down, until once more his tongue tasted the russet curls at the joining of her thighs. This was definitely not something her sisters had mentioned that their husbands practiced—and the Crais sisters had been quite thorough in their sexual education of Finnula while dressing her that morning. But it was something Finnula was fairly certain she could get used to.

It wasn't until her groans excited in him a similar longing that Hugo rose, shaking off her clinging fingers, which had fisted in his hair, and plunged himself into the tight warmth he'd been kissing moments before, finally making them husband and wife in truth, and wiping out any hope of an annulment. Finnula cried out in wordless pleasure as he drew back and entered her again, more deeply this time.

When release came, it crashed over both of them simultaneously, rocking Hugo forward again and again, driving Finnula back into the pillows with the force of his thrusts. Crying out hoarsely as wave after wave of pleasure rolled over her, Finnula didn't even hear Hugo's triumphant roar as he collapsed against her.

It was only when the two of them finally lay still, their hearts pounding against each other's, their breathing ragged, that they became aware of the sound of voices outside the solar's windows. Hugo raised his head from Finnula's damp throat. "What the hell . . . ?"

Then, when it became clear that the voices were those of their wedding guests, and that they were cheering, and calling up words of encouragement, Finnula felt herself turn crimson.

"God's teeth, Hugo! They must have heard you!" she whispered.

"*Me?*" Hugo looked distinctly amused, and not at all embarrassed. "I wasn't the one screaming."

"I didn't scream," Finnula cried, shocked. Then, doubtfully, she whispered, "Did I?"

Hugo only chuckled, and, moving from her, reached for the wolf pelt. This he pulled over her nakedness, as if, with it, he could shield her from the world. Then he slipped back into his braies and, barefoot, padded to one of the unshuttered windows.

Finnula rose up on one elbow, eyeing him curiously. "Whatever are you doing?" she asked the man who was now, for better or for worse, her husband in every sense of the word.

"Getting rid of them," he growled, shaking something in his hand that tinkled. "I'll not have an audience on my wedding night . . . even if it *is* too late." Then, calling out to the crowd below, he hurled a fistful of coins to the ground. "Take that, you ruffians," he cried. "And get gone!"

Appreciative squeals met his shower of coins, and Hugo was still chuckling as he drew the shutters closed. Finnula sank back against the pillows, sleepily admiring her husband's fine profile. Mayhap marriage to such a man would not be so bad, she thought. Mayhap he could be taught . . .

And when Hugo, extinguishing the wall sconces and once again stripping off his braies, slid beneath the wolf pelt and pulled her against him, she knew, with drowsy certainty, that there was no place else she would rather be. She fell asleep with her cheek upon his shoulder, lulled by the steady rise and fall of his broad chest.

# Chapter _Sixteen_

When Hugo woke the next morning, it was because his wife was sidling off the edge of the bed, taking such excruciating care not to wake him that it was obvious she was up to no good. Hugo immediately rolled over onto the trailing ends of her hair, and, feigning slumber, pulled her back into his arms. Finnula made no protest, which led him to believe that whatever she'd been up to would keep . . . at least until after he'd caught up on a few more hours of badly needed sleep.

When Hugo awoke again, it was almost midday and Finnula was conspicuously absent from his bed. She had not wandered very far, however. He could hear her throaty voice in the yard below his windows, barking out orders in the manner of someone well-used to doing so. Hugo did not have the slightest idea what she could be about, and was not at all certain that he wanted to know. He rose, however, and after a good deal of stretching and splashing cold water onto his face—it had never occurred to him that having a young wife was going to prove so physically taxing—he flung open the window shutters and blinked at the vivid spring colors that greeted him . . . the expanse of cloudless blue sky, the emerald of the treetops, and the bright copper color of his wife's plaited hair.

At first he thought it a trick of the strong sunlight that it appeared as if the yard below was filled with furniture, around which Finnula, followed by the galumphing mastiff Gros Louis, strutted—in her leather braies, he noted, grimly. But after he'd thoroughly wiped the sleep from his eyes, he saw that, indeed, his father's canopied bed sat in the middle of the courtyard, along with a number of other items from the late earl's solar. Hugo recognized a few shields, his father's water ewer, even a chamber pot, all piled haphazardly in the center of the courtyard. As he watched, his squire, Peter, came stumbling into view, staggering beneath the weight of the late earl's favorite chair.

"Very good, Peter," Finnula said. "Put it right there, by the bed."

"Yes, m'lady." Down went the chair, with a thump and a crack of wood that caused even Hugo, two stories above, to wince. "You want I should bring down that trunk in the corner by the window?"

"Yes, of course," Finnula replied, as if she were speaking to a particularly dense child . . . and Peter being Peter, Hugo didn't think she was far wrong. "Everything, Peter. I want everything brought down."

"Yes, m'lady." Peter turned, obeying Her Ladyship's commands with an alacrity that he'd never exhibited while serving

Hugo. Hugo, frowning, tapped his fingers against the stone window casement, and cleared his throat.

"Lady Finnula," he called down, pleasantly.

Old Webster appeared at that moment, dragging a ragged tapestry behind him. "'Ere ye are, m'lady. Where d'ye want it?"

"Oh, just drape it anywhere." Shading her eyes with a hand, Finnula craned her neck to squint up at Hugo. "Good morning, my lord," she called.

"Good morning, my lady." Hugo folded his powerful arms across his chest. "'Tis a pleasant day, is it not?"

"Verily," Finnula replied. "I trust you slept well."

"Like a stone, madam. So hard, in fact, I do not recall you mentioning that you intended to turn the house out this morn."

"Not the entire house, my lord," Finnula said, darting out of the way as a wench Hugo didn't recognize traipsed past, her arms full of his late father's clothing. "Only Lord Geoffrey's solar."

Hugo nodded. "I can see that. And might I ask, madam, what you intend to do with the items you've collected from there?"

Finnula, in a gesture Hugo instantly recognized as nervousness, pushed a few loose tendrils of red hair from her forehead. "Burn them, my lord," she called up to him.

Hugo oughtn't to have been surprised. Knowing how much she despised the late earl, it was a relatively mild gesture. Still, the fact that she had neglected to mention the matter to Hugo beforehand was rather irksome.

"I see," Hugo said, and he could not keep the disapproval from his voice. "I shall be down presently, Lady Finnula, to discuss this, er, bonfire with you."

As Hugo turned away from the window, Finnula's hoarse voice beckoned him back. "Might I suggest, my lord," she called up to him, a slight teasing note in her tone, "that you dress before coming down?"

Quickly glancing down at himself, Hugo realized he'd been addressing his wife—and, indeed, nearly his entire household staff—in his altogether. Grimacing, he stalked away from the window, only half conscious of the astonished cry that the sight of his naked backside elicited from Mistress Laver below. The cook, crossing the courtyard in order to consult with her new mistress concerning the evening meal, had to sit down and be fanned for several minutes before she recuperated from the shock.

Hugo was shaved and dressed in a matter of minutes, a skill he'd acquired during the Crusades, where sneak attacks by the enemy had necessitated rapid toilettes. Running a hand through his damp hair, he hurried down the stairs, observing that nearly all signs of the previous evening's festivities had been cleared away. New rushes had been laid upon the flagstones, and those had been doused with something sweet-smelling. The long tables were gone, with the exception of the one at which he and Finnula would partake of their regular meals. Because the day was fine, no fire had been laid upon the massive stone hearth. Instead, all the flowers from the night before were piled where a log ought to have been, making an eye-catching and pleasant-scented arrangement.

Hugo was so intent upon reaching the back courtyard, in which Finnula'd had all his father's belongings piled, that he didn't see the four-foot-tall impediment with which he collided as he came down the stairs.

"Hey there!" cried a pile of bed curtains at the base of the stairs. "Look where you're goin'!"

Hugo, backing up with alacrity, saw that the bearer of the brocade material was none other than his son, Jamie, who looked mightily indignant at being trod upon. Scrambling to his feet, the lad gave his jerkin a tug and said, "Just because I'm small don't mean I ain't here a'tall, you know." And then, grudgingly, "My lord."

Hugo looked down at the sulking little cuss and wondered how he could not have noticed the resemblance before. Though his memory of the boy's mother would probably never be much more than dim, his own features he recognized quite well. Particularly, he noted, the hazel eyes.

"Well, there, Jamie," he said, reaching down to help the boy get a firmer grasp on his load. "I apologize for that. Have you got hold of it, now?"

"Right enough," Jamie admitted. "Now if you'll 'scuse me, Lady Finn wants all this stuff out back—"

"Hold a minute there, Jamie," Hugo said, drawing the boy back with a hand upon his slim shoulder. "I believe there's something you and I need to get straight."

Obediently, the boy faced him, waiting with only the slightest expression of impatience on his face as Hugo settled himself on the bottom step.

"When I asked you, yesterday," Hugo began, hesitantly, "to whom you belonged, Jamie, you said—"

"You, my lord."

"Yes, that's right. You said that you belong to me, meaning, I assume, that you are my vassal—"

"Aye," Jamie said. "That I am. Like Mistress Laver."

"Well, yes, Jamie." Hugo stroked his chin. "But what I really meant was . . . Jamie, do you know who your father is?"

"I should think so," Jamie declared. "You."

Hugo nodded, relieved. "Yes, that's right. Me. Now, I've been away for quite a long time, and I realize that perhaps you've had things hard—"

Jamie looked as if his patience was wearing thin. "Lady Finn'll have my hide if I don't get back with these curtains."

"Well, stay a moment. I'll go with you and explain to, er, Lady Finn. What I want to say, Jamie, is that if there's anything, uh, anything that you need—"

"I need to get back to Lady Finn afore she kills me," Jamie asserted.

"Yes. Well." Seeing that there was no use pursuing the subject at the moment, Hugo rose and, taking the bed curtains from the boy, said, "Let me help you with that, anyway."

Jamie's face was a picture of delight. "Oh! You take that, my lord, and I'll run back up and get the others! Lady Finn'll be right pleased!"

Watching the boy scamper back up the stairs, Hugo shook his head. Somehow or other, Hugo was going to have to impress upon Jamie that he wasn't one of the servants. Though Hugo could not, in fairness to Finnula, name the boy as his heir, he could see the child properly—and prosperously—raised. The lad was going to have to be educated and apprenticed somewhere. Though what household would take him, filthy as he was, Hugo couldn't imagine. Mayhap Finnula, whom the boy seemed to worship, could induce him to bathe.

Gathering up the bed curtains, Hugo headed for the back of the house, carefully dodging scurrying chambermaids and frantic-looking laundresses, none of whom acknowledged his presence except by gasping and hurrying away. He could hear Mistress Laver barking orders at some hapless scullion, and if the aroma wafting from the kitchens was any indication of what awaited him for breakfast, he thought the cook hardly needed to scold anyone.

But he himself had some scolding to attend to before breaking his fast, and accordingly, stepped outside to find his wife instructing old Webster's newly hired assistant to hitch up the farm wagon, since she wanted all His Lordship's furniture carted to the south field where, she sweetly explained, it would be burned to the ground. Finnula was quite unconscious of Hugo's looming presence and didn't even turn around until the groom, gulping, pointed over her shoulder.

"I'm thinkin' 'Is Lordship is wantin' ye, Lady Finn," the rough-looking lad said.

Finnula spun around, spied the bed curtains in Hugo's arms, and cried, "Oh, lovely! Put those there, will you, my lord?"

Hugo dropped the material, then snaked out an arm and anchored it around his wife's waist. "Finnula," he said, through gritted teeth. "You and I need to have a talk."

"Not right now," Finnula said, squirming against him. "I've got work to do."

"I can see that you've been working very industriously indeed this morning, my love." Hugo's grip on her was inexorable, and she finally gave up twisting within it and eyed him, her gaze wary but her chin thrust out obstinately.

Glimpsing the fleeting surrender in her gray eyes, Hugo bodily hauled his wife out of earshot of the servants, depositing her on the far side of the courtyard, near the well. Once her feet touched solid ground, Finnula, catlike, set about adjusting her attire, tucking the ends of her white shirt back into her braies and flicking suspicious glances in his direction.

"You said at the millhouse," she began haughtily, "that Stephensgate Manor was mine, to do with what I chose—"

"But to burn all my father's belongings?" Hugo glowered at her. "Weren't you even going to consult me about my feelings on the matter?"

"*Your* feelings on the matter?" Finnula stamped a booted foot, her cheeks pinkening with anger. Her normally gentle gray eyes suddenly snapped fire as she jabbed a finger into Hugo's broad chest. "Your father was a miserable weak man"—she emphasized each word with a jab of her finger—"who allowed that *leech* Reginald Laroche to suck out his life's blood until all that was left was a half-crazed shell. Your father let that man rob and starve the very people he was sworn to protect, and then, to top it all off, he forced me to marry him against my will, died, and left me to be accused of his murder!" Drawing breath, Finnula dropped her hands to her hips and glared at him. "And you stand there and protest *your* feelings!"

Hugo frowned down at his obstreperous wife. His anger, if truth be told, was mostly feigned. What did he care about a lot of old furniture? But he couldn't allow Finnula to think that she, not he, was lord of the manor.

"And burning all of his belongings is going to remedy my father's mistakes?" he demanded, with what he considered intimidating gruffness.

Not very surprisingly, Finnula hardly looked cowed. "Burning all of Lord Geoffrey's belongings will make me happy," she informed him tartly. And then she added, with a sly glance at old Webster, who'd come stumbling into the courtyard bearing the late earl's saddle, "And 'twill make his subjects happy, as well. I'm sorry to say there wasn't much love lost between Lord Geoffrey and his vassals toward the end. Your allowing them to throw something of his onto an enormous bonfire just might make some of them forgive and forget. That, and the fact that you've dismissed Monsieur Laroche, will make them more accepting of you . . ."

"You think so, do you, wench?" Hugo couldn't help grinning at her. "And do you care whether or not my subjects accept me?"

She lifted her nose. "Certainly not. But 'twill make my role as chatelaine easier—"

Looking up at him, Finnula suddenly bit her lower lip, and laid a slim hand on his arm. Finnula so rarely touched him of her own accord—at least, without a knife in her hand—that Hugo raised his eyebrows, surprised by the gesture. He didn't have the slightest idea what caused Finnula suddenly to soften toward him, but all at once, she was looking up at him with something almost like sympathy in her eyes.

"I'm sorry to malign your father in this way, Hugo. I know that toward the end of his life he was . . . ill. But even before that, he was rather horrid—"

Hugo shrugged, amused. "I told you myself he was rather horrid, remember?"

She blinked up at him, and he saw the tenderness leave her face. "Oh, yes. That story about how your mother and father tried to force you to join a monastery." She laughed shortly, a laugh without mirth, and dropped her hand from his arm. "'Twas stupid of me not to have realized then who you were in truth. That's quite a famous story round these parts."

Hugo frowned again. So she was still sulking about Hugh Fitzwilliam, was she? Christ's toes, but he was beginning to hate that fictional knight. It seemed incredible, but he honestly believed the girl would have preferred to be wed to that lowly knight than to himself. What was he going to have to do in order to win over the ungrateful chit? True, he had her body, but her heart seemed to belong to someone Hugo himself had invented!

"Have your bonfire, then," he said, ungraciously and through gritted teeth. "Throw my own chair on it, if that will make you happy. I care not."

Turning, he strode away, and Finnula, to his chagrin, made no effort to stop him. He knew he was being foolish, sulking as if he were no older than Jamie, but it irked him that his wife, who was so demonstrative in bed—and in the bushes, for God's sake—should be so cold at all other times. It had not been so when he'd been her hostage. Why was it so now that he was her husband?

Hugo went inside to seek out some breakfast, and it was as he was eating it—not quite alone, for Gros Louis, seeming to have given up on his dislike of him, had joined him with a bone at his feet at the head of the long table in the Great Hall—that Peter approached, sweaty-faced and dirty from his exertions in the late earl's solar, to announce that John de Brissac was waiting outside the manor house gates for a word with His Lordship. Swallowing a last mouthful of pork and egg, Hugo rose to follow his squire, who seized the opportunity to complain of his treatment of late.

"I didn't leave London so I could haul furniture," Peter whined. "I'm not used to dirtying my hands performing common char labor. When am I to begin my training as a knight, my lord? I don't even have sword of my own—"

Hugo, who was in a foul temper, snapped, "You have a decent bed to sleep in, don't you?"

"Aye, my lord . . ."

"You didn't have three meals a day, and fine clothes, and a horse of your own, and a decent bed to sleep in when you were in London, did you?"

"Nay, my lord . . ."

"Those things are more important than swords."

"But I thought I was to be trained to fight." Peter was huffing from his attempt to keep up with Hugo's long strides across the stable yard. "I thought I was to learn swordplay in order to battle the enemy—"

Hugo snorted. "The enemy doesn't engage in swordplay,

my boy. The enemy's weapons are considerably more sophisticated."

"My lord?"

"The enemy uses winsome looks and swishing hips . . ."

"My lord?" Peter looked understandably confused. "Are you saying . . . Are you referring to *women*, my lord?"

Hugo had reached the gates by then, and he only shrugged. "Get thee gone, boy. I'll train you another day. For now, do as your mistress bids."

Peter, muttering darkly beneath his breath, hitched his shoulders and turned back toward the house.

John de Brissac, high upon his mount, looked surprised to see Hugo standing in the yard. "Ho, there, my lord!" he cried, dismounting with surprising quickness for so heavy a man. "Didn't mean to disturb you. Asked the boy to see whether or not you and your lady were receiving callers."

Hugo leaned against one of the useless stone turrets that guarded his home, enjoying the feel of the sun upon his face. "I suppose we are," he said. "At least I am. The Lady Finnula is otherwise engaged."

"Ah." The sheriff smiled knowingly. "Too modest to show her face after last night, eh? 'Tis the way with pretty brides."

Hugo snorted. "Not exactly, Sheriff. Modesty is not a virtue my wife seems to hold in much esteem. She is currently directing a team of laborers in removing my father's furniture from his solar, with the intention of burning it in a massive bonfire in the south meadow tonight."

"Is she?" There was no mistaking the glee in the sheriff's voice. "Good girl!" Then, with a cautious glance at Hugo, who was frowning, de Brissac amended, "What I meant was—"

"No, no, John." Hugo waved aside the older man's apology. "I can see by your enthusiasm that you think the idea a good one. I have been too long gone from here to know what is what. So you think it a wise plan?"

"'Tis a sure way to show the Matthew Fairchilds of this community that you mean to be a different sort of leader than your father," the sheriff thoughtfully observed.

"And all the wine and roasted pig I served last night was not proof enough?" Hugo asked, with a flash of humor.

"Ah, well, that was well and good, but this bonfire . . ." The sheriff chuckled, shaking his head. "'Twill be like bidding good riddance to bad rubbish, if you'll excuse the slight to your family, my lord."

Hugo, rubbing his jaw, frowned. "I think I see what you mean. 'Twill allow my vassals to feel as I did yesterday, when I closed the gates upon the Laroches."

"Precisely!" Noticing that Hugo was still frowning, John de Brissac slapped the reins he held against his side and whistled, low and long. When Hugo lifted an inquiring brow, the sheriff said, with a lopsided grin, "Well, my lord, to look at you, I'd hardly think you were a man newly wedded. I'm hoping that frown is from a headache brought on by too much wine last night, and not by your bright young bride . . ."

Hugo's frown lifted only slightly. "How did you guess?"

It was Sheriff de Brissac's turn to snort. "You forget, my lord. I was the one who was bid to stop the Fair Finn from poaching on your lands. That was like telling a man to stop the wind from blowing. Oh, yes, your Lady Finnula and I had many a long chat . . ."

"She hasn't chatted with me very much since she found out who I really am," Hugo growled. He slumped against the sun-warmed bricks, crossing his legs at the ankles. "Tell me, Sheriff. What is a man, returning to his home after a long absence, to do when he finds that he has a ten-year-old son by a woman he barely remembers, subjects who despise him, and a wife who will only admit to being 'fond enough' of him, despite the fact that he's made an honest woman of her?"

"Ah," John de Brissac grunted. "You're asking the opinion of a landless, childless bachelor, my lord?"

Hugo stared at the dirt. "I have no one else to ask."

The sheriff gave his horse a pat. "Be kind."

"Sheriff?" Hugo's eyes glowed almost gold.

"Be kind," John de Brissac repeated. "Be kind to the boy. Kind to your subjects. And kind to your wife. They'll come round. All of them. You forget." He gave Hugo a stealthy wink. "I know them all quite well. And there isn't a one who won't come to appreciate you, in time."

As he spoke, the sheriff lifted his head, distracted by some small noise coming from above them. Glancing up at the merlons that surrounded the rim of the turret against which Hugo leaned, John's face suddenly changed, and he barked out a warning even as he lunged forward. Throwing all his enormous weight against Hugo, John de Brissac shoved the younger man to the ground. Hugo, taken off guard, tumbled to the earth, the sheriff's larger body landing heavily across his . . .

. . . but not as heavily as the foot-long slab of solid rock that embedded itself into the dirt exactly where Hugo had been standing would have.

John de Brissac's mare reared in fright as the stone impacted, spraying dirt and grass, and both men shielded their heads as bits of loosened gravel rained upon them from above. When the brief shower ended, Hugo lifted his head, and, staring wide-eyed at the projectile, which, had the sheriff not acted so quickly, would undoubtedly have killed him, ground out, "What in the hell . . . ?"

John de Brissac was already struggling to his feet, reaching for his fractious horse's reins. "It's one of the merlons, my lord. Someone pushed it—"

"Pushed it, my ass," Hugo growled, rolling painfully to his feet. His body, where de Brissac had tackled it, throbbed. "Those towers always were a menace. As long as Finnula's redecorating, I should have them pulled down—"

"No, my lord," the sheriff puffed. He'd captured his mare, and was whispering soothing words into her flattened ears. "I think not. I heard footsteps from above, directly before it fell. Someone pushed that stone, I'd stake my life on it." His eyes bright, de Brissac shook his head. "My lord, someone is trying to kill you."

# Chapter Seventeen

on't be ridiculous."

Hugo, straightening, held on to the side of the turret for support. He wondered if, like Finnula that day that now seemed so long ago, he'd bruised a rib. The sheriff's girth was considerable, and he'd thrown all of it at Hugo in his anxiety to save him from being crushed another way.

"Who would want to kill *me*?" Hugo laughed, and then regretted it, when his side throbbed. "'Tis Laroche everyone despises."

"Apparently not everyone." The sheriff had managed to calm his mount at last, and now he stood with one hand shaded over his eyes, squinting up at the tower. "That merlon didn't fall. Someone loosened it, and someone pushed it. Come. The culprit is surely flown by now, but he might have left some sign. With these heavy rains, perhaps we shall find a footprint or two."

Now that the initial shock was over, Hugo found himself shaking his head in skeptical amusement. "No wonder you were appointed shire reeve, John de Brissac. You see crime even where one has not been committed!"

The sheriff said nothing. With a half-dozen strides, he was inside the gates, looking for the door that led up into the left-hand tower. Hugo, rolling his eyes, followed the portly investigator. His skepticism was shaken, however, when de Brissac found the door that led to the turret stairs yawning on its hinges. It had not been so when Hugo had passed it moments before. He would have surely noticed.

"These towers are not in daily use, are they?" questioned the sheriff sharply, as he knelt to examine the dirt at the foot of the twisting staircase.

"Nay," Hugo breathed. "They are not safe. The stairs sag and have not been repaired since my grandfather's day. My brother and I used to play in them as children, but—" He blanched, remembering the day of his return to Stephensgate Manor. Had not Jamie called down to him from this very tower?

As if he had read Hugo's mind, the sheriff lifted his head from his scrutiny of the dust and said, " 'Twasn't the boy. Wee lad like that wouldn't have the strength to push an entire merlon over. Slab o' rock that size weighs as much as me." Rising, de Brissac brushed dirt from the knees of his braies. "No, I see the boy's prints readily enough, but there are others here, all a-jumble. I'd say there were some visitors to these towers last night, durin' the festivities. Come. Let us climb up and see what there is to see."

The narrow wooden staircase was even more treacherous than Hugo remembered. Entire slats were missing, others rotting and warped, and the circular walls were covered with cobwebs and bird excrement. Creaking their protest as Hugo and the sheriff climbed them, the stairs threatened to give way beneath their combined weight. It was with relief that Hugo raised the wooden trapdoor that led to the dilapidated platform above. Inspecting the boards, Hugo thought them sound enough to hold his weight, and climbed through the trap to stand atop the watchtower.

Sheriff de Brissac, however, was not so trusting. He kept his enormous feet upon the staircase, his head and shoulders only through the trap as he squinted at the rotting planks.

"Aye," he growled, pointing at the jagged edge of rock where a rectangular merlon had once rested, the seventh in a series of eight. "See that pile of rubble there? Someone's been working on loosening that stone for some time."

Hugo knelt to examine the pulverized rock. It was clear that someone had spent long hours picking out the mortar between the merlon and the turret wall. It was a task that could only have been accomplished with a sharp metal tool and an indefatigable resolution to see it to completion. John de Brissac was correct. The merlon had not fallen from decay or natural ruin. Someone had intentionally loosened . . . and pushed it.

"Lord Hugo!"

Hugo straightened, and saw his squire standing in the stable yard below, looking about him idiotically. At Hugo's grunt, the boy looked up, then balked.

"Lord Hugo, what are you doing up there? 'Tisn't safe, you know. Monsieur Laroche told me that the very moment I arrived . . ."

"Laroche," Hugo murmured, and the look he darted at the sheriff was shrewd. "I'd quite forgotten about Monsieur Laroche."

The sheriff nodded briskly. "I'd best ride over to Leesbury

and see that the gentleman made it to his sister's safely. Perhaps something occurred to detain him—"

Hugo laughed. "Like an opportunity to murder his most despised enemy?"

"Lord Hugo," Peter cried, from below. "Is Lady Finnula up there with you? I cannot find her, and I need to know what she wants me to do with Lord Geoffrey's toilet articles—"

Sheriff de Brissac had already started down the rickety staircase, and Hugo ducked his head to follow. "Did you try the back courtyard?" he tossed over his shoulder. "That's where I last spied her—"

"She isn't there . . ."

Hugo shrugged and hurried after the departing sheriff, ducking his head to avoid spiderwebs and bat dung. When he reached the bottom of the twisted staircase, his talkative squire was there waiting for him, his jaw slack at the sight of the broken merlon.

"My lord," the youth stammered, hopping about wildly with excitement. "Somebody tried to kill you! Somebody is trying to kill you, my lord!"

"Close your mouth, you insolent pup." Sheriff de Brissac was annoyed. Besides, he still had a bit of a headache from the previous evening's revelry. "No one is trying to kill His Lordship. Anyone can tell these towers are falling to bits."

Hugo flashed the older man an appreciative glance. "Quite right, Sheriff. Peter, you are overexcited. Why don't you run and fetch old Webster, and have him direct someone to board up this door? It isn't safe in these towers, and I won't have Jamie break his neck playing up there . . ."

"Seems to me 'tis your own neck you ought to be lookin' out for, my lord," Peter said, with some indignation. "If you don't mind my saying so, only a fool'd think that there merlon fell on its own—"

"Are you calling me a fool, boy?" Hugo swung around, looming threateningly over his charge. The youth took an involuntary step backward, gulping.

"No, my lord!"

"Then get gone with you!" Hugo waved a dismissive arm. "Go and fetch Webster. Better yet, fetch a hammer and some nails and board up those doors yourself. No sense bothering the old man, when you're plenty able to oblige."

The squire balked. "But I'm helpin' Lady Finnula with the disposal of His Lordship's things—"

Hugo was in no mood to cater to his squire's sensitive nature. He turned and bellowed, with not a little ill feeling, "Off with you, boy! I care not to see your milk-white face again until the task is done!"

Peter's milk-white face went a shade paler, and without another word, the youth turned and ran for the stables, where Webster kept the tools. Sheriff de Brissac was still chuckling over Hugo's outburst when Finnula emerged from the house, wiping her hands on a piece of cloth.

"What's all the shouting about?" she demanded, strolling toward them. "I can hardly hear myself think."

Hugo was still fuming over his ward's thickheadedness. "That damned fool of a squire of mine. I have yet to hear an intelligent word out of his mouth, in all the weeks I've known him."

Finnula grimaced. There was no love lost between her and the boy who'd nearly broken one of her ribs. "Oh." She shuddered delicately. "Peter." Then, with a sly glance at the sheriff, she nodded. "Good morning, Monsieur de Brissac. You are looking well this morning. I'm surprised, I must say. I could have sworn 'twas you I heard laughing beneath our window half the night."

The sheriff, for the first time since Hugo's acquaintance with him, went red. Shuffling his massive feet, de Brissac hunched his shoulders and said, looking steadily at his own feet, "I admit I might have overimbibed last eve. The wine was flowing rather steadily. 'Twas quite generous of Your Lord and Ladyship—"

"Hmph," was all Finnula said, as she finished cleaning her hands, but it was clear she was stifling a smile at the sheriff's discomfort.

Anxious to change the subject, the sheriff lifted his head and said, eagerly, "Perhaps Her Ladyship saw someone come down from the tower earlier, and might be able to—"

Hugo quickly cut the older man off. "I assume you have breakfasted, my love," he said, wrapping an arm about his wife's waist. He ignored her raised eyebrows, pretending not to remember their tiff barely an hour before. "But what say you to sharing the midday meal with your husband? I thought we might ride to the millhouse and pay a call on your sister. She, too, after all, is newly wed."

Finnula, to his relief, smiled prettily at this suggestion, all rancor forgotten. "Oh! And I can welcome my new brother to the family. I had no opportunity yesterday—"

"And I shall make sure you come bearing gifts for him, and not arms," Hugo warned. Finnula frowned with disappointment at this, which sent the sheriff into guffaws.

"But you shan't be paying any social calls dressed like that," Hugo said, with mock severity. "Go and put on your finery. You are the wife of an earl now, and must be attired accordingly."

Finnula rolled her eyes but traipsed off obediently, slinging the cloth with which she'd wiped her hands around her slender neck like a scarf. Hugo glanced at the sheriff, to thank him for refraining from mentioning the broken merlon in front of the girl, but saw that de Brissac's attention was fully focused elsewhere. Following the older man's gaze, Hugo ground his teeth. It was his own wife's fetching backside that the sheriff found so absorbing.

All the more reason, Hugo decided, for the leather braies to join his father's belongings on the bonfire that eve.

Hooking an arm around de Brissac's neck, Hugo spun the larger man away from the sight of Finnula's retreating figure. "Come, John," he growled. "I have a need to see whether you lot consumed every last drop of ale in my brew house last night."

The sheriff seemed to recall himself, and coughed uncomfortably. "Ah," he said. "'Twould explain the pounding in my head were you to find every barrel empty."

"Unfortunately, the only explanation for my throbbing side is that I was hit by a sheriff the size of a cart horse."

Sheriff de Brissac's expression grew grave. "My lord, you had best face the fact that someone seems quite anxious to see you dead. I would advise the use of caution until I have had a chance to pay a call upon our friend Laroche."

"Caution," Hugo echoed, shaking his head. "I thought when I returned from Egypt I would have no more need for that kind of caution." Holding up both his hands, Hugo made a gesture that encompassed the entire stable yard and cloudless sky. "This is my home. Yet 'twould seem I needs fear for my life in my very bed!"

Sheriff de Brissac was thoughtfully stroking his beard, and Hugo did not miss the fact that the older man's eyes had strayed once more in Finnula's direction.

"Not your bed, I hope, my lord," the sheriff said. "You cannot mean that literally."

Hugo instantly saw de Brissac's meaning and glowered. "Certainly not," he said stiffly. "'Twas only an expression."

But he, too, found himself staring in the direction Finnula had departed, wondering if perhaps that was precisely what someone intended for him to think.

# Chapter Eighteen

Finnula would never approve of her sister's relationship with Jack Mallory. It had been established without anyone's knowledge save that of the two main participants, and conducted in secret. Mellana was not a girl to whom lies came easily, and so Jack must have been the one who'd insisted on subterfuge, which led one to believe his intentions from the start had not been honorable.

This, coupled with the fact that there was something distinctly distrustful about the man's face, caused Finnula to despise him. Perhaps it was only that his head was entirely too large for his small, wiry body. Now that she had such a fine specimen of a husband to compare him to, Finnula found Mellana's lover sadly lacking in both muscle tone and body hair. It pained Finnula to think that her sister was forever wedded to such a physical inferior.

But it wasn't just the musician's build that troubled Finnula. There was also his obvious affection for gewgaws, a love that rivaled even Mellana's. The minstrel was clad all over in velvet and ribbon. There were shiny bells upon his boots, and the buttons upon his jerkin were brass. Finnula even spied a ring upon his smallest finger! What sort of man dressed in such frivolous attire? Why, Hugo was a lord, but he dressed quite plainly . . . remarkably plainly, considering the jewels and precious materials he'd acquired in the Holy Land. Had he wanted to, Hugo could have outshone the king himself. So how was it that a common minstrel wore more finery than an earl?

Finnula did her best to hide her dislike for her sister's lover, however, for her husband's sake. On the ride over to the millhouse, Hugo had bade her to behave, and Finnula, anxious to assuage the guilt she felt over his upset about the bonfire, had assented. She felt quite badly about the fact that she'd forgotten to consult her own husband's feelings in a matter of such household importance. She was so used to doing exactly as she wished, whenever she wished, that it had come as a blow to her when she'd realized there was now another party she was obligated to consult in her decision making.

Still, it hadn't been easy not to knock Jack Mallory about the head. The bedroom that, up until yesterday, Finnula had shared only with her sisters was now Mellana's bridal bower, and Jack Mallory boasted of throwing out all the dried roses Finnula had hung from the roof beams, claiming that they made him sneeze. In addition, the minstrel did not seem the least enchanted with the idea of being a miller, and sneered at Robert at every opportunity. The fact that the coward was careful to sneer only when there wasn't the slightest chance of Robert seeing him do so made it all the worse.

Still, Finnula smiled graciously all through supper, responding calmly to Patricia's ribbings about her wedding night and the fact that, in her lavender samite gown, she seemed to glow. Finnula had no idea whether this was true, but she saw that Hugo's gaze strayed toward her often, and though at first she was certain it was because she had a piece of food caught in her teeth, she finally came to the conclusion that there was actual admiration in his glance. Could he, she wondered, actually find her attractive? It seemed incredible that any man would notice *her* when there was a beauty like Mellana in the room.

And yet even Jack Mallory, after several pitchers of ale, seemed to be grinning sloppily at her with alarming regularity. Finnula, discomfited by a sudden urge to ram her fist into the minstrel's midriff, excused herself and went outside. She was trying very, very hard to follow Robert's advice and act maidenly, in the dim hope that Hugo might actually come to feel something for her other than sexual desire, but she was finding it difficult indeed. How she longed to prick that troubadour's hindquarters with just one arrow from her quiver! And how she missed her braies. Even now, she was having difficulty with the hem of her gown, which seemed to drag woefully in the dirt. And there, there was another temptation! The elusive hawk that had been decimating Mellana's hen population was perched just a few yards away, again on the henhouse roof. And she had not brought her bow and quiver with her!

Rather than let the opportunity go to waste, however, Finnula spent a quiet half hour studying the bird of prey's habits, resolving to return to the millhouse surreptitiously upon the morrow expressly to kill the pest. The hawk, that was. Not Jack Mallory.

It was as she was planning the hawk's demise that Hugo's squire, Peter, strolled into the millhouse yard, looking for all the world as if he'd been invited to do so. Finnula, who still occasionally experienced a little tenderness in her side where the boy had struck her, eyed him mistrustfully but said nothing, hoping that he would go away without noticing her.

No such luck. Peter not only noticed her, her greeted her, and, though her salute was cold at best, he sauntered up to her with a smile.

"My lady," he nodded. "Right fair day, wouldn't you say?"

Finnula shrugged. She was in no mood for idle chatter. Peter, apparently recognizing this, asked her a question concerning the domestic arrangements she'd laid out for the staff that morning, and Finnula responded monosyllabically, enunciating clearly so that there would be no misunderstanding. It seemed odd to her that Peter would walk all this way merely to clear up a housekeeping dispute, and she couldn't help staring at him suspiciously.

The domestic puzzle cleared up, Peter nodded, then, to Finnula's dismay, leaned his backside against the very fence upon which she was sitting. Finnula glared at him, but the youth wouldn't go. Instead, he asked, in a deceptively toneless voice, whether she had heard any word concerning the Laroches.

"The Laroches?" Finnula's astonishment was difficult to disguise. "Do you . . . You don't mean Reginald Laroche and his daughter, Isabella?"

Peter affirmed that those were the very Laroches about whom he was concerned. "For," the boy said, matter-of-factly, " 'twould seem to me they've been very sadly used by His Lordship."

Finnula stared at the boy—who, if truth be told, was a year or two older than herself—and cried, "I like that! Sadly used indeed! I suppose 'twas Isabella who came to you with that lament."

Peter looked surprised, but attempted to hide the emotion. "Nay. Well, and what of it? There is a lady well-used to the finer things in life, suddenly thrown out of the home she has always known, to wend her way as best she can—"

Finnula snorted, though, now that she was the wife of an earl, such behavior really ought to have been below her. "Wend her way as best she can? But that is what Isabella Laroche does best! Never fear for Isabella, sir. She is like a cat. She'll always land upon her feet."

Seeing that the boy looked skeptical, Finnula's brow furrowed. What foolishness was this? Was the boy besotted with the ebony-tressed Isabella? Why did he come to *her* with his lament? There was naught she could do for Isabella. There was naught she *would* do for that conceited wench.

But Peter soon made it clear that not only did he think there was something Finnula *could* do, but something she *should* do.

"Couldn't you have a word with His Lordship?" Peter wanted to know.

"A word?" Finnula wished heartily she had remained indoors. Even Jack Mallory was better company than this. "What sort of word?"

"A word on the Laroches' behalf. A kind word or two from you, my lady, might make all the difference. I realize Lord Hugo is angry for what he perceives as the mismanagement of his estate in his absence, but even he must see that there were circumstances beyond his cousin's control at play—"

Finnula's gaze hardened. "Is this what Isabella told you?"

"Aye." Peter's throat moved convulsively as he tried to hold back tears. Isabella's recitation had obviously moved him deeply. "If you could have heard how sweetly she spoke of all the things her father did for His Lordship's vassals—"

"You forget, Peter," Finnula said, coldly. "I was one of those vassals. And I don't recall Monsieur Laroche doing anything for me but accusing me wrongly of murder, a crime for which I might have hanged had not Sheriff de Brissac taken my part."

That seemed to render Peter speechless for a moment. He stared down at Finnula, his Adam's apple still bobbing sporadically, and his pale eyes were filled with unshed tears. Though his ignorance was maddening, Finnula could not help feeling sorry for the boy, who was obviously tangled in the throes of first love. Surely she could not blame him for having so imprudently fallen in love with Isabella Laroche. Many a stronger man had done so, as well.

"Peter," Finnula said, as kindly as she could. She laid a gentle hand upon his arm. "I dare not speak a word of the Laroches to Lord Hugo. The very mention of their name causes his face to darken with rage—"

"But surely he will listen to you, my lady," Peter cried desperately. "For 'tis obvious he adores you—"

Finnula drew her hand away as if Peter had shocked her. "What say you?" she murmured, in some confusion. "You speak nonsense."

"Nay, my lady. Any fool can see that His Lordship loves you. His eyes, when they are upon you, are the color of the sun—"

Finnula quickly leaped down from the fence. "Cease your prattle. You know not what you say."

"I do—" Peter insisted, but something in her expression must have warned him not to proceed. Drawing away from her, the boy muttered, "As you wish, then, my lady."

Finnula was so flushed with embarrassment that she could feel the heat in her face. How dare that impudent boy spout such outrageous lies? And the fact that for a moment, she'd been fool enough to believe them . . . Oh, she would not easily forgive herself for that. Lord Hugo, in love with her? He had hardly known her a sennight. Such a thing wasn't possible . . . besides, he'd never said a word about harboring any sort of affection for her, not even in their most intimate moments.

The squire, perhaps noting her lack of composure, no longer pursued the subject. Instead, he thanked Finnula for her time and asked, politely enough, if he might trouble one of her sisters for a drop of ale to wet his throat before returning to the manor house, as the sun was high and day warm. Finnula pointed the boy in the appropriate direction, and then returned to the house. It would seem she was destined for bedevilment wherever she roamed, and she thought it safer to remain at her husband's side for the time being.

Inside the house, while Mellana looked on with worshipping eyes, Jack Mallory was singing a love ballad, a rather soppy one, to Finnula's mind. Four of her sisters—Camilla had returned home with her winemaker husband—and Robert's betrothed, Rosamund, sat at the minstrel's feet, seemingly enthralled by his performance. Even Patricia, usually so levelheaded, looked up in annoyance when Finnula banged the door, and shushed her.

Stifling an unladylike snort, Finnula tiptoed from the room, and found her husband in the kitchen with Robert, whither the two of them had gone to escape the minstrel's dulcet tones. There was no sign of Peter, which Finnula hardly thought strange. When the youth heard his master's voice, he seemed invariably to run in the opposite direction.

"Ah, there you are." Hugo grinned at Finnula, and slid to make a place for her on the smooth bench he shared with her brother. "A valiant effort, that."

Finnula sat down, eyeing him uncertainly. "What do you mean?"

"We both saw how close you came to pummeling him at

supper," Robert said, with a fond grin at his youngest sister. "And yet you restrained yourself. I see that marriage has begun to improve your disposition already."

Finnula stared, thinking they were speaking of Peter, then realized that it was Jack Mallory of whom they spoke. She shrugged uncomfortably. Neither youth was one whom she wouldn't gladly have pummeled behind her husband's back, and she wondered guiltily if that sentiment was entirely appropriate for the wife of an earl. Glancing up at Hugo, who was arguing good-naturedly with her brother over the most advantageous time of year to plant wheat, she checked on the color of his eyes. They were green. Peter had, of course, been talking nonsense in the yard, but it didn't hurt to make sure.

Jack Mallory's doleful little tune tinkled to its sad denouement—in which the lady fair flung herself into a river rather than live without her love—and Hugo, hearing Finnula's sister pleading for another love song, rose hastily and announced that they must be off. Robert rose with a shudder, saying he would rather see them to their horses than have to endure another of Jack Mallory's ballads.

Hugo and Finnula, not having expected to stay long at the millhouse, had tied their mounts near the water trough, and Robert accompanied them to their horses, expounding with great energy upon the changes he intended to make around the house once he was married, the most important of which was the construction of a separate cottage for Mellana and her drowsy-eyed husband, so that Jack Mallory's mournful tunes could go unheard by all but those who sought him out.

Helping Finnula onto Violet's back—the samite gown, though lovely, was hardly conducive to swinging in and out of saddles—Hugo grinned at the younger man's antipathy toward his newest brother-in-law, more pleased than ever that the minstrel had shown up in so timely a manner the day before. All of Robert's keen resentment was focused upon that unfortunate musician, instead of upon Hugo, who had, in fact, committed the greater sin, by stealing away the most exotic pearl in the Crais household.

That pearl, having whistled for Gros Louis, who came bounding up, was staring down at him, impatient to be away.

"Because," Finnula said, with uncharacteristic coyness, "I've a surprise for you back at the manor house."

Knowing perfectly well that the girl had no coin and could not, therefore, have purchased anything for him, Hugo assumed the surprise was of a romantic nature. She had, after all, spent the afternoon with her older sisters, and though he was convinced that what Finnula didn't know about lovemaking could be contained in a thimble, he supposed Fat Maude had mentioned something or other to one of the girls in the marketplace. Chuckling to himself, Hugo swung eagerly into the saddle, giving Skinner an encouraging kick with his heels.

But Skinner, instead of breaking into a brisk trot, as was his custom, whinnied loudly and, to Hugo's great surprise, reared with enough force that, had Hugo been a less experienced rider, he would have been sent sprawling to the grass.

"Whoa, boy!" he cried, to the fractious steed. "Easy!"

Skinner had not reared out of fright, however. Hugo had never known the horse to shy, not even from scorpions or raging Saracens bearing down upon them with scimitars drawn. The stallion, still whinnying as loudly as ever Hugo had heard him, bucked his hind legs, trying to pitch Hugo forward. Hugo clung to the horse with his knees, glancing frantically about him to see the source of his normally calm steed's distress, while Gros Louis barked frantically with alarm. It was Finnula, watching in horror from the placid Violet, who cried, "Hugo, jump! Jump!"

Hugo sent his wife a withering glance. All of her sisters, as well as Rosamund, the mayor's daughter, had hurried outdoors at Skinner's first shriek. He would be damned if he was going to make a fool of himself jumping from his own mount in front of half the village.

But Robert, scurrying out from under Skinner's flying hooves, seconded his sister's cry. "Jump, my lord! He wants you off, that's clear!"

Skinner, whom Hugo had long imagined to understand human language, seemed to second this statement by rearing even more violently than before, and Hugo, with resignation, slid from the saddle. He landed on his feet in the grass, but was forced to roll out from beneath the horse's flailing legs, and so when he rose, he was covered, for a second time that day, with bits of grass and dirt.

No sooner had Hugo slid from his back than Skinner calmed, and, looking a bit sheepish, trotted about the yard, snorting indignantly and tossing his noble head. Gros Louis, too, immediately quieted, and turned his attention on a tree, which he lifted a leg to water.

Hugo, his eyes on his horse, didn't see the slim projectile that hurled itself at him the moment he was on his feet once more.

"Oh!" Finnula cried, colliding into him with nearly as much force as the sheriff had earlier that day, only Finnula was a much lighter, much more welcome armful. "Oh, Hugo, are you all right?"

Surprised at the emotion trembling in the girl's voice, Hugo chuckled, smoothing back some flyaway strands of her bright hair. "Right enough." He winked. "'Twould take more than one of Skinner's temper to kill me, love."

Finnula's face had gone pale, despite the sunshine above. "Whatever was the matter with him? It was like he went mad!"

Robert had hurried over to the shaking destrier, and despite Rosamund's fearful plea for him to stay away from the awful beast, was running knowledgeable hands up and down Skinner's twitching legs.

"I can't find aught wrong with him, my lord," the miller said, straightening and shaking his head. "Nothing. It truly is as if the animal went mad."

"Not mad," Hugo said grimly. "Not Skinner. A saner mount I've never had."

"Then what?" Finnula's gray eyes, as they searched his face, were troubled. "Then what could have ailed him?"

Hugo tore his glance from his wife's concerned face, though he tightened his grip on her slim waist. "Look beneath the saddle blanket, if you would, Robert, and tell me what you find there."

Robert did as he was bid, and his sharp intake of breath was audible to all. "God's teeth!" he cried, plucking something from the stallion's back. "Look at that!"

Hugo's expression went even grimmer. Finnula, gazing up at her husband's face, felt a chill pass through her. She was very glad that look wasn't directed at her.

"A burr, is it, then?" he demanded.

"Indeed," Robert cried, in wonder, holding up a small, blood-ied thistle. "'Twas slipped beneath the saddle blanket and your poor mount's back. Bit into him something fierce, my lord, when you sat on him—"

Finnula withdrew her arms from her husband's neck and placed her fists on her hips. She was beginning to understand why her husband looked so grim. "But how did a burr work its way 'neath that saddle whilst we were dining? The horses never stirred from the fence post where we tied them, and there aren't any thistles growing there—"

"Someone put it there apurpose!"

The hoarse voice sounded from the tight cluster of onlookers in the millhouse door, and Christina shifted her pregnant belly to allow Peter to pass out into the yard. Seeing the young man's expression, Finnula felt her heart sink. Surely the squire would end up with Hugo's boot upon his backside before the end of the day.

"Someone put it there apurpose, I say," Peter bellowed, when everyone only blinked at him. " 'Tis like this morning, my lord, with the merlon. Someone is trying to kill you!"

Finnula stared up incredulously at Hugo. "What merlon? What is he talking about?"

Hugo said nothing, but if ever his eyes had burned the color of the sun, they did so then. Finnula had never seen so murderous a gaze, and was glad it was directed at the squire and not at her.

"A merlon from one of the watchtowers was toppled down upon Lord Hugo just this morning," Peter declared. "Would have killed him, too, had not the shire reeve shoved him out of the—"

"Silence, you bloody mongrel," Hugo roared, and in the mill-house doorway, Rosamund gasped, being unused to rough language. In just two strides, Hugo had the boy's head locked in a powerful arm, rendering further speech impossible. "You will shut your mouth and keep it shut until I get you back to Stephensgate Manor, where I intend to wear a hole in your insolent hide!"

"Hugo!" Finnula was furious. She darted forward, unconscious of her long hem dragging in the dirt, and faced her enraged husband squarely. "You release that boy at once! I want to hear what he has to say."

"He has naught to say," Hugo declared, not loosening his hold on the choking lad. "He is an impudent cuss who needs to be taught a lesson as to how comport himself around ladies—"

"Release him at once!" Finnula flew at her husband like a discontented sparrow. "What can you be thinking? How could you keep such a thing from me? Is someone trying to kill you? Is that what he said?"

Hugo, attempting to alleviate some of his wife's distress, loosened his headlock on the youth. Peter, in consequence, went stumbling away, clutching his aching throat and croaking piteously until he fell in a heap at the feet of a very surprised Rosamund.

"No one," Hugo panted, brushing his hands on his braies, "is trying to kill me, Finnula. Rest easy. I assure you that I intend to live long indeed, to torment you with reminders of the happiness you might have had with your Sir Hugh."

Finnula did not think this joke in very good taste, and she tossed her head and strode stiffly back to Violet, where she waited, impatiently, to be helped into the saddle once more, unable to mount unaided thanks to the tightness of her skirt. Hugo, chuckling at her indignation, followed her, and received, for his efforts at chivalry, a rather sharp kick to the solar plexus once his wife was seated. This only caused him to chuckle harder and wonder at the surprise that awaited him at home. He somehow thought it would be rather anticlimactic, considering the day he'd had.

Lord Hugo and his new lady were well out of earshot when Peter finally sat up, and, rubbing resentfully at his wounded throat, stared after them with an expression that would certainly have alarmed Finnula, had she seen it. Her brother, Robert, in a fit of foul temper, had hauled Jack Mallory down to the mill, saying that his new brother-in-law could sing just as easily carrying flour sacks as he could lounging upon the hearth. Mellana took bitter umbrage at this, and her sisters had hurried inside to comfort her. Only Rosamund, staring down at the suffering squire, remained, and her tenderhearted distress at seeing the poor boy so ill-used was touching.

"Oh, sir," she whispered, bending down to lay a slim white hand upon the youth's shoulder. "Is there aught I can do for you?"

"'Tis not I you need worry for, mistress," Peter said, bravely.

Rosamund looked perplexed. "I beg your pardon?"

"'Tis my lord who is in danger, not I. And he stubbornly refuses to see it!"

Rosamund bit her lush lower lip. "Sir? What say you?"

"You saw the attempt that was just made upon His Lordship's life, did you not?"

"You mean . . ." Rosamund's slender brows constricted. "You mean the burr beneath his saddle?"

"Someone laid that thistle there, just as someone, earlier today, tried to push a heavy stone upon His Lordship's head. Someone is trying to kill Lord Hugo."

"But who would want to kill His Lordship?" wondered Rosamund breathlessly. "Such an honorable and handsome man surely hasn't enemies—"

"Aye, but this enemy is the last, I fear, His Lordship would ever suspect."

Rosamund, looking down into the squire's face, read something in his expression that caused her to remove her hand from his shoulder and straighten.

"Oh, no," she gasped. "Surely not!"

"I fear 'tis so," Peter fretted. "Verily, I wish it were otherwise, but she has both motive and opportunity—"

"I cannot believe of it her! That is what they said when Lord

Geoffrey—" At Peter's knowing look, Rosamund gasped again. "No! You think . . . You think she really did kill Lord Geoffrey, and that now she is trying to murder his son, as well?"

Peter looked mournful. "Would that it were not the case, Mistress Rosamund, but I very greatly fear—"

"But why?" Rosamund was clearly horrified. "Why would she want to kill Lord Hugo?"

"She is not like other women, mistress," Peter said, slowly. "Why, I saw her brandish a knife at His Lordship. I saw her truss him up as easily as if he were a pig—"

"But to kill her own husband!"

"Finnula Crais is not natural, and cannot be expected to have the emotions of a natural woman." Peter shook his head. "Nay, Mistress Rosamund. I would say that Finnula Crais is a very dangerous woman. Very dangerous indeed."

Rosamund, looking down at him, swallowed hard. "'Tis true she is the best shot in Shropshire—"

"—and 'tis also true that she resents being married, as it keeps her from her hunting—"

"—and I saw her go out of the room after supper, alone. She could have slipped that burr beneath His Lordship's saddle!"

"And she was nowhere to be found when the merlon slipped this morning—"

"Oh!" Rosamund put both hands to her cheeks. "Oh, 'tis too awful!"

"But what can be done?" Peter looked down at his hands. "The shire reeve will never arrest her. Any fool can tell he is half besotted with her himself. I . . . I fear for my master's life, mistress."

"Yes," Rosamund said, softly. "I have seen Sheriff de Brissac's partiality for Finnula. He quite admires her, I fear."

Peter heaved a massive sigh. "Then all is lost."

But Rosamund, who had spent an entire year convincing her

father to allow her to marry Robert Crais, who was below her own station in life and saddled with six sisters besides, was not a girl to give up so easily.

"Nay," she said. "All is *not* lost. You leave it to me, sir."

"To you?" Peter's astonishment was great. "But you are only a simple maiden. How can *you* stop her, mistress?"

"Wait," Rosamund said, earnestly. "Wait and see."

And Peter, massaging his sore neck, was prepared to do exactly that.

# Chapter Nineteen

$\mathcal{F}$innula's surprise was not the kind Hugo had expected . . . at least, not exactly.

When they returned to the manor house, they were met in the stable yard by Mistress Laver, who slyly informed Her Ladyship that all was in order. Hugo was not in the mood for secrets, though he'd refused to answer any of Finnula's questions concerning Peter's statements back at the millhouse, and grumbled that she might do as she liked, but he intended to have a bath, feeling dirty from his fall and sweaty from their ride.

Finnula only turned up her nose at him, so Hugo strode into the house alone, and, after barking orders that hot water be brought to his solar, hastened there.

But when he entered his childhood chamber, he found that it, like his father's solar, had been stripped bare of furnishings. Everything was gone, from his clothing to the bearskin rug that had lain across the floor. Even the trunks that he had sent ahead from Cairo, the trunks to which only he had the keys and which contained a fortune in jewels and cloth, were missing. If they were sitting outside, waiting to be part of Finnula's bloody bonfire . . .

Hugo's bellow might have brought down the roof had Stephensgate Manor been less well-constructed. As it was, every servant in the household came running, but not his wife, whose name it was Hugo had shouted.

"Where," Hugo roared at Mistress Laver, who regarded him with more composure than any of the other staff, being well-used to his father's tantrums, "are my things?"

"Well, with your wife, I would imagine," was Mistress Laver's coy reply.

"And where is my wife?" Hugo demanded.

"In the lord's solar, I should think, where a proper lady would be."

Hugo thought he might suffer an apoplexy if someone did not give him a straight answer. Seeing this, Mistress Laver smiled and said gently, "The Lady Finnula had all your things moved to your father's solar, my lord. 'Twas quite gen'rous of 'er, I thought, considerin' what happened last time she was there. But she thought you'd be pleased—"

Hugo had turned away before the last words were fully out of the cook's mouth. His father's solar was quite a ways down the corridor, but he was at the heavy wooden portal in a few strides, and, lifting a fist to thump on it, realized that it was his own room now, after all, and laid his hand upon the latch.

His bed stood in a different place than his father's had, facing the row of windows on the south side of the solar, the fireplace on the opposite side. The trunks that had arrived before him from Cairo were stacked neatly in a corner. The bearskin rug was stretched across the floor before the hearth, and Gros Louis had already made himself at home there. The dog's tail thumped once or twice at Hugo's entrance. In the center of the room, Finnula was changing out of her lavender samite, into something less ornate, but not, he saw with relief, her leather braies.

"Was that you I heard caterwauling before?" Finnula asked, pulling the lavender gown over her head and awarding Hugo a tantalizing glimpse of her slim ankles and calves as the kirtle she wore beneath the samite hiked up a little. "Must you go about the house bellowing my name like that? 'Tis embarrassing, you know."

"I thought—" Hugo broke off, watching as she bent to scoop a plain yellow gown from her own trunk. The emerald he'd given her winked between her breasts on its silken cord. "I thought you had lain my own things upon the pile for the bonfire."

"Did you?" Finnula was concentrating mightily hard at working the lacings to the gown. "I said you were a fool to marry me. I didn't say *I* was a fool. Why would I throw out your things? 'Twas Lord Geoffrey I could not abide."

Hugo crossed the room to stand beside her. "And you had them remove his things to make way for mine?"

"You said your solar was drafty in the winter. And 'twas too small for your belongings, let alone the addition of mine. I thought it better to move in here." Finnula raised the gown to drop it over her head, but Hugo reached out, arresting the flimsy garment in one hand before it covered her.

Finnula looked up questioningly. "My lord? Is there aught the matter with the gown?"

With a rakish smile, Hugo tossed the garment over his shoulder. "Naught that can be remedied by your not wearing it."

Snaking out an arm, Hugo caught his wife about the waist and pulled her against him. Finnula, feeling the heat of his body through the muslin of her kirtle, looked up at him with amusement in her gray eyes.

"You called for a bath," she reminded him.

"There isn't any reason why I must bathe alone." He grinned down at her. "Have you any objections, my lady?"

Finnula actually burst out laughing. "None at all, my lord."

# Chapter Twenty

*I*f the entire village of Stephensgate had turned out for Hugo and Finnula's wedding, then the entire population of Shropshire gathered together for the bonfire the following night. Or so it seemed to Hugo. He was surprised by the number of people who wished to witness the destruction of his father's property, and a little ashamed that so many should harbor such contempt for the late earl. Hundreds of people, very few of whom he recognized, flooded the south meadow directly after Vespers—everyone from Rosamund's father, the village mayor, to Fat Maude, the village prostitute, who greeted Hugo with a lascivious wink, despite her advanced years.

It wasn't very long before the vassal who tended the field appeared at His Lordship's elbow to complain that the grass was all being trodden down and what was his flock to eat for the rest of the summer?

Hugo provided for the shepherd's losses rather more generously than necessary, because, thanks to the pleasant afternoon he'd spent in Finnula's company, he was in a mood to be obliging to all. True, his new wife had a few vexing character quirks, such as an infuriating independent streak and a tendency toward obstinacy. But in every other respect she was exactly what Hugo had always looked for in a woman, and never found, till now. And she was entertaining in the bath, as well.

Since the wedding celebration had not quite depleted Stephensgate Manor's wine and ale supply, Finnula had instructed Mistress Laver and her nieces to see that all who attended the bonfire received a cup, and spirits, in every sense of the word, were high. In the purple twilight, the air that was heavy with the scent of spring flowers was soon fragrant with spilled ale as well.

"'Tis a boisterous lot you've assembled here, my lord," observed Sheriff de Brissac, his own cup clutched securely in a gloved fist. "'Twould seem the Lady Finnula was correct in thinking this torching of your father's goods would warm more than hands."

Hugo grunted noncommittally, though he had long ago come to realize that Finnula's plan had merit.

"I understand there was a second attempt made on your life," was de Brissac's next remark.

"Bloody rot," Hugo growled. "A burr 'neath my mount's saddle, 'tis all. Hardly life-threatening."

"Oh, I wouldn't say that. I've seen many a good man lose his life in a fall from a horse."

"Well, I didn't fall."

"Nay, but someone wanted you to." De Brissac's deep voice

lost its teasing tone and became serious. "I fear for you, my lord. Someone wants you dead, and he will not rest until his goal is achieved."

"Do not speak of it anymore," Hugo said, as he observed his wife approaching. "I do not wish to alarm Finnula."

The sheriff's eyes followed the slim figure of the new Lady of Stephensgate. "I fear, my lord, that I have heard her name bandied about as the culprit behind these vile pranks."

"Whoever says so can go to the devil," Hugo declared, with sudden savagery. His hand went to the scabbard at his belt. "And I will be more than obliged to hasten his journey."

"That is not the way, my lord," de Brissac chastised. "'Tis not the gossipers who are to blame, but the man who is trying to kill you—"

"And I tell you there is no such person. Be silent on the subject, now."

Finnula, her long red hair loose about her shoulders, approached them, a coy smile on her lips and a jug of wine in her hands. Hugo had not failed to notice that she was still acting strangely complacent, with glimmers of her former outspokenness breaking through this new, ladylike facade only occasionally. He supposed he had Finnula's interfering sisters to thank for that, and wondered how long he was going to have to put up with it.

"Sheriff, I fear your cup runs low," his wife purred, with a glance in Hugo's direction to see if he registered how docilely she was behaving. "Allow me to replenish it."

His eyebrows raised in surprise, Sheriff de Brissac held out his empty flagon, and Finnula, for all the world as if she wanted nothing more from life than to spend it refilling men's chalices, poured him a generous serving of wine. "There," she said with satisfaction, when the cup was full. Turning soft gray eyes upon Hugo, she asked, "And you, my lord? Do you require replenishment? For, if memory does not fail me, I believe you exerted yourself strenuously this afternoon."

Hugo grinned. Despite the outward trappings of propriety— the rust-colored bliaut she wore over a kirtle of gold—Finnula was still, underneath it all, the Fair Finn, and no amount of sisterly advice was ever going to cure her of that. It still seemed incredible to Hugo that the huntress he'd first seen garbed in a pair of braies could look so stunningly feminine when she wanted to. Though the form-fitting bodice of the gown left little to the imagination, the skirt was full enough to hide all that the braies had not, a fact that Hugo found immensely satisfying. Now that she was his, Hugo wanted no man save himself to enjoy the sight of Finnula's slim legs.

It was for this reason that he planned to eliminate the source of this anxiety.

"Aye," he said, his hazel eyes as green as the emerald she wore beneath her kirtle. "A drop of wine would ease my parched throat very well."

Finnula's grin was as wicked as his own as she leaned forward to replenish his cup. When the vessel was full, Hugo slipped an arm round her waist and turned to the great crowd that had gathered round the towering pile of his father's belongings.

"Good people of Stephensgate," he cried, holding his flagon aloft. He did not have to say anything further to gain the attention of his vassals. All eyes turned toward the new earl, and the crowd quieted in order to hear what Lord Hugo had to say.

"Yesterday," he said, in his deep voice, "you were all witness to my marriage—" Applause, accompanied by hoots and some interesting catcalls. When they had quieted down again, Hugo continued. "This evening, I have the pleasure of your presence at another moment of historic importance. For tonight ends your vassalage to my father and his bailiff, Reginald Laroche, and begins my assumption of the duties of lord . . ."

More applause, which Hugo held up a hand to silence.

"And for my first official act as Earl of Stephensgate, I declare that all outstanding tithes due to my household be forgotten—"

Such an outcry arose over this announcement that it was several minutes before Hugo could regain his audience's attention. Finnula, at his side, looked up at him with such wonderment in her eyes that he bent down and kissed her heartily, and when he lifted his head again, the crowd had quieted enough for him to continue.

"And I would ask you all to join me now in putting to rest the memory of my father," Hugo said, in a more somber tone. "It grieves me that Lord Geoffrey was not the sort of man of whom a son could be proud, and I"—here his eyes searched the crowd for Jamie, who, though somewhat cleaner than before, still looked as little like the son of an earl as a pig keeper—"I can only hope that my sons, as well as all of you, will have reason to feel differently toward the new Lord and Lady of Stephensgate . . ."

Removing his arm from his wife's waist, Hugo gestured to Peter, who stood nearby with a flaming torch held high. Peter hurried forward and thrust the torch into his master's hand. Turning toward Finnula, Hugo bowed, and presented the end of the burning branch to her.

"My lady," he said, in a voice only meant for her. "You will do the honors, of course."

Finnula's smile was, of all things, shy, and he did not believe that diffidence was feigned. "I thank you," she whispered hoarsely. Gingerly taking hold of the torch, she approached the pile of furniture and clothing, which had been soaked with oil earlier in the day for speedier conflagration.

It took only a single touch of the torch to ignite the great tower. Finnula stared like one enchanted at the first licks of orange flame, and when she didn't move away from the suddenly roaring inferno, Hugo stepped forward and steered her gently back.

Finnula wasn't the only one whom the sight of the flames subdued. The rabble which had so raucously cheered Hugo's every sentence had gone eerily still as the fire grew, engulfing seemingly innocuous objects, a chair, a stool, with savage intensity. The wood snapped and popped in protest as it burned, but that was the only audible sound in the meadow. Had he not seen it for himself, Hugo would never have suspected that such a large group of people could remain so still.

It did not take much to break their spell, however. From out of nowhere, Jamie came scurrying up, and hurled, with a grunt, a thick leather belt onto the fire.

"There!" the lad cried, with evident satisfaction as flames engulfed the strap. "And good riddance!"

Sheriff de Brissac, grinning at the boy's vehemence, noticed Hugo's questioning glance and explained, "That's the strap your father used to take to 'im when he misbehaved."

Horrified, Hugo watched as dozens of other people, inspired by Jamie's action, moved forward to throw their own personal reminders of the late lord onto the fire. He saw a horsehair shirt begin to smolder, a metal collar attached to a chain growing red from the heat, a block of wood that looked as though it had come from a stockade turn to cinder. Scores of bits of parchment, the markings on which the owners undoubtedly had never been able to read, fluttered from work-roughened hands onto the flames. These, he knew, were the bills of tallage his father and Reginald Laroche had presented to these illiterate peasants. Hugo had never liked his father, had never held him in any sort of esteem, but at the sight of those slips of parchment, he felt, not for the first time, ashamed of the man who had sired him. Fortunately the heat from the fire hid his burning cheeks.

Then all at once, the stillness was broken. Cheering erupted as someone threw a bundle of straw-stuffed clothing onto the fire. A face had been crudely drawn on the sack that made up the mannequin's head, and Hugo recognized Reginald Laroche's curling mustache. Somewhere, Jack Mallory's rebec sprang to life, and a spritely tune joined with the laughter in the air.

Turning to his wife, upon whose shoulders he'd laid his arm, Hugo asked, hesitantly, "Do you think . . . Is it better now, then, do you think?"

Finnula darted a swift glance at his face before looking away. "Aye. Better, I think."

Hugo felt some of his grief lift at her smile. Playfulness swiftly followed, and he asked, teasingly, "Then shall we add another reminder of days gone by to the fire?"

When her gaze again lifted to meet his, it was with wariness. "What reminder?" she asked suspiciously.

Wordlessly, Hugo reached into his jerkin and withdrew a tightly folded bundle. Finnula eyed it with growing unease until Hugo shook it out, revealing her leather braies. Then she let out a cry of outrage.

"You'll burn them over my dead body," she declared. "Return those to me at once!"

Laughing at her indignation, Hugo held the trousers easily out of her reach simply by lifting his arm. "Nay," he teased. "They, too, symbolize a time that has passed. Your maidenhood is over, and 'tis time you faced the fact—"

"What am I to ride in?" Finnula demanded, stamping a slippered foot. "What am I to wear while hunting?"

"You will wear attire suitable for the wife of an earl," Hugo said firmly.

Finnula was so angry, she looked ready to claw his eyes out. Her cheeks were flaming near as hot as the fire. This was his Finnula, as he had first known her. Gone was the pretense at gentility. His grin widened to a smile of delight at the realization that the Fair Finn was back.

"How dare you?" she raged, spitting mad. "How dare you take what's mine? I only wore what was most comfortable to hunt and ride in! Why is it that a man may wear what he likes," she demanded, "but a woman must cover herself from head to toe?"

Truthfully, Hugo had no answer for that . . . He began to doubt if his plan was, indeed, such a sound one after all. But he dared not back down now.

"Nay. I brought with me from Egypt silks enough to make up a wardrobe for a queen. You may hire a seamstress to create all the bliauts and kirtles that you like, but no more braies."

"Fie on your silks! What care I for fine clothes? I want only what's mine. Now, give them to me!"

Hugo, with a final shake of his head, and before he could change his mind, threw the offending garment deep into the fire. Finnula let out a shriek fit to wake the dead. Indeed, many a head turned, expecting no doubt to see a banshee, not the Lady of Stephensgate in the throes of a magnificent temper.

"Oh!" Finnula cried furiously, as her beloved leather braies were enveloped in flames. "Oh, you . . . you . . ." Finnula seemed at a loss for an epithet foul enough to suit her purposes. Whirling upon Hugo like a fishwife, she spat, "You . . . *bastard!*"

With that, she spun on her heel and stalked angrily away. John de Brissac, who had watched all that had passed between husband and wife with interest, now exhaled gustily.

"My lord," he said, shaking his head. "You are a braver man

than I. Only a rare few have tangled with the Fair Finn and emerged unscathed. The Laroches, for instance . . . until your return."

Hugo attempted a chuckle. Although, truly, he did not feel as happy as he'd thought he would, watching the leather trousers burn.

"She is not so fierce as she has led you all to believe," he said, with a conviction he did not actually believe. "Why, I have seen more ferocious kittens—"

He would have said more, but at that moment, a familiar sound distracted him. He looked up sharply, his reactions instinctive, honed from years of warfare.

He saw the projectile before it struck him, before he heard Sheriff de Brissac's warning shout. The pointed shaft came streaking out of the flames of the bonfire, and though he threw up an arm to ward it off, the arrow embedded itself into his shoulder with enough force to knock him off his feet.

"My lord!"

Sheriff de Brissac was at his side immediately, along with a half dozen other stunned onlookers. Hugo, on his back in the grass, blinked up at the concerned faces and thought it ironic that after a decade of battles in foreign countries, he should finally be felled in his own sheep meadow. He opened his lips to verbalize this, but John de Brissac made a gesture for him to be silent.

"My lord, do not attempt to speak," the sheriff urged, lifting Hugo's head and sliding his own short cape beneath it for use as an impromptu pillow. Calling over his shoulder, John shouted, "You over there. Run and fetch Lady Finnula, at once. And you, get Father Edward, quickly!"

Hugo grinned, though he felt the pain now. It drummed in his temples. "Father Edward, Sheriff?" he quipped. "Surely 'tis not so grave as that . . ."

"I told you to be still," the sheriff snapped. "Where is the Lady Finnula?"

"I reckon she isn't far, Sheriff," one of his deputies assured him.

"Then get her, for God's sake."

"Are you certain you shouldn't be the one fetching her, sir?" The deputy pointed at the shaft in Hugo's shoulder, which he found his neck too stiff to turn to look at. "See the colors of the quill."

Hugo saw the sheriff look . . . and turn pale.

"What is it, John?" Hugo struggled to rise to his elbows, but anxious hands pushed him down again, and besides, he felt as if all his limbs had turned to stone. "What is it? What about the quill?"

When the sheriff said only, "Someone, anyone, find the herbalist—" Hugo reached up, and grasping de Brissac by the tunic, brought the older man's head down toward his own.

"Tell me," he rasped. "Tell me, or I swear I'll rip your heart out."

"The quill," John whispered. " 'Tis purple and white."

"So?"

"Lady Finnula's quill tips are all dyed purple, my lord."

Hugo, despite his pain, nearly burst out laughing. "You can't be serious. She would never—You can't think Finnula—"

"I think nothing of the kind. I beg you, my lord, be still. You are losing blood . . ."

Hugo knew he was seriously injured, more seriously than he'd ever been before. He'd lost all peripheral vision and could only see what was directly before him, which, unfortunately, was John de Brissac's face. He was still in possession of his wits, however, and it took only a moment for the reason behind the sheriff's grim expression to sink in.

"Don't let them," Hugo said, his fingers tightening on John's tunic. "Don't let them take her—"

"Nay, never fear, my lord." John's voice was soothing. "I will see to it. She will not be harmed."

"People will think—"

"I know what they will think. Leave it to me. 'Tis my fault. I was detained by business in town today, and did not have time to go to Leesbury to check on Laroche. I'll take care of everything. Rest easy, my lord . . ."

Hugo hardly needed that kind of encouragement. His eyelids had grown so heavy that he could no longer lift them, and he felt as if he was sinking deep into the peat below him.

"Hugo!"

The horrified accents in the voice rendered it almost unrecognizable, but Hugo knew the speaker, nonetheless. The last thing he saw before darkness overcame him was Finnula's face, white with fear even in the glow of the fire, but beautiful, as beautiful as the first time he had ever looked upon it.

"Hugo! Oh, no!" She sank to her knees at his side, her hands clasping his. "Hugo!"

He tried very hard to tell her something—he knew not what—but his tongue, like his limbs, had turned to lead. And then his eyelids fell closed, and he knew no more.

# Chapter Twenty-one

$\mathcal{F}$innula saw Hugo's head fall limply to one side, and she let out a wail that seemed to have been wrenched from the depths of her soul.

"Oh, no!" she cried, desperately clinging to her husband's fingers. "No, Hugo, no!"

"My dear." Sheriff de Brissac's hands were heavy on her shoulders. "My dear, there is naught you can do. Leave it to those who can help him—"

Finnula struggled to break free from the sheriff's restraining grip, and only stopped her fractious twisting when her brother, Robert, broke through the stunned crowd and, his face paling at the sight of Hugo on the ground, took her by the arm. By then the village herbalist had found his way through the throng, and

Finnula watched with bated breath as the old man bent over her unconscious husband, examining the wound with a critical eye.

"'Tis deeply embedded." Old Gregor leaned back and sighed, after a pause that was, to Finnula, dreadful. "But it missed the heart."

"Will he live?" asked the sheriff softly, because Finnula had buried her face in her brother's shoulder with a sob.

"Only God can say with any certainty," was Gregor's highly unsatisfactory reply. Finnula, in Robert's arms, began to weep angrily as the herbalist made his patient ready for transport back to the manor house.

"What happened?" she demanded through her tears, her hands balled into fists. "Who can have done this to him?"

"There will be no telling that tonight, my lady," Sheriff de Brissac said gravely. "What is important now is that he is moved indoors, and given a chance to recover—"

"What is important now is that the person who did this is discovered!" declared someone from the crowd of onlookers that had gathered round the fallen earl. All eyes turned upon the speaker, and he straightened to his full height. Finnula was surprised to see through her tears that it was none other than her husband's squire, Peter.

"Aye," she agreed, her voice shaking with emotion. "Peter speaks rightly. We must find out who did this—"

"I think that is fairly obvious," Peter interrupted rudely. Finnula, taken aback, said nothing, but she felt her brother's hands tighten on her shoulders.

"What say you, boy?" Robert demanded, angrily. "You dare—"

"Aye, I dare," Peter scoffed. "I dare accuse your precious sister of attempting to murder Lord Hugo!"

In a flash, Robert had released Finnula and lunged at the

younger man. Only Sheriff de Brissac's swift actions prevented another murder from being attempted before their very eyes. But even as the sheriff separated the two men, another threw down the gauntlet.

"The boy speaks the truth!"

Finnula gasped. Rosamund's father, Miles Hillyard, the mayor of Stephensgate, stood in the red glow of the bonfire, his lined face a mask of rage.

"Aye," Hillyard cried. "The truth! My daughter told me how it was just this afternoon. Two attempts made on His Lordship's life already today before this one, and Finnula Crais had opportunity both times—"

"This is madness!" Robert declared. The roar from the bonfire was nothing compared to the roar in the miller's voice. "You know not of what you speak. My sister would no sooner try to kill her husband than—"

"Is that so?" The mayor looked smug. "And what of Lord Geoffrey? Was she not married to the late earl, and did he not die mysteriously on their wedding night?"

"Aye," cried a shrill voice, and Finnula's sister Patricia, followed closely by Christina and Mellana, pushed her way through the crowd until she stood before her sister's accusers. "That he did. But not because our Finn killed him!"

"No one ever proved Lord Geoffrey was murdered," Robert stormed.

"No one ever proved Lord Geoffrey died of . . . of. . . ." Mellana blinked up at Robert for help. "What is it called?"

"Unnatural causes. And that was a different matter entirely! What possible motive could Finnula have for killing Lord Hugo? Look at her, you old fool. Anyone can see she loves him."

Whether Miles Hillyard did not appreciate being called an old fool by his future son-in-law, or whether he was simply fed up with having his declarations second-guessed, he paid no more heed to Robert Crais and his sisters than one might to a nest of sparrows.

"Sheriff de Brissac," the mayor said loudly, "I demand that you arrest that girl on suspicion of having attempted murder—"

There was a collective gasp from the crowd, quickly followed by a number of shouts of indignation and protest. Finnula, however, was oblivious to it all. Her hands pressed to her mouth, her gaze never left her husband's supine body. *If he dies*, she thought. *If Hugo dies . . .*

Matthew Fairchild shoved his way to Robert's side and shouted, "See here! You can't arrest the Lady Finn! Any simpleton can tell that arrow wasn't shot by her—"

"Oh, any simpleton could tell that, could he?" Miles Hillyard looked decidedly testy by now. He was a wealthy man, and one who did not take kindly to criticism. "Kindly inform me how, then, since I must be a simpleton."

"Gladly." Matthew gestured to Lord Hugo's body as it was being loaded onto one of the litters that had transported the ale from the manor house. "Had the Lady Finn wanted him gone, she'd have hardly used an arrow from her own quill. 'Twould be clear evidence of her guilt!"

Peter, sidling up to Hillyard's shoulder, laughed shortly. "That's precisely what she'd *want* you to think—"

"Finnula is the gentlest creature I've ever known," Patricia declared staunchly. "She'd no sooner injure a man than cut off her own arm—"

"Gentle!" Peter scoffed. "I'll show you gentle! She caught me in a tree snare. I barely escaped with my own life!"

"You know very well that was only because she was trying to

capture Lord Hugo," Mellana chastised him, shaking a finger. "She couldn't very well tie him up with you about—"

"Mellana," Patricia said sharply. "You aren't helping."

"And she never would have done such a thing," Mellana insisted, ignoring the warning tone in Patricia's voice, "if I hadn't asked her to. Finnula's the most loving, loyal sister anyone ever had."

"Loving!" Peter shook his head incredulously. "Was it lovingly, then, that I heard her abuse His Lordship with the most vile language directly before he was shot? She called him a bastard!"

The crowd murmured at the truth of this. Everyone had heard Finnula's strident cursing, though none had known the cause of the outburst. Finnula made no move to defend herself. She was not even aware of what was going on around her. *If Hugo dies*, was all she could think. *If Hugo dies . . .*

"I can *prove* that it wasn't Finnula that shot that arrow," Mellana insisted staunchly.

Sheriff de Brissac, who'd been watching the proceedings with unmasked anxiety, nodded encouragingly. "Go on, then."

"If Finn had really wanted her husband dead," the blond girl said, with careful emphasis, "she wouldn't have missed."

The mayor let out an exasperated snort. "Are ye blind, madam? She didn't miss! She hit him!"

Patricia, seeing Mellana's meaning at last, cried, "But she missed his heart. Don't you see? Finnula's the best shot in Shropshire. She wouldn't have missed such an easy target, at such close range—"

"Bah!" Hillyard threw his hands into the air. "This is madness! Sheriff de Brissac, will you arrest that girl, or will I have to do it myself?"

John de Brissac inhaled deeply, his gaze meeting Finnula's. She lowered the hands she'd pressed to her mouth. The flames from the bonfire were not so high now, but in their orange glow, she could still see the body of her husband, as it was carried toward the house. All of her attention was focused on the slow rise and fall of that immense breadth of chest. *If Hugo dies . . . If Hugo dies . . .*

She, too, would die. And not because she'd be hanged if found guilty of his murder.

"I must go with him," she murmured, starting forward, but the sheriff flung out a hasty arm, barring her path.

"Nay, Finnula," he said, in a surprisingly soft voice for so large a man. "Let Gregor tend to him. There is naught you can do—"

Finnula shook her head, completely dazed with anxiety for her husband. "No, no. You don't understand. I must go with him. I am his wife."

"You cannot go, Finnula." Sheriff de Brissac reached for the cloak he'd laid beneath Lord Hugo's head and, shaking it out, laid it now over Finnula's shoulders. She seemed quite unconscious of the gesture, and stood staring after the departing litter.

"I must go," she repeated, but when she took a step toward the manor house, Peter leaped at her, his face twisted with malice.

"Stay where you are, murderess!" he cried. "Sheriff, you cannot let this woman out of your sight! She will run away and hide in the woods, for she knows them better than anyone—"

Startled, Finnula backed away from the squire, until she felt Sheriff de Brissac's hands on her shoulders. Then she froze, staring with wide eyes at her accusers. The roaring in her ears was not the sound of the flames behind her, but seemed to come from inside her own head, as she recalled, only too vividly, a scene not unlike this one, which had occurred almost exactly a year before.

"Lady Finnula is not going anywhere, boy," boomed Sheriff de Brissac. She stood so close to him that she felt the vibrating rumble of his voice against her back. "Not thanks to your impudence—"

"Impudence!" The lord mayor took umbrage at the sheriff's tone. "John, there is no impudence in the case. The girl's never been quite right in the head, anyone here can tell you that. What kind of woman dresses in such a scandalous manner? What kind of woman spends her days poaching instead of sewing?"

"You've eaten game poached by my sister often enough, Lord Mayor," Patricia reminded him with a sneer.

Robert strode forward, his fists clenched impotently. "This is madness," he cried. "I will not allow it. Someone here shot Lord Hugo, but 'twas not my sister! Now, will none of you do anything to find the true assassin?"

"There is no need to look further than this," Mayor Hillyard said shortly. "The wench is obviously guilty. We ought to have seen her hanged a year ago, when she poisoned Lord Geoffrey—"

The crowd murmured at this.

"There is no obviousness about it!" Robert declared. "Did anyone here *see* my sister draw a bow this night? Is there anyone who can positively identify my sister as the one who shot Lord Hugo?"

The crowd was silent, all except for Peter, the squire. He stepped forward with a challenge of his own. "Can any man here say they saw *anyone* draw a bow this night?"

Robert was not finished, however. "My sister wears no quiver, nor has any bow been found. Who is to say where the arrow that felled Lord Hugo came from? The doors in Stephensgate Manor are not locked. Anyone could have crept inside and taken one of my sister's shafts—"

"Anyone, yes," Peter agreed. "But who better than Lady Finnula herself?"

"This arguing is pointless," declared Mayor Hillyard. He pointed at Finnula, who stood with her hands at her sides, her face turned toward the manor house. "To the stockade with her! The girl must stand trial. If Lord Hugo dies, she will be charged with murder. If he lives, with attempting to commit murder. For either crime, she will hang—"

Sheriff de Brissac stepped forward at that, moving his bulk so that it blocked the mayor's view of Finnula. "That," he rumbled menacingly, "will be quite enough, Lord Mayor. I shall remove Her Ladyship to my own home—"

"To your home?" The mayor laughed shortly and without humor. "For what purpose? She must be locked in the village jailhouse, like any criminal—"

"She is the wife of the Earl of Stephensgate," Sheriff de Brissac reminded the mayor. "The jailhouse is no place for a lady."

"No place for women who murder their own husbands?" Mayor Hillyard had gone red in the face with impatience. "Sheriff, you disappoint me. You, too, have fallen under the witch's spell! Finnula Crais is a menace, a harpy who preys upon—"

Sheriff de Brissac held up an impatient hand. "You forget yourself, Miles," he said quietly.

It was Patricia who stepped forward and, her eyes burning with hatred, lit into the mayor. "I know it rests ill with you that your daughter is to wed my brother, sir," she whispered, menacingly. "I know that you intended Rosamund for a much richer man, or at least a man with a better standing in the community. How convenient for you that Lord Hugo was shot, and apparently with my sister's bow—"

Mayor Hillyard's eyes narrowed. "What say you, madam?"

"Need I repeat myself? For I will gladly do so, only louder, so that all these folk might hear how you abandoned your better judgment for the sake of sparing yourself a son-in-law with such relations—"

The mayor sputtered indignant denials, but John de Brissac interrupted wearily.

"I am reeve of this shire," he reminded everyone. "Appointed such by the king himself. The lord mayor does not make the laws here. He abides by them, like any other God-fearing man. And I say that the Lady Finnula shall not be taken to any jail."

Miles Hillyard looked ready to argue the fact, but he closed his mouth with an audible snap when Finnula's brothers-in-law, accompanied by a half dozen of Lord Hugo's vassals, loyal to the woman who had helped their families through the long winter, broke free from the crowd and strode toward him. Crossing arms heavily sinewed from toiling the earth over chests made brawny from years of hauling wheat and livestock, the farmers glowered down at the corpulent mayor, while Patricia's husband shoved an indignant finger at him.

"Miles," he said, evenly. "You ain't never settin' foot in my pub again."

The mayor stammered something, but was interrupted.

"'Er Ladyship ain't goin' to no bleedin', rat-infested jail," one of the farmers announced, and the others agreed, employing language of varying degrees of obscenity.

Mayor Hillyard, whose red face had blanched at the sight of the burly farmers, held up two hands, palms out. "So be it," he cried. "So be it. But if Lord Hugo dies, and she escapes, let it be on your heads, not mine."

Finnula, clutching the sheriff's cape about her shoulders, had watched the arguments concerning her guilt as dispassionately as if they concerned some other woman, and not herself. All her concentration was focused on the manor house, which she could see in the near distance. She blinked when the sconces in the lord's solar were lit, and offered up a prayer that Hugo be spared much suffering. *If he should die,* she thought, over and over again, *then so shall I.*

Her sister Patricia, her face a mask of irritation, turned toward her and hissed, "What is wrong with you, Finn? Where's your mettle? These people are saying such things about you, and yet you stand there, dumb as a statue. Tell them you didn't kill anyone. *Tell them!*"

But Finnula, who'd never before had a problem finding her tongue, could not, even to save her own life, utter a sound. The lights in the windows of the lord's solar flickered, but she saw no other movement within. When Sheriff de Brissac finally approached her, looking as shamefaced as if he himself had accused her, she lifted tear-filled gray eyes upon him and nodded mutely when he informed her that he was placing her under arrest. The sheriff seemed as disturbed by her silence as her sister was, and he barked for his mount to be brought round with uncharacteristic asperity.

"Oh, Finnula!" Mellana, her hands clasped to her breasts, sniffled miserably. "I'm so sorry you're to be arrested again! And 'tis all my fault. If I hadn't asked you to capture a man for me to hold for ransom, none of this—"

"Mellana," Patricia said sharply. "Shut your mouth."

Brynn, too shy to have taken part in the argument over Finnula's arrest, spoke up for the first time. Laying gentle hands upon her youngest sister's arm, she whispered, "Finnula, dearest, tell me what I can do for you. Of course I shall look out for Lord Hugo, but what else? Is there aught I can bring you while you are in the sheriff's house?"

Finnula was still wholly incapable of speech. She saw that

Sheriff de Brissac's horse had been brought round, and that he and her brother were standing by the mare, waiting patiently for her to finish her good-byes. Obediently, she started toward them, ignoring her sisters' clinging hands.

"This will not be borne," Robert ground out, his gaze darting from Lord Hugo's grinning squire, who, with the mayor, was congratulating himself on a job well-done, to his pale, trembling sister.

"Fear not, Miller Crais," Sheriff de Brissac murmured. "The truth will out. And 'tis better that your sister remain with me. Whoever is trying to kill Lord Hugo will not stop until he is well and truly dead, and 'tis likely he'd be only too glad to dispatch Her Ladyship as well. She will be safer at my home than here at the manor house."

Robert agreed, and added, "'Tis His Lordship for whom I fear . . . I always thought 'twas Reginald Laroche that killed Lord Geoffrey, but now 'twould seem the enemy wears the smile of a friend."

"I shall post men outside Lord Hugo's solar," the sheriff said emphatically. "No one shall be admitted save the herbalist. Unless his enemy is a ghost and can walk through walls, the earl ought to be safe enough until he recovers . . ."

Both men fell silent as Finnula, pale as the ghost the sheriff had been referring to, approached, four of her sisters trailing anxiously behind her. The crowd of spectators had thinned considerably since Lord Hugo had been felled; concerned mothers had hauled their children home to bed and out of the line of fire of stray arrows. But many of their husbands had stayed, and now somberly observed the arrest of the woman to whom many of them owed, if not their lives, then a good deal of prime venison.

The mayor, standing with arms akimbo in the ruddy glow of

the bonfire, which had nearly burned itself out, called, "You'll be needin' some rope, eh, John? Peter, my lad, run and fetch a length of the stuff—"

"That won't be necessary, Miles." Sheriff de Brissac swung himself into his saddle, then bent down from his horse to hold out a hand to his fair prisoner. "Step upon my boot toe, my dear." Finnula did as he requested, lifting her skirts with one hand and grasping his large fingers with the other. "That's right," the sheriff said with satisfaction, as she sprang nimbly into the saddle before him. "Just like last time, eh?"

The dismal smile with which Finnula greeted this small joke soon faded altogether as Mayor Hillyard's voice rang out.

"Sheriff! When you arrested Fat Maude last week for that lewd display of nudity she exhibited in front of the Fox and Hare, you did not invite her to sit before you in the saddle!"

"No," Sheriff de Brissac replied mildly. "I did not. Winnie wouldn't have been able to stand Maude's weight." As the crowd of onlookers chuckled, John de Brissac leaned past Finnula and gave his mare an affectionate pat on the neck.

"Sheriff." The mayor frowned. "Your prisoner ought properly have her wrists bound, and be forced to follow you and your horse on foot—"

"Oh, Father!" For the first time, Rosamund, who'd been a mute witness to the proceedings, spoke up. "Surely such precautions are unnecessary!"

"Unnecessary? The girl is a murderess! What's to keep her from slipping a knife into the good sheriff's heart, eh? She's already destined to hang for one murder. What's one more?"

"Father!"

"Faith, child, *you're* the one who begged me to have her arrested." Mayor Hillyard shook his head. "And now you take her side?"

"Father!"

Rosamund turned tear-filled eyes upon her betrothed, but Robert had been paying close attention to their conversation, and said curtly, "Nay, do not cut your father off, Rosamund. I long for him to finish what he has to say."

"Well." The mayor coughed, flattered that someone was finally listening to him. "When Rosamund returned from the millhouse this afternoon with such wild tales about falling merlons and burrs under saddles, I hardly knew what to believe. But I must say I am not in the least astonished by tonight's turn of events . . . especially taking into consideration your sister's long-standing, flagrant contempt for all that we men cherish in the fairer sex."

"I see," Robert said, and turning toward Rosamund, bowed coldly. "Madam, I can only assume that, considering your behavior today, you wish to be released from our betrothal—"

Rosamund gasped. "What? Robert, no!"

"I release you, then, and have only to wish you a long life and much happiness." Glaring at her father, Robert turned away from Rosamund. "You have certainly made it most clear that my own is of no consequence to you."

With that, Robert strode away in the direction of the manor house. While his sisters looked on in astonishment, the woman he was to have married burst into tears.

"Oh, Father!" Rosamund cried. "Oh! What have I done?"

"Hush, child. Don't take on so. You're well-rid of the chap. He wasn't half good enough for you. Now, Sheriff," the mayor continued, as if they hadn't been interrupted. "About your prisoner. Hadn't you ought properly to bind her wrists at least?"

Sheriff de Brissac was in no mood for further catering to the lord mayor's whims. He said, "And hadn't you, Miles, ought properly to be tending to your own duties as mayor? Please allow me to treat my prisoners as I see fit."

Puffing up indignantly, Mayor Hillyard shook an index finger up at the mounted man. "I shall appeal to the king, John. Wait and see if I don't. Your partiality for that young woman will be your undoing . . . Wait, where are you going? Come back here. Did you hear me? I said come back here!"

John de Brissac ended the argument by simply riding away, Finnula sagging dismally in the saddle before him.

# Chapter
## *Twenty-two*

When the man who had called himself his father was shot with the arrow with the purple tip, Jamie had crept away and hidden, knowing it was his fault.

It was Jamie's fault because he'd known about the danger. He had seen the person who'd pushed over the merlon. He had known that someone was trying to hurt Lord Hugo. He ought to have told the sheriff, who had taken him fishing before. He ought to have at least told Lady Finn, who never complained about him not having had a bath and had even given him lessons in how to hunt and draw a bow. He ought to have told his father himself.

But he hadn't told anyone. Instead he had hidden, like a baby, underneath the table where they'd set up the beer barrels. And by the time he'd felt brave enough to come out, both the Sheriff and Lady Finn were gone, leaving him *no one* to tell what he knew. He was no better than the tabby cat that licked the milk pails clean. He hadn't done anything to stop his father from getting hurt.

Until now.

Now his father was lying on the great bed in Lord Geoffrey's solar, and an old man was hovering over him, doing strange things to him. The old man had told Mistress Laver that Lord Hugo wasn't going to die. And that's when Jamie had fetched the sword that had been hung on one of the bedposts.

Lugging the heavy weapon behind him, Jamie crouched down in the shadows before the door to his father's solar, intent on keeping out the person who wanted Lord Hugo dead. He was too small to heave the sword at anyone, but he would hold it, anyway. He could trip someone with it. He could swing it at someone's legs. He could stop them from hurting his father some more. Soon the sheriff and Lady Finn would come back, and then Jamie would tell them what he knew. In the meantime, he would protect his father. He would keep him safe.

No one saw Jamie in the shadows. No one ever saw Jamie, unless he wanted to be seen. That was because Jamie had learned, long ago, that the only way to avoid Lord Geoffrey's wrath was to not be seen by him. And so he'd learned to disappear, to blend in with shadows, to be silent as a wraith. He hid well, melting into walls. Not being very clean helped, of course. No one noticed his white face, because it was always covered with dirt.

After Lord Geoffrey had died, instead of not hiding anymore, Jamie took to hiding from Monsieur Laroche and his daughter. Though the bailiff had never beaten him, it was only because he'd never been able to catch him. Mam'selle Isabella had been a different story. She was quick, with long fingernails that sank into Jamie's skin. Holding him by the arm, Mam'selle Isabella would hit him with the back of her hairbrush. Once the Lady Finn had caught her at it, and had threatened to take the hairbrush to Mam'selle Isabella. Mam'selle Isabella had continued to beat Jamie after that, but only indoors, where there was no chance of Lady Finn seeing her.

Crouching in the shadows with his father's great sword, Jamie waited confidently for the sheriff. Now that he knew Lord Hugo wasn't going to die, he was not so afraid. In the days since Lord Hugo had come, Jamie hadn't been beaten once. No one had even *threatened* to beat him. He had not wanted Lord Hugo to die. And that was why he was so ashamed of himself for not telling what he had seen.

But now he would tell. He would guard his father's life, and he would tell what he'd seen. And then everything would be all right.

Inside his father's solar, the old man was still doing mysterious things to Lord Hugo. Mistress Laver was helping him, holding a basin of hot water and saying things like, "Oh! Should ye be doin' that now, Gregor?" and "But what if ye were to put it this way, Gregor?"

The old man only grunted in response. Old Gregor did not like women. Jamie was forced to agree with him there. With a few exceptions, women were a continual source of strife in Jamie's life.

When he heard footsteps on the stairs, Jamie sank deeper into the shadows, but took a firmer hold on his father's sword. He hoped it was the sheriff, or even the Lady Finn, but he saw that it was neither. It was the boy Peter, the one Lord Hugo had brought to the manor house from London. Peter thought a great deal of himself. Though he hadn't yet hit Jamie, Jamie thought it was only because Peter felt himself to be so much above him. Jamie didn't think much of Peter's velvet tunics and London accent. He would have liked the older boy better if he hadn't complained so much his first few days after arriving.

Peter, lighting upon the top of the stairs in his fancy boots, saw that the door to Lord Hugo's solar was open, and headed toward it.

Heaving the sword over his head, Jamie let its weight carry the blade forward until, with a resounding clang, the sword struck the flagstones directly before the threshold to the solar—and just inches from Peter's toes.

The older boy stared down in astonishment.

"What the hell d'you think you're doing?" Peter demanded, in a strangled voice. "You could have cut my foot off!"

Jamie only glared up at him. "You are not to enter my father's room," he said firmly.

"Your *father*!" Peter laughed. "I like that! Lord Hugo, *your* father?"

Mistress Laver, hearing the disturbance in the corridor, came bustling out of the solar.

"What's this, now? What's this?" Seeing Jamie with Lord Hugo's sword, she frowned. "What's the matter with you two boys, playin' at yer games when 'Is Lordship is 'overing on the brink of death? Jamie, give me that—"

With a yank, Mistress Laver took the heavy sword from Jamie, and, glaring at Peter, said, "I'm ashamed of the both of ye. You, Peter, should know better. You should be settin' an example for the young one. Now be quiet, and let old Gregor do his work."

The heavy wooden door did not slam behind Mistress Laver, because she was too concerned for her patient to make that much noise. But it did close very firmly. Jamie stared at the portal, and wondered what he was going to do now.

"What were you doing with Lord Hugo's sword?" Leaning

against the wall, Peter folded his arms and stared down at Jamie. "Did you think I was going to try to hurt him?"

Jamie pressed his lips together to keep himself from speaking. Peter noticed, and observed, "I'm a good deal bigger than you, boy. I could make you talk if I wanted to."

Jamie started to sidle backward, knowing that if he could shrink back into the shadows, he would be able to disappear again. He knew he should lie, but lying was not something he did well. He was much better at hiding.

"What is this about Lord Hugo being your father?" Peter was smiling, but Jamie knew better than to let his guard down because of a smile. Mam'selle Isabella had smiled a great deal, as well, and then she'd gone straight for the hairbrush.

"Has Lord Hugo acknowledged that you're his child?" the older boy demanded. When Jamie failed to respond, he laughed. "I can't imagine he much liked that, coming home to find his bastard running about like a half-wild thing, covered in dirt and God knows what. So, tell me. Has he called you son?"

It occurred to Jamie that beating the son of an earl, even a bastard son, was not something much smiled upon. If admitting that Lord Hugo had, indeed, called him son would spare him a beating, then Jamie would confess to it readily.

"Aye," he said, his voice gravelly from disuse. "Aye, Lord Hugo called me his son—"

"Is that so?" Peter grinned, his face shadowed in the light from the wall sconce. "So if Lord Hugo dies, you're his heir?"

Jamie didn't know what the older boy was talking about. Instead, he reevaluated his position, and decided that he was likely to get beaten anyway, earl's son or no. He continued sidling backward.

"Well? Answer me, boy. Did Lord Hugo say anything about

you inheriting?" Peter rubbed his chin. Earlier, Jamie had noticed that the squire did this often, even though there was no hair growing there. "Nay . . . Nay, he would have had legitimate heirs enough from that red-haired bitch. There'd be no need to claim you. But we mustn't take any chances . . ."

Jamie turned and started to run. He didn't know what made him run, only that something in the older boy's tone of voice sent the hairs on the back of his neck rising.

Peter chased after him, laughing.

*I*t wasn't until they were a good distance away, and well out of the mayor's earshot, that the Lady of Stephensgate broke down, sobbing fitfully into her hands. With what would have been comic awkwardness, had the gesture not been so pathetic, the sheriff raised a hand to pat her shaking shoulders, in a manner not unlike the way he often patted his horse, Winnie. If she not been so miserable, Finnula would have laughed.

"There, there," John de Brissac murmured soothingly. "Things are not as bad as all that. You mustn't let Mayor Hillyard upset you so. After all, Lord Hugo still lives . . ."

"But for how long?" Finnula sobbed.

"As that old hermit said, only God can tell. But he is a strong young man. He ought to have a few good years left in him, if you don't wear him to the bone."

Finnula cried even harder at this reminder of her behavior following her husband's tossing her braies into the fire. "Oh," she sniffled, swiping at her wet cheeks with the backs of her hands. "I called him such names!"

"Indeed you did. Fortuitous to his would-be assassin, that was. You certainly *looked* angry enough to kill him."

"I was," Finnula confessed. Then she gasped, twisting in the saddle to look up at the bearded man. It was dark on the road they traveled, the newly risen moon half hidden in the thickly leafed branches of the trees that flanked the wheel-rutted path. Still, she could see the sheriff's face well enough.

"But you cannot think I would have done such a thing!" she cried. "Killed my husband over a pair of braies? Oh, surely not!"

"I think nothing of the kind." She saw the sheriff smile in the wan moonlight. "But somewhere in that throng was someone who wanted Lord Hugo very dead indeed."

"I cannot think who it could be." Finnula sighed. She had recovered herself somewhat, and sat a little straighter in the saddle. "Who could hate Hugo so much as to want him dead?" she wondered. "He has only been back in Stephensgate these few days . . ."

"I think I have a very good idea who might be behind it all," Sheriff de Brissac said. "Strangely enough, however, he wasn't present tonight to accuse you again, as he did a year ago."

"You mean Reginald Laroche?" Finnula shook her head. "But why would he want to kill Hugo? For forcing him to leave the manor house?"

"'Tis reason enough."

"But what else could he have expected Hugo to do? Monsieur Laroche cheated and robbed Lord Geoffrey, mayhap even killed him—"

"Indeed. And Lord Hugo humiliated and threatened him for doing so."

"But that is not reason enough to kill a man!"

"Men have been killed for many a stupider reason," Sheriff de Brissac observed.

"But—"

"'Tis possible that Monsieur Laroche thinks that, with Lord Hugo out of the way, he would inherit the title—"

"But that would be impossible," Finnula said, her tears forgotten. "There's Jamie—"

"Has Lord Hugo declared Jamie heir? I think not. Laroche has more claim to the title—"

Finnula gasped. "'Twould be criminal!"

"'Twould be most convenient for Reginald Laroche, who has devoted so many years to the estate, and has so many friends at court . . ."

"Has he?" Finnula was surprised. She couldn't imagine Reginald Laroche having any friends at all, particularly wealthy ones. But then she supposed that wealthy ones were the only kind he'd tolerate.

"Indeed. His sister, with whom he went to live in Leesbury, is married to the cousin of the queen's favorite lady-in-waiting—"

Finnula's spirits had returned with enough to force to allow her to snort sarcastically at this piece of information.

"Scoff not, my lady," the sheriff warned. "'Tis connections like that which aid one in winning the king's favor—"

"Any king who would favor Reginald Laroche over Lord Hugo is a fool," Finnula declared, with feeling.

The sheriff, she felt rather than saw, since the night was dark indeed, grinned. "Ah, my dear. You will never make a proper earl's wife unless you learn to curb that tongue of yours . . ."

Finnula frowned, chagrined. Was she forever to be reminded of how inappropriate a wife she was? 'Twas unfair, woefully unfair. Here she was, under arrest for a crime she did not commit, while her husband, whom someone was trying to kill, languished unconscious some miles away. A fortnight ago, her worst fear had been that Sheriff de Brissac might arrest her for poaching. Now she was being accused of attempted murder, and the very man who had arrested her was trying to aid her in discovering the true murderer's identity. She hardly knew if she was the most fortunate creature in the world, or the least.

"You must stop Laroche, John," she breathed, using the sheriff's first name unconsciously. "He won't rest until he has what he wants. He's already killed once . . . Oh, Hugo is in such danger! If only you'd release me! I'd find Reginald Laroche in a snap—"

"Lord Hugo is not the only person in danger from Reginald Laroche, my dear." Sheriff de Brissac chuckled. "Which is the primary reason why, without a single witness to confirm that you drew a bow, you are under arrest. The last thing this community needs is you, gallivanting after your husband's enemy—"

"But—"

"Cease! I myself will find Monsieur Laroche upon the morrow—I am certain I can do so without your aid, Finnula—and then we will have the truth."

"And tonight . . . Tonight you'll return to Stephensgate Manor, and stay with Hugo, and see that . . ." Her throat closed up, as tears threatened once more. ". . . See that he is not . . ."

"Indeed I shall, my dear." Again, John de Brissac awkwardly patted her on the shoulder. "I shall not stir from his bedside."

Finnula, relieved, suddenly began to feel the effects of her very long, very trying day. She sagged once more in the saddle, grateful for John de Brissac's supporting arm. As Winnie plodded along the dark road to the sheriff's home just outside Stephensgate proper, Finnula listened distractedly to the frogs and crickets that chirped from the woods alongside the road, comforting sounds that always reminded her of home. Of course, her home was no longer at the millhouse, but the night sounds remained the same, whether she was sleeping in her attic bedroom with her sister, or in a lord's solar with her husband.

Then she heard something that sent a chill down her spine, and she straightened fearfully. The sound was neither frog nor cricket, and it had come from neither the sheriff nor his mount. Craning her neck to look behind them, at first she saw nothing.

Feeling her sudden stiffening, Sheriff de Brissac asked gently, "What is the matter?"

"I do not know," she whispered. "I feel as if someone were following us. I thought I heard breathing . . ."

Sheriff de Brissac pulled his mount to a halt, and, as if Finnula's fear was contagious, he laid a hand upon his sword hilt. "Who goes there?" he shouted, into the darkness. "Reveal yourself, or feel my blade—"

The heavy breathing continued. Finnula felt as if her heart had stopped beating, she was so afraid. Had Reginald Laroche followed them from the manor house, intending to dispatch bride as well as groom? Or was there some foul specter waiting there in the shadows? Finnula did not believe in ghosts . . . much. But considering how her day had been going, 'twould not have surprised her overmuch had one leaped from the gloom . . .

The moon, which had slipped behind a cloud, suddenly burst upon them, and in its silver light, Finnula saw that they were followed not by Reginald Laroche, or by any ghost, but by her own mastiff.

"Gros Louis!" She was so relieved, she began to weep once more, even as she laughed. "Oh! 'Tis Gros Louis!"

The dog, panting heavily from his exertion to keep pace with the sheriff's horse, frolicked in the road, delighted at hearing her call his name. Sheriff de Brissac looked down at the capering beast and removed his hand from his sword.

"You have many loyal supporters, my lady," he observed, his amusement tinged with relief. "If I recall, this animal followed us home the last time you were arrested."

Finnula smiled fondly at the memory. "And your mother kept him in the kitchen, where he ate all the butter." To Gros Louis, she cooed, "Such a good dog! Oh, Sheriff, mayn't he stay with me again?"

Sheriff de Brissac shrugged philosophically. He was not accustomed to allowing his prisoners to bring their pets along to jail. Then again, he wasn't accustomed to bringing his prisoners home to his mother. And Madame Clarisse de Brissac was going to be happy about neither his prisoner nor her pet.

During the long ride home, Sheriff de Brissac decided the best course of action would be for him to deposit Finnula with his mother as quickly as possible, then return to the manor house posthaste. The benefits of such action would be twofold: One, he would be able to keep an eye on the victim, and ensure that no more attempts were made on his life. And two, he wouldn't have to listen to Madame de Brissac complain about Finnula and her dog.

This decision bolstered his spirits all the way to his front door. It was only when that door opened that he began to have second thoughts on the wisdom of leaving his prisoner alone with his mother. While of the two, Reginald Laroche was the more dangerous, it was quite possible that Madame de Brissac, too, had the mind of a killer. But her weapon of choice was her tongue: She chose to bore everyone within earshot to death with her incessant complaining. On the whole, John de Brissac preferred arrows as being more efficient instruments of death.

# Chapter Twenty-four

*W*hen Lord Hugo finally regained consciousness, the sun was high in the sky, pouring in through the arched windows and making the solar overly warm.

Turning his head, which felt as if it had been stuffed with lamb's wool, Hugo saw that there was a fire in the hearth, adding to the chamber's uncomfortable warmth. In addition, wolf pelts had been piled on top of him until it felt as if an entire pack of the wild beasts had lain down upon his chest.

Hugo tried to lift his arms to push the pelts away, but he was too weak to so much as make a fist. What the hell, he wondered, had they done to him? His shoulder throbbed painfully, but it was his head that ached the most. His mouth was as dry as if he had recently been eating sand, and there was a stabbing pain behind his eyes. His worst hangover in Egypt hadn't been this bad.

"Ah, you're awake!"

There was no mistaking that booming voice. Hugo winced as the sound of it reverberated around inside his tender head.

"De Brissac," he muttered, through clenched teeth. He closed his eyes against the glare of the bright sunlight. "Get these damned pelts off me before I suffocate."

"Gladly, my lord, gladly."

Hugo exhaled with relief as the heavy furs were removed. Shrouded only in a sheet, he risked opening an eye, and found his entire line of vision filled with the sheriff's hairy face and broad shoulders. He lowered his eyelid with a shudder. "Where is my wife?" Hugo demanded, irritably. "Why is it that I wake to find *you* at my bedside and not her?"

"Do you not remember, my lord?" John de Brissac's voice was entirely too loud for Hugo to bear. He groaned and tried to bury his head more deeply into the pillows. "Ah, that's correct. Perhaps you were not conscious at the time. You have been unconscious nigh on two days now, my lord. We quite feared for you, Mistress Laver and I."

Hugo spoke through gritted teeth. "Where . . . is . . . my . . . wife?"

"Safe. Quite safe. You needn't fear for her. Well, except perhaps for her disposition, which does not seem improved by forced inactivity. My mother, 'tis true, has found much employment for her around the house, but Lady Finnula is one who craves the outdoors—"

Hugo opened both eyes at that and fastened an incredulous gaze upon the sheriff.

"Your *mother*? Why is my wife in the company of *your* mother and not here, tending to me?"

"Because she's under arrest, of course."

"Under arrest?" Hugo was so surprised that he forgot all about his pain and discomfort. Struggling to sit up, he found that his limbs, though sluggish and slow to obey, were at least still functional. "Under arrest, did you say? For what crime?"

"For attempting to murder you." Sheriff de Brissac held up a chalice. "A cool draught, my lord, for your parched throat?"

Hugo, with a swiftness astonishing for a man so grievously injured, knocked the chalice from the sheriff's hand, sending the water cascading to the floor. The metal cup banged upon the hearthstones.

"Damn you," Hugo cursed. "Stop playing games with me. Tell me what happened, man, and do not spare me. You say Finnula has been arrested?"

Looking a bit sheepish, Sheriff de Brissac bent to retrieve the chalice. "Aye," he said.

Hugo was furious. "If you have put her in that decrepit hovel you call a jailhouse, I swear to God, I will kill you—"

"Nay, my lord. Your wife is being held in my own home, with none but my mother as warden, though, if truth be told, a less formidable guard could hardly be found . . ."

"You *arrested* her? Dammit, man, you know it was not she that shot me!"

"I know it, my lord." John refilled Hugo's cup from a jug on the bedside table and handed it to him. "'Twas not I that accused her, but the lord mayor. And upon consideration of the matter, I deemed it wisest to remove her, in the event that whoever had attempted to kill you chose to next take out his wrath upon your wife."

Hugo, holding the water-filled chalice in a hand whose trembling he could not control, said simply, "The lord mayor dies."

"Nay, my lord. You cannot kill a man for standing up for his convictions."

"Indeed?" Hugo sipped the water, and felt it slide, cool and soothing, down his aching throat. "When his convictions involve my wife, I believe I can."

"Then I would have to arrest you, too, my lord. And you I would have no qualms about locking up the jailhouse, rats be damned."

Hugo drank again, then, dismayed to find that the simple action of lifting a chalice to his lips had exhausted him, handed the cup to the sheriff and sank back down against the pillows.

"And when I refuse to press charges against her," he said. "Will you then release her?"

"Nay, my lord. I will not." Without asking permission, Sheriff de Brissac lowered his enormous bulk onto the side of Hugo's bed. The jostling sent shooting pains down Hugo's left arm, but he was too caught up in the conversation to notice overmuch. "'Tis better that Lady Finnula stay where she is at present."

Noting the grave expression on the sheriff's normally jovial face, Hugo said, "You have not told me all. Do so, now."

Sheriff de Brissac sighed. "'Twas our belief—mine and your lady's—that the culprit behind the attempts on your life was none other than Reginald Laroche . . ."

"Of course," Hugo breathed. "I should have thought of that before. The last thing he said to me was that I had not heard the last of him—"

"Indeed you had not. For I believe now it was his intent to kill you, and then see your lady hanged for the crime."

"He dies." Hugo shrugged, then instantly regretted the gesture as pain shot through his chest, radiating in waves from the wound in his shoulder.

"'Tis not so simple as that, my lord. You'd have to find him before you kill him, and it is like he has vanished from this earth—"

Hugo's grin was sarcastic. "What? The man is not with his sister in Leesbury?" He sounded mockingly astonished. "And

I would have expected him to wait there meekly for you to arrest him!"

John grimaced. "I was a fool to think he would go quietly. The sister in Leesbury says she has heard from neither Laroche nor his daughter in a sennight. Wherever they intended to go after you threw them out, 'twas not there."

"And so Laroche is at large, while my wife stands accused of crimes committed by him." Hugo's grin vanished. "'Twill not be borne, John. As soon as I am well again, I will hunt down the scurrilous dog myself, and sever his throat."

"Aye," John agreed, heavily. "But you will not find him. I have searched every hostel, every barn, every field between here and Leesbury, and found naught to point me in the direction of Laroche and his spawn. I tell you truly, my lord, he has vanished."

Hugo's brow constricted. "'Tis not difficult for a man to hide himself under such conditions, but there is the daughter to think of. Mademoiselle Isabella is not a young woman to take kindly to hiding in a fetid stable or lean-to. I would imagine that wherever they are, she would insist upon some degree of comfort."

"But I have inquired at nearly every house in the county, and no one has seen them—"

"No one has admitted to it. But the man lived here years and years. Surely he has *some* friends."

"One friend too many, I fear." John sighed.

Hugo fixed him with an apprehensive stare. "I like not your tone, John. What now have you not told me? What friend has deserted me and gone to Laroche?"

"No friend, I expect, and no surprise to anyone. But none of us have seen your squire Peter since you were shot."

Hugo had not anticipated that. Peter, gone over to the enemy? It hardly seemed likely, considering the enemy's relative poverty. The boy was overmuch fond of luxury. He had complained nonstop of the discomforts of the road during the journey from London. Why would such a boy leave the manor house for the unease of living in hiding?

"Are you certain?" Hugo asked, hesitantly. "Absolutely certain? I think it strange . . ."

"As did I, which is why I searched the chamber where the lad had been sleeping. He took everything, my lord, including his horse. He is gone, and, I think, not likely to return."

"Back to London," Hugo said, with certainty. "Aye. He missed the city—"

"Nay, my lord." The sheriff fixed his gentle brown eyes upon Hugo's face, and there was something almost pitying in his gaze. "Not London."

Hugo, who could not remember ever having been pitied before in his life, found that he did not much appreciate the sentiment. Irritably, he snapped at the sheriff. "What do you mean, not London? Where else would the boy go? He had nothing, nothing that I did not give him, including his wages. He did not much trouble to keep his dissatisfaction hidden. It seems likely he just gathered up his things and went back home—"

"And do you not find it strange, my lord, that he did so directly after you'd been shot?" The sheriff's voice was kind. "Do you not think it odd that he did not stay even a day after that, to see whether or nay you lived? And after he accused your wife, publicly, of being the one who shot you—?"

Hugo's eyes narrowed. "What say you, de Brissac? Did he dare—"

"I think the boy was not the innocent you'd like to believe," the sheriff interrupted, quietly.

Hugo was already shaking his head incredulously. "But *why*? Why would my squire want me dead? He could gain nothing from my demise . . ."

"Nay, but his paramour would."

"His . . ." Hugo's voice trailed off, then hardened on a single word. "*Isabella?*"

"'Tis the only explanation I can think of," de Brissac said mildly. "Laroche has nothing, nothing that would tempt such a lack-witted young jackanapes. Except, of course, his comely daughter. A lad like Peter might do much to win the approval of such a woman. Even attempt to murder his own master, so that her father could inherit . . ." Hugo started to shake his head in mute denial, a gesture the sheriff dismissed with an impatient wave of his hand. "*Yes*, my lord. Think on it. When Finnula kidnapped you, you sent the boy ahead, no doubt to rid yourself of his annoying presence. He was in the company of the Laroches for some little time before you arrived, but 'twas enough. His loyalties were easily won, possibly because Laroche wined and dined him, but probably because Isabella seduced him . . ."

"Seduced that boy?" Hugo blurted out. "Not her. She would consider him beneath her prodigious talents."

"Not had her prodigious talents been rejected by you." The sheriff wagged an index finger knowingly. "Did she not try to, er, win your sympathies, my lord?"

Hugo stared at the sheriff, realizing for the first time that beneath the heavy beard and jolly belly of John de Brissac lurked a keen observer of human behavior, a man very well-suited indeed to his job. Slowly, remembering the scene he had come upon when first entering the manor house—Peter drunk, and wearing the new gold necklace—he nodded.

"Yes. She came to me," he admitted. "The night before my wedding—"

"And when you, er, informed her that you were not interested, she turned instead to the boy. Although she had probably been working on him long before she ever came to you . . ."

"But I still don't understand why," Hugo declared. "What could she have hoped to get out of it? My *squire*? He has *nothing*!"

"No, indeed, Peter had something Isabella and her father wanted very much. He had your trust. He was able to move about the manor house at will, without causing comment. He was the perfect pawn in their murderous game."

Hugo knit his brow. "Are you saying—"

"Aye. It wasn't Reginald Laroche who pushed over that merlon, or set that burr beneath your saddle, or shot that arrow. 'Twas your squire, Peter."

"Of course." Hugo's fingers curled into fists of rage, but he was so weak that he could not raise them from the sheets. "I'll kill him. I'll find him, and then I'll kill him—"

"Aye," the sheriff agreed calmly. "Can't you see it, my lord? A ready slave the boy would be in the hands of a schemer like Isabella. She asks him to kill you, but to be certain to make it look as if Finnula did it, and gets rid of two birds, as it were, with a single stone. You are dead, your wife hangs for your murder, and Reginald Laroche becomes the new Earl of Stephensgate. For they will have guessed that surely you have not yet had time to put a will to parchment. And so your father's will is what the courts will have to abide by, the one placing Laroche as heir, in the event that you did not return from the Crusades." Shaking his head, John chuckled. "Ah! The wily devil. Laroche has more balls than I ever gave him credit for."

"Balls I will cut off, when I get my hands on him." Hugo was furious now. Hugo could feel rage flowing through his veins, and could not stay abed a moment longer. He flung back the sheet, only to see that he was naked beneath it. "Damn!" he cried. "Who took my clothes?"

"Mistress Laver, I expect. But where do you think you're going, my lord?"

"To find that bastard Laroche, and run him through," Hugo replied, in some surprise, as if the answer were obvious enough to any fool. John de Brissac, however, laughed at him.

"Is that where you go, then? And how do you expect to find him, my lord, when neither I nor all of my men have had any luck?"

"Neither you nor your men have the incentive I do. I want my wife back."

"At peril of your life, my lord? For if you continue thrashing about in this manner, you will surely reopen your wound."

"I do not know what you're talking about, de Brissac." Hugo did have to admit that, upon swinging his long legs over the side of the bed, he felt a bit light-headed. But he had been more gravely injured in Acre, and had recovered in less time.

"Old Gregor told Mistress Laver that you were to stay abed a week," John remarked, watching Hugo's weak efforts to rise. "You lost a considerable amount of blood, you know, when they dug out the arrowhead."

"You'd like that, wouldn't you, you old goat?" Hugo demanded, with a humorless chuckle. "You expect me to stay abed a week while you have my wife locked up in your own house? Not bloody likely. Fetch me a tunic and some braies from that trunk yonder."

John de Brissac looked offended. "I will have you know, my lord, that your wife has been suitably chaperoned by my mother every minute of her stay in my home—"

"I wouldn't doubt that," Hugo snarled. "Madame de Brissac probably longs for just such a daughter-in-law."

"What? A daughter-in-law who cannot sew, will not clean, and likes her food ready-made?" The sheriff laughed. "You know not my mother. She considers your wife perfectly useless. Had I brought her home as *my* bride, my mother would have turned her out of the house by morning."

"She might have tried." Hugo grunted. "But Finnula's fairly handy with sharp objects, you know . . ." Hugo would have said more, but at that moment the light-headedness that had been bothering him became something considerably more serious. His vision swam blackly, and he found himself unable to sit up a second longer. Sinking back against the mattress, he groaned as his headache, which had lessened somewhat since waking, returned in full force. The pain was of such intensity that it blinded him.

Sheriff de Brissac was not in the least alarmed by the patient's sudden relapse. He chuckled and, reaching for the wolf pelts, drew them back over Lord Hugo's naked body.

"Serves you right," he said. "Accusing me of lusting after your wife! Like I said before, you can't kill a man for his convictions, only his actions. And I'd never lay a hand on Finnula. Like as not she'd cut it off if I tried."

Hugo only groaned miserably. The sheriff shook his head, perfectly unsympathetic.

"Rest easy, my friend," he suggested. "And leave all to me. I will find Laroche, your bride will be returned to you, and all will be as it should."

"The boy," Hugo moaned, lifting a listless hand.

"Peter? Aye, him, too. I'll find them both soon enough, never fear."

"No." With a tremendous effort, Hugo reached out and managed to close his fingers over the sleeve of the sheriff's leather jerkin. De Brissac looked down, bemused. "Not that boy," Hugo rasped. "The other one."

De Brissac blinked confusedly. "What other boy, my lord?"

"My . . . son."

For the first time, the sheriff looked less than self-confident. "Jamie," he murmured. "Aye. Jamie."

"Where is he?" Hugo wanted to know. "Has someone been watching him? He, too, might be in danger . . ."

"Jamie," the sheriff murmured once more, and it was clear from the stricken expression on his round, bearded face that no one had thought of Jamie in quite some time.

Hugo let go of the sheriff's sleeve and sank back against the pillow, cursing his own weakness. "Find him," he growled, from between teeth gritted in fury. "Now."

# Chapter Twenty-five

*I*n the three days that she'd been a prisoner in the de Brissac household, Finnula had received nearly nonstop instruction in the housewifely arts. She had been forced by Madame de Brissac to perform such tasks as her sisters had always gladly undertaken, leaving Finnula free to hunt. Madame de Brissac's horror over the fact that Finnula was unskilled in even the simplest household chores, like churning butter and spinning thread, had been profound, almost as great as her shock over the fact that Finnula refused to cover her bright hair with a wimple, even though she was wed nearly a week. Madame de Brissac waxed eloquent on the subject at every opportunity, which, since Finnula was not allowed out of her sight, was approximately every five minutes from dawn until dusk. Finnula had been forced, if only to shut the woman up, into complying with Madame de Brissac's scheme of making the Lady of Stephensgate the perfect chatelaine.

By the end of the third day of her incarceration, Finnula had learned to make cheese as well as butter, bake a passable loaf of bread, mend any tear in any article of clothing, thread a spindle, and work a loom. She'd also received tutelage in the instruction of household serfs and had spent many laborious hours being taught to memorize a single passage out of Madame de Brissac's prayer book, a passage that dwelt heavily upon Eve's lack of judgment in the Garden of Eden and how women were solely responsible for the downfall of mankind.

Finnula bore with these hardships only because she knew that it was either Madame de Brissac's bullying or jail, and though she feared neither rats nor lice, upon the whole she disliked small, enclosed spaces. While she intended never to touch another spindle upon her release from the de Brissac household, she thought the passage from the prayer book might prove a valuable weapon the next time she chose to tease one of her sisters, who were frequent, though disbelieving, visitors to the de Brissac cottage. Never had any of them seen their youngest sister bear such rough handling so meekly. Patricia even whispered that Finnula was a fool not to try to escape, and offered her own services in an attempt to do so, services Finnula declined.

Still, despite the meekness, Finnula could not admit to being anything but miserable in her incarceration. She tried to tell herself that it was because she'd once again been wrongly accused of a crime she did not commit. She even told Brynn, who inquired worriedly after her pallor, that it was the effect of being so long indoors. She did not tell anyone that her unhappiness was due to her anxiety for her husband. She was careful that, though she cried herself to sleep each night—because even after having been wed to him so brief a time, she could not sleep without Hugo's arms around her—she cried silently, so that Sheriff de Brissac and his mother would not hear her. She told no one, and she thought no one guessed, how very much she missed her husband, and worried about him, and prayed for him.

But John de Brissac could not miss the fact that each night when he returned home from his turn guarding Lord Hugo, Finnula was waiting for him just inside the door to his cottage, wearily enduring his mother's criticism in her impatience for news of her husband's recovery. He saw how pale she had grown in just a few short days, and though to spare her embarrassment he pretended otherwise, he was perfectly aware that she sobbed into her pillow every night.

That fact, more than all of Lord Hugo's swearing and threats, was what pricked most at John de Brissac's conscience. Finnula's secret tears were the reason behind his running his men ragged in his frantic search for the Laroches, his appeal to the king for even more manpower, his frequent outbursts of ill temper, and even, upon one occasion, his striking the lord mayor full in the mouth with his glove. The girl's worry and sorrow wore upon him like bristles from a horsehair shirt, and it was for that reason that he returned home the fourth night of her imprisonment with a heart even heavier than usual.

Finnula recognized his chagrin at once, and hung back, fearful to hear more bad news. Madame de Brissac, however, took no notice at all of her son's reticence, and flew at him like a scolding blue jay.

"And what do you think this flibbertigibbet did all this day long?" she demanded, pointing a plump finger accusingly at Finnula, who, wearing a plain gown her sisters had brought her, sat silently upon the hearth, sorting thread. "Nothing. Nothing except gossip with those sisters of hers, who are no better than they should be. It seems the pretty one, the one who got herself in the family way with that troubadour, couldn't keep him, for all he married her a week ago. Disappeared into the night he did, taking all of the money Lord Hugo gave to her with him, along with his rebec, and Kate, his donkey. Apparently, the honest life of a miller was too dull for him, and so off he went, without a word. And many pretty tears did Mistress Mellana shed, for all she's better off without him—"

Sheriff de Brissac, wearily removing his boots, raised his eyebrows at Finnula, though he could not say he was particularly surprised. "Is this so?" he asked.

Finnula looked up from the bright threads she held and nodded, gravely. "'Tis true, I'm afraid. I do not think we shall ever see Jack Mallory again. Or, if we do, 'twill be at the end of my brother's blade, for he is like to kill him . . ."

"That I do not doubt." John turned his attention back upon his boots. "That is another missing," he grumbled.

Finnula heard him, and lifted her head sharply. "Another? Who else is gone? I know you search for the Laroches and for the boy Peter, but who else?"

Madame de Brissac cared no more that Finnula had married the Earl of Stephensgate than she cared that the sun set in the west. To her, Finnula would always be simply one of the miller's daughters, even if she married the king himself, and so was not an equal to her son, and never would be.

"How dare you speak to the sheriff in that bold and brassy tone, young lady?" she demanded. "Lower your eyes and do not open your mouth unless addressed first. Do you not ken that you are amongst your betters?"

John de Brissac cast his mother an aggrieved look and asked if there was not any ale in the house. When Madame de Brissac replied in the positive, he asked her whether she could not fetch him a cup, and when Madame de Brissac tartly inquired why Finnula could not fetch it for him, instead of his aged mother, John de Brissac threw one of the boots he held very forcefully against the wall, driving the old woman screeching from the room.

The effect this action had, besides ridding the sheriff of his nagging matriarch, was to force a smile out of Finnula, who had been longing to throw something in Madame de Brissac's direction for days.

"You missed," she pointed out.

"I know it." The sheriff grunted. "Not all of us are gifted with your aim."

Finnula winced at this reminder of why she was a guest in his household, and John immediately wanted to kick himself for his blunder.

"What I meant was . . ." he said, but Finnula held up a tired hand.

"I know what you meant. Now tell me what it was you could not say in front of your mother. Is . . . is Hugo—" She swallowed, then went bravely on. ". . . Is Hugo worse?"

"No, no." Disgusted with himself, John strode across the room and flung himself onto a bench before the hearth. "Listen, Finnula. 'Tis not Lord Hugo for whom I fear, but Jamie."

"Jamie?" she echoed. "What of Jamie?"

"No one has seen nor heard from the boy since the night . . . since the night your husband was shot. Lord Hugo fears that perhaps some mischief has befallen him—"

"Some *mischief*?" Finnula stood up so swiftly that the balls of thread that had rested in her lap launched themselves, bouncing about the room. "'Tis not mischief Hugo fears, but murder! Have they murdered Jamie, Sheriff? Has someone hurt him, do you think?"

John de Brissac sighed heavily. "I fear it to be so. In all his life, the boy has never before been so long gone from home and hearth. 'Tis my fear—and Lord Hugo's, too—that perhaps the squire, Peter, took Jamie with him when he left—"

"But Jamie would not leave the manor house with him," Finnula said firmly, "except by force."

"I know that. Which is why I have redoubled my efforts at discovering where the Laroches hide. But 'tis all in vain thus far. There is no sign, not even a hint of their whereabouts—"

With an anxious sound, Finnula turned from him and quickly paced the length of the room, her long skirts making soft swishing noises against her legs. In the slanting light of the setting sun, which glanced into the room from a west-facing window, John could see that her expression was one of earnest concentration—the same one she wore when holding prey within her sights.

"What measures have your men taken at hunting for Jamie?" she inquired, after a pause.

John hesitated, then replied, with brutal honesty, "They have dragged the river. They have beaten the underbrush in the woods. They have searched every haystack—"

"Then you think him likely dead." Her voice was cool.

". . . Aye."

"And have you tried hounds?"

"Aye." Standing abruptly, the sheriff reached into his pocket, pulling what looked to Finnula like a scrap of cloth from the pocket of his jerkin. Then she recognized that it was a tunic Jamie had often worn. The garment was filthy. It had probably never once been washed. In this particular case, that was a blessing.

"They scented on this," the sheriff said, holding the small shirt between his large, hairy hands. "But never got farther than the woods before breaking off in confusion—"

Finnula stepped forward and drew the garment from his fingers, inspecting it closely. "Gros Louis could track him farther," she said flatly.

"Indeed he could. But you know the dog will track for none but you, Finnula."

Finnula bit her lower lip, not daring to look up at the sheriff. "And you would not . . . you would not allow me . . ."

"Do not even think it." Abruptly, the sheriff took the small tunic from her hands, and stuffed it back into his pocket. "What you ask is impossible. Until I have a confession from Reginald Laroche and the squire, I cannot allow you to so much as set foot outside that door." Seeing Finnula's crestfallen expression, John de Brissac heaved a sigh. "Do not look at me like that, Finnula. You know Miles Hillyard wants nothing more than to see you hang."

Finnula made a face. "I do not ken why he hates me so. He ate the venison I brought him all winter readily enough."

"Mayor Hillyard hates only to look foolish, and the fact that no one was arrested for the murder of Lord Geoffrey made him look foolish indeed. He intends to see that this time around, someone pays for the crime. Whether 'tis you or another, it matters not, but it must be *someone*. 'Tis not a personal grudge against you, Finnula, though 'twould seem convenient for him that his daughter is no longer to wed so lowly a man as your brother, Robert."

"Aye," Finnula agreed quietly. Running her hand thoughtfully along the stone mantel, she sighed. Hearing the soft sound, Sheriff de Brissac looked up from his inspection of his own fingernails and cleared his throat.

"What is it, Finn?" he asked, not without some trepidation. Finnula wore an expression he did not recognize, and he thought he had seen her every mood.

"Reginald Laroche wants only one thing," Finnula said matter-of-factly. "And that is to see Lord Hugo dead and himself placed as the Earl of Stephensgate."

"Aye, that's so," John admitted with shrug. "What of it?"

"So in order for him to get what he wants," Finnula said, "Lord Hugo has to die. When he does, Monsieur Laroche will reveal himself."

"Aye. But Lord Hugo isn't dead, Finnula, and if my men and I have our way, no one will be able to get near enough to him to do him any harm."

"But supposing," Finnula said, "that Lord Hugo was not to recover from his wound. Supposing—just supposing—Lord Hugo were to die tonight . . ."

Sheriff de Brissac stared down at the girl in horror. "Know you what you say? Are you suggesting—"

"—that we announce publicly that Lord Hugo has died, and that I am to hang for his murder," Finnula finished for him, shortly.

"But—"

"That news will bring Laroche out of hiding far sooner than any effort on our part to find him."

"But 'twould be a lie!"

Finnula looked impatient. "Of course 'twould be a lie! Think you I meant we should kill my husband in truth? Are you a lack-wit?"

Taken aback at being called a lack-wit, the sheriff could only stammer wordlessly as Finnula paced the room, outlining her plan.

"'Twould be a simple thing to convince the world that Hugo has died. Keep him out of sight and do not let even Mistress Laver know he yet lives. Orders for a coffin can be sent, and plans laid for a fine funeral. Word spreads that Lord Hugo has died of his

wound, and that I am to hang. The Laroches return, with Peter.
You promptly interrogate them, and, when the truth comes out,
because the boy Peter will crack like an egg, I assure you, arrest
them for kidnapping and attempted murder. How difficult is that
to understand?" She shot him a disdainful look, remembering all
the times he'd threatened to arrest her for significantly less than
murder.

Sheriff de Brissac shook his head. "But will your husband go
along with it? He was a soldier, remember, long before he was
ever an earl. For a man of his nature to play dead . . .'twill not sit
well with him . . ."

"Would he rather his son die?" Finnula's asperity was ill-
disguised. "I think not. Explain it to him as I have explained it to
you, and he will agree to the scheme readily enough."

Sheriff de Brissac lifted a hand to his beard and stroked it, obviously deep in thought. To Finnula the pause was dreadful. She
knew her plan had merit; indeed, it was the only way she could
perceive of ever catching a man of Reginald Laroche's cleverness.
She liked John de Brissac, liked him very much indeed, in spite of
the fact that he had arrested her and subjected her to his horrible
mother.

But she was not certain he'd agree to her plan. If he did not,
Reginald Laroche would forever remain a free man, and would
forever represent a threat to her and Hugo and, God willing, any
children they might have.

Suddenly, John de Brissac lifted his head and, piercing her
with his stare, nodded. "Aye," he said.

She raised her eyebrows. "Aye?"

"Aye. We'll do it. I'll speak to Lord Hugo first thing in the
morning."

Finnula stamped a slippered foot. " 'Twill be too late! You must
speak to him tonight!"

The sheriff looked surprised. "Tonight? Whatever for?"

"The longer we dally, the greater the chances that Jamie will perish. 'Tis possible they are holding him alive, John!"

"Nay, Finnula," the sheriff said, his regret palpable in his voice. "I think it hardly likely . . ."

"But 'tis possible, is it not?"

" 'Tis possible, I suppose, but—"

"Then he must die tonight! Tell him. Tell Hugo that tonight he must pretend to die, and news of his demise must be spread first thing in the morning—"

Startled by the girl's vehemence, John held up both hands, palms outward, and said, "Very well. Very well, my lady. 'Twill be as you command. I will go at once. Only hand me my boots, if you will be so good—"

Finnula was glad to do so, since it was as the sheriff was bending down, tugging on his boots, that she slipped a hand with lightning quickness into his pocket and drew forth Jamie's ragged tunic, which she swiftly shoved within her wide sleeve. When John de Brissac straightened, he bellowed to his mother that he was going out, and stomped toward the cottage door, pausing only to take one last, long look at the Lady of Stephensgate.

"Think you this will succeed?" was all he asked, with a look that was so eager Finnula would have kissed him—had she not been married to another, of course, and his face not covered with bristles.

"I think so," she said, feeling a momentary pang of guilt.

"Good." The sheriff turned and strode away, into the purpling twilight. And Finnula, leaning against the doorjamb, sniffed the air, pleased to note there were no clouds in the sky nor any hint of rain. It would be a fine night, she thought, for hunting.

*F*innula waited only until darkness fell, encompassing the land in long blue shadow and lending her the cover she needed to escape. She did not think it necessary to delay her journey until the sheriff and his mother retired for the night. Doing so would mean hours wasted, valuable time better spent searching for Jamie. Once she made the decision to go, Finnula could not wait.

Since she had no braies, she wore the darkest bliaut she owned, of midnight blue with muted silver trim, and a kirtle of dove gray that, though light in color, was mostly hidden by the gown. Forsaking a wimple for her trusted braid, she was ready to leave at once, and opened her window shutters to climb out upon the thatched roof of the smokehouse.

Gros Louis saw her at once, banished as he'd been to the yard, Madame de Brissac not being able to stand the sight of him after last year's butter debacle. A well-trained dog, he did not bark, but stood happily wagging his tail until Finnula was safely upon the ground. Then he rose onto his hind legs, placing his forepaws on her shoulders, and licked her face until she moved away.

She had no knife, no bow, and no quiver; no supplies, in the event that they were forced to spend the night out of doors, and no coin to purchase any. All she had was the heavy emerald, hidden in the valley between her breasts, and that she wouldn't have parted with for all the money in the world. Still, the only trepidation she felt was for the sheriff's sake, since he would surely be chastised when it became known publicly that she had escaped.

But if she was able to find Jamie before morning, as she hoped to, perhaps her absence need never be known beyond the walls of the de Brissac cottage. For she would return to her prison as soon as she'd satisfied herself on Jamie's account, and there await her punishment. 'Twas the honorable thing to do.

Creeping from the yard, Finnula trod as silently as a wraith in her velvet slippers. Gros Louis was nearly beside himself with delight at the prospect of this unexpected hunting trip, and he conducted himself as well as a dog aquiver with excitement could be expected to. They avoided the road, of course, and stuck to well-traversed trails through the woods, heading in the direction of Stephensgate Manor. There was no moon yet to guide them, but Finnula knew the land as well as she knew the lines on her own palms, and they made rapid progress despite the uneven terrain, the stinging brambles and occasional stream.

By the time they reached the demesnes of the manor house, the moon had risen, and, though still tangled in the lower branches of the trees upon the horizon, its silver light was already both a boon and a disadvantage: Though Finnula could see better by its light, she herself could also more easily be seen, and that, above all, was something she wanted to avoid.

But though her intention had been to skirt the edges of the property on which the manor house was situated, she was completely unprepared for the hypnotic pull Hugo's presence had upon her. A single glance showed her that a light burned in the window of the earl's solar, and she found herself drawn toward it. She felt a lovelorn fool. She had to shake herself, and drag her eyes from the window, in order to proceed according to plan.

She turned her back upon the manor house and trudged to the very spot where, Sheriff de Brissac had explained, Jamie's scent had been lost by his own hounds. Drawing the boy's soiled tunic from her sleeve, Finnula presented it to Gros Louis, who sniffed at it curiously.

Words were not necessary between huntress and hound. The mastiff had accompanied Finnula on too many midnight hunting trips not to know what she wanted him to do. Lowering his snout to the ground, the dog sniffed the fresh spring grass, nosing through dead leaves and sheep dung. Then, his heavy ears lifting, but his nose still upon the ground, he began to move, jogging swiftly into the cloying darkness of the woods.

And Finnula, lifting the hem of her gown, followed.

# Chapter Twenty-seven

ike bloody hell I will!"

Hugo was sitting up. He felt stronger now, had been feeling better with every passing hour, ever since he'd sent that damned old man and his foul-smelling poultices away. Hugo didn't know what was in them and he didn't care, either. All he knew was that they were sapping his strength as sure as leeches sapped the blood. He was convinced that the only thing that had kept him from dying was his very strong resolve to kill Reginald Laroche before doing so.

"My lord," Sheriff de Brissac said, with forced patience. "'Tis the only way—"

"Find another, then." Hugo felt like hurling something, and the only thing handy was a pitcher of water at his bedside. And so he heaved that, angrily, at the far wall, where the clay jug shattered satisfyingly. Water made a dark arc across the flagstones. "I will not play dead," Hugo bellowed. "If you can't find my son, then I will damned well look for him myself. Mistress Laver! Mistress Laver, fetch me my sword!"

Sheriff de Brissac sighed. He hadn't expected Lord Hugo to agree to Finnula's plan. The fatal flaw in it was that it depended upon a man of action to forcibly remain inactive for a significant period of time. Hugo would never agree to it. John felt a fool even suggesting it.

And then, with a feeling of dread, the sheriff wondered why Finnula, who surely knew her husband better than he did, would ever have considered such a course of action as viable. Surely it would have occurred to her that Hugo would say no. She must have known that her husband was not a man to allow others to take action while he waited.

When the pounding on the solar door came, Sheriff de Brissac was the only person not surprised by it. He turned slowly, his fingers stroking his beard, already trying to determine a course of action under these new developments.

"Sheriff!" One of de Brissac's deputies, a good man, though young, burst into the solar, panting as if from having ridden a good distance. "Sheriff! 'Tis the Lady Finnula, sir. Your good mother . . . your good mother reports that the Lady Finnula has flown!"

Lord Hugo was no longer sitting up in the bed. He was standing beside it, his hazel eyes glowing green, greener than the stone the sheriff had glimpsed around Finnula's neck.

"What?" Hugo breathed, but in the solar, his whisper was as loud as any shout. "*What?*"

John de Brissac brought his hand down from his beard and shoved it into the pocket of his leather jerkin. The boy's tunic was gone, as he knew it would be before he even felt for it. The little hussy. The scheming little hussy.

"What do you mean, the Lady Finnula has flown?" Hugo demanded, no longer whispering. "What does he mean, John? Where is my wife? *Where is my wife?*"

John de Brissac pointed to the window. "Out there, my lord," he said, gesturing to the dark landscape that surrounded the manor house. "Out there."

# Chapter
## Twenty-eight

She found him well before dawn.

He had not gone far. She and Gros Louis walked for only a few hours. Not that the way had been easy. There was no path, only thick brambles that tore at her long skirts and hands, through which Gros Louis, with his short fur, slipped as easily as a fish through water. He lost the scent a few times, but by then Finnula had found what none of the sheriff's men had managed to see: that the way was marked by broken twigs and crushed undergrowth. People had been here before her, several of them, and they had made little effort to hide their tracks. This deep into the woods, there was naught but brambles and wolves, each assiduously avoided by hunters and berry gatherers alike. Reginald Laroche had evidently known this, and used that knowledge to his advantage.

The moon had not even set by the time the dog sat back on his haunches and softly whined. Placing a hand on the beast's wide head, Finnula knelt beside him, peering through the darkness at that which Gros Louis had led her to.

She was not surprised that the sheriff's men had missed them. The cave was not a well-known one. She remembered it from her childhood as a place in which they'd been warned not to play. A child had been lost forever inside it, it was rumored. The fact that wolves lived inside it during the harsh winter months was no rumor. That was why it was called Wolf Cave.

But 'twas not wolves that occupied the cave this eve—or at least, not of the four-legged variety. The rock formation had been transformed by human hands into a spot nearly as homey as Stephensgate Manor. A bright fire danced on the rock lip just outside the cave's entrance, casting a golden light throughout the small clearing. In that light, Finnula recognized Reginald Laroche's horse, along with the squire Peter's, grazing peacefully to one side of the clearing. Across the cave's mouth had been hung a velvet curtain, to keep out the wind that fluttered the newly washed clothing hanging on a line stretched taut between two nearby trees. Finnula recognized one of Isabella Laroche's low-cut bliauts, and realized that it must be she who slept behind the velvet curtain, along with her father. Peter the squire had apparently been assigned first watch, but he was doing very little watching, dozing quite comfortably instead on a carpet by the fire. Beside him, Finnula saw with relief, slumbered Jamie. A Jamie who seemed very much alive. They would not trouble themselves to bind the wrists and ankles of a dead boy.

Now that she had found them, Finnula was quite certain as to how to proceed. She would, of course, turn back, and alert the sheriff. That was undoubtedly the best plan, as she had no knife or quiver. It would have been tempting to waylay the squire and loose Jamie . . . which she was certain she could have done without waking either of the Laroches.

But not weaponless.

Exhilarated as she was from her long walk—exhilarated and reluctant to give up her newfound freedom so soon—she had to go back. It was hard to believe she had not been on her own in the out-of-doors since she'd captured Hugo. She had certainly not gambled on losing her freedom in curtailing his. Mellana cried that she was responsible for Finnula's predicament, but Finnula blamed only herself. She had badly misjudged Hugo's character that day in the tavern. He was not a man she could control.

Perhaps that was why she had fallen so desperately in love with him.

It was Gros Louis, however, who changed things suddenly. The dog, as exhilarated from his long trek as his mistress was, happened to see a rabbit a few feet away, and reacted with pure instinct. With a low growl, the dog launched himself, an act that startled one of the horses, causing it to lift its head with a sharp whinny. The noise roused the squire, and Finnula ducked, suddenly finding herself in very grave danger of discovery.

"What—" Peter was on his feet, no doubt feeling guilty at having fallen asleep on watch. Peering out into the darkness, he saw Gros Louis's great silver head thrashing back and forth as the dog broke the rabbit's neck. With a swift intake of breath audible even to Finnula, Peter cried, "Christ's toes!"

To her dismay, Laroche staggered out from behind the velvet curtain, swiftly adjusting his tunic, which apparently had hiked up in the night, while balancing a drawn sword in his other hand. "What is it?" he cried. "The sheriff?"

"Nay." Peter pointed a trembling finger. "'Tis a wolf, sir, the biggest one I've ever seen!"

"Damn," the bailiff swore, his eyes wide as they took in Gros

Louis's bloodied muzzle. "Well, don't just stand there, boy. Fetch something to throw at it."

"What, throw something at that?" Peter was appalled. "He'll come up here and sink those teeth in me next!"

Grunting, Laroche bent down and found a fist-size rock. Finnula gasped as he hurled it at Gros Louis, but she needn't have worried for her hound. Reginald Laroche could not have hit a duck in a barrel, his aim was so bad. The stone flew harmlessly past Gros Louis's head, and the dog, busily devouring his prey, failed even to notice the missile.

"Oh!" Isabella Laroche came out from behind the curtain, rubbing her eyes prettily. "Oh, what is it? What is wrong?"

"A wolf," Peter informed her, in a voice Finnula had not heard him use before. It was deeper than his normal speaking tone, and Finnula supposed he thought it manlier. "Never fear, though, mademoiselle. I'll not let it harm you."

Isabella Laroche didn't look the least bit afraid, however. She flung back some of her long, loose hair, and approached the edge of the rock lip. Though she slept in a cave, she wore one of her diaphanous nightdresses. Her bed robe, tightly cinched around her waist, did nothing to hide the curves of her voluptuous body, Finnula noted.

The minute her gaze focused on Gros Louis, Isabella gave a snort. "That's no wolf," she said scathingly, turning to go back into the cave. "That's Finnula Crais's dog."

Finnula, crouching in the brambles, dropped her face into her hands in despair.

"*What?*" Both Laroche and Peter spun around to stare at Isabella, who blinked back at them as if they were simpleminded.

"You heard me," she said. "That's Finnula Crais's dreadful dog. I think I'd know it. She never goes anywhere without it. Get rid of it, why don't you? Nasty thing."

Finnula lifted her head in time to see Isabella turn around to go back to her bed, not in the least suspecting the effect her words had upon her father and Peter. Both men stared at each other, and then down at the dog.

"If the dog is about," said Reginald Laroche, in a tone that sent shivers up and down Finnula's spine, "then can its mistress be far behind?"

"But that's impossible," Peter scoffed. "Finnula Crais is in jail!"

"And her dog just happened to wander in this direction?" In the firelight, Finnula caught a glimpse of Laroche's yellowed teeth flashing beneath his dark mustache. "Nay. She is near, I can feel it. At any moment, I expect an arrow to come streaking out of the night—"

Peter looked hastily over his shoulder, as if anticipating a shaft in the backside. "Verily, sir? But it cannot be! We took such care—"

Laroche waved Peter to silence with a flick of his fingers. His dark gaze scanned the woods in which Finnula hid. She felt those eyes come to rest upon her, then move restlessly on. He had not seen her. Not yet. But he knew she was there.

Oh, yes. He knew she was there.

His next action confirmed it. Reaching down, the bailiff snatched Jamie up by the arm, hoisting the boy roughly to his feet. With a coldheartedness with which Finnula would not have credited him, had she not seen it for herself, Laroche pressed the edge of his blade to the boy's throat. Jamie, dazed from both fear and his abrupt awakening, whimpered softly. Laroche called out, into the darkness, "Show yourself, my lady. I know you are there. Show yourself, or the boy dies."

Finnula's fingers curled into fists so tight that her fingernails nearly broke the skin of her palms. She felt physically ill. Sweat had broken out along her hairline, and the night breeze, which was actually quite warm, felt cold as ice to her. Knowing she had no alternative, she rose from her protected hideaway, and glided out into the light of the clearing, oblivious to the thorns that clung to the material of her skirt. As she approached the rock lip, she saw a variety of expressions cross the faces of those who stood before her. Laroche looked triumphant, Peter incredulous, Isabella angry, and Jamie . . . Jamie burst into tears.

"No!" he cried, struggling piteously in Laroche's grasp. "No, m'lady! Go back! Go back!"

Finnula didn't pay the boy any heed. She walked until she stood directly beneath the grinning mask of Reginald Laroche, and after a quick glance at Jamie to see that, though scared, he was basically unharmed, she lifted her face to meet the bailiff's gaze.

"Ah," cried Laroche delightedly. "Look what we have here, Isabella! The Lady of Stephensgate, come all this way to pay a call upon you!"

Isabella glared at Finnula. "Kill her, Father," she said.

"Ah, my bloodthirsty daughter." Laroche laughed. "You must forgive her, Lady Finnula. Isabella has quite a temper, you know."

Finnula maintained enough presence of mind to say, quite calmly, though through fear-whitened lips, "Gros Louis. Go home. Go home."

Before anyone could make a move, the great mastiff was loping away, his pink tongue lolling. Finnula watched with satisfaction as her pet disappeared into the thick bracken, and did not see the hand that descended toward her until it was too late.

The blow caught her full on the side of the head and sent her reeling. She would have fallen if a hard hand hadn't reached out and caught her by the arm to jerk her upright. Dazed, the left side of her face aflame, Finnula lifted her head, and saw a furious Reginald Laroche glowering down at her from atop the rock outcropping.

Before the man could say a word, Finnula found her tongue, and lashed out with, "The sheriff and his men follow me. They will be here anon. You had best release us at once."

"My dear." Reginald Laroche had let go of Jamie, who'd collapsed against the rocks. Now, keeping a firm hold of Finnula, he squatted upon the stones in order to meet her gaze. "You are such a very dreadful little liar. What am I to do with you?"

"Kill her, Father," Isabella suggested, again.

"Indeed, she will die." Laroche reached out and lifted a fine tendril of red hair that had escaped from Finnula's braid and lay across her cheek like a streak of blood. Examining the auburn curl, the bailiff said, his breath hot on Finnula's face, "That has always been the plan. Or at least, 'twas what we decided the day my fool cousin Geoffrey married you, my dear. But then he so conveniently perished before he could get you with child, and we thought we were safe." Laroche sighed gustily. "And then our beloved king had to go and ransom his brave crusaders, following which *you* took Hugo prisoner yourself . . . though I doubt by doing so you expected to find yourself chatelaine of Stephensgate Manor once more. What could I do then, but employ the same plan that had worked so well before? Of course, 'twas more difficult this time, since I'd been banished from the manor house, and could not employ poison, as before—"

Finnula listened to this speech with growing dread. She would not, she knew, be hearing this frank confession, were it not absolutely certain that she was not going to be allowed to live long enough to repeat it. This suspicion was confirmed when Isabella interrupted her father impatiently.

"Kill her *now*, Father," Isabella insisted. "Do not waste time on pretty speeches. Kill her and let's to bed! I'm *so* tired."

Peter looked more than a little surprised at Isabella's vehemence. "Kill her, in cold blood?"

Isabella rolled her eyes. "What say you, boy? You were willing enough to kill Lord Hugo and let her hang for it. Why balk at killing her yourself?"

"But—" In the glow from the firelight, it was evident that Peter was blushing. Was it possible, Finnula thought, that he was having second thoughts about his ladylove? "But to kill a woman . . . like with the boy. 'Tis wrong. Not very chivalrous. When we first set out together, monsieur, you said nothing of killing women and children—"

"Idiot," Isabella spat. "Kill her now, Father, and bury the body. No one will find her this deep into the woods. People will think she ran away to escape hanging for the murder of her husband—"

"But Lord Hugo yet lives," Peter burst out. "They will not hang her, for the earl yet lives!"

"Hard I've tried to forget it," Laroche grumbled. "Had you played your part right, boy, he'd be well and truly dead now. I am starting to think you did not aim to kill after all . . ."

"I told you, Father," Isabella cried. "Send me back to the house in the morning to finish His Lordship off. 'Twill be simple. They none of them suspect me. If Hugo is truly as ill as they say, 'twill be but the work of a moment to suffocate him with his own pillow—"

Finnula could stand it no longer. She felt a killing rage within her, but, weaponless, was helpless to save herself or anyone else, for that matter. Instead she said, her voice shaking, but with anger, not fear, "Kill me, if you must. And Hugo, too, if you can, which I doubt. But spare Jamie. He is just a child. Killing him will gain you nothing."

"Nothing?" Laroche tugged on the lock of hair he held. "Jamie is your husband's heir, my dear. In order for my plan to succeed, there must be no heir but me."

"He isn't legitimate." Finnula shrugged, with dissembled indifference. "Hugo cares naught for him. The child will never inherit. Let him go. He will run away, never again show his face at Stephensgate Manor. All the world will think him dead." She dared not look at Jamie's face as she spoke, and hoped the boy knew she was lying to save him.

Laroche laughed, but gently. "You plead so eloquently for a life not your own. I am not so interested, I confess, in the boy's death, as in yours. His claim is far shakier than any progeny *you* might yet birth. And yet, 'tis necessary to kill you both, to secure what should be mine." Laroche nodded, as if to himself, and rose to his full height. "Yes. That will be the way of it, then. Peter, find some of that rope we used to keep the boy from escaping. We will dispatch the Lady Finnula at once, the way the hangman would have, had she ever stood trial."

Finnula stared, completely taken aback. She had not supposed that they would kill her with so much swiftness—and coldness. She fretted more over killing a stag than this man did over killing a woman. She knew then that Jamie stood no more chance of surviving capture than a fatted suckling pig.

Suddenly Isabella's face filled her field of vision, as the older girl peered down at her, gloating. "Little fool," she said, and laughed at Finnula scornfully. "To think my father would let one of your husband's bastards go free! He'd have killed him long ago if your husband's pathetic squire hadn't put up such a fuss about it."

Finnula shot a glance at Peter, to see how he bore this statement. He would not meet her gaze.

"Is that why Lord Hugo had to marry you?" Isabella demanded. "Because you're carrying another one of his bastards?

Fool! Now you will hang and the boy will die and I will take my place as chatelaine of Stephensgate Manor. And a more proper lady I make than *you* ever did," she sneered, "with your orange hair and leather braies and wild ways!"

Isabella ought to have known better than to taunt someone who had absolutely nothing left to lose. Or, at least, she ought to have waited until Finnula's wrists were bound before insulting her. Instead, Isabella found a fist launched in her direction that she was not agile enough to duck. Finnula's knuckles connected solidly with Isabella's nose, making a highly satisfying crunching noise that nearly drowned out a great crashing of bracken that occurred in the woods just beyond the clearing where the cave rose. Horses whinnied, and Finnula, drawing back a throbbing fist, heard Gros Louis's bark, and her own name bellowed in a voice she knew only too well.

"Finnula!"

Her jaw slack with disbelief, Finnula turned at the very moment that Skinner, bearing a pale but very resolute Hugo, leaped into the clearing.

# Chapter Twenty-nine

*N*o amount of cajoling, pleading, or threats on John de Brissac's part had any effect whatsoever on Hugo's resolve to join in the search for his wife. The Earl of Stephensgate was dressed and mounted upon his horse before the sheriff could even summon his men. Impatient to be on his way, Hugo did not wait for the sheriff's entourage, and headed into the woods, armed with only his sword and a grim determination to shake Finnula silly when he got his hands on her.

Not that he blamed her for taking action when all around her seemed wallowing in confusion. It had become clear to him, those days he'd spent upon his back, how it was that a man like Reginald Laroche could abuse his power for so long, without a single person rising up to say nay. All it took was one man, just one, to declare that something was not right, and others would follow.

But Finnula had been the sole dissenter in a village of over a hundred people, and because she was a woman, her dissension meant nothing . . . or rather, it pegged her for an eccentric, and when next came the time to blame someone for something, her former dissension was now used as proof against her.

But the Mayor Hillyards and Reginald Laroches of the world were exactly the sort of people against whom Hugo had been fighting all his life, in one form or another. The time for him to lay down his sword and live in peace had not yet come.

But when he entered the dark woods where, according to de Brissac, Jamie's scent had been lost, he was suddenly seized with a certainty as to the boy's location. The boy had gone to Wolf Cave, that desolate place, the one place every boy in the village had been forbidden to explore. Hugo and his brother had climbed those monstrous rocks many a time, though had never worked up the courage actually to enter the dark cave. Of course . . . if the Laroches were looking to hide somewhere in the area where no one would think to look, Wolf Cave was the logical place.

And Finnula certainly knew these woods well enough to have figured that out. Like Hugo, she'd need neither moonlight nor a torch to find her way to that place.

But what she'd had to guide her infallibly was Gros Louis. And when Hugo saw that massive beast streaking toward him in the pinkening light of predawn, barking his alarm, his heart had nearly exploded in sudden fear. Why was the dog alone, and why was he running *from* his mistress? Unless, of course, she had ordered him to do so . . .

Hugo shouted a command, and the dog halted, looking up at him with a face that bore a great deal more intelligence than

Hugo had ever credited any animal before. His tail wagging energetically, Gros Louis turned and began streaking back in the direction from which he'd come, not even looking behind him to assure himself that Hugo followed. This fact, more than any other, struck Hugo as peculiar, and he spurred Skinner into a gallop, though with low-lying branches and unsteady footing, the horse moved with a slowness that, to Hugo, was maddening.

He did not know what he'd envisioned he'd find when he reached the clearing in which the cave was situated. He certainly expected to find Finnula, though in what state, he hardly dared guess. But when Skinner broke through the last of the brambles and pines and burst upon the unsuspecting participants in what looked to Hugo to be a scene straight out of a Greek tragedy, lit by the lavender light of an early dawn, he could only gawk.

Atop the rock lip that led to the cave's opening crouched Isabella Laroche, clutching her nose, from which blood was flowing freely. Fists cocked, above her stood none other than Finnula, her red hair flying about her head like an aurora. Lying prone beneath her was Hugo's squire and would-be assassin, Peter, looking very much as if he'd just been kicked in the chest, and not far from him, holding a length of rope that he'd tied into the semblance of a noose, stood a very startled Reginald Laroche. Slumped some few feet away lay a small bundle that Hugo could only assume was the boy Jamie.

All five people gaped at Hugo, who, his sword having already been drawn sometime back, stared at them with the blade aloft, uncertain as to whom he ought to cut down first. He ought to have known that Finnula, weaponless, would have already gained the upper hand. Now he felt a ridiculous and almost overwhelming desire to burst out laughing.

The impulse died immediately, however, when Laroche, the first to recover from his astonishment, leaped onto the outcropping and flung an arm around Finnula's slender neck, dragging her toward him.

"Good evening, Lord Hugo," the older man quipped, the point of his jeweled dagger aimed at the hollow of Finnula's throat. "What a pleasant surprise. If we'd known you intended to pay us a call, we'd have put on our finery, would we not, Isabella?"

Isabella only moaned, ineffectually trying to stanch the flow of blood from her nose with the hem of her bed robe.

"Hugo," Finnula said, her voice a rasp thanks to the pressure Laroche was exerting upon it. "Hugo, what are you doing here? You oughtn't be out of bed. You're not well!"

Hugo smiled at his wife's scolding. It had been some time since she'd last chastised him. "Well enough," Hugo replied mildly. "And the sheriff and his men follow me. They will be upon us anon."

"Precisely what your wife said." Laroche chuckled. "You two are naught but a pair of liars. You deserve one another. How touching that you shall die together!"

Hugo cleared his throat. "As I was saying, the sheriff and his men will be upon us anon, and will undoubtedly arrest you, Laroche, which will deprive me of the pleasure of slitting your throat myself. So I suggest you release my wife and take up a sword, since I intend to kill you now."

"You think me a fool, cousin?" Laroche's grip on Finnula tightened, and she was no longer capable of speech. Her gray eyes, however, spoke volumes, as they flashed angrily in the firelight. "I know there are few handier with a blade than yourself. You are as good a swordsman as this one is a markswoman—"

"Think you so? Even with a wounded shoulder in my sword

arm?" Hugo turned so that the bandage beneath his white shirt was obvious. "Look, even now, blood is soaking through the padding. I am a wounded man, Laroche, and yet you are too cowardly to fight me?"

"I shan't fight you, wounded or no. I know you won't dare lay a hand on me while I hold such precious cargo, and so I beg your leave to depart—"

"Fight him, Father," Isabella begged, through her blood-soaked fingers. "Do fight him. He insulted me most grievously! Peter will help you, won't you, Peter?"

Peter, still trying to draw breath from having been evidently kicked in the chest by Finnula, gasped, "No."

Isabella threw him a startled glance, her dark eyes wide with astonishment. "*What?*"

"I said no." Peter, to Hugo's surprise, was glaring at Laroche. "Let her go, monsieur. This has gone far enough."

Laroche swung around to stare at the boy. "*What?*" he blurted out, in an unconscious imitation of his daughter. "Have you lost your mind, boy?"

"No." Peter shook his head, his blond hair falling over one eye. He swept the lock back impatiently. "I've only just regained it. This isn't right. None of this is right. I believed you, monsieur, when you told me Lord Hugo was naught but an uneducated second son, who through sheer luck rose to the title of earl. I believed you when you said you'd make a far better Lord of Stephensgate than he ever would, with his coddling of peasants and the highly unsuitable woman he took as wife. But I know that Lord Hugo would not kill a woman in cold blood. And I know that Lord Hugo would not murder a child. In your cousin, monsieur, I have a found a man of true refinement and chivalry, and 'tis to my shame I did not recognize it before." To Hugo, Peter said, his eyes glittering brightly with unshed tears, "My lord, I have erred greatly. I am more sorry than I can ever say—"

"You should be." Hugo grunted. He kicked his feet free from the stirrups and dismounted, wincing as the action jarred his injured shoulder. "For I intend to thrash you, young one, within an inch of your life, for what you did to my wife."

"To your wife?" Peter's mouth fell open. "But I tried to convince them to spare her life, my lord! What did I ever do to your wife?"

"Nearly broke her rib, for one thing, the day we met her," was Hugo's calm explanation. "But I'd have forgiven you that if you hadn't then proceeded to see her blamed for crimes which you yourself committed."

Peter bent his head in shame. "Very well, then, my lord. I will await your punishment."

"Indeed you will." Hugo drew off his riding gloves slowly, as if doing so caused him pain. "I took you into my house and home, and in return, you gave me naught but your contempt. 'Twould grieve your father, who was my friend, to hear of this."

"Thankfully my father is dead," Peter murmured.

Hugo nodded. "Thankfully, yes. As you will wish you were, when I get through with you. Now, cousin, you will choose your weapon."

Reginald Laroche's surprise at Peter's defection was so great that his grip had loosened perceptibly upon Finnula, who readily seized the opportunity to send one of her elbows deep into his gullet, and thus remove herself from the man's grasp entirely as he buckled in pain. Throwing herself on top of Jamie, she grabbed the boy, then jumped with him down from the outcropping.

He did not appear to appreciate her rescue attempts overly much, however, when she landed on top of him.

"Oh, Jamie," Finnula cried, when their bodies collided against each other, in the soft peat. "Are you all right?"

"I don't know." The boy grunted, blinking up at her. "Could you untie me?"

"Are you mad?" Hugo inquired of his wife, rushing over to stand guard over the two of them. "Truly?"

"No, but I think you are," she snapped, as she struggled in the semidarkness with the ropes that bound the boy. "You're wounded, and your cousin's desperate, and you intend to fight him? Do *not*—"

"Thank you, my love," Hugo interrupted, patiently, never taking his eyes from Laroche, who still stood indecisively atop the rock outcropping, trying to regather himself after Finnula's blow. "But I shall have my revenge."

"Revenge!" Finnula's throaty voice was filled with scorn. "He is not worth it, Hugo! Leave him to the sheriff."

"He killed my father," Hugo said. "And he would have killed you, had I not arrived in time."

"What say you, cousin?" Reginald Laroche, his breath finally caught, leaped down from the rock wall and went to stare up at Hugo, his black mustache twitching. "You challenge me for the seat of Stephensgate?"

"Aye," Hugo said, flexing his sword arm experimentally. It seemed hale enough. "You beat me, Laroche, and the title is yours."

"Hugo!" Finnula was horrified.

But Hugo knew that this was the sole incentive with which he could tempt his cousin into an honorable duel. His desire to see the older man's blood flow was so strong that it almost staggered him.

But the man had caused him naught but trouble since he'd set foot in Shropshire, and Hugo would have peace at last.

After a moment's hesitation, Laroche grinned toothily. "You are my witnesses," he declared, turning to face his daughter and Peter. "You heard what he said. He loses, and the title is mine."

"Kill him, Father," Isabella said venomously. "And when you are through, kill the bitch he married as well." Darting a glance at Peter, she added, "And it wouldn't hurt to kill this traitor as well."

Reginald Laroche grinned, seemingly pleased by his daughter's bloodthirsty nature, and drew his sword. "Come then, cousin," he taunted. "Let us see who the next Earl of Stephensgate shall be in truth."

Hugo, who had been hearing such crashing in the woods behind him as to indicate that de Brissac and his men were on the way, was relieved to have the opportunity to kill Laroche before their arrival. With a reassuring smile at Finnula, whose face looked pale in the steadily growing light of dawn, he stepped forward, ready to intercept his cousin's attack.

Grinning, Reginald Laroche held aloft his blade, and sank into a fencer's stance. Hugo stared at him as if at one demented. Hugo was not a fencer. He was a fighter. His blade was heavy, and he swung it purposefully. There was no feinting in Hugo's technique, no parrying. Thrusting was all he knew, and he did so, aggressively.

But his opponent was not a soldier. Reginald Laroche had trained at swordplay at some faraway French court. The older man was lighter on his feet than Hugo, and faster, too. That much became evident when Hugo, irritated by Laroche's bouncing back and forth upon the balls of his feet, wielded his blade in an arc meant to lop off his opponent's head. Laroche easily ducked the swing, and laughed triumphantly as he danced away from Hugo, unscathed.

"Getting tired, cousin?" Reginald teased.

"Tired of watching you bob about like a puppet on a string," Hugo growled in response. "Why don't you stand still, Laroche?"

"So you can run me through? I think not."

Finnula, having unloosed Jamie, stood off to one side of the clearing, watched in a frenzy of anxiety. "Take care, Hugo," she called occasionally, when Laroche's blade swung too close to her husband's head. She could see that Hugo was tiring already, that it was harder and harder for him to lift his heavy sword. The fool! What could he have been thinking, challenging someone in his condition? 'Twould serve him right to be cut down.

And yet Reginald Laroche's skills with a weapon were nothing compared to Hugo's, war-weary as he was. Had the Earl of Stephensgate not been suffering from that injury to his sword arm, he would have felled the older man in a single blow . . . or at least, that's what he told himself. As it was, the duel lasted long enough for Sheriff de Brissac and his men to break through the underbrush and arrive in the clearing with considerable confusion.

"What goes here?" John de Brissac demanded, as the sound of clanging metal and panting men filled the morning air as thickly as the dew.

"Well, Sheriff," Finnula said. "Hugo is out of his head, and says he shall give up the title if his cousin wins—"

Sheriff de Brissac dismounted wearily, gathering Winnie's reins and holding them loosely in a gloved hand. "I ought to have known that if anyone could find him, it would be you, Finnula. You should have been loosed at once to follow Laroche's foul trail . . ."

"Please, Sheriff! They'll kill one another!"

"I'm quite certain that is the point, my dear. Though, in the name of the law"—he sighed—"they ought to be stopped."

"Oh!" Finnula gasped as Laroche, with a powerful swing, sent his blade ringing against the one Hugo lifted at the last minute to avoid injury. "Sheriff! Will you do something? They must be stopped!"

"And yet," Sheriff de Brissac said, watching as the two men lunged at each other, "I would not rob your husband of this opportunity to avenge your honor."

"What?" Finnula reached up to cling to the sheriff's arm. "Oh, John, no! Hugo doesn't care about my honor. No, you must stop them—"

But the sheriff was unmovable, and Finnula could only watch, miserably, as her husband engaged in a cat-and-mouse battle of blades. She was certain that, having risen so recently from the sick-bed, Hugo was the weaker man, but it appeared that in strength, the two were thus equally matched . . . until, of a sudden, Laroche began to fade. Finnula watched, hardly daring to hope, as Hugo, with a burst that indicated that he'd only been conserving energy throughout the fight, pressed his adversary back against the lip of the outcropping, where Isabella stood.

"Tell me, *cousin*," sneered Hugo, neatly slicing open Laroche's tunic but not leaving a mark upon his smooth and hairless chest. "Was it you who poisoned my father?"

Laroche was panting too hard to reply, but Hugo did not seem to notice. His blade danced across either of Laroche's gaunt cheeks, leaving lightly oozing scratches that emphasized the older man's pallor.

"Was it you? Or your bitch of a daughter? Poison is a woman's weapon, after all. Was it you who killed him?" Hugo continued to swipe at Laroche until he had the man cornered, backed up against the rock wall and only feebly heaving his sword. It was the work of but a moment for Hugo to fully disarm him. But then, instead of throwing his own sword away in victory, Hugo stepped forward and gathered the edges of Laroche's tunic together in one hand, bringing the smaller man forward until his face was just inches from his own.

"Admit that you killed my father," Hugo growled, menacingly. "Admit it, man."

Laroche knew he was beaten, and had naught left to lose. He laughed, a frightening sound that caused Jamie to bury his face in Finnula's skirt, even as she, in turn, looked up beseechingly at the sheriff.

"Aye, I killed the old man," scoffed Reginald Laroche.

"And laid the blame upon the woman I love?" Hugo's voice was deadly quiet.

"Aye." Laroche laughed. "As she'd have been blamed for your death, if that stupid squire of yours had been better able with a bow."

A roaring sounded in Hugo's ears, and his vision swam before his eyes. His face had gone ruddy with rage. Finnula saw it, saw his broad shoulders trembling with the effort he was making not to rip his cousin limb from limb. Untangling herself from Jamie's clinging grasp, she rushed forward, laying gentle fingers upon her husband's quaking limbs.

"Nay, Hugo," she said softly. "Nay, do not kill him. Your killing days are over. Let others be his judge."

Hugo turned a glowing eye upon her, and she saw that his hazel eyes were gold now, not green, as they'd been seconds ago. His lips parted, and he croaked, "Why?"

"Why?" she echoed. "Why what?"

He spoke with an obvious effort. "Why should I not kill him?"

Finnula, for the life of her, could not think of any reason that Hugo should not kill the man, except that for all her skills with a bow, she abhorred violence and bloodshed, and could not stand to see even this man she despised die before her, and at her husband's hands. Not after what she'd heard him say, which, though she still was not certain she believed her own ears, was that he loved her. Tears gathering beneath her eyelashes, Finnula whispered, "I know not. Only do not do it. Come home with me. Come home with me and love me as I love you."

She felt the quivering in his muscles lessening by degrees, and then, all at once, he released Laroche, and wrapped those powerful fingers around her own shoulders instead, as if he was relying now upon her strength to support him. She was only half aware that Sheriff de Brissac had stepped forward to take charge of his prisoner—his *new* prisoner—for all her attention was focused upon her husband. It had been too long since she'd last been in his arms. She was comforted by the hardness of his chest beneath her cheek as he pulled her against him, and the sinewy strength of his arms tightening around her.

When he tilted her chin up to gaze down into her face, Finnula saw that Hugo's eyes were every bit as golden as the sun, just rising over the horizon. But instead of the worldly confidence she was used to seeing within them, she saw uncertainty. When he did not kiss her, she wondered if perhaps she had not heard him correctly. Was it not she he loved? Had she spoken hastily, assumed too much?

Embarrassed, she began to attempt to extricate herself from his embrace, but to her surprise, Hugo eagerly snatched her back, though the worried look did not leave his eyes.

"D-do you . . ." he stammered, like one choosing his words with special care. "Do you . . . forgive me, then?"

Finnula gazed up at him in confusion. There was nearly a week's old growth of beard upon his jaw, and he looked a bit like the way he had the day she'd met him, when he'd been nothing more to her than a hostage for Mellana.

"Forgive you?" she echoed. "For what?"

"For burning your braies."

Finnula could not help laughing. "I forgive you," she said. "Do *you* forgive *me*?"

"For what?" Hugo asked bewilderedly.

"For holding you for ransom," she exclaimed.

"Oh, that," Hugo said, his arms tightening around her. "There's naught to forgive there. 'Twas the pleasantest time I ever passed, those days I was your hostage. 'Tis my fondest hope we'll return to the Spring of St. Elias for another swim—"

She silenced him with a kiss, though it was hard to do properly while she was laughing so much.

# Chapter Thirty

*A*s it happened, though she fitted herself promptly with new ones, Finnula was not able to wear leather braies for long, in any case.

A scant six months later, she had grown too round with pregnancy to fit into even her old kirtles. Her sisters were quick to supply her with their own, particularly a still guilt-ridden Mellana, who gave birth to a baby boy and quickly regained her old figure . . . though Jack Mallory never returned to Stephensgate to appreciate it.

To the surprise of none but Mellana, however, Sheriff de Brissac's admiration of her waist, when trim or otherwise, was great, and when not sharing a cup with Hugo in the manor house's Great Hall, John de Brissac could invariably be found at the millhouse, helping Mellana with her son and her chickens. It was thought that as soon as Madame de Brissac passed away—which, thanks to a troublesome case of gout, was to be sooner rather than later—the sheriff would make an offer for Mellana's hand, something he'd never dared to do while his mother yet lived.

And it was thought by many—including Finnula—that Mellana might just accept, and happily.

Finnula was determined not to let motherhood stand in the way of her new duties as Lady of Stephensgate, and despite the ungainly size of her stomach, she personally delivered to every one of Hugo's vassals a haunch of venison for Michaelmas. Speculation ran rampant as to whether the Fair Finn had actually shot the meat herself, but as everyone had grown used to the sight of the earl and his lady roaming the countryside in search of game, they all assumed she had, seeing as how she was by far the better shot.

Hugo, thanks in no small part to his wife, proved a popular and well-liked lord. He found that, once the trouble of his cousin's trial and subsequent hanging was past, he was quite capable of leading the peaceful existence he'd always wanted. He was particularly heartened by the fact that, through some foul-up, his squire Peter and the Lady Isabella managed to escape the sheriff's men, and had presumably fled to Scotland, where they were undoubtedly living in great discomfort . . . but, as Hugo pointed out to Finnula upon occasion, they were at least *living*.

Finnula pretended that she did not know that Hugo had bribed the sheriff's men to allow the pair to escape, since she was quite proud of her husband for not doing as he liked and killing the lot of them.

Had they known of it, their leader's happy domesticity would have appalled those men whom Hugo commanded during the last Crusade. What little they did see of it when, shortly before Christmas, a group of them appeared at Stephensgate Manor, came as a blow. Finnula was in the Great Hall with Mistress Laver, oiling one of her bows, when a new groom scampered in to announce the arrival of five strangers.

"And like as if they come straight from the 'Oly Land, m'lady," he cried. "Wif faces tan as leather and right shiny chain mail!"

"Well," Finnula said, with a shrug. "Let them in, then."

The men who entered might have been knights, but judging solely by their manners, one would hardly have called them chivalrous. They tramped noisily into the hall, tracking snow and laughing heartily, already clearly drunk from a spell at the tavern. Spying Finnula by the fire, they staggered to a halt, remembering themselves, and Mistress Laver, casting a disapproving eye over them, called out tartly for the master to be fetched.

"Eh, there, pretty lady," slurred one of the knights, whose brown beard was every bit as bushy as Hugo's had been when she'd first laid eyes upon him, as he leered at Finnula. "Would this be Stephensgate Manor, then?"

Finnula replied, calmly, "It would, and it is."

Grinning appreciatively at this impertinent reply, the knight hooted. "Saucy one! And would there be a Hugo Fitzstephen a-livin' here, then, Miss Cheek?"

"There would," Finnula replied. "He shall be here anon. Will you be seated, and wait for him? I can have some ale brought to you while you wait, or wine if you prefer."

The men only stared at her, and then finally one of them burst out laughing, and said, with a chuckle, "I'll suck down a cup, if you'll sit beside me, lass, and let me look into those silver eyes of yourn."

Mistress Laver inhaled sharply. "Sir! Do not you ken—"

"I ken that this here lass is the most fetching little miss I've seen in half a year," declared the brown-bearded knight, and before anyone knew what he was about, he had Finnula about the waist, which was still slender except where her belly swelled, and had placed a wet and bristly kiss upon her silken cheek.

Finnula's reaction was instinctive. She seized the jeweled dagger she wore low upon her girdle and, quick as a cat, placed its point into the knight's neck, exactly where his pulse beat.

The man froze, his arm still around her, and Finnula saw his Adam's apple bob as he swallowed.

"Try that again, sir," Finnula said, in the same polite tone she'd employed before, "and you'll be sucking down that cup from a hole in your neck."

She broke off, as the familiar ring of Hugo's boot heels filled the Great Hall.

"Finnula," he bellowed, stamping his feet to rid them of snow. "What's this I hear about visitors?" Striding into the Great Hall, a clean, well-dressed Jamie trotting behind him, Hugo was too busy drawing off his fur-lined gloves to notice the suddenly sobered group of men by the fire. "Your brother sends his regards, my love. If I'm not mistaken, you'll see him wed come springtime. Rosamund came to call while we were there, ostensibly to see Mellana, but if I know women, she'll have that betrothal ring back on her finger again before Easter—"

Hugo staggered to a halt when he saw the men before the fire. "Damn," he swore softly. "If my eyes don't deceive me . . ."

His voice trailed off as he noticed the highly suspect manner in which his wife was being held by one of those men. When he observed the knife glinting in her hand, a slow grin spread across his clean-shaven face.

"Well, gentlemen," he said laughingly. "I see you've met my wife."